# IN THE MOOD

Also by Keith Waterhouse

# IN THE MOOD

Keith Waterhouse

Michael Joseph
LONDON

First published in Great Britain
by Michael Joseph Ltd
44 Bedford Square, London WC1
1983

ISBN 0 7181 2224 0

Printed and bound by Billings & Sons,
Worcester

# 1

I lived in a different country once. Nothing there was the same as now. All that happened then, if it happened here, would be strange and fresh.

Everything was sharper. Cigarette smoke had a pungency it has since lost. Even stale beer smelled full-bodied and good. Girls' breasts were whiter. Like alabaster, we said, though none of us knew what alabaster was in that long-ago place. The air was as crisp as apples, and all the sad songs were sweeter, then.

Youth was our visa to this country. Although we were only visitors, yet it had no other inhabitants while we were there, or none that we recognised. There were those whose shadows were thrown across our path sometimes but they were to us as aborigines must have been to the old settlers. Alice in Wonderland dodoes waddled self-importantly about with bunches of keys on chains, membrane-thin pterodactyls flapped the ledger-dust off their wings, troglodytes drew academic gowns around themselves like shrouds, fossils propped up on the benches of bowling greens followed us with their petrified stare. They were nothing to do with what we were. These were our years and this was our green land. It is all far off from what we have become.

My name is Raymond Watmough, pushing fifty, successful in my small way as a travel agent, married happily enough to my former secretary with a son already grown and feeling his way in the family business. It is remarkable, absurd, and, when I reflect upon it, a little frightening, that my wife's position as my wife instead of someone else's who might have left her or made her a millionairess or a dypsomaniac, and the particular assortment of genes and chromosomes that in some other combination might have brought my son into the world not my son as he is but a mongol or a genius at mathematics, and the circumstance that I am such a person as I have become, earning so much a year, weighing so many stones and pounds, living in such and such a house in such and such a neighbourhood, with so-and-so and the so-and-sos as friends, and driving such and such a car, all stem from a single, smiling glance from a balcony in that country I once lived in. Realising now how casually forged and slender was the first link in this chain-armour of consequences that makes up most of the habiliments of my present rank in life, I can see that the supposedly formative years of my childhood were little more than a mechanical process of physical growth and accumulation of calcium, and that my true character and real destiny were respectively defined and moulded in that one instant, in less time than is needed to establish a chocolate soldier in a comic opera.

If this territory of improbable happenings could have had but one name, Ruritania would have been as good as any. But it did not have one name. It depended on where you were when you discovered that you lived there. To us, it happened to be known as Grippenshaw. And still is, I believe, to those who live there now, although it has been cocooned by another name, the Metropolitan District of something, I forget what, and its carpet mills are fallen into ruin and its gritstone streets have been cut through to make shopping malls and car-stacks. None of this matters. Even if not a stone had been changed, there is nothing there that we who lived there then could reach out and touch and be back in that country as it was. It has gone, or we have gone, it makes no difference which.

Not that the carpet mills were ever very much to do with us, or the gritstone terraces either. Our workaday lives were spent in, mooned away in, first the colleges and then the banks and commerce houses of the town. Our homes, places of shelter rather, where we repaired to sleep or eat some food and change clothes and experiment with a new hair parting, were on rising ground where the cobbles and tarred setts gave way to bitumen, and the curving streets had names like Winifred Drive, Pearl Grove, Edith Close, or, when the builders had run out of womenfolk, Elm Tree Gardens, Parkview Gardens, Laurel Rise. These were scented streets, giving off as distinct an odour of anticipation as a woman drenched in perfume. I would bottle that scent and market it had it not long ago evaporated. It wafted over you directly you stepped out into this country of ours through the sunburst wooden gates

2

of Rosedene or One-O-Nine or Casa Mia: a heady pot-pourri of privet, creosoted chestnut palings, woodsmoke, fog or plum blossom according to season, hot cinder-dust from the railway cutting, the pungency of Argosy Fish Saloon batter and vinegar forever lingering under the glass canopy of The Parade, that colonnaded crescent of shops next to the Crag Park Avenue Congregational Chapel, which itself subscribed a drowsy, sinful bouquet from the tall weeds that flourished behind it; and the minty touch of freshly cut grass, and the lawn-mower oil, and the frost-smell that even the warmest evenings seemed to have when the moon would soon be full. It promised everything, that scent.

Most of our country was contained within the inner range of this aroma before it became diluted in the brackish town-smells below us or the moorland tang above us or the washing-day fumes of new brick and builders' sand from the housing estates beyond the golf course. As well as the cul-de-sac closes and groves of laburnum and bay windows, and as well as the concrete forecourt of The Parade that was lapped with flickering waves of creamy white light from the fluorescent tubes in Moffat's Radio & Electrical, this perimeter encompassed the orange-brick Royal Coronation branch library with its campus-like esplanade of green rubberised tiles where we strutted like Romans in their forum; and, across the huge grass roundabout, where the hissing trolley-buses turned round on a spider's web of overhead wires, the Clock Ballroom, built like an aircraft hangar on what was otherwise a piece of waste ground planted with a huge painted sign that said FESTIVAL OF BRITAIN 1951: SITE OF GRIPPENSHAW PAGEANT OF PROGRESS; and opposite, the Gainsborough Cinema rising bulkily from its plain of tarmac; and the more modest Gem Picture Palace squashed between the petrol pumps and the coal depot down by the station, where it was handy for the Argosy Fish Saloon's rival, the Mermaid Supper Bar, with its three tile-covered tables for consumption of eatables purchased on the premises; and the red gravelled avenue that promenaded us down to Crag Park; and the municipal tennis courts; and Grippenshaw Girls' High School; and the tin hut with an asbestos roof that was the Youth Guild on Wednesdays and Fridays but did not exist for us on other nights of the week when it was for the use of boy

3

scout gargoyles and choral society fossils; and the alley of weeds between the Youth Guild hut and the back of the Congregational Chapel; and the unlit telephone box on the corner of Iris Crescent and the other one on the corner of Pearl Grove; and all the long shadows beyond the yellow pools of lamplight, and the leafy nooks and crannies.

There was as much for us there as a planter in some far-flung colony might have found in the clubrooms and verandahs of the rest compound. But we had our outstations too. From Crag Park, with its own rhododendron smell of expectancy, the fossils of the bowling green, shading their rheumy eyes, could look down upon the town at the glass roof of the covered market and at the Cloth Hall and the ponderous civic buildings, and the last of the damson Grippenshaw Corporation trams rattling to extinction across the Aire Bridge; and if the sulphur pall did not hang too low in the river valley they were supposed to be able to count thirty-eight mill chimneys and thirty-nine chapels and tabernacles. We saw none of that. But from the same promontory we had a view of the mouldering green dome of the raffish Palace of Varieties; the milk bars and cafeterias of the main street, Sheepgate; a panorama of terrace-end pubs and wine lodges where none of the dodo landlords would know our aborigine fathers; the neon sign of the Mecca Locarno palely glowing in the tea-dance afternoon; and the name of the Paramount Cinema spelled out vertically in bare electric light bulbs. It held the excitement of Broadway.

Down there, too, behind the Cloth Hall and above the new Infirmary, were the tall glimmering windows of the Grippenshaw College of Commerce. All summer long the topmost ones, ratcheted open to an angle of forty-five degrees, had reflected the blood-orange sun as it sank behind the distant Pennines. They were closed now, and the black iron gates padlocked. Summer term, the last one for us, was over. We had been given our proficiency certificates in Pitman shorthand, book-keeping, touch-typing, English and commercial French, and with them, our papers of full citizenship in the new country. Equipped as junior clerks, but feeling like voyagers, we set out to explore this land of ours.

The trail had already been blazed. One smouldering, oppressive Friday morning at the tail-end of that last term, having missed the No 17 Market Street trolley-bus I habitually caught with Douglas Beckett and Terry Liversedge, and which would have deposited me virtually at the College of Commerce gates, I took the next one, the 19A Circular. That meant alighting at Rabinowitcz the Jeweller's Corner and hurrying through the arcades of the town as their carillons sounded the hour, or, chancing that a particular set of traffic lights would be at red, remaining on the platform either to hop off near the Central Library and take a short cut through the Corn Exchange next to it, or face the long walk back up Infirmary Hill.

Chance is all. The lights were at red, I took the short cut through the Corn Exchange, and so saw Audrey.

The Corn Exchange, at that time in that country, was still in use as such. On Fridays the pterodactyl chandlers set up a Stonehenge of varnished wooden stands around the great circular chamber and for a morning you could believe yourself in a small market town as you saw the dodo farmers and merchants thwacking their gaitered legs with sticks and trickling samples of grain through their fingers. On other days the mosaic-tiled arena was given up to cage bird shows or exhibitions of model locomotives, or left to echo the footsteps of gargoyle clerks as they criss-crossed the dusty searchlight-pools of sunshine beaming in through the dormer windows of the domed copper roof.

But the offices that ran all round the iron-balustraded balcony no longer belonged exclusively to corn merchants. One by one they had been let off to the sort of small businesses you found in the town's ramshackle Victorian office buildings such as Bank Chambers and Town Hall Chambers: estate agents, mail order companies, import and export agencies, dye-stamp suppliers. One of these firms was Moult & Sumpter, travel organisers, whose name was emblazoned in a fan of gold lettering on a frosted balcony door immediately above the grand main entrance of the Corn Exchange.

Hurrying through the side doors on Town Street and crunching across a carpet of strewn grain between the varnished stands where the pterodactyls and dodoes leaned and loitered, I felt insignificant with my school satchel slapping against my blazer, and embarrassed by the blazer itself. I stopped to throw on the mac I was carrying against the

5

promise of summer rainstorms, and to gather up the reins of my satchel so that I could carry it like a briefcase.

As I glanced up at the big clock over the main doors it was as if the minute hand, lurching up to ten past, was directing my sightline towards her as she came out of Moult & Sumpter's and swung along the balcony carrying coffee mugs in a wooden filing tray. She wore a green bolero twin-set affair of a type I had already made a surreptitious study of on a saunter through the Junior Miss floor of Clough & Clough's department store. The jacket would peel off easily enough but the jumper, buttoning only on the shoulders, would have to be slipped over her head. Care would have to be taken not to ruffle her tightly-permed red hair. But the full ballerina skirt, unlike some of the pencil-slim jobs you were beginning to see around, looked as if it would slide off smoothly without the need of any awkward fumbling with the straps of her high-wedge leatherette sandals. I was glad to see, from the way her stomach plumped out gently in reaction to the pressure of the tray against her waist, that she probably wasn't wearing a girdle. I would not have known where to start on a girdle and had been advised by Douglas, when the land-horizon of this strange new country first began to loom up ahead of us, to have nothing to do with any chick who wore one.

Although the floor of the Corn Exchange below her balcony was milling with dodoes and pterodactyls, she singled me out at once unerringly, like to like, recognising her own kind. But I must have cut an incongruous figure as I stood there gawping up at her like a school-prefect Romeo in my absurd maroon blazer, knock-kneed from the effort of clasping my satchel between my legs while I struggled to manipulate a clenched hand through the torn sleeve-lining of my mac. I had rather she had not seen me in that situation, yet if she hadn't she would not have paused and smiled fleetingly, before vanishing with her tray of coffee mugs into a tiled, steam-billowing recess that served as a still-room. The swirl of her skirt revealed a hem of creamy lace.

All in that moment, full and complete, a scenario for the summer's pleasures fell into my head, commencing with my haunting the Corn Exchange each lunchtime and at the close of office hours until I had picked her up, or alternatively ringing her five or six times a day – she was bound to be in charge of the switchboard – and badgering her for a blind date under the Bovril sign on Rabinowitcz the Jeweller's Corner; continuing with visits to the Paramount, Lounge and Gaumont Coliseum cinemas, a Saturday evening or so at the Clock Ballroom and Sunday afternoon walks in Crag Park, and with kisses becoming ever more urgent in some convenient twilit no-man's-land before my sprint for the last trolley-bus home from wherever she lived in Grippenshaw (or out of it – she could have lived over in Halifax for all I cared); and culminating in her lying naked in long grass.

As to this ultimate venue: a relief map of the West Riding had already projected itself upon the retina of my mind, the section to the north-east of Grippenshaw coming into focus under the magnifier as the Perspex parallel rulers unfalteringly pivoted in on some neglected smallholdings where a field beyond an obscure copse lay fallow: it was barely a quarter of a mile from a road serviced by the dark blue Textile District buses but was neglected by walkers and lovers probably because of the proximity of the corporation sewage farm.

Concurrently, a timetable for the seduction, with astronomical footnotes, was piecing itself together: the longest day was already behind us; after the end of term on the coming Thursday, when the nights would already be drawing in, I should become more or less my own master as to how long I stayed out at night; by the beginning of September, with lighting-up time well on the right side of eight o'clock, we should be getting an hour of dusk and a good hour and a half of thorough darkness each evening before she began to get distracted by anxiety about getting home; and in mid-September there would be the harvest moon. I had a run-up of ten weeks.

At once, and still in the same instant that it took for that flash of lace to pirouette into the still-room, I had the enterprise costed. The packet of three gossamer contraceptives I already had, from the machine outside the rubber goods shop in Aire Bridge Passage; but there would be cinema seats to pay for, dance-hall tickets, incidental refreshments, an extra twenty cigarettes a week if she smoked, a sweet-ration allowance of chocolates if she didn't. There would be fares to pay – perhaps, if the rain came on while we lingered in a darkened telephone

7

box too far from the bus stop, the cost of a Silver Line radio taxi. I could see it working out at a good pound a week, certainly more than pocket money would run to. I would be well advised to find a job where I could start at once rather than, as so far taken for granted, after the annual caravan holiday in Colwyn Bay with my aborigine parents.

A last wild fancy seared my brain as I shrugged the mac over my shoulders and gathered up the strap of my satchel. Perhaps, with the house to myself, I could tempt her into it and ravish her on the uncut moquette, a full two months ahead of schedule? An unlikely prospect, made no less remote by the certainty of surrogate aborigines being given keys to the house or even left in custody of it; but worth the thought.

The fevered moment passed and I hurried on my way. But a lever had been released and the bulging flood gates had swung open. Ever after, for so long as I lived in that country, I do not believe I experienced another waking thought, and precious few sleeping ones, that did not directly or obliquely touch on acts of lust.

# 2

'She's my type,' I reported to Douglas and Terry Liversedge. Though barely half-past nine yet, it was like a brick kiln in the College of Commerce assembly hall. An insulating layer of cloud had unfolded beneath the July sun, muffling the distant shunting-yard sounds of thunder. The sticky heat made us restless. We lounged against a cool radiator by the notice-board, thinking our thoughts and wishing we could smoke.

Whenever Douglas and Terry Liversedge were mentioned in the same breath, it was in that order and that style, so that those who didn't know them sometimes took them for brothers. Doreen Theaker and Betty Parsons had thought so at first upon asking someone their names at the Clock Ballroom Saturday afternoon dancing class. No one could say why Douglas Beckett was always known by his Christian name only and Terry Liversedge by his name in full; it was just the way they were billed, like an act at the Palace of Varieties. It should have been the other way round, since Douglas had always lived very much in Terry Liversedge's shadow. Although I was a friend of them both, each was the other's best friend, inseparable except by the intervention of anything in skirts. But far from being brothers, they could not have been more unalike.

Terry Liversedge, with his straw-coloured hair set in Brylcreemed ridges, his College of Commerce tie flopping like a cravat, and patches of real leather on the elbows of his blazer, had the Picture Show Annual looks of a rising young film star. He had begun to smoke a pipe and when he clenched it between his even white teeth the jawbones stood out and his cheeks were gaunt. We envied Terry Liversedge, Douglas and I – Douglas more than I, I expect. Whereas I was reasonably presentable, though with no outstandingly attractive features beyond a greyness of eye which some girls took to (or at least Doreen Theaker had), Douglas was downright ugly. His dark skin was dirty-looking and studded with moles and warts, mercilessly compounded by a persistent adolescent rash.

(Both Terry Liversedge and I having been spared such blemishes, Douglas held that he had been issued with the acne ration for the three of us.) His black hair hung in lifeless hanks and he always had the beginnings of a moustache and sideboards even when nicks and scratches revealed that he had been shaving. Slightly built in the first place, so that he looked older than his body, he had become shorter still from affecting an academic stoop that had by now solidified almost into a hump.

But Douglas had no trouble getting girls – or 'getting off with the chicks' in the argot of our country. He had a theory about this. (Douglas had many theories.) Just as it was common knowledge that it was easier to get off with a plain chick than a pretty one, by virtue of her being grateful for the attention, so Douglas held that the getting-off process was easier for an ugly type like himself than for a handsome one. This was because all chicks were like the Japanese, they feared loss of face: and so they would prefer a Douglas who wouldn't stray to a Terry Liversedge who had the run of the field.

It had not worked out quite like that so far. On Duck-walk forays in pursuit of giggling threesomes around Crag Park boating lake, in the moonstruck, calf-love puberty we were leaving behind us now, Terry Liversedge had always got the blondest and buxomest one, I the passable brunette, and Douglas the one with the glasses. He did not complain. He had had no trouble getting off with a chick – and he was able to boast that he was proving simultaneously the two corresponding theories about the attractions of being ugly.

'What's she called?' asked Terry Liversedge idly, pulling on a chewed pencil as if it were the stem of his new briar. Or perhaps not so idly. It was, after all, something of a landmark occasion – the first time any of us had been involved, or anyway was setting out to be involved, with a chick who wasn't still at school. Not counting the mill-girls who had scorned and spurned us and demanded to be shown our little willies, the night a youth known to Terry Liversedge had got us into their works social.

I could see he was impressed. 'Don't know yet,' I shrugged. But I was to learn before the day was out. Audrey Marsh. Of one of the thirty-six Marsh families in the Grippenshaw directory, assuming she was on the phone.

'And she works where, do you say?'

'Moult & Sumpter, that travel firm,' I said, foolishly jumping into the trap. So far I'd only said that she worked in Corn Exchange Chambers. Now Terry Liversedge would know exactly where to find her. 'And don't you go sniffing round there,' I warned him, 'because I saw her first.'

'Play your cards right, Raymondo, and she'll take you on a dirty weekend to Morecambe on staff discount,' said Douglas, voicing an idea that had already occurred to me. 'Where does she live, by the way?'

'Give me a chance, Duggerlugs, I haven't even spoken to her yet.' Soon I would have thirty-six addresses to conjure with. Marsh A.B., 14 School Lane, Grippenshaw 5. Marsh A.R., 105 Cartmell Drive, Grippenshaw 12. Marsh B., Rev., The Vicarage, St Wilfrid's Close, Grippenshaw 9. Vicar's daughters were supposed to be hot stuff. 'Anyway, what does it matter?'

'It's of paramount importance, mon brave!' counselled Douglas with great urgency, hunching his frail shoulders and smiting a wart-encrusted fist into his palm. 'It's one thing taking a High School dish to the local flicks, knowing you can get her up against the privet in Crag Park Avenue on the way home. But these working bints expect to be taken to the Gaumont Coliseum or the Mecca Locarno – and there are no privet hedges in the middle of Sheepgate.'

True enough. And it was probably not permissible to get her down a back alley then dump her at the bus station. 'So I see her home and we find a shop doorway or somewhere.'

Douglas thrust his black-whiskered chin forward and raised a solemn finger. 'Quite. And you wait half an hour for a Textile District single-decker out to Top Moor Grange or wherever she lives. Every minute standing in that bus station and every minute sitting on that bus is a waste of *valuable snogging time!*' Again Douglas smote his palm, this time in a distinctly lascivious manner.

'Never mind, youth, I'll take her off your hands if you like,' said Terry Liversedge. Not a chance. But I was grateful for Douglas's caution. This was all new territory and we should have to pool our knowledge and learn from one another as we went along.

We automatically straightened up like schoolboys, then

self-consciously resumed our elaborate lolling postures around the radiator at the recollection of who we were now, as Miss Cohen, the shorthand teacher, walked down the assembly hall on her way to one of the form-rooms. Something rustled as she passed, probably a starched petticoat under the flared cotton dress that could be unzipped to the navel and then slid gently over her hips. Miss Cohen, or Rebecca Redlips as we had called her ever since Terry Liversedge had discovered her first name, was the only one of the staff who was not a troglodyte.

Terry Liversedge puckered his lips to release a soft phwit-phew whistle. 'Do you think if I agree to come back next year and take my Advanced Certificate, she'll let me do her?'

*To do:* that was another much-used verb in our argot. Its only definition, so far, related to what one hoped to do rather than what one did. The basic sentiment, 'I would like to do her', had many yearning declensions: 'I wouldn't mind doing her', 'She wants me to do her', 'I'm going to do her'. But there was no past participle. I do, she does, I will do, I can do, but never I have done. We meant to change all that.

No more Latin, no more French, no more sitting on the old school bench: all we had to do now was hand in our books, clear out our desks and undergo the advice of the careers troglodyte who was seeing us in alphabetical order. Then we were supposed to go for our job interviews, returning only to swop notes and smuggle bottled beer into the end-of-term party.

Our future was pretty well mapped out: eighteen months as dogsbodies with the banks or building societies or insurance companies, a two-year swan on National Service, then back as second-rung clerks on annual increment until those reaching the top of the ladder became branch managers of Lloyds or the Pru, and the plodders grew round-shouldered over their ledgers.

That was for the likes of Douglas, Terry Liversedge and me. The girls, it went unquestioned back in that time, became shorthand typists, mostly for solicitors of whom there were uncounted hordes in the Georgian terraces off Bank Row. The bright ones became secretaries and the lucky ones would marry their bosses.

12

There were not many we would have tipped for such a future in our year's intake. It was noticeable that the real pick of Grippenshaw, those we would want to *do*, went to the private secretarial college in Cloth Hall Lane, while only the ones with moustaches, puppy fat or astigmatism were washed up at the College of Commerce. Or perhaps it was a case of the grass being greener. We outnumbered them three to one and tried not to think of them much, since they were a source of some embarrassment. All of us had arrived at Grippenshaw Commerce at the age of fourteen, released from our one-sex council schools as monks and nuns from their cloisters, and had at once set about forming attachments in a manner and of a kind we now wished to forget. Notes had been passed under desks and Valentines dropped into satchels, pink-faced emissaries had accosted pink-faced victims to blurt, 'Raymond Watmough wants to know if you'll go out with him' – or worse, the challenge had been flung down first-hand, only to be received with the wild response, 'Go where?' Sweaty palms had surreptitiously been wiped on red plush. Hands had finally been grasped like nettles but no one had known the routine for unclasping them. Kisses had taken off but missed target. The grapevine crackled with incestuous cross-references: A, going out with B, had it made known to him that B would prefer to be going out with C, who was going out with D, who wished to go out with A. After a term or two of this, when all the secrets had been told and everyone had been betrayed by rote, there were few in the first year who could look the opposite sex in the eye. There-after, by mutual unspoken agreement, we trawled for our talent at Grippenshaw Girls' High or the secretarial college, while the girls cast their sights on the gorillas from the nearby Tech.

The clouds looming closer to the high windows were black now. Someone had clicked on the overhead lights. The assembly hall, with its sprawling knots of idlers and the more energetic types playing table tennis, had a Christmas-like atmosphere that only the mugginess of the day denied. A youth called Appleton emerged from the form-room that the careers troglodyte had taken for his cave and called, 'Arkwright, then Armstrong!' It was going to be a long wait for those of us in the W's.

13

'Why don't we go down to the cloakroom for a quick drag before he gets to the B's?' I suggested to Douglas Beckett. He nodded. Douglas lived at the Chocolate Cabin on The Parade and so he was rarely without a twenty packet of Capstan Full Strength.

'Just a tick,' murmured Terry Liversedge and inclined his head slightly, at the same time contorting his face as if in great pain. Following his tortured glance I saw Miss Cohen re-approaching, this time shepherding a shuffling coven of gym-slipped lumps she had rounded up to study the list of situations vacant on the notice-board. The girls did not get any careers advice: Miss Cohen creamed off the top shorthand speeds for the solicitors and insurance offices, while the rest were thrown into the carpet-mill typing pools where they would become proficient at making tea.

It was just conceivable that the erotic soundwaves emanating from Miss Cohen were created not by the rustle of her petticoat but by the velvet rasp of her stocking-tops rubbing together as she walked. Such fevered pleasure as I was about to derive from this speculation was blanketed, however, by sheepishness at the sight of Victoria Leadenbury among her charges.

Victoria Leadenbury, with a once-intriguing lisp that now seemed next door to a cleft palate and a squint-rectifying shield masking one lens of her National Health glasses, was still so podgy that she seemed to have been stuffed into her maroon gymslip like a polony into its skin. Two years had now elapsed since we were exchanging letters every day, but some of the passages were still etched on my mind like the image of a light bulb long after it has been switched off. *'Well precious I haven't much more to say just now except that I liked the last part of your letter about you loving me with every atom of your heart – it's poetical.'* I met her good eye, then we both looked away hurriedly.

My averted glance fell on Terry Liversedge, who was preening himself as one did before approaching a possible catch at a Youth Guild social. Having adjusted the hang of his blazer and patted the terraced straw ridges of his hair, he ingratiated himself in front of Miss Cohen.

'Yes, Liversedge?' Smaller than Terry Liversedge, she tilted her chin to look up at him. With her black bobbed hair and crisp, rustling summer dress, she looked more like a Spanish dancer than a teacher.

'I just wanted to thank you for all you've done. I'm only sorry my shorthand speeds aren't better.'

With a nod to acknowledge the tribute, Miss Cohen said with just a touch of archness, 'Well, that's in your own hands, isn't it?'

Douglas and I exchanged imperceptible winces, having a good idea what was coming.

'Yes, I'll have to get some practice in during the holidays.' I could see Terry Liversedge's Adam's apple take a leap before he plunged on. 'I was just wondering if you ever, you know, give *private lessons*.'

The girls clustered around the notice-board froze, their gasps and giggles put into cold storage until Miss Cohen had gone. Douglas raised his black eyebrows and rolled his eyes ceilingwards. Miss Cohen regarded Terry Liversedge levelly for what seemed like minutes before she spoke.

'You haven't *quite* left school yet, you know, Liversedge. Since you're so concerned about your shorthand speeds you can do me twelve pages of Pitman exercises by Monday.'

She flounced off, rustling. The pent-up giggles exploded, the huddle around the notice-board jack-knifing like marionettes into a hissing, nudging, shoulder-heaving heap. Douglas and I simultaneously expelled long exhalations of breath.

'You bloody madman, Liversedge!'

'You want your head read!'

Terry Liversedge shrugged. 'Worth a try.' As, in one respect, it probably was. By the end of the day everyone in Grippenshaw Commerce had heard about Terry Liversedge trying to get off with Miss Cohen, and by nightfall a story had reached the Youth Guild that he had asked a teacher if he could do her. It couldn't do his reputation much harm.

Pawing and jostling one another as they whispered and sniggered like the fourteen-year-olds we had once held sticky hands with, some of Miss Cohen's squad of job-seekers barged against the notice-board, dislodging drawing-pins and bringing down a flurry of papers. A sheet of foolscap fluttered to my feet. I picked it up and was about to hand it over when I saw that the only one upright among a scrum of girls stooping to retrieve the scattered papers was Victoria Leadenbury,

15

blotchy with embarrassment. In my own confusion I affected a close interest in the document I had been on the verge of giving to her. It was headed 'Filing/invoice clerks etc., some typing, s/hand not essential.' The vacancies tabulated were evidently the dregs of what was on offer: a petrol station, a wholesale butcher's, the accounts department at Clough & Clough's – the kind of dead-end jobs that would suit someone like Victoria Leadenbury until Mr Right came along and she left with a canteen of cutlery and a card wishing her every happiness. My eye skimmed the list until it reached the last entry:

> Assistant to existing secretary, customer accounts, postage, filing. Moult & Sumpter, the Travel Specialists. 1A Corn Exchange Chambers.

There was some other stuff about hours and wages and the congenial atmosphere but I didn't take it in. I nudged Terry Liversedge.

'What, youth?'

I showed him the Moult & Sumpter entry. 'Existing secretary, man! That dish I was telling you about! I'm quids in!'

Douglas, looking over Terry Liversedge's shoulder, shook his head elaborately, his thick lips pursed in discouragement. 'Badger'll go spare.'

He would too. Badger, the troglodyte who taught commercial geography, was the careers adviser we were all waiting to see. The drill was that while he sat riffling through a sheaf of appointment cards for the various firms claiming to be able to offer golden opportunities to bright juniors, you told him what you aspired towards, if anything. Dismissing any choice of career outside his gift, such as newspaper reporter or actor, he then selected two or three cards according to your supposed range of abilities, and you went for your interviews. Only if you botched all these, and subsequently failed the aptitude tests for one of the Grippenshaw Corporation sinecures which he held in reserve for his duds, were you supposed to address yourself to the vacancies listed on the board. It was a sign of failure.

Terry Liversedge took the sheet of foolscap out of my hand.

'Anyway, these are all dames' jobs.'

'It doesn't say so, does it? We can but try. If Badger gets up to the W's while I'm gone, tell him I've joined the Foreign Legion.'

Sheet lightning like a camera flash flooded the long dark windows, then the thunder rattled them as I clattered down the steps to the cloakroom. Halfpenny-sized raindrops began to splash and steam the asphalt as I hurried along Town Street buttoning my mac.

# 3

Probably if I kept my mac buttoned to the throat, she wouldn't see my College of Commerce blazer and remember me as the clown whose contortions had made her smile this morning. But was I sure that her remembering me wouldn't be to my advantage? She was probably a few months my senior, since she was already a wage-earner while I hadn't left school yet, so perhaps my fumbling performance with the torn sleeve and satchel might have appealed to her mothering instinct, if she had one. Douglas always said that if they started to mother you, you were away.

I would leave it in the lap of the gods. But I was glad, anyway, that I did have my mac, for it would be coming down in sheets before I reached the Corn Exchange.

It was by no mere chance that I was prepared for rain on what had started as a blazing July morning. I had become a keen student of the weather forecast, on which the strategy for evening or weekend so often depended. It was pointless lashing out twice times one and tenpence at the Gainsborough if it was going to be dry enough and warm enough to sit for nothing in Crag Park; fruitless to embark on a moorland walk if the grass was too damp to lie on. Not that I had so far been on grass-lying terms with anyone, but I lived in rising hopes.

Once, though, the weather forecast had been wrong, and I had stood with Doreen Theaker all one Sunday, for nine hours, under the dripping eaves of an electricity sub-station on the edge of Throstle Moor, waiting for the drenching rain to stop. Saying good-night in the telephone box on the corner of Pearl Grove the previous evening, she had more or less admitted under questioning that there were times when she felt like going further than French kissing and that it was only guilt and terror that made her push away the hand that remorselessly inched towards her breasts. One of those times, I was convinced, was now – for why else would she have agreed to the long bus-ride out to the moors? If only the rain would cease and we could find some dry or near-dry bracken under a crag, a persuasive, exploratory tongue would do the rest.

I tried, while we waited, to put in some preliminary work on breaking down her reluctant scruples, but she was inhibited by the possibility of mobile peeping toms on the deserted moorland road and would not even let me put my arms around her and press her against the damp steel door that gave us shelter. 'No, wait, Ray, there's a car coming,' would be her parry to each thrust. There never was, but the implied promise in her injunction gave me hope, and I spent the day in a mounting delirium of anticipation.

The morning dripped by. The hourly buses came and went. The noon one from Ilkley nosed out of a blur of mist along the glistening ribbon of tarmac and there was ample time to catch it and be sitting in the back row of the Gainsborough before the first performance of *Twelve O'Clock High* had even started. But although she wanted to see the picture because she went on Gregory Peck, Doreen refrained from suggesting a move, and that too bolstered my expectations. Her plaid waterproof remained tightly buttoned. Perhaps she was naked under it. I licked what I took to be a trickling raindrop off my upper lip and it was salty. I was sweating, for all that the day was so cold that I had to dig my nails into my palms for fear of their growing too numb to negotiate her buttons.

Doreen said something about the rain easing off, an observation that seemed to me so packed with wishful thinking that she might as well have added, '. . . so you should soon be able to throw me down in the heather.' Now I could feel the sweat pricking my forehead. I grew so feverish as ever more lustful images danced through my hot brain that I felt like a malaria victim trapped in a jungle swamp. But the rain was not easing off, it was getting worse. The hours passed. When we had grown nauseated with hunger, and the bell for evensong was sounding in some unseen dales parish behind the darkening horizon, we saw the lights of a Textile District bus sweep a brow of moorland, and so we stumbled across the sodden ling to the lonely request stop.

If this had indeed been one of the times when Doreen felt like going further, then it had passed, for as we took damp leave of one another in the Pearl Grove telephone box she

19

would permit only the chastest of kisses. Doreen Theaker's breasts and I remained strangers.

Moult & Sumpter's was a small, old-fashioned office with varnished board walls decorated with posters for holiday camps and Lake District coach excursions. The glass panels overlooking the Corn Exchange were frosted, so that typists passing along the balcony on their way to work would be seen only in silhouette. But that was not the first thing I noticed. The first thing I noticed was that she had removed the bolero jacket which now hung on the back of her chair, and that the button nearest to her neck on the right shoulder of her jumper was unfastened, whether by accident or design, exposing a sliver of flesh. She was thumping a typewriter at a desk facing on to the small shop-style counter at which, damp mac steaming, I stood, her doubtlessly crossed legs concealed by a modesty panel. Two pterodactyls in Burton suits sat on opposite sides of a big central table, scribbling and picking at pieces of paper from a huge pile. Another and more ancient pterodactyl lurked in a glass-partitioned cubicle, only his bald head visible above a rolltop desk.

It was evidently her task to receive callers, for after I had cleared my throat once or twice she was the one who looked up from her work, registered surprise that the door noisily opening and shutting should have resulted in someone entering the office, then crossed to the counter, skirt swinging slightly.

She looked even more surprised when, wishing I had cleared my throat one more time, I attempted to give speech. I was finding increasingly that striking up a conversation with any strange member of the opposite sex, particularly one upon whom I had designs, induced a bloating of the tongue and a tendency to garble my words. Hence, when I tried to say that I had called about the vacancy, it came out as, 'Oh, glub morning, I've crawled amount the vagrancy.'

After a puzzled frown, she exposed uneven teeth which threatened to scrape the lips of anyone French-kissing her. 'Oh, I see. Only you do know they were advertising it as a position for a young lady?'

She had a mill-girl's voice but with the ironed-out vowels of the secretarial college. Not very ironed-out: the six-month

20

crash course by the sound of her. It was all right by me so long as she pronounced her aitches. Douglas held, and I was inclined to believe him, that if they didn't pronounce their aitches they probably didn't wash themselves down there all that often, and that there were all sorts of infections you could pick up that weren't necessarily the ones that made your nose drop off.

I thought she was quite encouraging. Putting the firm in the third person as 'they' suggested that if it had been left to her, she would have advertised the position as one for a young gentleman. She was resting her elbows upon the counter, so that a small flap of her jumper fell forward where her shoulder button was unfastened. I could see part of her collar bone.

Without looking up from his heap of paperwork one of the pterodactyls said to her, 'Is he from the College of Commerce, ask him?'

I cleared my throat again. 'That's right.' I saw from her faintly mischievous half-smile of reminiscence that she now recognised me from this morning. Had the pterodactyls not been there she would probably have said something on the lines of, 'I *thought* it was you when you came in, but I didn't like to ask,' and the ice would have been broken.

I had begun to reflect that since we were already on the verge of getting along famously there was no real need for me to pursue the job any longer, when the pterodactyl who had spoken, who was to turn out to be Mr Sumpter, pushed up his glasses and surveyed me, and having uttered one or two hums and hahs reiterated what I already knew about them really wanting a young lady who would be junior to Miss Marsh here. Why, he wanted to know, was I so keen to work for them?

More for her benefit than his, as she swirled back to her desk, and also because I could hardly tell him I didn't want the position at all now, I stammered piously that I had read how more and more people would be taking holidays abroad in years to come, and so I wanted to learn all I could and become a travel agent. That would show her I had a serious side. It would make her more interested.

He cackled pterodactylically that I shouldn't believe all I read in the papers. But after making one last valiant effort to put me off by warning that I needn't think travel agents lived

21

glamorous lives or spent all their time gadding off to romantic places, he did get to his feet and start asking me questions about my qualifications. Then I was taken into the elder pterodactyl's den and asked the same questions all over again by Mr Moult, the senior partner. Finally they called in the remaining pterodactyl, identified as Mr Eppersley, the cashier, who asked them yet again, and upon hearing my claim to understand double-entry said, 'Well, it would certainly be a help to have someone who can do a bit of book-keeping. But how would he feel about being under Audrey?'

The job was mine. All three of them, talking across my head, began to ramble on about wages and annual increments and holiday arrangements, but I hardly listened. I was going to be under Audrey.

I was taken across to her desk and ponderously introduced, my hand touching her hand, with the words, 'This young man so much wants to be *under* you, Audrey, that we haven't the heart to turn him away.' The pterodactyls smirked at what they supposed was the mildest of sexual double entendres, little knowing what wild cavortings they were calling up in my head. Audrey, catching the insinuation, smiled. It was a smile full of mischief and directed at me. The same picture that was in my mind must have flitted through her mind too to provoke that smile. I would remind her of it when we lay exhausted, smoking cigarettes, in the field of long grass near the sewage farm.

As Douglas had predicted, the careers troglodyte, Badger, was furious and demanded to know what I thought I was doing. I repeated woodenly what I had said to the pterodactyls about wanting to learn all I could and become a travel agent. He was unimpressed. 'Quite the Thomas Cook!' he sneered, then started going on about all the plum jobs I could have had if I hadn't taken my future into my own hands. There was one with the Bank of England in Leeds which he said he had been holding up his sleeve. It seemed that by keeping my nose clean I could have finished up in Threadneedle Street. I let it all wash over me. As he chuntered on, I was thinking of being under Audrey with all her shoulder buttons undone.

I compared career notes with Douglas and Terry Liversedge. They too had disappointed the Badger troglodyte, though perhaps not on the same catastrophic scale.

Terry Liversedge, assessed as having excellent prospects provided he could curb a tendency towards impertinence and not look upon himself as cock of the walk, had been sent to the National Provincial Bank, with the second-fiddle Pennines Linen Bank as his reserve in case he failed to make a good impression. The interview, he reported, was a piece of cake. He was offered a post on the spot and accepted it, though with some subsequent misgivings after noting what he described as a shortage of talent when taken on a conducted tour by an assistant pterodactyl.

As he crossed Bank Row on his way down to the Lyons' in Sheepgate for a celebratory coffee, it was with some disdain that Terry Liversedge registered the grimed Doric frontage of the Pennines Linen Bank. The appointment card with its College of Commerce crest that one was supposed to present when going for interviews was still in his blazer pocket. He was about to tear it up when he noticed a chick of about his own age entering the bank.

She wore a completely transparent mackintosh over a navy blue dress, on the buttoning arrangements of which he was unable to enlighten me. She was bare-legged, with mud splashes on her trim ankles and calves. Terry Liversedge saw himself wetting a finger in her mouth and erasing them for her, gradually working his way upward until he reached the backs of her knees, perhaps the foremost of the secondary erogenous zones.

The bank's swing doors were wedged open to draw in the sweet rain-washed air after the morning fug. Terry Liversedge, wandering after her into the marble coolness, saw her commencing some complicated transaction with paying-in books and bundles of cheques, obviously on behalf of her employer. From the tooth-baring reception bestowed on her by the cadaver at the till, this was clearly a regular, possibly even a daily, routine. What Terry Liversedge further registered, taking in the clerical comings and goings in the great pillared expanse beyond the public counter, was that unlike the National Provincial, the Pennines Linen Bank employed a high proportion of talent.

Observing all this and enjoying these pleasant surroundings, Terry Liversedge now saw that he himself was

23

observed – by a mummified dodo draped in the uniform of a commissionaire. 'What are you on, son?'

On impulse he produced the interview appointment card he had nearly torn up. Three quarters of an hour later he left the Pennines Linen Bank by the staff door, having accepted a position as a postage clerk at seven and sixpence a week less than the National Provincial were offering.

Thirty years on and wretchedly married (he was advised that divorce would affect his promotion prospects), Terry Liversedge is sub-manager of the Huddersfield main branch of what is now called Norbank, his chances of a full managership having dwindled to nothing when the Pennines Linen was absorbed by the Northern Bank Ltd. The College of Commerce form-mate who took the post he was originally offered by the National Provincial is now Grippenshaw manager of NatWest.

As for Douglas: it transpired that the Bank of England plum which the Badger troglodyte claimed to have been keeping up his sleeve for me, he had first kept up his sleeve for Douglas, and had flown into a rage when Douglas refused even to consider it. Though derided as spineless, Douglas's excuse that Leeds was too far away and that he would feel lost in a big city had a good deal of substance to it. He held that the talent in big places like Leeds tended to turn up their noses at smaller places like Grippenshaw, so that being regarded as yokels and speaking in a broader accent than theirs made it doubly difficult to get off with them. There was also the factor he had already warned me against, that of too much travel cutting into valuable snogging time.

In disgust the Badger troglodyte packed Douglas off, without any further option, to the Grippenshaw Permanent Building Society, where he was taken on as an office boy. In 1975, not yet forty, he became its youngest-ever chief executive.

But all such things were long before us on that July tea-time of 1950 as the sun steamed the rain-puddles off the wide rubberised paths criss-crossing the greensward in front of the Royal Coronation branch library, where we loitered on the low wall smoking one after another of Douglas's cigarettes, out of reluctance to enter the bay-windowed lairs of the aborigines and be interrogated about what employment we

24

had been offered and which we had accepted, and the pay and the annual increments and the potential for advancement; and in celebration that we were our own masters now and we knew that we had arrived in our own country at last.

Hugging their stacks of pony and ballet books, chicks in tight-buttoning blouses and stiff, hook-and-eye-fastening, belt-buckled High School gymslips drifted up and down the brick steps of the library or lingered hopefully in small groups on either side of the glass-bricked entrance lobby. But we barely glanced at them now, for we had dared to begin to aspire to something more than the fumbling embraces and glancing kisses that would be the most we could hope for from the talent encountered on the Monkey-walk, as the library's criss-crossing boulevard was known to distinguish it from the boating-lake Duck-walk. I pulled deeply on my cigarette and thought of Audrey Marsh and what she might be wearing on our first date; Terry Liversedge was crumbling a Capstan Full Strength into his pipe and thinking about the chick he had followed into the Pennines Linen Bank with mud-splashes on her legs; Douglas, swirling smoke down his hairy nostrils, thought luxuriously about a Mrs Duckworth, the general manager's secretary at the Grippenshaw Permanent Building Society, who he said had been very nice to him and might in due course want to seduce him.

'Get in there, youth,' encouraged Terry Liversedge. 'All things are possible with the older woman.'

'So long as the older woman doesn't happen to be a certain Rebecca Redlips,' I murmured, blowing an almost perfect smoke-ring.

'You never know, youth, you never know,' responded Terry Liversedge, unabashed. 'She hasn't seen my shorthand exercises yet.'

Pipe clenched in his jaw, the gaunt profile tilted for the benefit of the Girls' High School talent, he rummaged in his satchel and extracted a shorthand notebook. Spiralling open the pages, he passed it across.

'Twelve pages she asked for, and twelve pages she will get.'

The Pitman shorthand was copperplate, each consonant of the required thickness and in the correct position on the feint-rule lines, each diphthong and vowel precisely indicated, the loops and hooks immaculate, each grammalogue impeccable, so that there could be no ambiguity or misreading of the text. *'I would like to do you,'* Terry Liversedge had begun. *'Slowly my fingers would caress your throbbing nipples until they were erect before my gaze . . .'*

Douglas and I read in silence, one of us placing a restraining finger on the corner of the page whenever the other was ahead of him. I spoke only once, when I reached an unusual outline.

'What's this?'

Terry Liversedge leaned across and ran the stem of his pipe down to where I was pointing.

'Cunnilingus.'

'I think it should be a short oo vowel instead of a U diphthong.'

'She'll know what it means, youth,' said Terry Liversedge, retrieving the notebook.

Douglas made a great show of pressing the back of a swarthy hand against Terry Liversedge's temple. 'Temperature seems normal. Has he fallen on his head recently to your knowledge, Raymondo?'

'You may scoff, Beckett. For all you know, Rebecca Redlips is gasping for it. This could just do the trick.'

'You're not going to give it to her!' I exclaimed.

'I'm *hoping* to give it to her, youth, let me put it that way.'

With an obligatory 'Har har!' at the laboured double entendre, I said, 'You know what I mean.'

'Oh, the *shorthand*! Why not? She's not going to get it till the last day of term – I'll keep saying I've forgotten it. By the time she gets round to reading it we'll have left. You never know, youth – I might find her waiting for me outside the Pennines Linen Bank!'

'Pigs might fly.'

'Oh, ye of little faith. I'm telling you, kiddo – all things are possible.'

He was never going to show his Pitman fantasy to Miss Cohen, of course, but Terry Liversedge was right about one thing. All things were possible. As we sat on the hot brick wall that surrounded the library greensward, passing Douglas's last cigarette one to the other, promise hung about our heads like a heat haze. That evening vapour of expectancy was already tingeing the air, gathering in and blending with the tobacco smoke and the sharp tangs of high summer: melting

26

tar, rain, grass-cuttings, and the smell, perhaps imaginary, of girls' lately-shampooed hair. All was possible.

# 4

But first there was a melancholy duty to be done.

Douglas always said that the civilised way to go about it would be to clap hands three times and declaim, 'Begone, I divorce thee.' But that was not the way of the Monkey-walk and the Duck-walk. The convention was that when someone had to be brushed off they were given a brush-off card. You made the card yourself: a small piece of pasteboard the size of a playing-card on which you had carefully drawn, in Indian ink, a picture of a sweeping-brush. Everyone knew what it meant. It was a terrible thing to do to a person – it was reputed to have the same effect on some recipients as the Black Spot in Treasure Island – but you had to be cruel to be kind. Or so it was said.

We had our cards ready. We had agreed that it was best to get it over and done with at once. We were starting our new lives now and we did not want any impediments from the past to hold us back. Besides, it was only fair to them, so that they would know where they stood after the holidays, when our blazers had gone to the jumble sale and we wore the herringbone jackets and flannels of wage-earners and doers of women.

'Don't look now,' I thought I had better murmur to Terry Liversedge.

'Trouble?'

I nodded. Betty Parsons, still wearing her High School uniform though it was evening now, was approaching The Parade in a long diagonal across Crag Park Avenue from the end of Winifred Drive where she lived. Terry Liversedge didn't turn round. He would not have done at the best of times and certainly wasn't going to now.

We were waiting for Douglas outside the Chocolate Cabin. We had had our tea and fended to another day the business of explaining to the aborigines why the jobs we'd landed were not quite the plums they'd been led to believe were our

28

entitlement. Doubtless Douglas would be doing the same up in the flat above his own aborigines' shop. With any luck he would acquire a fresh packet of Capstan Full Strength on his way out.

Though the sunlight still filtered through the sloping glass canopy and its black iron pillars were still hot to touch, night on The Parade was tuning up like an orchestra. At the Congregational Chapel end, outside the cycle shop, gargoyle bike-riders circled the cemented concourse or balanced their front wheels in the empty racks and combed their hair while waiting for the Youth Guild along the adjacent cinder path to open. The Argosy Fish Saloon behind its stained glass galleon windows was already palely lit and sizzling; soon, as the sun went down, its arc of light would draw in the available talent like moths. A youth in a Fifty-Shilling Tailors' suit grimaced and squeezed his spots in the reflection afforded by the blue roller blinds of the Post Office. Similarly kitted out, and similarly inspecting himself in the window of the Maypole Dairy next door, another youth eased his tight white collar with a signet-ringed finger and worked his brilliantine-polished head around like a tortoise. A chick in a cloth coat, too thick for the weather but ideal for lying on, paced up and down, her rouge and lipstick blue in the humming fluorescent glow of Moffat's Radio & Electrical. Waiting for their dates, all three ignored one another. They were older than us. They would be starting their evening in the Parkview Arms near the bottom of the avenue, but they would certainly not be finishing it there: the ditch that ran behind the back gardens, known as Lovers' Leap, would testify to that when gargoyle archeologists made their smirking explorations tomorrow morning. They ignored us, too, but in a lordlier manner than they ignored each other. Little did they know we were of their number now.

It was generally acknowledged that Betty Parsons was not a bad piece of homework. Terry Liversedge had clicked with her at the Clock Ballroom Saturday afternoon dancing class and no one had had a look-in since. She was as tall as he was, with a confident prefect's walk to match his long-legged stride, firm features that mirrored his, waving corn-coloured hair that complemented his straw ridges. Told that they could be taken for brother and sister, Terry Liversedge had made a lascivious noise at the back of his throat and growled that it was a good job they were not; for Betty had a generous mouth and well-developed breasts, and it was his boast that by kissing her for prolonged periods until his lips were almost numb, he had five times succeeded in touching one breast and on two occasions both of them. Since that was seven times as far as Douglas or I had ever got, we affected not to believe him, but it was probably the truth. In his shoes I would have thought twice about giving Betty Parsons the brush-off before making at least equal progress elsewhere, but that was his business, not mine.

She reached the cycle shop at the other end of The Parade and stood against one of the iron pillars with the sun coming through the glass canopy and catching her hair. She ignored the bucking-bronco bike-riders showing off in front of her with the same aloofness as the older youths and the chick in the cloth coat ignored us. She rocked gently up and down on her low heels, hands thrust deep into her blazer pockets. I thought of Terry Liversedge touching one of her breasts five times and both of them twice.

'You're fizzing mad, man,' I said.

'Got to be done, youth.'

Though she knew he was standing there by the enamelled *Argus* and *Yorkshire Post* placards that formed a small fence between the Chocolate Cabin and the Post Office, she would not come any further. That was because I was there: and now, as he emerged from the shop giving us the thumbs-down sign to indicate that he was cigaretteless, so was Douglas. The system was that if your date happened to be with friends you did not approach but waited, as a protection against possible ridicule. That wouldn't have happened in Betty Parsons' case but she observed the rule all the same.

'Not even five stinking Woodbines?' I asked Douglas glumly. One thing I meant to take up when I started getting wages was chain-smoking.

Douglas dug into the pocket of the sports jacket he had changed into. 'I knew he wouldn't let us down!' crowed Terry Liversedge. But he produced not a packet of twenty but a stamped envelope. He showed it to us. It was addressed to Alma Tipper.

Alma Tipper was the surviving member of a trio Douglas,

Terry Liversedge and I had clicked with on the Duck-walk many Sundays ago now. He had stuck with her because she was slightly lame. Douglas held that all lame girls were either active or potential nymphomaniacs. But the potential had never been realised.

He pressed his thick lips to the envelope. 'Farewell, my lovely . . .'

I protested, scandalised: 'You're not *posting* the frigging thing, are you?' There was no rule against posting a brush-off card but I had never heard of anyone doing such a thing.

Douglas held the envelope at arm's length, gesturing histrionically. 'Parting is such sweet sorrow . . .'

'Waste of a twopence-halfpenny stamp,' said Terry Liversedge. Then a disturbing thought struck him. 'Listen, Duggerlugs. This doesn't let you off the hook, you know.'

'Hook, mon capitaine? I know of no hook.'

'We had an agreement.'

So they had. Douglas was going to present Terry Liversedge's brush-off card to Betty Parsons, while Terry Liversedge delivered Douglas's brush-off card to Alma Tipper. It was a recognised procedure.

'Null and void, old top, old bean, old boy,' said Douglas airily. 'An agreement has to have a consideration. I thought you were supposed to have studied commerce.'

Terry Liversedge pretended to ruminate. But then he lunged forward and before Douglas could stop him had grabbed the letter and thrust it into the pillar box outside the Post Office.

'There's your consideration, *old* top, *old* bean. I've posted it, so technically I've delivered it. Now it's your turn.'

'No dice.'

'You rat, Beckett!'

'Raymondo'll do the dirty deed, won't you, mon brave? Then Terence can return the compliment with Doreen Theaker.'

I shook my head slowly and positively. They sometimes cried when handed a brush-off card. I didn't want to see Betty Parsons cry. 'I'll tell you what I'll do, Douglas, I'll arbitrate. You did have an agreement, so get going.'

So in the end Douglas took the neatly-drawn brush-off card from Terry Liversedge, palming it as if about to do a conjuring trick, and walked across to where Betty Parsons was waiting by the cycle shop. Terry Liversedge, producing his leather comb-case and steel mirror, turned his back on the scene, but I watched as Douglas exchanged a few words with Betty and handed her the card. She looked at it. The bike-riding gargoyles had ridden off whooping along the cinder path by now and I was glad about that, for they might have known what the card was and jeered at her. Betty Parsons handed the card back to Douglas: that was unusual, they nearly always tore it into pieces. Then she said something to him – 'The condemned person's last words were, "Just tell him it was nice while it lasted," ' reported Douglas – and walked away, taking the same long diagonal route across Crag Park Avenue as when she had arrived. She walked with her usual upright, confident step but as she reached the other side of the avenue and turned into Winifred Drive, her proud shoulders drooped and I thought they had begun to shake as she moved out of sight along the privet hedges.

The three of us crunched off down the cinder path to the Youth Guild hut behind the Congregational Chapel, Douglas and Terry Liversedge to inspect the available talent and I to meet Doreen Theaker. The brush-off card I had prepared was in my top pocket. Scissoring two fingers I drew it out so that a margin of it was visible like a pocket handkerchief. I wanted her to notice it and speculate on it so that getting the brush-off would not come as a complete shock.

'Good luck, youth,' said Terry Liversedge, running his steel comb along his temples.

Summer was not the Youth Guild's busiest season and anyway it was still early. The trogolodyte whose function was youth leader had not yet arrived to organise his discussion group on whether girls should do National Service or whatever treat he had in store, and so the bare and girdered hall still reverberated with the sound of clattering boots as the gargoyle bike-riders scrambled aimlessly on and off the concert platform, and with a jangled, perpetual rendering of 'Chopsticks' from the near-derelict piano. Four bullet-headed council-school gargoyles were perched in a row on a trestle table, sitting on their hands and swinging their mottled legs as they waited for a turn at table tennis. Doreen Theaker and a concave-chested youth in a Fair Isle pullover called Geoffrey

Sissons, who claimed to belong to the Communist Party, were finishing a game. She wore her grey chalk-striped skirt that zipped down the back and a buttonless high-neck sweater. Her breasts bounced provocatively as she lunged backward and forth to meet his wild half-volleys.

There was little other talent to speak of. Douglas and Terry Liversedge looked disconsolate.

'Reckon you're the ones who are going to need the good luck,' I murmured, and having made sure that Doreen had seen me I went and waited outside the hut among the weeds and cinders. Soon, following a long-established pattern, she came out and joined me, shrugging on her green High School blazer over her sweater. We never spent our evenings at the Youth Guild but usually arranged to meet there so that Doreen could truthfully tell the aborigines at home that that was where she was going.

We went on one of our usual walks: along Crag Park Avenue through the park gates and left along the wide rhododendron alley that presently narrowed to a footpath. Here, as I had been hoping she would not, Doreen slipped her arm through mine. The park's scents were heavy and orchid-sickly after the day's rain. The far-off sound of children playing that is only to be heard in parks evoked the usual sweet melancholy. None of this was making my mission any easier.

Instead of leading her off down one of the stony detours that would take us into the bluebell woods, I steered Doreen, rather to her surprise it seemed, all the way along the rhododendron path until we came out at the clearing where the bowling greens were. We went to the far edge of the clearing where it fell steeply away to form a grass cliff, and sat on one of the park benches overlooking the town. White clouds drifting under the evening sun caused a gently rippling shimmer, like a still sea, on the far-off glass roofs of the carpet mills.

We had not spoken much so far. Doreen always insisted that she liked long silences as they enabled her to think, though what she was thinking she would never say. Until this evening, I had continued to hope that sooner or later she would confess to thinking the same as I was thinking. But it was too late now.

I decided to tell her about my job at Moult & Sumpter's.

33

Since she had shown no sign of recognising the tip of white card protruding from my top pocket, that should help me ease the conversation around to the subject at hand. She was politely interested and asked several questions about the place and the people I would be working with. Putting off the moment, I answered them over-fully, though without mentioning Audrey.

Finally, and unexpectedly, Doreen squeezed my arm and said, 'Well, I think you're very clever, Ray, and I hope you'll be very successful. Many congratulations.' With which, to my surprise, she kissed me lightly on the cheek. Though she was not averse to kissing, it was the first time she had taken the initiative, even in so token a manner.

Prevaricating further would only make it worse. I pulled the brush-off card out of my pocket and said, in a gasping voice resulting from having taken too inadequate a deep breath, 'So. What all this is leaning up to, I'm affray, Doneen, is that I'm sorry very but I've gone to give you this.' It was not quite what I had meant to say but she would get the gist. And I handed her the card.

She took it carefully between finger and thumb and studied it. It was a very well-executed piece of work. I had taken the joker out of a pack of cards and stuck a gummed label over it cut to size. The rounded corners, I thought, gave it a touch of class. Unlike some of the dashed-off cartoon-like efforts I had seen, my Indian-ink portrayal of a sweeping-brush had been carefully and faithfully drawn with a mapping pen, each bristle finely etched, so that it looked like an illustration from a Victorian ironmonger's catalogue. It was a superior brush-off card and I was quite proud of it.

'Don't think I'm not grateful, Ray,' said Doreen in the amused, mock-grave voice she would have used to thank a small child for the gift of a pebble, 'but what am I supposed to do with it?'

She didn't know what it was. She was the only girl in Grippenshaw who had never heard of a brush-off card.

I said with an indignation born of desperation, 'You must have seen one of these before, surely to God?'

She fingered the card, turning it over, looking for the joke.

'I can see it's been a playing card, but why has it got this picture of a broom pasted over it?'

34

I was beginning to feel like someone who had thought it was easy to drown kittens in a pail but can still hear them miaowing.

'It's not a broom, it's a brush.'

'Brush, then. I still don't get it.'

I took another deep breath, a proper one this time. 'It's what's known as a brush-off card.'

She continued to look at the card blankly, until at last she smiled – a rueful, the-joke's-on-me smile – and slowly and repeatedly nodded her head to show that she comprehended now.

'The penny's dropped. It means I'm getting the brush-off.'

'I'm ever so sorry, Doreen,' I said wretchedly. 'If I'd thought you weren't going to know what it was I would have put it in some other way.'

'Don't be *silly*!' She sounded warmly reproving, as if she were already in my debt for far more consideration than she deserved. 'It's my own fault, for being so slow on the uptake. I was just being stupid.'

I hadn't expected her to apologise for being given the brush-off. I tried to give her the same kind of rueful smile she had given me, but I could feel from the muscle spasms that it had come out more like a leer. 'Sorry and all that,' I mumbled. 'I wish it didn't have to happen, but it does, so there we are I'm afraid.'

Still looking at the card as if admiring a little present, she asked, now suddenly flat and miserable, 'Am I allowed to ask why?'

I floundered, trying to tell her that we belonged to separate worlds now, with different horizons and a different time-scale even: that she would still be confined to her small corner with homework and exams and aborigine curfews to preoccupy her, while I had become a free agent, able to stay out as I pleased and rove anywhere, though with obligations to workmates to spend evenings with them in pubs and such places as required by convention. It didn't sound convincing, perhaps because although it was the truth it was not the complete truth, and Doreen rightly paid no attention to it.

'So it's not anything I've done?'

'No, of course not.'

She fell silent. Now she was looking ahead of her at the mill roofs, breathing heavily so that out of the corner of my eye I could see the slack of her wool sweater tauten as her breasts heaved. I darted a shifty glance to her face but there were no tears to see. Now that the worst was over and I was feeling better, I felt cheated by the absence of tears. I could not account to myself why it would have distressed me to see Betty Parsons crying, but to have made Doreen Theaker cry seemed no more than my due.

'Then is it something I *haven't* done?' asked Doreen, plainly having had to screw up courage to ask the question.

At first I wasn't altogether clear what she meant. We were not being very successful at communicating with one another this evening.

'I'm not with you,' I said warily.

Her voice low, her dry eyes downcast: 'That Sunday when we went up to Throstle Moor and it rained all day. Would it have made any difference if it hadn't rained?'

I was going to get pipedreams out of this. Really detailed pipedreams, elaborately constructed like airships. I was going to reconstitute that day slowly, step by step. Getting off the Textile District bus. Walking up the heather, hand in hand. Finding, after a search, a suitable protected spot, then sitting down, then lying down. Unbuttoning her waterproof.

Would it have made any difference? It hadn't made any difference in the case of Terry Liversedge, who had touched one of Betty Parsons' breasts five times and both of them twice. But I wasn't Terry Liversedge.

With real regret I said, 'There have been other days since then, Doreen.'

'I didn't want to look cheap,' she said in a low voice.

I considered, seriously and soberly, the likely consequences of taking Doreen into the bluebell woods now. Without question, we would do what we hadn't done on Throstle Moor that Sunday. I could be having that experience within, say, four minutes.

Against that, she would cry afterwards, the kind of tears I didn't want to see, and say something like, 'Tell me I haven't still got the brush-off, Ray.' And the situation thereafter, although perhaps much improved, could not be the one I was looking for. Doreen, with the distractions, commitments and restrictions I had already catalogued, could not match my own aspirations. Under the qualified new regime that it seemed to me she was now offering, it would be possible when she asked, 'What are you thinking?' to tell her in some detail, and perhaps act upon it to a limited extent. But she would never be able to understand that I was thinking it full-time.

'Come on,' I said gruffly. 'I'll buy you some chips on the way home.'

'Shouldn't I be buying my own chips now?' she responded with a wry perkiness that was quite heart-wrenching for a second. As we got to our feet she took a last look at her brush-off card. 'I didn't know you could draw,' said Doreen, and put it in her shoulder-bag as carefully as if it were a pressed flower.

We walked Indian file along the path through the rhododendrons and she did not take my arm even when the path widened. Nor did we speak at all until we were back in Crag Park Avenue, when Doreen said, 'Ray, is it all right if I ask you one more question?'

'Fire away.'

Without any tinge of humiliation, as if simply seeking a point of information, she asked bluntly, 'Is it true that Douglas Beckett swopped me with you for a second-hand electric razor?'

Oh, that. Yes, in essence it was true. In fact it was true in substance. What had happened was that Doreen and Betty Parsons had made up a twosome to the Clock Ballroom afternoon dancing class on the one Saturday that I, who had had my eye on Doreen since catching her looking at me in the Royal Coronation branch library reading-room and deciding that she was my type, had been unable to go. I had contracted to weed the next-door widowed fossil's garden in exchange for her late husband's broken-down Remington electric dry-shaver. But Douglas and Terry Liversedge had gone; and so when Terry Liversedge clicked with Betty Parsons, Douglas got Doreen Theaker, for all that he was already encumbered with Alma Tipper, who did not go dancing because of her lameness.

The following Saturday morning I was taking the electric razor for repair to Moffat's Radio & Electrical when I ran into Douglas, who at once coveted it. After some haggling we reached an agreement that if I gave him the razor, he would give me Doreen. Accordingly, at the Clock Ballroom dancing class that afternoon, Douglas and I contrived to swop partners with a clodhopping dexterity that fooled neither of them. The deed, however, was done, and it was I who had the last stumbling waltz with Doreen. As for Douglas's side of the bargain, the electric razor had made no noticeable difference to his hirsute appearance.

'No, it's not true, and I wish Douglas had never said it, even as a joke. It so happens that I sold him the razor on the same day I met you at the Clock, and that's all there is to it.'

That sounded convincing enough, I thought. It seemed to satisfy Doreen, for she went on, 'The reason I ask is that Geoffrey Sissons asked me to go out with him earlier.'

'He did, did he?' I said, quite coldly. Geoffrey Sissons had been too premature by half. It was well-established that you did not ask chicks to go out with you if they were already going out with somebody else. As a Communist and a stickler for principle, Geoffrey Sissons should have known this.

'I just wanted to make sure you haven't swopped me for anything,' said Doreen, quite apologetically.

I put as much warmth as I dared back into my voice. 'Come off it, Doreen.'

We had reached The Parade and the welcoming lights of the Argosy Fish Saloon. If we ate our chips in the cycle shop doorway we could say our last good-night at the top of the cinder path and then I could join Douglas and Terry Liversedge and look at the talent.

'I don't think I want any chips,' said Doreen. 'I think I'll just pop back to the Youth Guild for half an hour.'

And play table tennis with Geoffrey Sissons. Which meant that I couldn't go back to the Youth Guild too, and had nothing to do for the rest of the evening except eat a bag of chips by myself. For the first time, watching her go with what looked to me like a spring in her step, I felt a pang at what I was losing.

# 5

The arrangement with Moult & Sumpter, a letter signed with a pterodactyl scrawl confirmed, was that I should start on the Monday after coming back from the caravan holiday in Colwyn Bay. I would have preferred to start at once, on the Friday morning if they wanted me to, but they would not hear of it.

The Colwyn Bay holiday passed in a fidget of restlessness and boredom. There was a certain amount of talent on hand but mainly in twos: it was difficult to click if you were not likewise one of a pair, especially when hampered by aborigines. I went for long walks along the promenade or sat about in deck chairs, to the extent that the aborigines began to fear I was ill or apprehensive about starting work.

I was thinking alternately about Audrey and Doreen. In the first few days I thought mainly about Doreen and what might have been on Throstle Moor had the day been dry, and what it would be like now on the sands, by moonlight. But by the beginning of the second week Doreen had begun to recede and I was thinking mainly about Audrey and wondering whether she was at that moment thinking about me and trying to decide what she would wear for my first day at the office. Perhaps she would dab perfume behind her ears – if so, I would know at once that she was interested. The time dragged by. I found a scrap of paper and pencil and worked out that in 9,678 minutes I should be walking through the door of Moult & Sumpter's.

In the event it was in 9,635 minutes, or a full three-quarters of an hour early, that I arrived at the Corn Exchange – so early that the building was not yet open and I had to wait twenty minutes or so for a uniformed dodo to appear and fuss open the big doors. Then another twenty minutes of pacing the balcony in my new squeaking shoes before the first of the Moult & Sumpter pterodactyls arrived to admit me. He was closely followed by the other two, by which time I had already been established at a small, splintering desk, seemingly

39

recovered from a rubbish-dump but placed gratifyingly near to Audrey's. She was now nearly a minute late.

The pterodactyls took up their own places, leaving me to twiddle the knitted tie that picked out the greens in my Horne Bros Lovat tweed jacket, and wish I had tied it in a Windsor knot. Eventually one of them, Mr Sumpter, said across his cluttered table to Mr Eppersley, the cashier pterodactyl, 'He might as well try his hand with the Inward Post book, mightn't he?' The other, scooping up a sheaf of opened and unopened mail and producing a Dickensian-looking register, commenced to instruct me in how to sort the letters into different heaps and enter them in the book under different headings. I tried to pay attention, but it was now coming up to twenty-past nine and Audrey had still not arrived.

It could be that she was notorious for her bad timekeeping. She would roll up at half-past to a chorus of joshing recrimination, my contribution to which would be the conspiratorial smile of a potential ally. If she had not arrived by half-past it meant she had flu. Suddenly, perhaps nudged by the schoolroom smell that all offices seemed to have, I was back in my first term at the College of Commerce with my eye swivelling between Victoria Leadenbury's empty desk and the wall clock.

On the stroke of half-past the Sumpter pterodactyl flung down his fountain-pen with an exclamation. 'Blast! You do realise we've let Audrey go without showing him where to make the coffee?'

Let Audrey go. My dismay must have showed, for the Eppersley pterodactyl sniggered roguishly, 'Oh dear, he wishes he hadn't joined us now!' He did not know how close he was to the truth. 'It's all right, lad,' he went on, still twinkling. 'She's only gone on holiday, if you can hold out for a week.'

One hundred and sixty-seven and a half hours. I was not sure that I could.

I was shown the filing-cabinet drawer where Audrey kept the coffee mugs and the jar of Bev and powdered milk, and directed to the throbbing water-heater in the still-room off a half-landing. I loitered there as long as I dared in case any other typist from any other office came by with a tray of coffee mugs, petticoats swirling. But none did. It was going to be a long week.

Terry Liversedge had begun work at the Pennines Linen Bank that same day, and Douglas at the Grippenshaw Permanent Building Society the week before. We had arranged to meet in the lunch-hour at a place Douglas had found where you could have an adequate snack for about a shilling. The Kismet Café, it was called, a pleasantly gloomy chamber occupying the basement of one of the Victorian office buildings, with fake oak panelling and tables marked out as chequerboards where dodo solicitors' clerks played chess over their morning coffee and biscuits. The boiled-pudding smell was lightened by the fragrance of orange pekoe wafting in from the tea warehouse across the hot street.

It was gratifying to be smoking cork-tipped cigarettes and studying menus in a proper restaurant like businessmen, and we agreed to make it a regular institution. It was a pity, though, that the Kismet was so male-dominated – the office chicks, we were to find, either queued up for salads at Clough & Clough's cafeteria or stayed at their desks nibbling crispbreads and apples. It could also have been a drawback that most of the waitresses were fossils, but we had the luck to be served by one who wasn't. She was small and dark and looked to be in her early twenties. She reminded Terry Liversedge of Jane Powell, though Douglas and I thought she was more like Lana Morris. Her name, Douglas had learned, was Madge. The black dress she had on under her white apron did not have any visible fastenings, but as to that it was unlikely she would wear her uniform on a date, though it was to be hoped she would retain her black sheer rayon stockings. She was my type. Douglas and Terry Liversedge thought she was their type too, and we decided that this would be our usual table. We lit fresh Craven A's and ordered Welsh rarebits.

We compared experiences at our places of work. Or rather Douglas and Terry Liversedge did, for I had nothing to report.

'Can't move for crumpet, youth,' bragged Terry Liversedge. 'There's at least three who are definitely panting for it, not including some very distinct possibilities I haven't had the chance to size up yet. Sheila, that's one of them. She's been giving me the eye all morning. The only drawback is, she's got what her best friends won't tell her about. BO.'

'Musk, that could be,' advised Douglas. 'The powerful

41

odour secreted by female animals when on heat. It's rare in humans unless they have an unusually high sex drive.'

'Oh, she's gasping for it, no doubt about it.'

'Then get stuck in, mon capitaine. You could always wear a war-surplus gasmask.'

'What about that bird you followed into the bank in the first place?' I asked. 'Any joy there?'

Terry Liversedge looked blank.

'The one with the mud-splashes on her legs that you were raving about. The one that made you change your mind about going to the National Provincial.'

'Oh, her.' He had forgotten all about her. 'No, the thing is, youth, you can't see the front counter from where I sit, and even if you could they'd take a dim view of my nipping out and asking one of the customers for a date, wouldn't they? So I'll just have to make do with the available talent.'

For Douglas's part, there was talent in plenty in the Grippenshaw Permanent Building Society's typing-pool, but unfortunately it was on a different floor from his, and so he had made little contact so far. However, one of his duties was to pick up the outgoing mail from the general manager's office several times a day, and this had given him ample opportunity to study Mrs Duckworth, the secretary. She was almost certainly a nymphomaniac. Waiting for letters to be signed, Douglas had observed her habit of sitting with crossed legs, swinging her ankle back and forth. This near-simulation of the sex act was meant, consciously or not, to arouse the male at whom the ankle-swinging was aimed – in this case, Douglas. It was Freudian, he explained. He had not as yet pursued his advantage with Mrs Duckworth, since older women liked the stimulation of making the running themselves. He was awaiting developments.

'And your little chickadee's gone on her holidays, has she, Ray?' mused Terry Liversedge unkindly as he pushed away his plate and began to fill his pipe with Cut Golden Bar from a new oilskin pouch. 'She'll be flat on her back under the pier by ten o'clock tonight.'

I thought of that remark at ten o'clock that night as I slumped in a chintz-covered armchair listening to a Home Service detective play for want of anything better to occupy me. It was strangely unsettling, being indoors with no homework to do. I had nothing to read, for all the books in the house were clean ones. There were some copies of *Lilliput* with pictures of naked girls draped in fishnet up in my bedroom, but I could not be bothered unscrewing the plywood panel that blocked up my fireplace where I kept them. The 9,300 minutes before Audrey's return were passing slowly.

The novelty of working for a living took only a day or two to wear off. The Corn Exchange, which had always seemed a lively place on my short cuts to the College of Commerce, was dull, with a high pterodactyl and dodo count and little talent to be seen. It was interesting when Friday finally rolled round to look down from the balcony at the weekly corn market, but there were no farmers' daughters in the throng. The real highlight of the week was getting our first wage-packets and splashing out on the full two-and-ninepenny set menu at the Kismet, thus eliciting from Madge the remark, 'It's good to tell it's payday, isn't it, lads?' This at once put us on chaffing terms, where previously even Terry Liversedge had been diffident about trying to exchange banter with Madge.

I heard myself saying with thick-tongued heaviness, 'Don't worry, Madge, there'll still enough plenty be for taking out with tonight.'

I was stumbling over words as if they were boulders in my path. It was because she was an older woman in sophisticated surroundings and also because Douglas and Terry Liversedge were listening. It wouldn't be like this with Audrey.

'You what, love?'

'He's got his dad's false teeth in again, Madge,' Terry Liversedge chipped in. 'What he's trying to say is we'll have plenty enough left over for taking you out on the town tonight.'

'Where are you all taking me, then? The Hotel Metropole dinner dance?'

'If you like, sweetheart.'

Feeling myself blushing, I stared at the menu and had no further truck with Madge. Terry Liversedge, on the other hand, kept up the badinage all through lunch, not only when Madge appeared at our table but even when she was bustling past it, tray held high, to serve someone else. He seemed able to tailor each bit of chaff so that it fell perfectly within her hearing range yet gave her ample time for a word in reply over her shoulder before moving out of earshot. At first Douglas tried to join in but his speech was too slow and convoluted. He was no match for Terry Liversedge's quickfire prattle about whether we should wear evening dress with carnations in our buttonholes, whether Madge would prefer to be picked up in the Rolls or the Bentley, and so on. When she came to make out our bills Madge said to Douglas and me, 'You'll have to bring him in on payday more often if this is how it takes him.' It was a real compliment and this time it was Terry Liversedge who blushed, but out of gratification. He left Madge a shilling tip.

I did not begrudge him his little moment, for reading between the lines it was apparent that he was having surprisingly little success with the talent at the Pennines Linen Bank.

His answers were evasive: 'Trouble is, youth, when you look at them close to, half of them are about ninety. Well past it, I'm afraid.' What about the three who were definitely panting for it? 'They are, but they're the sort who play hard to get. Life's too short, youth.' And Sheila, with her BO or musk, who had been giving him the eye? 'Cockteaser. I can spot 'em a mile off.'

'Smell them a mile off, don't you mean, old bean, old boy?' said Douglas drily. Not that he had anything to write home about. He had yet even to exchange two words with any of the talent from the Grippenshaw Permanent Building Society typing-pool. On the Mrs Duckworth front he had revised his earlier impression. What Douglas was now saying was, 'I'm very much afraid she's frigid.' Behind this new thinking was a study of her body movements while she was busying herself about the office. Douglas had become convinced that she was encased from neck to kneecaps in the type of all-embracing elastic armour known as 'the passion-killer'. When she stretched up to a shelf or bent over, he said, she seemed completely solid under her dress, reminding him of a plywood Mrs Noah in a toyshop ark. It was very off-putting.

I could afford to be sympathetic to Douglas and magnanimous towards Terry Liversedge. By the time I got back to the Corn Exchange after lunch there would be only 241,200 seconds before I saw Audrey. Unlike the Pennines Linen Bank

44

and the Grippenshaw Permanent Building Society, which the other two had found swarming with youths of their own age, Moult & Sumpter harboured no potential rivals. Further, Audrey did not wear passion-killers. 'I'm quids in,' I said. But to myself.

That first payday ended on a depressing note. By way of celebration we had decided to spend the evening on a pub-crawl. Accordingly, having met at the Kardomah after work for toasted teacakes and milk, which Douglas said would line the stomach against the ravages of alcohol, we started at the Raven, an obscure little beerhouse in Back Cloth Hall Lane. The tiny taproom, empty except for a leather-skinned fossil half asleep over a glass at its single beaten-copper table, smelled like the crates of returned beer bottles we had sometimes rummaged among behind the off-licence in Station Approach. It was a pungent, nostril-searing smell that alerted the taste-buds.

Terry Liversedge had been in a pub before, while on holiday in Blackpool, and so Douglas and I left him to do the ordering. We lined ourselves up along the small bar, leaning against it confidently enough although the foot-rail pressed unexpectedly against our shins. There was no one in attendance.

'What are we all having?' asked Terry Liversedge over-loudly. 'Rum and pep or what?'

'I think we ought to start on beer and work our way up,' murmured Douglas. Nodding, I drew Terry Liversedge's attention to a free-standing placard on the bar counter: '*Insist on Buckton's Dinner Ales.*'

A shirtsleeved and waistcoated dodo, carrying an unfolded *Grippenshaw Evening Argus*, emerged from a back room in response to our coughs and shufflings.

'Could we have three Buckton's Dinner Ales, please?' said Terry Liversedge unwaveringly.

'Out,' said the dodo.

'You should have asked for three halves of bitter,' counselled Douglas as we slunk out of Back Cloth Hall Lane into Cross Street.

'If you know so much about it, Duggerlugs,' snapped Terry Liversedge, 'you can do the fizzing ordering yourself.' But we had no nerve left to continue the pub-crawl. The first house at the Palace of Varieties, another treat we had promised ourselves, had already started, and so we took ourselves off to the Gaumont Coliseum. Richard Widmark in *Night and the City*. The cinema was packed with clerks and shop assistants on Friday-night dates and all around us, when the lights faded up after the Gaumont British News, there was a stir of movement as powdered faces were lifted from padded shoulders, and arms that had been stealthily exploring ribcages or hips were brought into neutral position on the backs of seats.

'We must look like three frigging monks,' said Terry Liversedge, gloomily puffing at his pipe.

Possibly. But so far as I was concerned, there were now less than 220,000 seconds of the celibate life left to serve.

# 6

The V of the slip–over cotton jumper she wore above a tailored flannel skirt, side-zipping, showed her neck vermilion from sunburn, and her nose was peeling. I knew she had been to Bridlington from the red-letter-day arrival of a postcard of the boating-lake addressed to 'all at Moult & Sumpter'. Drawing-pinned to the wall, it was now noticeably convex from my repeatedly curling it forward to re-read the message on the back. In a cramped, sloping scribble that contrasted intriguingly with all the schoolgirlish rounded hands I had known, she had written, as a PS to the usual holiday banalities, 'How is Ray getting on with Old Faithful?' This was not, as I at first thought, a daring reference to one of the pterodactyls – it was Moult & Sumpter's nickname for the bubbling water-heater in the still-room.

There was much to be read into the message. Not only was she thinking about me in Bridlington, but she wanted me to know that she was thinking about me, hence the apparently innocuous enquiry. The esoteric mention of Old Faithful, initiating me into an office joke, was a small masonic-type gesture indicating a desire for shared intimacies. The choice of the familiar diminutive 'Ray' magnified that desire almost into a yearning. For once, the conventional salutation, 'Wish you were here,' throbbed with meaning. Quids in.

As on my first day at Moult & Sumpter's I got to the Corn Exchange early, in the hope that Audrey would arrive before the pterodactyls and we could chat about our respective holidays and exchange a joke about Old Faithful. After a few more such pleasantries during the day, I could perhaps fall in with her as she walked to her trolley-bus stop after work. I would make this seem casual and natural. Not until about Wednesday would I ask her what she was doing on Friday evening.

But Audrey did not turn up until the stroke of nine, by which time two of the pterodactyls were already installed. There was some joshing about her sunburn, to which I was not encouraged to contribute, then the senior pterodactyl arrived and we settled down to our daily routine, which in Audrey's case commenced with making the coffee.

So far she had been in the office for over five minutes without speaking to me or even looking in my direction. But I knew it was only the shyness which in our country often took the form of elaborate ostracisation.

As she clattered her tray of mugs out of the filing cabinet near my desk I said, 'Do you need any help?' I had rehearsed the words and spoke them carefully, slightly slurring only the word 'need' which I had substituted at the very last moment for 'want'.

Audrey gave me the secret half-smile that was private to our country and excluded the pterodactyls, and shook her head. I noticed, as she stooped over the filing-cabinet drawer, that she wore a slim silver chain around her neck, its pendant concealed in the cleft below the V of her jumper. A person could idly toy with that chain, affecting curiosity as to what was suspended from it, gradually delving further and further towards the concealed pendant.

I did hope it was a pendant and not a crucifix. Douglas had delivered a solemn warning against Catholic chicks, saying that their insistence on coitus interruptus, or the rhythm method as he believed he had heard it called, made doing them a chancy and unsatisfactory business.

One of the pterodactyls made a laboured joke about Audrey needing to look to her laurels after my success as surrogate coffee-maker, to which she riposted in her rounded-off mill girl's voice, 'If he's all that good he can go on making it.' Then, standing by my desk with the pressure of her tray producing a soft bulge to her girdleless stomach, just as when I had first encountered her, she spoke to me directly for the first time since that day a month ago, 'D'you take sugar, Ray?'

'Yes, please, two lumps or three?' I said idiotically. But at least my gabbling had the effect of re-eliciting the half-smile.

'Which?'

'Two or three, I really don't mind,' I insisted, trying to make the slip sound intentional. She gave me a look of humorous mock-exasperation, but I could see that there was a little real exasperation there too. I ploughed on. 'Give me two, then if it's too sweet I can always put another lump in.'

'You mean not sweet enough, don't you?'

I was saved from further imbecilities by a pterodactyl cry of, 'Oh, go and make the coffee, Audrey, for heaven's sake, and put him out of his misery!' She departed, leaving me at the mercy of some ponderous ribbing about tongue-tied swains, love's young dream and suchlike nudgings. But at least I was making headway, and she had called me Ray. I would have to find a way of working her own name into the conversation.

But once we had got through the coffee interlude ('Thank you, Audrey . . . No, Audrey, it's just right, Audrey, thank you. Not too sweet, Audrey, and not too not sweet enough') there was little chance for further exchanges. I had already registered that apart from desultory outbreaks of chaff it was not a very gregarious office.

The truth was that we were kept too busy for socialising. Although there were few callers, most public enquiries being dealt with by the firm's booking-office in the private coach station down by the market, there was a lot of mail to be got through, and the pterodactyls were constantly on the telephone to hotels and holiday camps or on the direct line to the booking-office. Audrey handled these calls from the little PBX board by her desk, and I, crouched over my Inward Post book, pricked up my ears whenever the telephone buzzed. Ineptly managing the switchboard myself during her absence, I had dreaded some cock-of-the-walk male voice asking if it could speak to Miss Audrey Marsh, please. There had been no such call, but of course any regular boy-friend would have known she was on holiday. I listened now. She took two brief personal calls, to a background of reproachful breathing and slamming shut of ledgers by the pterodactyls, but they were evidently from girl-friends, and her making an arrangement to accompany one of them on a shoe-buying spree on Saturday afternoon suggested that she was not overburdened with social engagements. True, Saturday evening was yet to be accounted for, and I had an apprehensive moment when she answered a buzz on her switchboard with, 'Hello, light of my life, have you missed me?', but it was only the manager of the booking-office. He had called in once or twice and he was a pterodactyl. Touch wood, I was still quids in.

But not making much progress – as, since they clearly weren't either, I didn't mind admitting to Douglas and Terry

Liversedge when we met in the Kismet at noon. Audrey and I had been told to stagger our lunches as the pterodactyls did, which meant she would be going out the moment I got back and not returning until two, leaving me only three and a half hours to make some kind of impression upon which to build the next day. On my performance so far, I could look forward only to a repetition of the morning's coffee-break inanities during afternoon tea.

'You want to get your finger out, youth,' admonished Terry Liversedge. 'Always supposing this dame's all you've cracked her up to be, if you don't get in there someone else will. It might even be me, the way things are going.'

Even if we did not exchange another word all afternoon, I would definitely get as far as walking her to her trolley-bus stop.

At twenty-five-past five Audrey picked up her handbag and trotted off along the balcony to the Ladies'. At five-thirty the pterodactyls closed their ledgers, capped their fountain pens and snapped their spectacles away in chamois-lined cases. The Eppersley pterodactyl said to me, as he had said for five consecutive evenings and as he evidently meant to say every night for so long as I worked at Moult & Sumpter's, 'Haven't you got a home to go to, young feller-me-lad?', which was the signal for me too to clear my things away. I did it slowly, so slowly that as Audrey came back through the door the Sumpter pterodactyl dumped a pile of Highland coach tour brochures on my desk with the words, 'If you're not in all that much of a hurry, laddy, I wouldn't mind getting these off tonight. Mr Moult won't be locking up for a few minutes.'

'Poor you!' mouthed Audrey in secret sympathy. Perhaps, when she had got her cardigan on over her jumper, she meant to stay behind and help me.

Audrey picked up her bag again. 'Good night, Mr Moult. Good night, Mr Sumpter. Good night, Mr Eppersley. Good night, Ray.'

'That's quite all right,' I appeared to have replied. And she was gone.

Tuesday was an improvement. I spilt coffee on the Inward Post book, affording myself the opportunity of asking Audrey where she kept the blotting-paper. She introduced me to the stationery cupboard and spent far more time than was necessary pointing out carbon paper, typewriter ribbons and other items. We had quite a chat about stationery. That morning she was wearing a light two-piece suit in blue cotton, the side-buttoning skirt sunray-pleated to display her legs to anyone chancing to follow her up a spiral staircase. I wondered if she made a practice of wearing something different every day or whether it was for my benefit.

I made my plans and when five-thirty came I was ready. I had already had the signal from the Eppersley pterodactyl and cleared my desk. As Audrey slung her bag over her shoulder and began, 'Good night, Mr Moult, good night, Mr Sumpter, good night, Mr Eppersley – ' I cut in, nearly word-perfect: 'No need for me to say good night to me, Audrey, I'm coming with you. Good night, Mr Moult. Good night, Mr Sumpter. Good night, Mr Eppersley.' The pterodactyls were exchanging knowing simpers as I held the door open for her but I didn't care.

As we walked along the balcony to the clattering steps that led down to the main entrance of the Corn Exchange, Audrey, to my relief, took the initiative.

'How do you like working at the joke-shop, then?'

'Oh, very nicely. I think it's bestly interesting work.'

She either ignored or didn't notice the new adverb that had formed on my lips like one of Douglas's warts. 'I wouldn't go as far as that. Still, they're better than some firms you hear about.'

I said, enunciating very carefully, my mouth opening wide as if I were doing an elocution exercise, 'Have you worked there long, Audrey?'

'Too long. Well, good night, Ray.'

I was so stunned, and she moved so quickly, that she was passing through the big main doorway of the Corn Exchange before I saw, very slightly in retrospect like an instant playback, what was happening. A brunette of about her own age, wearing a three-button swagger coat that could quickly be wrapped around her naked body should some hikers come by while we were lying together in the gorse, was waiting for her by the varnished directory-board at the bottom of the steps. She was my type. As Audrey took her arm and they moved away she tilted her head round to give me a curious, I hoped predatory, up-and-down look.

Audrey had the best legs, though. I stood on the steps of the Corn Exchange, waving out the match that had lit one of the Markovitch box of twenty-five Black and White I had hoped to share with her, and watched the pair of them chattering their way arm-in-arm along Exchange Row, Audrey's sunray pleats swinging like a hula-skirt. Perhaps they were talking about me.

'You're going about it the wrong way, youth,' Terry Liversedge saw fit to warn over lunch next day.

I didn't think so. Arriving at Moult & Sumpter's that morning I had found her waiting on the balcony while one of the pterodactyls fumbled for his keys. I took my opportunity.

'Enjoy the picture last night, Audrey?'

'Who says we went to the pictures?'

'Well, if meet you friend straight from work, there's not Elsie many places you could be going.'

'That's what you think.'

Never mind that she must be convinced by now that I had a speech impediment, we had had a conversation. And I didn't care whether she'd spent the evening at the pictures or watching the hands of the Cloth Hall clock go round. The quids-in point was that she'd spent it with a girl-friend, not a boy-friend.

'I'm afraid that's where you could be making a very grave error, mon brave,' said Douglas, cutting into his Welsh rarebit.

'How can I be, man? I saw them going off together.'

'He's as thick as a brick,' said Terry Liversedge. 'They were off to meet two blokes, dozey! Isn't that right, Doug?'

'I very much doubt it, old bean, old boy, or they wouldn't have bothered to meet one another first,' said Douglas superciliously, to Terry Liversedge's manifest annoyance. Terry Liversedge was getting very short-tempered of late. It was frustration, Douglas told him. 'They might have been *hoping* to meet two blokes, which is not quite the same thing. But it's what you have to watch out for, Raymondo.'

'I don't know what you're rambling on about,' I said sulkily. Perhaps I was suffering from frustration, too.

'That's because you don't listen!' snapped Douglas. Perhaps all three of us were. 'All right, let's take it step by step. What is the only reason two chicks go to the pix together?'

'They've both got a crush on Van Johnson. I don't know, Douglas. You tell me.'

'To get picked up.'

Undeniable, but unacceptable. 'Not necessarily,' I said distantly.

'Then answer me this. Why do two chaps go to the pix together?'

'How do I know? They might be nancy-boys.'

'You're whistling in the dark, youth!' Terry Liversedge came in with, as if he'd already made Douglas's point himself instead of missing it altogether. 'What you've got there is a tart who's panting for it so much, she's going out night after night looking high and low for it, and you're letting her slip through your fingers.'

I let this wild surmise go unchallenged, contenting myself with, 'No I'm not, I'm breaking her in gradually.'

'They don't go for that, kiddo. That's what I keep saying – you're going the wrong way about it.'

Always the first to finish his meal, Douglas had shovelled his Welsh rarebit away and was tapping one of the oval Abdulla Turkish he now habitually smoked against the gunmetal cigarette-case he had just acquired, the elegance of the gesture being marred by the unsightly growths on the back of his hand. 'There's one infallible approach if you're prepared to take a calculated risk,' he said. 'It's been statistically proved that if you go up to twenty-five dames and say, "Excuse me, but I would like to do you" straight out, you'll get the come-on from at least one.'

'Why don't you try it out on Madge?' I asked Terry Liversedge, following his carnal stare. She was standing at a nearby table, waiting for two solicitors' clerk dodoes to choose between the soup and the half-grapefruit. Terry Liversedge said, still eyeing her black stocking-seams, 'Are you sure it's only twenty-five?'

'It might be a hundred,' said Douglas hastily. 'Besides, we want to come here again.'

Reluctantly, Terry Liversedge came back to earth. 'I'm not suggesting you go as far as that, youth, but there is a right way and a wrong way of getting off with a chick, you know.'

I winked at Douglas. 'Get Errol Flynn!'

'Credit where due, mon brave. You must admit Terence's

devastating technique has all the Pennines Linen Bank talent eating out of his hand,' said Douglas with silky malice.

'Listen, Duggerlugs, I could have at least six of those bints this very day, if I wanted to. I just happen to be choosy. Anyway, look who's talking! I haven't noticed the Grippenshaw Permanent Building Society talent exactly queueing three deep for you to get their knickers down. So shut it.'

Douglas and Terry Liversedge glowered at one another while Madge came to clear our plates away. 'Cat got his tongue today?' she said to me.

I said, 'He's got a problem big on his mind, Madge.' I was about to add an elephantine rider to the effect that he was trying to think up the best way of asking her for a date (or more likely that he was trying to think out the last way of taxing me for a bait), but she had whisked herself off.

There was no point in trying to change the subject, since there was no other subject we wished to talk about. I said pacifyingly, 'All right, Terry, I'm always willing to learn. How would *you* go about getting off with this dame?'

Mollified, Terry Liversedge said, 'I'm not sure I ought to give away my trade secrets.'

'Please your frigging self, my friend.'

'All right, youth, I'll tell you what I'll do, seeing it's you. I'll tell you how to click with this dish if you do me a small favour.'

'What small favour?' I asked warily.

Terry Liversedge took out the shiny mock-crocodile wallet he had just bought for himself in Clough & Clough's menswear department. He extracted from it a folded sheaf of pages torn from a shorthand notebook. 'Look after this for me.'

I glanced at the neat Pitman outlines.'. . . *Then, as my hand travelled lightly up your creamy thighs. . .*'

'I thought you were going to give this to Rebecca Redlips?'

'I still am, youth, but I thought all things considered it'd be better if I left Commerce first. I'm just waiting till they start the winter term.'

'You want certifying. Why are you trying to palm it off on me?'

'Because my old lady knows Pitman. If I'm sitting in the lounge and my jacket's in my bedroom, I shit a brick every time she goes upstairs.'

'Go on, then,' I said, stuffing the pages in my pocket. I didn't mind being the custodian of Terry Liversedge's outpourings, in fact I quite looked forward to reading them again. In private. 'Now what's this magic formula of yours?'

'It's simple, youth. All you've got to do is arouse their curiosity.'

'How?'

'Tell her if she feels in the pocket of your flannels you've got a big surprise for her,' suggested Douglas with unusual coarseness.

'Quiet, Duggerlugs, this is serious! Now I'll tell you what you do, youth. This brunette chick you say she goes around with. Ask her what her name is.'

'Why?'

'That's what *she'll* want to know. And what you say is, "Oh, because my oppo Terry Liversedge wants a date with her." You can crack on I was waiting for you outside the Corn Exchange last night and asked who she was.'

'I may be slow on the uptake,' I said, 'but what good does that do me?'

'You *are* slow on the uptake, Ray, because shall I tell you what'll happen? She'll go straight to her mate and tell her what you've said. And this dame'll be so curious about who this Terry Liversedge is when he's at home, that do you know what she'll say? She'll say, "Why don't you tell them both to meet us outside the Paramount on Friday night?" The beauty of it is that instead of you having to think up ways of asking your bird for a date, she'll be asking *you* for one!'

It seemed a circumlocutory approach to me but Terry Liversedge had a persuasive way with him. And his lack of success at the Pennines Linen Bank apart, he did have an impressive record at clicking. 'D'you think it'll work?' I asked Douglas.

'She can only fall about with hysterical laughter, old bean, old boy,' said Douglas, signalling to Madge to give him change out of a ten-shilling note.

'And you'd really go on a blind date with this dish?' I persisted to Terry Liversedge, giving him the chance to change his mind. 'I mean, not that she's got a face like the back of a tram-smash, but you must be fizzing desperate to go out with a chick you've never set eyes on.'

'I am, youth.'

'We're all desperate,' said Douglas mournfully. 'Ask her if she's got a sister.'

# 7

The next few days were purgatory.

After my tactical discussion with Terry Liversedge I was determined to speak to Audrey on the lines suggested that very evening as we left the office. I did not bargain for her leaving early to post a registered letter. Nor did I bargain for Terry Liversedge skulking in wait at the bottom of the Corn Exchange Chambers steps.

'What did she say, youth?'

'I haven't asked her yet.'

'What are you waiting for? Ask her, Ray! We could have been going out with them tomorrow night if you'd done what I told you to do.'

Although we had given up our College of Commerce custom of travelling into town together, he was waiting for me again at the trolley-bus terminus in the morning. 'Right, kiddo, today's the day. You know what you've got to say, don't you?'

He hectored me all through lunch at the Kismet Café. 'I don't understand you, Watmough. You've got two birds as much on a plate as this poached egg on toast and you won't even lift a finger to let them know we're interested.' I knew he would be hanging about the Corn Exchange that evening. I dodged out through the side doors and jumped on a moving 19A Circular.

It was no use. The more Terry Liversedge pestered me the less I felt able to go through with it. Even practising in my head, I couldn't get the words right. 'Oh, by the boy, Audrey, you know that friend I saw you met with when we stepped down the steps on Tuesday Monday.' Every time I anticipated speaking to Audrey my tongue felt like liver.

On Friday morning, under the disapproving glare of the pterodactyls, I stiltedly accepted my first personal call on Audrey's switchboard.

'Hello? Raymond Watmough speaking.'

'It's me, youth. I've got to make this quick, while the

57

sub-manager's out having a leak.'

'Oh, yes?'

'Have you asked her yet?'

'Not at the present moment, no.'

'Are you going to?'

'I hope to, in due course.'

'Listen, youth, her name's Audrey, isn't it?'

'I believe so, yes.'

'Right. If you haven't asked her by lunchtime I'm going to ring her up and ask her myself. And if you think I'm joking, just you wait.'

'I see. Thank you very much.'

'Just get her asked and stop bollocking about.'

'Thank you very much. Good bye.'

It was the pterodactyls who saved the day for me. As I replaced the receiver I became aware that the Eppersley pterodactyl was standing impatiently at my elbow, brandishing a parcel of brochures. 'You haven't been round to our booking-office yet, Raymond, have you?'

'No, Mr Eppersley, but I've a good idea where it is.'

'Why doesn't Audrey go with him, then she can show him how to do the log sheets and so on in case he ever has to do holiday relief over there?' chipped in the Sumpter pterodactyl.

It was as if he'd invited me to take Audrey to the pictures followed by a Sunday afternoon walk in the fields near the sewage farm. Even as she slipped on the cardigan that would protect her white jumper from grass stains, a ploy formulated in my mind, every detail worked out. The walk to the coach station would take us down Sheepgate, past the Paramount cinema. Drawing Audrey's attention to the 'Forthcoming attractions' poster I would say, 'Oh, by the way, Audrey, I don't know whether you've seen that but it's very good, according to what I've heard.' I would rehearse this speech to myself several times before giving voice to it, at the same time making sure that we were not walking so quickly as to induce breathlessness. Then, according to her answer, I would either say, 'Oh, well in that case I wonder if you feel like seeing it, say next Wednesday, Thursday, Friday or Saturday?' or, 'Oh, well, it was worth a try. And I suppose as bad luck would have it you've seen that picture at the Gaumont Coliseum as well?'

Once we had started discussing the actual arrangements, I

might do Terry Liversedge a favour. 'I don't suppose you'd like to make it a foursome?' I would say. 'Only a friend of mine wants to meet that friend of yours who's a friend of yours.' No I wouldn't. Stuff Terry Liversedge.

As we walked down Exchange Row, Audrey gave me prattling potted biographies of the pterodactyls and dodoes we should be encountering in the Moult & Sumpter booking office. She seemed very much at ease with me, which put me at ease too; but I confined my side of the chatter to monosyllabic interjections, to be on the safe side. Mentally, I was going over my lines.

It occurred to me, as we turned into Victoria Street, that the Paramount showed only new releases, and so I should have to redraft my speech to eliminate the passage about not knowing whether Audrey had seen next week's film. I would have to say, 'Oh, by the way, Audrey, I don't know whether you've read anything about anything in the *Picturegoer,* but it's supposed to be very good.' Or rather, 'Oh, by the way, Audrey, I don't know whether you've read anything about that picture in the picture, but it's supposing to be every good.' Or rather . . .

Through the area railings of Victoria Chambers, the Gothic sign pointing down to the Kismet Café came into view.

'That's where I have lunch,' I ventured.

Audrey looked down at the restaurant's criss-cross leaded windows, appearing genuinely interested. 'Oh, so that's where you go. I wondered where you took yourself off to every day.'

I allowed myself a deep, luxurious breath. If Audrey spent my lunch hour sitting at her desk wondering where I had gone and who I was with, then asking her out should be the merest of formalities. 'Oh, by the way, Audrey, I don't know whether you've read anything about that particular film in the *Picturegoer* . . .'

But we did not go past the Paramount. Audrey chose to keep straight on along Victoria Street where it crossed Sheepgate, not turning until we reached Market Street. We were almost at the coach station before I had completed a further reworking of what I had to say.

We were cutting through the covered market. Audrey was saying something about how she loved the smell of slab toffee from the sweet stalls although she would never dream of eating it. I knew I was under-rehearsed but if I didn't do it now it would be hanging over me all the time we were at the Moult & Sumpter booking-office, and I would be too wretched and washed-out to seize my last chance on the way back. I said, heart pounding, 'Oh, by the way, talking of sweets, there's a picture on at the Paramount.'

I didn't look at her but the half-smile would have touched her lips. 'It'd be funny if there wasn't, seeing it's a picture-house.'

'Ah, yes, but I meant is it was a good one.'

'It's not all that hot, actually. All right if you like Danny Kaye but as it happens I don't.'

I had to plough on, the text of what I was supposed to say next swirling loosely about in my head like anagrams. 'Oh, well that's my bad luck, Ben, because there's always the Gaumont Coliseum.'

'Oh dear me,' said Audrey, and stopped. We were in the sawdust-sprinkled lane of the market where all the fish stalls were, slab upon white marble slab laid out with glistening lemon soles and cod and halibut steaks. Ever after, the stench of wet fish was to remind me of this moment.

'I'm very sorry, Ray, but if you're asking me for a date, I'm very sorry but you're too late with your barrow.' It was comforting that there could be times when Audrey too had trouble with her syntax.

'Oh, I see. I didn't know you were already steady.'

'It's more than going steady. I've been engaged for three months.'

She couldn't be. The first thing I invariably did after noting how their clothes unfastened was to look at the third finger, left hand. I had checked.

'I know what you're thinking,' said Audrey. She put her hands to her neck and drew out from under her jumper the delicate silver chain that had featured so prominently in my recent imaginings. What I had always seen as a pendant was a slender ring of pale gold, emblazoned with a cluster of crushed diamonds in what looked to me the shape of a bow tie. Twelve guineas. There were tray upon tray of the things in Rabinowitcz the Jeweller's windows. 'My mam and dad won't let me get officially engaged until I'm eighteen in

60

February, so this is where I keep it. I wear it on my finger when Ronnie comes home on leave.'

'So he's doing his call-up, is he?' That would put him at getting on for two years my senior at least, with a world of experience behind him. I had had no chance from the start.

'Yes, he's in the RAF. Stationed over at Skipton-on-Swale, so it's not too bad. He gets home most weekends.'

'Oh, well, worth a try,' I said, and managed a semblance of the rueful grin I supposed was expected of me. It was a difficult feat to achieve, for I could not remember ever having been so cheesed, as Audrey's RAF fiancé might have put it. It was not the fact of committing myself to Moult & Sumpter's on a false premise that depressed me, it was that I had wasted so much time on the wrong scent. It was now five weeks since I had given Doreen Theaker her brush-off card and I was as far from my goal as I had ever been.

Audrey misread my woebegone expression. 'Sorry, Ray. I know some girls do go out with other lads when they're engaged, but I don't happen to believe in two-timing.'

We walked on and out the other end of the market. Across Airebridge Road was the coach station. One of Moult & Sumpter's cream and green streamlined coaches was just pulling out, laden with fossils on a pensioners' outing. The dodo behind the wheel sounded his horn, and Audrey waved.

There was something I had to say next. I knew it would be unsuitable in the unanticipated context but I was programmed to say it. It was out of my hands.

'Oh, by the way, I've been meaning to ask you, Audrey. That friend of ours that I saw you with this night. I was wondering what's her name was.'

Audrey shot me an acid look. 'I'll say this for you – you don't believe in letting the grass grow under your feet, do you?'

'No, I was only wonderling,' I said, feeling pink, and since we had now reached the Moult & Sumpter booking-office and she didn't respond further, I left it at that. The only remaining embarrassment now would be the walk back to the Corn Exchange. Audrey solved that by saying, after she had introduced me to the dodoes and pterodactyls inhabiting the booking-office, 'You might as well go straight to lunch from here, mightn't you, Ray? I'll leave you to get the hang of things.' And to my relief she departed.

'So in other words, you've buggered it up!' exclaimed Terry Liversedge, throwing down his fork.

'What do you mean, buggered it up! She's engaged, man! I can't make her unengaged, can I? How is that buggering it up?'

'You didn't get *me* fixed up, though, did you? No, you naffing didn't! Pull the ladder up, that's you, Watmough.'

'I did try, Terry. She jumped to the conclusion I was trying to get a date with this bird for myself, because I couldn't get one with her.'

'And that's what you call not buggering it up, is it? You're like a tart in a trance, youth.'

We were at a very low ebb. Douglas, who had taken to ordering a black coffee after his daily Welsh rarebit, toyed moodily with his cup. He had hardly spoken since taking his seat with the news that he had been given a massive brush-off by one of the chicks from the Grippenshaw Permanent Building Society whom he had encountered in the lift. With more candour than either I or Terry Liversedge could have summoned in his place, Douglas told us exactly what she had said when asked for a date: 'Off your knees, small fry – we don't go out with office boys.' It was evident, concluded Douglas glumly, that she was speaking on behalf of the entire typing-pool.

Madge scribbled our bills on the pad that hung from her waist on a length of string. For a woman in her twenties she had a very slim waist. It could be worth betting her that her waist could be spanned with two hands.

'You're a lively-looking lot today. Anyone'd think it was Monday, not Friday.'

'It might just as well be Monday, Madge.' I admired the way Terry Liversedge could get over the stumbling block of 'Monday, Madge' with such ease.

'What, stood you up for tonight, has she?'

'No one to be stood up by, that's the trouble. I'm a free agent, Madge.'

'Well, there's always the Metropole, my love.' Terry Liversedge in white tie and tails escorting Madge to the Hotel Metropole dinner dance had become a running joke between them.

'The Metropole?' Terry Liversedge pretended to misunder-
stand. 'Right, you're on, Madge. Which shall it be – the bridal
suite or just a common-or-garden double bedroom?' I
marvelled less at his audacity than at his articulation.

'Get away with you. You wouldn't know what to do when
you got there.'

Madge, unruffled, moved around the table collecting our
florins and sixpences. 'Who wouldn't? Don't be too sure!'
pursued Terry Liversedge, but she had tired of the game and
declined to go on with it.

That should have warned Terry Liversedge but he never
knew when enough was enough. In his own defence he
claimed later that he genuinely thought Madge might have
been giving him the come-on, and that he had reached a point
where he had to clutch at straws. As we were pushing out
through the swing doors, he muttered impulsively, 'I'll catch
you up,' and doubled back into the restaurant.

Douglas and I waited on the steps leading up to Victoria
Street. Through the leaded windows we saw Terry
Liversedge approach Madge at the cash-desk where she was
counting out coins against the counterfoils on her bill-pad. He
took her by the elbow and drew her aside. They were quite
close to the wall and it cannot have helped Terry Liversedge
that Madge was able to see Douglas and me with our noses
flattened against the window.

'Speaking as one who passed his Boy Sprout lip-reading
badge,' murmured Douglas, swarthy hand shading his eyes to
get a better view, 'I'd say we'd better start looking round for a
new lunch venue.'

'Why, what's he saying?'

'Something like, "Don't mind my asking, Madge, but what
would you say if I told you I'd like to do you?"'

'The stupid crow – he's cracked up at last.'

Douglas didn't have to lip-read Madge's reply. 'Be your
age, you dirty young devil!' she could quite clearly be seen to
explode after several thunderstruck seconds. Then, giving
Terry Liversedge a push, she flounced out of sight, only to
reappear in the basement-well below us as the swing doors
were violently thrust open and Terry Liversedge was
propelled through them. 'And I suppose you two put him up
to it!' screeched Madge as he swaggered up the steps after us.

'Well, you don't come in here again! Any of you!'

'Ah well,' said Terry Liversedge as we hurried away along Victoria Street like small boys who have been pressing doorbells, 'one down and twenty-four to go, eh, Douglas?'

Having the quality of some of our schoolday scrapes, the episode quite cheered us up. We were still in high spirits when we met after work in the foyer of the Palace of Varieties, in plenty of time for the six o'clock first house.

It was not to last, although our euphoria was to carry us well through the first half of the show, whose title, *Eves Without Leaves*, promised much. We had never been allowed into the Palace before, thanks to the Watch Committee's insistence on a lower age limit of eighteen, but this time our bespoke suits and Tootal ties and cigarettes, supplemented by the pork pie hat which Terry Liversedge now affected, swept us past the box-office dodo without query. Once we had been admitted, as Douglas had pointed out, we were unlikely to be asked to show our identity cards when ordering drinks, provided we went the right way about it. Jubilantly we made for the red plushness of the circle bar, to drink halves of bitter and study our elbow-lifting reflections in all the caryatid-encrusted mirrors.

From the programme that Terry Liversedge had bought to scrape acquaintance with an usherette, we saw that the 'Eves' of the title was an exaggeration. There was one nude only, who would be following the crosstalk act in the first half and the juggler in the second. We sipped our beer meditatively, enjoying the bouquet, until muffled laughter began to percolate through the heavy velvet curtains that cut the bar off from the circle, then we drank up with a flourish and wandered out with elaborate nonchalance.

We stood at the back of the circle, leaning against the brass rail on folded arms with the casualness of regular patrons, tapping our feet and puckering our lips into a soundless accompaniment as the comedians signed themselves off with a chorus of 'Music, music, music'.

A front cloth of crushed silk-like material fell, washed in pink light, a tinny fanfare trumpeted up from the orchestra pit, and the disembodied voice of a northern troglodyte trying to sound like a southern one boomed through an off-stage microphone: 'Ladies and gentlemen, in her first appearance at the Palace of Varieties this evening, the delectable Wanda will portray in all their classic beauty those lovely daughters of the Greek god Zeus, the nine magnificent muses. First, it is with very great pleasure that we introduce you our audience to the beautiful Clio, the muse of history!'

None of us had ever seen a naked woman outside the pages of *Lilliput* and *Health and Efficiency*. Suddenly dry-mouthed, it seemed to me important to make it appear to the nearby plum-uniformed dodo with epaulettes like scrubbing-brushes that it was a commonplace sight. As, to the accompaniment of scraping violins, the crushed silk curtain began to divide slowly like a twitching blind in a Crag Park Avenue bay window, I stifled a world-weary yawn and looked up with careless curiosity at the cherub-painted ceiling, the sweep of my gaze taking in Douglas who was moistening his thick lips and Terry Liversedge whose knuckles glistened white as he abstractedly tamped his pipe. Both were staring mesmerically ahead. I allowed my own unhurried, panoramic glance to reach the proscenium arch just as the divided curtain fell again, affording me a confused glimpse of some chiffony material cascading over a plinth.

'Next, ladies and gentlemen, the charming Calliope, the muse of epic poetry.'

As one who has grudgingly decided that he might as well see what he has paid to see, I kept my eyes on the stage as the curtain parted again, revealing first the plinth, then limbs draped with pink chiffon up to the hips, then a torso looking remarkably like an imperceptibly breathing edition of all the *Lilliput, London Opinion* and *Health and Efficiency* photographs I had ever seen, except that Wanda was clutching a scroll to represent epic poetry and her long blonde hair was crowned with a laurel wreath. A smattering of applause, in which we did not join, and the crushed silk fell back into place.

'And now, ladies and gentlemen, the delightful Thalia, the muse of comedy.'

The same chiffon-protected pose, with the laurel wreath still in position but a Greek-chorus mask substituting for the scroll. I focused on Wanda's breasts, hoping for a return of the dry-mouth sensation, but they seemed curiously lifeless. That would be the Watch Committee's doing: the statuesque poses had the eye-feasting potential of an exhibit in the Grippenshaw

Borough Museum.

As the delicious Terpsichore, muse of dance, was superseded by the voluptuous Urania, muse of the stars, my expression of boredom was no longer simulated.

'. . . And finally, ladies and gentlemen, the wonderful Wanda's accolade to the beauty of all the beauties. It is our pleasure to present to you here this evening that supreme heart-stopping lovely, the proud and mysterious Melpomene, muse of tragedy.'

The violins sawed away and the crushed silk drapes rose. Still she stood on her plinth but the chiffon had fallen about her ankles. The laurel wreath was gone and the blonde hair fell about her shoulders where her head was bowed tragically. I ran my prematurely languid eye up and down Wanda's at last completely naked but still completely marble body, and it was only as it came to rest on her long hair and what I could see of her face that my heart belatedly raced. I was seeing not an unassailable vaudeville star who would be departing for the fastnesses of Bradford and Sunderland when her week was up, but Betty Parsons of Grippenshaw Girls' High School who would not be straying very far from Winifred Drive.

Terry Liversedge too saw the resemblance after I had pointed it out. 'What wouldn't I give to do that one!' he said wistfully during the interval, holding his glass up to the light as he had seen the fossils doing. The beer did not have the same kick as the first glass, for a slow gloom was settling upon us. After Wanda's next and last appearance in the second half, as Venus In All Her Guises, the dead weekend and all the working days beyond it stretched before us like desert sand. We would have nothing to look forward to at all.

'Who does she remind you of?' I said.

'I couldn't say, youth, I didn't get round to looking at her clock.'

'Get an eyeful of her in the second half, then, and tell me if she doesn't remind you of Betty Parsons.'

Terry Liversedge considered, then nodded slowly. 'You're right, Ray. You're not wrong.'

A faraway look came into his blue eyes and I knew what he was thinking even before he confessed it.

'Do you know what? When I think what I could be doing to that bint at this very minute instead of standing here with you two, I begin to realise that brushing her off was the biggest mistake I've ever made.'

'It's never too late, mon capitaine,' said Douglas.

Terry Liversedge swilled beer around his glass moodily. 'I'm afraid it is, youth. She'll be going out with some other lucky devil by now. That's the trouble, you see – I've given her the taste for it. She can't do without it.'

Considering that he had only five times fondled one of Betty Parsons' breasts and both of them but twice, I thought he was exaggerating the case against himself. But I knew how he felt. My own thoughts had drifted from Betty Parsons to Doreen Theaker who would be out this evening with Geoffrey Sissons. I was conjecturing how soon it would be before she was admitting to him that there were times when she felt like going beyond French kissing, and whether it would keep fine for them on their first outing to Throstle Moor.

'Raymondo's round, I believe,' said Douglas, pointedly placing his empty glass on the bar counter in front of me.

I took out my new wallet, real leather as against Terry Liversedge's mock crocodile. 'I don't know about you lot but I'm going on to shorts. Who wants a rum and pep?'

# 8

Then it all seemed to start coming right at once.

Woozily, that Friday night, we had decided on a council of war. Something had to be done. We had set off on what was supposed to be a momentous journey, yet here we were, drifting.

We convened on Saturday afternoon by the park boating-lake, selected not as an old haunt but because it was handily near the perimeter of the Cragside municipal golf course, and on the fourth rum and peppermint the night before Terry Liversedge had floated the notion of hiring some clubs and taking the game up. Douglas and I had enthusiastically endorsed the idea, a pleasant vision of mixed sixsomes with partners in Gor-ray skirts pushing into the background the uncomfortable realisation that its underlying purpose was to give us something to do on the long blank weekends.

In the light of day the proposal seemed negative and even maudlin. We were not done for yet. But with the golf scheme shelved, the boating-lake as a venue was seen at once to be a bad mistake.

The keen autumnal air and the glinting sun, with a hint of distant bonfires already permeating the full-blown rhododendron smell, at once touched the park with life yet distanced its sights and sounds as with an invisible screen so that it had the unreality of an animated steel engraving. Yet while the swooping of kites and the keeling-over of model yachts and the children's shouts all seemed to be going on behind an immense sheet of glass, it was a different kind of remoteness that separated Douglas, Terry Liversedge and me from the concrete circumference of the boating-lake even as we strolled around it. We had walked the Duck-walk a hundred times or more, on Saturday or Sunday afternoons like this, eyeing as we did now, and being eyed by, the shoulder-quaking, arm-shoving twosomes and threesomes straggling anti-clockwise to us. But now it was like watching a pageant. This was our country and we were in it, but we were not of this region of it any longer.

'Mine's all right but I don't go much on your two,' said Terry Liversedge automatically as, with the standard up-and-down, side-turning looks, we peacock-sauntered past a fanciable one, a presentable one, and the one wearing glasses who would do for Douglas. But his heart wasn't in it any more and I was glad he didn't make the tongue-clicking sound that would have told them we were interested. Clicking on the Duck-walk now would have been on a par with playing in the sandpit on the tarmac playground through the glass wall.

Following Terry Liversedge's lead I was trying out a pipe. While he stood by the lake's edge combing his breeze-ruffled hair I re-lit it, ignoring the exaggerated nose-wrinklings of a pair of rouge-daubed mill-girls wobbling by on their high heels like children playing dressing-up games in their mothers' shoes, and not responding to their loud and leaden attempts at repartee.

'Pooh, can you smell burning varnish, Mavis?'

'Smells more like somebody's hair on fire, if you ask me owt.'

Douglas too had taken up a pipe, a meerschaum in his case, and he had indeed singed a stray black lock while adjusting the flame of his petrol lighter. He was not amused. 'It's like a kindergarten down here,' said Douglas brusquely. 'Come on, let's move.'

Usually it was Terry Liversedge who led the way but this time we followed Douglas. Striding out across the grass, pipes jutting all at the same aggressive angle, and shedding three catherine-wheel trails of sparks and smoke, we affected not to hear the diminishing sound of derisive laughter as we put the Duck-walk behind us.

'Do you know what all that reminded me of?' said Terry Liversedge. 'Trying on an old school sports shirt again and finding it's two sizes too small.'

Puffing knowingly and nodding, Douglas and I acknowledged the unaccustomed sagacity of this observation, though all it conjured up for me was a picture of Terry Liversedge preening in front of his wardrobe mirror. Why had he been trying on his old school sports shirts? I was prepared to bet Douglas privately that he had at last bought the cravat he had been hankering after and was looking for something to go with it.

'And the Youth Guild'll be just as bad,' he went on. 'So if anyone's thinking of suggesting we go to that social tonight, forget it. I don't go in for cradle-snatching.'

I had been thinking of mentioning the Youth Guild social but Terry Liversedge was right. Doreen Theaker would be there with Geoffrey Sissons, and Betty Parsons and Alma Tipper with whoever they were going out with now. There was a chance of finding talent of a sort but there was an even bigger chance of our standing around the Youth Guild hut like three spare parts.

'There's always the Clock Ballroom,' I suggested tentatively.

'H'm,' hedged Douglas.

'Possible, possible,' hedged Terry Liversedge.

Their lukewarmness was predictable and understandable. If we had outgrown the Duck-walk and the Youth Guild, we had yet to demonstrate that we were ready for the Clock Ballroom. We had been two or three times on Saturday afternoon dancing-class half-price tickets, lured by the big-band siren sounds and the sight of streams of talent in flared dance-frocks that would billow around their waists as they defied the ban on jitterbugging; but it had usually been a disastrous experience, unless we had gone in escorting partners, when it had become a pointlessly expensive one. Most of the unaccompanied talent, we had found, consisted of gum-chewing hard cases from the carpet mills who made a regular circuit of the town's dance halls: The Rex on Wednesday, the Mecca-Locarno on Fridays and the Clock on Saturdays – like gypsies working the fairs. Their first object was to dance, which they did with grim concentration, selecting their partners from only the most proficient of the sharp-suited, Don Ameche-moustached junior troglodytes and National Servicemen with berets tucked into their epaulettes who cruised restlessly around the clusters of gilded cane chairs on the periphery of the maple-sprung floor. Anyone still taking tango lessons or seen to be counting to himself when negotiating the foxtrot got short shrift. I had seen Terry Liversedge, on our last foray to the Clock, approach a sequin-sheathed brass-blonde in what he had observed to be the approved manner – gliding towards her with arms outstretched, crooning 'Bewitched, bothered and bewildered' and rolling his eyes – only to be told, 'Get on home, your mother wants your boots for loaf-tins.'

'I think we should hold the Clock in reserve,' said Douglas.

'So do I, but I thought I'd mention it,' I said.

'Oh, well, if you two have already made your minds up, there's no point in even talking about it,' said Terry Liversedge as if aggrieved. 'So what's the plan of action, then?'

'I'm thinking, I'm thinking,' said Douglas.

We passed through the great coat-of-arms-emblazoned gates into Crag Park Avenue. The cobbled crescent forming the entrance to the park was lively with vendors selling kites, balloons and paper parasols, and a threepenny-bit-brandishing throng around Petrocelli's ice-cream cart. My mouth burning with backfired tobacco ash, I could have fancied a vanilla wafer if left to myself, and so I guessed could Douglas and Terry Liversedge if left to themselves. We contented ourselves with sly, covetous looks as we walked past, pipes puffing; until Terry Liversedge grabbed my arm with a hoarse cry of 'Other side, quick!' and hustled Douglas and me across the Avenue.

Professing to study a privet hedge topiaried into the shape of battlements, Terry Liversedge jerked his head back viciously to take in Petrocelli's ice-cream cart. 'I told you she'd get herself fixed up, didn't I? It's that Ralph Driver who works in the library. I must say she hasn't wasted much time.'

Two of Petrocelli's customers were just detaching them-selves from the cluster around the cart, clutching ice-cream cones, his plain, hers strawberry. Ralph Driver from the Royal Coronation branch library, though in shirt-sleeves, carried a folded mackintosh, the only purpose of which could have been to spread out over a bed of leaves or soft grass. Betty Parsons, the first time I had seen her not in school uniform, wore a full-skirted blue gingham dress, back-fastening, that could fall about her hips like chiffon, later to slip down about her ankles. *And now, ladies and gentlemen, the loveliness of Betty Parsons daringly combines with the genius of the great artist Botticelli to bring you the devastating beauty of Venus, Goddess of Love, rising from the sea in all her nudity.*

'I expect she was taking out a new library book and thought she'd kill two birds with one stone,' murmured Douglas unkindly. Terry Liversedge pretended not to hear him.

She did not see us. Her long-limbed, straight-backed prefect's walk took her to the park gates, her escort's free hand seeking her free hand as they turned along the rhododendron alley, licking their ice-cream cones in what Terry Liversedge, for one, seemed to think was a lascivious manner.

'Do you know what I wish, youth?' he said to me as we moved off again up Crag Park Avenue. 'I wish you'd never reminded me how much she looks like that Wanda bint at the Palace last night. I keep thinking of her stripping off, and all the things I could be doing to her. Just like that jammy crow'll be doing as soon as he's got a threepenny ice-cream cornet down her throat. It's driving me round the twist, Ray, I don't mind telling you.' It was beginning to drive me the same way, but I thought it would be imprudent to admit it.

We reached the corner of Wendy Rise where Terry Liversedge lived, and stood tapping out our pipes on the enamelled street sign. No one cared to review our options for the evening, for they were pretty-well non-existent. We could not go to either the Gainsborough or the Gem Picture Palace for fear of having to play gooseberry to couples we would know in the back row. The Youth Guild social and the Clock Ballroom were out for their different reasons. With the aftertaste of rum and peppermint still lingering, we had no stomach for the Saturday-night pub-crawl that had seemed such a good idea in the circle bar of the Palace of Varieties. We could always stay in and make model aeroplanes.

'I'm giving very serious thought to going swimming after tea,' I said diffidently. 'I haven't been to Cragside Lido on a Saturday night for ages.'

'Neither have I, because I haven't fizzing had to up to press,' said Terry Liversedge. 'You'll get nothing there, youth.'

'We'll get nothing standing on the corner of your street, either!'

We were snapping again. 'I thought you were supposed to be thinking,' snarled Terry Liversedge, turning on Douglas.

'I've thought,' said Douglas.

There was an irritating pause while Douglas waited, as he always did, for one of us to prompt him.

'All right, Einstein – give,' I said.

Douglas allowed the thick horn-rimmed spectacles he now affected to slide down his nose. They were his reading-glasses really but he had taken to wearing them all the time even though they caused him to bump into things. Grasping the Wendy Rise street sign like a lectern, he began rhetorically: 'What is the object of the exercise?'

'To find some crumpet,' said Terry Liversedge sourly.

'Not only to find some crumpet, mon capitaine, but to find the kind of crumpet that is going to be whimpering and gibbering and slobbering for it in the shortest possible time. Where, we have to ask ourselves, is that crumpet most likely to be available?'

'Come on, Duggerlugs, get on with it.'

'Let us apply logic, my friends. We are seeking three dames who want it but are not getting it. Now what is the well-known psychological condition of dames who want it but can't get it?'

I was not familiar with the breed. 'You're the one who's supposed to have read Freud, Douglas.'

'They're frustrated, aren't they? The same as we are. So out of all the places where a frustrated chap might wander, where is he most likely to meet a frustrated dame?'

We considered the question earnestly. I suggested the women's prison up on Top Moor. Terry Liversedge plumped for St Joseph's Convent near the College of Commerce. Douglas ruled them both out on grounds of inaccessibility by the male sex.

'Where, then?' asked Terry Liversedge.

'Church,' said Douglas.

I exchanged an eyebrow-shooting glance with Terry Liversedge, who then ostentatiously stalked off along Wendy Rise as if washing his hands of the discussion and going home. Folding his arms, Douglas complacently awaited his return.

Terry Liversedge retraced his steps with feigned reluctance, as if giving Douglas a last chance. 'And I thought *I* was going crackers! All right, Duggerlugs, I'll buy it. Why should a frustrated dame take it into her head to go to church? To get off with the vicar, I suppose.'

'Very probably,' said Douglas. 'Or the choirmaster. Or anything else in trousers – such as three new members of the congregation.'

'You've got evidence of this, have you?' I asked, interest beginning to stir despite my scepticism.

'It's very generally known, mon brave. There's a certain type of repressed nympho who's too nice and well-brought-up to go out and get herself picked up and shafted by the nearest lorry-driver, which is what she'd dearly like to do, so she goes to church where it's possible to talk to strange bods and still be respectable. Once she's clicked, of course, all that pent-up frustration comes out.'

I could see that Terry Liversedge was wavering too, though he was determined to remain scornful. 'Does Dr Kinsey know about this, Douglas? How come we've never come across any of these nymphos at the Youth Guild?'

He was thinking of the Youth Guild's affiliation with the Crag Park Avenue Congregational Chapel, of which all three of us were supposedly members although we had not set foot in the place since our Sunday School days. While there was no obligation for Youth Guild members to attend chapel, any young nymphomaniac Congregationalist seeking sanctuary under its tin roof would almost certainly have been encouraged to join the Youth Guild. But none had come our way.

'We're talking about St Chad's parish church, not the Congregational Chapel. It's a question of different atmospheres,' said Douglas authoritatively. Concluding his case, he prodded his outstretched left palm with a wart-noduled index finger. 'You see, with this particular type of nympho, the Church of England service actually acts as an aphrodisiac. It's what gets them going, like Spanish bullfights do with another type of nympho. So by the time you click with them, they're really in the mood.'

Terry Liversedge and I affected to ponder, not wishing to admit outright that we were persuaded.

'What do you think?' I ventured. He grunted dubiously.

'Mark you, I don't promise results,' said Douglas. 'But if we do strike lucky, there's one slight problem. Once they're on the job they're insatiable.'

'That's the least of our worries, kiddo.'

# 9

And with Sunday evening upon us it was Terry Liversedge who was the first to arrive outside St Chad's, even though Douglas and I were there a good half hour before we reckoned the service would begin, to allow a covert analysis of the available talent.

The parish church, a blackened Gothic mass with a stump tower rising from a dishevelled graveyard, was in the older part of the neighbourhood beyond the station, where stone cottages still stood among the pebbledash. Meandering back late from our monastic Saturday night swim at Cragside Lido, we had plumped after long deliberation for the evening rather than the morning service, on Douglas's submission that the material we were looking for would be feeling more restless by nightfall; but we could not be bothered dragging ourselves down to St Chad's to look up the hours of service. We were going by the timetable posted outside the Crag Park Avenue Congregational Church. As Terry Liversedge said, they probably all opened at the same time, like cinemas.

I happened to catch up with Douglas in Station Approach and we strode to St Chad's together. Like me, he had given some thought to his dress. He was wearing his customary off-duty sports jacket, but with the trousers of his Price-rite Tailoring dark suit, newly pressed, and a pair of patent leather shoes, dancing pumps really, that he had bought off a second-hand stall behind the covered market. The outfit was completed by a starched-collar blue striped shirt with pin-check tie held in place by a new chromium tie-clip with dangling chain.

I had an exactly similar tie-clip, bought at the same time from the same shop in Town Arcade, but in the end I had opted for tossing my tie casually over my shoulder as if picked up by the breeze. I too wore my sports jacket but with flannels, deliberately left baggy, and my tartan shirt and sandals. Where Douglas had for once larded down his lank black hair until it looked like a rubber bathing cap, I had combed mine out to fall carelessly over one eye. I was aiming for the bohemian effect.

'Though I don't know why we bother,' I said as we rounded the corner into Church Street, Douglas limping somewhat because his patent leather shoes had begun to pinch his feet. 'Any crackling that's on offer, we both know who's going to get first pick.'

Holding up his steel pocket mirror and patting ridges of buttery hair into place, Terry Liversedge lounged by a cottage wall opposite the parish church's rustic-looking lych-gate. Though minus his pork-pie hat for once, he looked very smart. He had had the idea of unstitching the crest from his old College of Commerce blazer, creating an American-style maroon jacket that teamed up nicely with his cavalry twill trousers and chrome-buckled crepes. And I was right: Terry Liversedge had acquired a cravat, a yellow silk one imprinted with red dragons rampant. He wore it tucked into the neck of a black shirt.

'Get Van Johnson,' I said, tossing back a lock of hair.

'Get Veronica Lake,' said Terry Liversedge. He took one more look in his steel mirror and slipped it back into his top pocket, well-satisfied with his appearance as he had every right to be. The pipe clenched between his teeth and tautening his cheekbones really did set off his profile to good effect.

Douglas and I filled our pipes and lit them. We had evidently judged the time of the evening service correctly, for we could hear the first sad notes of the organ striking up, and a dodo in a long black gown, presumably the verger, was darting through the rickety gravestones and into the church. The churchyard threw off the rhododendron scents of the park combined with the mustier smells of old stone and dead flowers: anticipation mingled with melancholy.

'I'm still not sure about this, youth,' said Terry Liversedge. 'All I've seen going in so far are two old women who look as if they've come for one another's memorial service.'

'Fret not,' said Douglas complacently.

Around the bend of the pavement skirting the church wall hobbled a fossil in a heavy cloth coat that hung on her frail body like a turtle's shell. 'There goes yours, Douglas,' I said, as her broom-handle legs, with stocking wrinkles standing out like veins, conveyed her painfully through the lych-gate and up the church path.

In the wake of the female fossil came two male ones in best suits, clawing at their tight collars, and behind them, two more female ones, obviously their wives, dressed against any possible sudden drop in the temperature in matronly swagger coats, gloves and hats.

'I'll tell you what, Duggerlugs,' said Terry Liversedge uneasily. 'You go in and keep a place for me, and you can have first crack at anything that's in there already. Before I commit myself, I'll wait outside and see what turns up in the talent stakes from now on.'

'I did say no results were promised,' protested Douglas.

'Too true, youth. The way things are going you'd have to promise miracles to get me in that church.'

I said softly, 'What about this, then?' Fetching up the rear of what was seemingly a family procession, and accompanied by a cloth-cocooned aborigine who was probably her mother, was what Douglas at once accurately categorised as a very nice piece of homework. Full red lips and jet black hair under a blue pillbox hat contrasted with a creamy complexion unusual in a rouge-orientated town. She was the right age, upwards of sixteen or so, and my type. She was exceptionally neatly dressed, wearing real nylons with white court shoes that matched her kid gloves and handbag, and a powder-blue suit so immaculate that she would surely wish to remove it herself and fold it carefully on top of her discarded petticoat. Her hat and gloves she could perhaps keep on.

'Bloody hell fire!' was all Terry Liversedge could say as we watched her turn in through the lych-gate. Her seams were perfectly straight. She had very good legs.

The church organ was bashing away at full blast now. It looked as if we had seen the last of the congregation arrive, for there were no more straggling fossils – and no more very nice pieces of homework. Terry Liversedge licked a palm and pressed back a ripple of blond hair. It was such a foregone conclusion that I had half a mind to leave him to it and go try my luck at the First Church of Christ Scientist down in the town.

'Come on, then, what are we waiting for?' said Terry Liversedge, adjusting an unsatisfactory fold in his cravat. He led the way across Church Street, scattering sparks as he knocked his pipe out against the arch of the lych-gate. I did the same, and my pipe snapped neatly in two, the bowl rolling away under the stone bench.

'You should never do that,' said Douglas unnecessarily, tamping out his own pipe with a nicotine-stained thumb and slipping it smugly into his pocket. His patent leather dancing pumps were causing him no little pain by now, reducing him to a bow-legged hobble as he fetched up the rear along the weed-sprouting path up to the church porch.

Never having been in an Anglican church before we were unprepared for its spaciousness and grandeur, outclassing even the Gainsborough cinema. Its echoing flagstone floor, cool stone pillars and neon-sign-flashing stained glass were in rich contrast to what I remembered of the drab green plaster walls and plain schoolroom windows of Crag Park Avenue Congregational. Only the eucalyptus smell of polish, super-imposed on a dank wash-house odour, linked them.

The black-gowned dodo at the door handed us prayer books and hymn books and we tiptoed into the body of the church, Douglas having to point like a ballet dancer so as not to crack the patent leather of his aching shoes. As my eyes grew accustomed to the gloom and I took in bank upon bank of empty, dark wooden pews, I was surprised at the smallness of the congregation. There could not have been more than twenty people in the church, most of them scattered about the first three or four rows, far away down the centre aisle near the pulpit and altar. Our notion of skulking at the back had to be abandoned.

Luckily she was sitting, or as it turned out kneeling, in the last occupied row of pews, with only her aborigine mother for company. We shuffled into the row behind, positioning ourselves somewhat to her left so that she would be able to turn round and choose one of us without cricking her neck. We could see now that she was praying, her head bent to expose a milky band of flesh between her black hair and blue collar. Douglas nudged me fiercely and grimaced both at me and Terry Liversedge, to urge us to take note of this evidence of the interplay between religion and nymphomania.

At the organ, two bony dodo hands protruding from a billowing mass of white fabric continued their seemingly aimless exploration of the keyboard. Shufflings and throat-clearings reverberated, every smallest sound magnified; you could almost hear the rasp of chin on starched white collar and the creaking of tea-rose corsets, as one fossil after another turned round to stare at us. I supposed, though with increasing uneasiness as I saw that we had become a whispered talking-point, that they were merely unused to strangers augmenting their small congregation.

She had finished her praying and taken her seat, and now she too looked round with simulated casualness, appraising the three of us. We gazed back avidly, but to no response. She picked up her prayer book and opened it, and Terry Liversedge, doubtless to ingratiate himself with her in the event of her glancing round again, did the same.

'What do we do when it starts?' he whispered, holding the prayer book up to his mouth as soundproofing.

'Just watch what everybody else does,' whispered Douglas.

I wasn't so sure it was going to be as simple as that. As the stares and mutterings continued, I was more and more convinced that something was wrong. I opened my own prayer book and leafed through it, then looked up again to find her smiling round at us, responding, as I could have guessed even if I could not have seen, to the suggestive leer which Terry Liversedge called his 'come-on look'. As she turned back he mouthed 'We're in!' and made a soft clicking noise with his tongue.

There was a sudden ripple of activity as several youngish-looking gargoyles of either sex in the front rows, prompted by the dodo in the black robes, began to detach themselves from the congregation and move towards the open space in front of the pews. At the same time a troglodyte in various flowing garments, who would be the vicar, was emerging in what seemed to be a one-man procession from some vaulted chamber off a side aisle. Our view of the proceedings was temporarily obscured as the dodo at the organ unexpectedly became animated and abandoned his five-finger exercises for a robust and recognisable hymn tune, whereupon the remaining fossils started to rise in twos and threes. We too got to our feet. The troglodyte had brought himself to a ceremonial stop to face the group of youngish and self-conscious gargoyles, who could now clearly be seen. All of them wore stiff best clothes and one of them was cradling a gargoyle baby contained in a cascading bolt of creamy white lace.

79

My open prayer book shielding my mouth, I gestured Terry Liversedge and Douglas closer.

'Has the penny dropped?'

'What, youth?'

'We're at a fizzing christening!'

Terry Liversedge's eyes swivelled only momentarily to take in the proceedings involving the gargoyle baby, then clicked back to feast on the slim powder-blue skirt where it clung to a curving hip-line. 'I don't care if we're at a funeral – I'm staying.'

Douglas, as dismayed as I was, hissed, 'All I can say is, don't blame me if we end up as three flaming godfathers.'

The fossils were shuffling back into their seats, one after the other like falling dominoes. We followed suit.

*'Dearly beloved, forasmuch as all men are conceived and born in sin. . .'*

The troglodyte dronings, ricocheting around the high-raftered ecclesiastical stratosphere in distorted echoes, seemed to go on a long time. Sporadically the fossils uncertainly bobbed to their feet or bowed their heads in mumbled prayer. The christening was a very ragged affair. Unable to follow Douglas's advice to do as everyone else did, since the majority had no more idea what to do than we had, we took our lead from the seasoned churchgoer in the powder-blue suit, interpreting her every response and genuflection as a sign of advanced nymphomania. During some protracted negotiations around the font, when the baby gargoyle commenced to cry, she quite openly looked round and shot us a wide and accommodating smile. Even on the most conservative reading there was collusion in that smile, suggesting a bond of sympathy at the small, shared vicissitude of the gargoyle baby's grizzling. As Terry Liversedge had said, we were in. Or rather, one of us was.

Presently the dronings petered out and the fossils, with rather more alacrity than they had so far displayed, rose to sing hymn No 651, 'Sweet infancy, O heavenly fire'. It was not a hymn that had featured in our school assembly repertoire and so Douglas, Terry Liversedge and I were able to contribute even less than the rest of the congregation. After half-heartedly miming a line or two I allowed my attention to wander from my hymn book as I tried idly to identify a fragrant burning smell that had begun to impregnate the damp, eucalyptus-tinged air. Vague on Anglican ritual, I had an idea that it could be incense.

Though the full red lips could be seen moving, I had listened in vain for the sound of her voice. Now, however, as the incense smell grew more pungent, she unexpectedly and astonishingly turned full round towards us, and, gustily singing *'O heavenly joy, O great and sacred blessedness, Which I possess, So great a joy, Who did into my arms convey?'* brazenly pointed at us with a gloved forefinger.

Terry Liversedge, unable to believe his luck, prodded himself in the chest, mouthing, 'Who, me?' Still singing, she shook her head with frowning vehemence, gesticulating even more insistently. It became plain that she was pointing at Douglas, or rather at Douglas's jacket. His pocket was on fire.

Sheepishly, Douglas drew out his smouldering pipe, dragging with it a wispy trail of aromatic Punchbowle tobacco. Inhibited by his surroundings, he was diffident about tackling his scorched pocket with undue energy. He gave it one or two ineffectual pats. Smoke billowed through the charred cloth like steam out of a ventilator. Tugging the pocket open with one hand, and about to delve into it with the other, he realised he was encumbered by his still unextinguished meerschaum. He rammed the pipe in his mouth, with the unfortunate side-effect that it looked as if he were smoking in church, then plunged his liberated hand deep into his smoke-swirling pocket, only to withdraw it with a suppressed yelp as if having grabbed a red-hot coal. Waggling a hairy hand vigorously, Douglas withdrew.

Terry Liversedge and I, stepping out into the aisle to let him shamble past, watched him half run, half limp towards the church porch in his crippling dancing shoes, then, exchanging an amused and patronising lifting of the eyebrows, resumed our places, anxious to see what she had made of the exhibition. Her face was hidden in her hymn book, but as hymn 651 ended with a flat Amen, we could see that her shoulders were quaking.

After a brief resumption of the troglodyte droning, the fossils began to gather up their commodious handbags, gloves, scarves, walking-sticks and other accoutrements as the gargoyle baby was conveyed by its attendants to a side-chamber.

'What do we do now?' muttered Terry Liversedge.

'I think it's like a wedding – you have to wait till they leave,' I hazarded. What concerned me more was not making a hash of the pleasantry I was working on for her exit. 'Sorry about that,' I would say as she paused, with any luck, to exchange a smile at the Douglas débâcle. 'It's not that he's a pyrotechnic but we can't stop him playing with matches.' No. 'Sorry without that. It's not that he's a pyromaniac but. . .'

As it turned out, while smiling readily enough, she did not pause at all, so that there was time only for Terry Liversedge to get in with, 'If you see Guy Fawkes outside, tell him we'll be out in a minute,' before she had moved on in a waft of unidentifiable scent, or perhaps musk. Tagging behind her, however, her aborigine mother did pause, and address herself mainly to me. 'Excuse me for being nosey, lads, but I've been racking my brains trying to place you. You're not on our Jack's side of the family, that I do know.'

'No, sorry without that, we thought we were early too for the proper serving.'

'Pardon, love?'

The translation furnished by Terry Liversedge was presumably passed down the line of curious relatives, for as we traipsed out in the wake of the last straggle of fossils and gargoyles, one of them standing in the porch passed a hearty remark about our getting into training for when we were fathers ourselves. Then the troglodyte in the vestments detached himself from a gaggle of them who were cooing at the baby gargoyle and swept across to shake our hands, effectively barring our way. We had been about to move determinedly in on Douglas, who was standing halfway to the lych-gate in animated conversation with the putative nymphomaniac in the powder-blue suit, waving his arms about and doubtlessly giving her an exaggerated account of his incendiary adventure. Whatever yarn he was spinning her, he was making her laugh a lot.

'It must have been very confusing for you, boys,' the troglodyte was saying. 'We've had quite a run on christenings today, so this last one was running a little late. But you know, you did arrive awfully early for evensong.'

'Just a bit,' said Terry Liversedge.

The troglodyte droned on about it being better to be too early than too late, how gratifying it always was to see new faces, especially youthful faces, and how he hoped we would still be staying for the service.

'We'll come back,' I said. They were getting on awfully well. She was doing the talking now. Douglas, lighting his meerschaum, was sucking his cheeks in to make his swarthy profile look gaunt like Terry Liversedge's.

'Hardly worth leaving, for the sake of twenty minutes or so. Rather than kill time, fellows, why not make yourself known to Mr Culbert, my verger, and ask if he'd like you to put out the hymnals. Tell him you've been press-ganged!'

There was no escape. 'I'll just get our friend,' said Terry Liversedge grimly. But even as he beckoned savagely, Douglas was limping towards us up the path. She had turned away and was moving towards the lych-gate with the posse of gargoyles escorting the baby. The troglodyte drifted across to see them off.

'Another fine mess you've gotten us into!' I mimicked as Douglas approached. I saw no point in not making light of it.

But Terry Liversedge was in no mood for shrugging off the fiasco with wisecracks. 'Come on, Duggerlugs. It's all because of you that we've just been roped in as fizzing sidesmen or something, so you can do your share.'

'Sorry, old bean, old boy. Pauline's only dropping in on the christening tea for half an hour, since they're not close relatives, so by the time I've popped home and changed my shoes I'll have all my work cut out to meet her at the top of Station Approach and take her for a walk.'

As Douglas directed his crippled feet towards the lych-gate, proving that it is possible to hobble jauntily, the St Chad's church bells began to peal.

# 10

With the Kismet Café out of bounds, we were unable to agree
on another lunch venue. Terry Liversedge fancied Clough &
Clough's cafeteria where, according to what he'd heard, there
was so much lunchtime talent on offer that clicking was easier
than pulling up radishes. Douglas would eat only where he
could get his daily Welsh rarebit and black coffee, which he
had decided to make an unbreakable lifetime habit. I favoured
varying the locale from day to day, on the basis that we never
knew whom we might pick up.

The custom of meeting for lunch having thus fallen into
disuse, it was not until mid-week that we saw one another
again, in the main lounge of the Hotel Metropole after work.
This was Terry Liversedge's idea. For reasons that remained
obscure – I suspected he had been indulging himself in
fantasies of an alliance with Madge, seeded by the daily banter
about the Metropole dinner dance which she had now brought
to an abrupt end – he had lately done some exploration of the
Metropole's public rooms. The lounge, he had discovered,
had two attractions. One was that you could sit there without
buying anything for as long as you pleased. The other was that
you were likely to be accosted by prostitutes of riveting chic
and beauty, who were tolerated by the management as a
convenience for the fossil guests.

After we had been accosted by beautiful prostitutes we
meant to eat a fish and chip supper at the Majestic Fisheries in
Sheepgate before finding out if we could get served at the
Wine Lodge opposite Rabinowitcz the Jeweller's Corner. If
we could, the Wine Lodge was so noisily big and crowded
that, practising midweek economy, we should be able to get
away with nursing a half-pint apiece all evening, while
studying the Woodbine-smoking, port-wine-sipping perox-
ide blondes in imitation leopardskin box-jackets who represented the other end of Grippenshaw's sector of the
prostitution market.

Crossing Town Square towards the somewhat alarmingly

imposing façade of the Hotel Metropole, I hoped Terry Liversedge's information on its beautiful prostitutes was more reliable than his information on the talent just waiting to be plucked like radishes in Clough & Clough's cafeteria, where I happened to have eaten my solitary lunch. That the talent was there in abundance couldn't be denied: every typing-pool in Grippenshaw must have been represented in the queue for tongue salads. What Terry Liversedge hadn't thought to point out was that the talent arrived in groups of four or five and occupied tables for six. To take up the remaining place and attempt social intercourse was as foolhardy as throwing open the door of the ladies' powder-room at the Clock Ballroom and asking any sequined mill-girl at random for the last waltz. I was cheesed with Terry Liversedge.

Entering the Metropole was an even more awe-inducing experience than entering St Chad's church, to which atmospherically it bore some resemblance. At least there hadn't been a uniformed dodo on duty outside St Chad's. I looked ostentatiously at my watch as if checking an appointment, stumbled over the top step, and passed through a large tiled area of panelled wood and desks and counters that resembled a bank, into an even larger, carpeted area of hanging tapestries and basket chairs, glass-topped tables and ferns in Benares-ware pots, that looked like the set for a film I had once seen at the Gem called *Weekend at the Waldorf*. Fossils of either sex sat about taking tea or sipping gin-and-tonics, but there were no beautiful prostitutes that I could see. At the far end of the lounge, partly concealed behind thickets of greenery, some violinists of Colwyn Bay pier standard were playing what was probably Strauss. I hoped they weren't planning on passing the hat round.

I took the nearest vacant chair at the nearest vacant table and perched on the edge of it, as in a doctor's waiting-room. I took out a packet of Black Cat and pushed it open at the wrong end, scattering cigarettes on the floor. As I stooped to pick them up a venerable dodo wearing a dusty tail-coat and carrying a Benares-ware tray to match the plantpots came up and asked if there was anything he could get me. 'It's right all, I'm waiting just for Mr Liversedge,' I said. I was relieved to see Douglas entering the lounge.

We had spoken only briefly and with customary guardedness on the telephone since the weekend, so I was not up to date on his progress with Pauline – Pauline Batty as it seemed her full name was. But I feared I was not to be spared a detailed bulletin.

Pauline had turned out to be a dentist's receptionist. Dentists' receptionists enjoyed a general reputation in Grippenshaw equivalent to the one that female churchgoers were supposed to have according to Douglas's specialist knowledge. My feeling of personal cheesedness deepened as I saw how flushed and excited he looked, like someone who has won the big prize in a raffle.

Douglas helped himself to one of my cigarettes – like me, he had concluded that a pipe didn't suit him. 'I'm afraid this is only a courtesy visit, mon brave. I've got to meet Pauline outside the Gaumont Coliseum at six.'

Contemplation of an evening alone with Terry Liversedge did nothing to lift my spirits. But at least I would be able to berate him at length on the non-availability of clickable talent at Clough & Clough's cafeteria, or of beautiful prostitutes in the Hotel Metropole.

'You're working fast, aren't you? How many times have you taken her out so far?'

'Oh, just for a walk on Sunday and the pix on Monday. She had to stay in last night to wash her hair.'

'And, er – ?' Pauline's readiness to be dated no fewer than three times in four days, not to mention Douglas's willingness to shell out for two sets of cinema tickets out of one week's earnings, indicated that spectacular inroads were being made. Terry Liversedge would be asking bluntly, 'Have you got your end away yet?' but I hoped I had more finesse. 'Are you getting anywhere?' I asked.

'Progressing, progressing,' said Douglas in an irritatingly self-satisfied manner. Inhaling deeply, he lolled back in his basket chair, so relaxed and pleased with life that I thought for an alarmed moment he was about to put his feet on the table. 'She's wonderful, Raymondo, she really is. I've never met anyone like her. No, I really mean it this time.'

The rider, as well as the testimonial it was meant to buttress, was standard with Douglas in all his encounters. Even the very dregs of the Duck-walk leftovers he had habitually been saddled with were reportedly wonderful, though he remained inscrutable on detail. The effect, probably intended, was to make me and even Terry Liversedge ponder on the possibility that we had not, after all, got the best of the bargain.

But this time Douglas really did sound as if he truly meant it. Behind his thick library-frame glasses, his dark eyes shone with gospel intensity. Perhaps Pauline Batty's nymphomaniac potentiality had already been realised.

'Shall I tell you what she's like?' he went on, unusually unreticent. 'You know where Iris Crescent is, don't you?'

'No.' Surely he was not about to claim to have been deflowered in the street?

'Yes you do, it runs off Station Approach. And being a crescent, you can go in at either end – the top end or the bottom end.'

'Get on with it then, Duggerlugs. I didn't ask you to draw me a map.'

That, however, was precisely what Douglas proceeded to do. Taking out his Biro he sketched a rough arc on my cigarette packet, marking one end with a cross.

'This is the top end of Iris Crescent. Walking back from Crag Park you naturally come to this end first. So that's where I kissed her good-night on Sunday.'

It seemed months since I had last kissed anyone good-night. Come to think of it, it *was* months. It was getting on for eight weeks since I had last felt Doreen Theaker's lips on mine.

'Oh, we're getting a blow-by-blow account, are we?' I said with leaden lightness.

'Au contraire, mon brave, we will draw ze veil on ze gory details.' Douglas now moved his pen to the other end of the arc and described a small square. 'This is the phone box at the other end of the crescent. No light bulb. Very convenient place for saying good-night.'

'I thought you just said you were at the top end.'

'That was on Sunday. This is on Monday. Coming back from the Gem, which end of Iris Crescent do we reach first?'

'The bottom end. So you got her in the phone box. It's all right for some, isn't it?' I spoke with ill-concealed envy.

Douglas tapped the cigarette packet with his pen. Reading-glasses glinting, he thrust his head forward. 'Ah, but before that, my friend, what was it she said?'

'I don't know. "Be gentle, Douglas, it's my first time"?'

87

Ignoring the tasteless falsetto jeer, Douglas went on, his voice now touched with wonder: 'I'll tell you her exact words. I'll never forget them, Raymondo. We'd just been making another date for tonight when she suddenly said, "Incidentally, just because we're at this end of the crescent instead of the other one, it doesn't mean to say you can't kiss me good-night again." '

Douglas, with a swaggering wriggle, leaned back in his chair. He looked convinced, and had certainly mesmerised me into being transiently convinced, that Pauline had all but pulled him into the privet with a cry of 'Do anything you want with me!' Perhaps, in the darkened phone box afterwards, she had indeed breathed something along those lines?

The spell was broken by the arrival of Terry Liversedge, who came bounding into the Hotel Metropole lounge as if it were a cinema foyer. The dodo in the black tails, serving pewter tankards at the nearby table, squinted round magisterially as he drew back a chair with a clatter and flopped into it.

'I can spare you exactly five minutes. Sorry to let you down, gang, but you'll somehow have to struggle along without my company tonight. I've got a date with Esmé.'

I saw, with a wrench of envy, that he had the same triumphant, raffle-winning air as Douglas.

Dutifully I asked, 'Who's Esmé when she's at home?'

Terry Liversedge, with the exaggerated sigh of genial exasperation he always affected when delivering news of a fresh triumph, as if he were having to spell it out unnecessarily, said, 'Esmé Carpenter!'

I left the next part of the litany to Douglas. 'We don't know any Esmé Carpenter, mon capitaine.'

'Yes you do. Or at least you know of her. Cast your mind back, youth. Why am I slaving away at the Pennines Linen Bank instead of lolling back in a cushy billet at the National Provincial, having grapes dropped into my gob?'

I saw the light. 'You mean that dame you followed into the bank – the one with mud-splashes on her legs?'

'I don't mean the charwoman, do I? Esmé Carpenter, her name is. I happened to be charging into the bank after lunch, late as usual, just as she happened to be coming out. So of course, I accidentally on purpose bump into her. I'm meeting her outside the Gaumont Coliseum at six.'

'Snap,' said Douglas, his dark face for once quite pink with pleasure.

It did not yet sink in that I would be left to spend the evening on my own. What was immediately sticking in my throat was the speed and effortlessness with which Terry Liversedge, if he was to be believed as I was sorry to say he was, always seemed to make his conquests.

I said, trying not to sound grudging, 'You don't mean to say you made a date right there and then, in the middle of the bank?'

'I could tell you I did, youth, but I'd be a liar. No, when I picked up the paying-in books she'd dropped, I saw where she worked. Lippincott's – that sheet-music shop in Town Arcade. So as soon as I got the postage-room to myself I rang them up, and by happy chance she answered. I said I hoped I hadn't laddered her nylons, and she said what are nylons when they're at home, and I said oh, can't you afford nylons, I might buy you a pair if you come out with me tonight, and we took it from there.'

'It's an established technique,' said Douglas knowledge-ably. 'One of the surest ways known to man of getting off with a dame is to ring her up and whisper sweet nothings, even if you've never met her. It's a well-known fact.' He talked as if he spent much of his daily life making assignations by telephone.

With a cruel glint in his blue eyes Terry Liversedge dug two pennies out of his pocket and proffered them to me. 'He's right, Ray. He's not wrong. You'd better have this to make a phone call with, if you're at a loose end tonight. Don't say I never give you anything.'

Masking my humiliation I accepted the coins and flipped one of them in the air in a debonair manner. It missed my outstretched wrist and fell noisily onto the glass-topped table. 'Don't worry about me,' I said with forced gallantry blended with sarcasm. 'Heads I'll pick up a tart in the Wine Lodge, tails I'll splash out on one of these high-class broads you swore blind would be trying to pick us up in here.' I would have done, too, had I had considerably more than ten-and-six in my possession, and had I been sufficiently briefed on how to go about it. And had the promised high-class prostitutes been in evidence.

'Don't you believe me, youth?' Any challenge to Terry Liversedge's worldliness was always a point of honour with him. He craned round the back of his chair and looked with feigned casualness around the big lounge, his eye finally settling on a middle-aged female fossil in a severe grey-flannel suit who was sitting alone near the waltz-playing violinists, drinking tea.

'That's one, for a start.'

She was as old as an aunt and looked like a headmistress. 'Don't talk fizzing wet, man.'

'Suit yourself, youth. What about that one over there, then?'

I followed his imperceptible nod. A younger fossil in a flowered dress, but a fossil nonetheless, was sipping gin with a serge-suited fossil. They looked like man and wife.

'What, that one with her husband?'

'She's just picked him up, kiddo. I saw her go and sit down with him.'

'Balls.'

Terry Liversedge, affecting an injured air, slowly swivelled his head in a panoramic sweep of the lounge, counting the while. 'One . . . two . . . three . . . four . . . There's at least five broads in this lounge who are definitely on the game, youth. Maybe more.'

'Balls.'

'All right, what do *you* think they are, then?'

'How do I know? Half of them look like schoolteachers.'

'So does Rebecca Redlips, youth, but I bet she could give you and me and Douglas lessons,' said Terry Liversedge with coarse gusto.

Douglas, turning in his chair, but to look at the sunburst clock over the arched entrance rather than to give any of the alleged prostitutes the once-over, said, 'You're not trying to make out Rebecca Redlips is on the game, are you?'

'She could be, Duggerlugs, for all I know. You know she's left Commerce, don't you?' I had heard that Miss Cohen had unexpectedly not returned to the College of Commerce in the new term. A wild rumour stemming from the Youth Guild had it that she was pregnant. A wilder one, probably put into circulation by himself, had it that Terry Liversedge was the father. 'That reminds me,' he said to me. 'I hope you've still got that shorthand epic of mine, because I might still send it to her if I can find her address. If I'm desperate, that is. I'll have to see how I get on with Esmé.'

With a suggestive clicking of the tongue, Terry Liversedge rose. To Douglas he said, 'Did you say you were meeting your bird at the Gaumont Coliseum as well? We'd best be making tracks.'

A little shamefacedly it seemed to me, as if they felt they were leaving me in the lurch, Douglas and Terry Liversedge took themselves off. They should have had nothing to feel guilty about, since it had always been our rule that any arrangements between us were subject to any more attractive arrangements that might turn up in the interim. But they were right, I did feel let down, and I blamed them both for doing to me what I would have done to them.

Fighting off the desolation I knew would soon enshroud me like a wet flannel, I wondered how I was going to spend the empty evening. I looked idly around the lounge, counting possible prostitutes. Where Terry Liversedge had reached a total of five, I reached seven. He was, I now concluded, right: they probably were on the game. Just because they weren't wearing hoopla-stall ear rings and mock-leopardskin box-jackets didn't mean they weren't tarts. It was probably a condition of their using the Hotel Metropole lounge that they were discreet.

The one in grey flannel who looked like a headmistress was the only one of them sitting on her own. To my surprise, for she didn't look like a smoker, which went to prove that appearances could be deceptive, she had just taken a tortoiseshell cigarette-case out of her bag. Perhaps in a moment she would come across and ask me for a light.

'This isn't a public waiting-room, you know, young man.' With a start I became aware of a Benares-ware tray hovering at my eye-level, clutched by two gnarled and freckled hands extending on bony wrists from frayed white cuffs. 'If you want to stay you'll have to order something, a soft drink or something.'

I jumped to my feet as if stung. 'Sorry, I was just going, actually.' But the tray still hovered, and the old dodo's watery eyes looking accusing. I plunged my hand into a trouser pocket, knowing that I possessed only three half-crowns, a florin and a shilling. I would have to trust to luck that it was the shilling my fingers closed on: with the Benares-ware tray thrust under my nose like the St Chad's church collection plate, I wasn't going to spend time feeling the milled contours of one coin after another. I tossed a coin grandly onto the tray. It landed with something less than a ringing sound, and I saw that it was one of the pennies Terry Liversedge had jokingly given me to make a telephone call.

It seemed an interminable distance to the archway that would lead me out of the lounge, across the tiled reception hall and out into Town Square and oblivion. I could feel the reproachful boiled eyes upon me as I trudged through the thick carpet. Then I became aware that someone else was looking at me. She had seemingly emerged from the Ladies' across the room and like me was heading for the archway, but now she had stopped. She looked very much younger than any of the others, and her brunette hair fell loose instead of being piled up on her head as most of them had theirs. She was my type. She was carrying a light raincoat and wore a blue glazed rayon dress, fairly close fitting, with a rounded neckline but with no fastenings visible. Taking the dress off, though, would almost certainly be a task she would wish to attend to herself. The raincoat would not be needed, not that there was any grass for miles, for she would have her own room near at hand. Probably, if the management were as accommodating to this sort of thing as Terry Liversedge said they were, she might even have a room in the hotel. I could explain that although I was short of funds at present, I could always come back on Friday.

'Hello,' she said. A pleasant voice: I was surprised it wasn't brassier.

'Oh, hello!'

She looked as if she expected me to continue. I didn't know what to say next. On reflection, any mention of money, particularly any mention of not having any money, would seem crude and clumsy. I would try something a little more urbane. 'I'm sorry, my dear,' I could say. 'The flesh is willing but the spirit is weak, I mean the spirit is willing but the french is weak, owing to because unfortunately having too much to drunk.' Given my usual form, it would at least have the merit of sounding convincing.

92

I moistened my lips in readiness for whatever might stumble out of them.

'You don't remember me, do you?' she said.

I assumed that was her standard line of patter. I was probably expected to respond with something on the lines of, 'No, baby, but I bet I won't forget you in a hurry.'

'Of course I do.'

'No reason why you should – we only saw each other for about five seconds. Still, I suppose I must have made a good impression or you wouldn't have asked Audrey Marsh what my name was.'

Coming down the Corn Exchange steps. Audrey's friend in the three-button swagger coat. And she had given me the once-over as they walked off arm-in-arm. My type.

'She never told me, though,' I said, astonished at the ease with which I managed to manipulate my tongue around such a complex sentence.

'I knew she wouldn't. Wait till she wants me to do *her* a favour, that's all.'

She had said something very warm and flattering there, if I could only unravel it. I would put that little compliment away and savour it later.

'What brings you to the Metropole?' I asked. It was a question I wanted to get out of the way, although I was sure that the possibility of her replying, 'Oh, I'm on the game, actually,' was remote, even if it happened to be true.

'I work here. I'm a receptionist. Well, trainee actually. I'm in the office at present. If it comes to that, what are you doing here?'

'Oh, just meeting some friends.'

'Left you in the lurch, have they?'

'No, they've taken some selves off to the pictures.'

'Lucky for some.'

We had meandered out of the lounge into the tiled reception hall. Now she was standing with her legs slightly apart, the light raincoat draped across her clasped hands in front of her. It was not the stance of one who is about to move on after a passing word with an acquaintance. She was quite relaxed and seemed to be enjoying talking to me, and if I was not mistaken, was on the verge of fishing to be asked out. My command of English waning by the second, I sought some simple words.

'I still know your don't name.'

'Do you always talk Double Dutch, or only sometimes? It's Janet. Janet Gill. And I know what your name is – It's Raymond Watmough, isn't it?'

'That's bright.'

She must have asked Audrey. They would have had quite a discussion about me, probably. Audrey would have told her, I suppose, that I'd asked her out and been given the brush-off.

Janet was looking at me steadily. There was amusement in her brown eyes, but she wasn't laughing at me.

'*I'm* not engaged, even if Audrey Marsh is. And in case you should get round to asking – no, I'm not just going on duty, I'm just coming off duty.'

Douglas would hear of this. Pauline, after only two dates, had said, 'Incidentally, just because we're at this end of the crescent instead of the other one, it doesn't mean to say you can't kiss me good-night again.' But Janet, who three minutes ago I had never spoken to in my life, had said, '*I'm* not engaged, even if Audrey Marsh is,' and then gone on to point out that she was coming off duty and was therefore free for me to do more or less what I pleased with her. It was game, set and match to me, in my view.

'In that case, what are why waiting for?'

'What are why waiting for?' she laughed, friendly mocking. '*I'm* waiting for someone to take me to the Paramount. If he happens to like Bette Davis. *All About Eve* – it's supposed to be good.'

'You wouldn't prefer the Gaumont Coliseum, would you, Janet?' I asked flawlessly.

Terry Liversedge, on his first date with Esmé Carpenter, would have splashed out on the three-and-sixpennies. Douglas, after exposing Pauline Batty to a scratchy Old Mother Riley film at the local fleapit on Monday, would probably have felt obliged to do the same, to show he wasn't a cheapskate. Seven bob plus ices and trolley-bus fares would leave me with barely half-a-crown to see me through Friday, but it would be worth it. I could make do with ten cigarettes tomorrow and do without lunch. 'Oh, greetings, chaps.' I would say. 'Fancy seeing you here. Oh, by the way, this is Janet.'

# 11

Such was my preoccupation, during the next few crucial weeks, with making a steady territorial advance down the front of Janet Gill's dress, that I saw little of Douglas or Terry Liversedge. Their own free time, in any case, was more or less fully spoken for in pursuit of the same obsessional targets with Pauline Batty and Esmé Carpenter respectively.

The possibilities of an occasional sixsome fizzled out after only one such evening when it emerged that Janet thought Terry Liversedge conceited, Esmé thought Douglas ugly, Pauline thought I was tongue-tied, Douglas thought Janet was laughing at him, I didn't take to Esmé, and Terry Liversedge found himself uncomfortable in the presence of Pauline. This crosshatching of prejudices was quite usual in our dealings with talent, and was barely discussed. Nor was such progress as we might individually have been making with our own particular partners.

Our occasional brief meetings after work, usually in the Sheepgate Lyons' or Kardomah as handiest for the Paramount, the Gaumont Coliseum or Rabinowitcz the Jeweller's Corner which were the usual points of rendezvous for dates in the town centre, were mainly of a business nature. Either they were to do with the lending or returning of small sums of money or, with a view to stretching our wardrobes, with exchanging or borrowing jackets, ties, pullovers, sports shirts, and Terry Liversedge's cravat. Sometimes one or other of us had a need to sell something. Thus, at different times, Terry Liversedge acquired Douglas's gunmetal cigarette-case and my real leather wallet, Douglas acquired Terry Liversedge's mock-crocodile wallet and the cuff-links that Doreen Theaker had given me for my sixteenth birthday, and I acquired Douglas's new shot-silk treasury-note-case. Such transactions kept us in touch.

However, one week when Janet, Esmé and Pauline all three chanced perversely to pick on Friday as the only possible evening to stay in and shampoo their hair, we paid another visit to the Palace of Varieties. Seasoned theatregoers now, we watched only the striptease in the first act and the Seven Faces of Salome in the second, and spent the rest of the time in the circle bar. Terry Liversedge had discovered a new drink, Irish whiskey and ginger ale. Soon we grew talkative. Or Terry Liversedge did:

'So how are you getting on with Pauline, the nympho of St Chad's, Duggerlugs?' he asked, tapping out a Camel. Ever since biting through the stem of his pipe, Terry Liversedge had smoked only American cigarettes. As soon as he had learned to flick a Camel or Philip Morris into his mouth straight out of the packet, the gunmetal cigarette-case once belonging to Douglas would be back on the market. I would probably buy it.

'Fine, fine, fine.'

'She doesn't like me, does she, youth?'

'I wouldn't say that, old bean, old boy. I think she has the impression that you don't like her.'

'I don't, to tell you the truth.'

'That's your hard luck, my friend.'

'You don't mind me saying that, do you, Douglas?'

'Yes he does,' I said.

'No he doesn't. You don't, do you, Duggerlugs? Anyway, it's not really that I don't like her, it's just that I haven't had a chance to get to know her yet.'

'You're not going to get the chance, either,' said Douglas.

Expelling smoke down his nostrils and giving me a knowing leer, Terry Liversedge crowed 'Aye aye!' in the nudging manner of the Palace's check-suited comedians. 'Keeping her to yourself, are you, Duggerlugs? So how well do *you* know her? Eh? How well do you know her?'

'Well enough.'

'Aye aye! Did you hear that, Ray? – "well enough". Come on, then, youth – spill the beans!'

'Sorry, mon capitaine, I make it a rule never to bandy a lady's name in the mess.'

'Ah, don't give me that bull, Duggerlugs! Have you got to first base, second base, or hit the jackpot? That's all we want to know.'

I was enjoying this. It was man's talk. The toasted tobacco scent of Camels smouldering between nicotined fingers, the headache-inducing bouquet of the Irish whiskey and the Christmassy whiff of ginger ale, with the circle bar's accumulation of stale taproom smells, all combined into an aromatic fog that reminded me of the sealed upper deck of the last trolley-bus home on Saturday nights. It was the smell of a good night out.

'Hold your horses while I get them in,' I said to Douglas. I picked up the three thick spirit glasses with clutched fingers like an amusement arcade grab-crane, as I had seen the potman do, and went over to the long mahogany bar. I bought three Irish whiskeys and one ginger ale and decided to treat us all to a packet of Smith's crisps. They would go down well with Douglas's confession.

'Just ask your friend to keep his voice down. They'll hear him out in the circle if he talks much louder,' said the white-aproned dodo.

I conveyed the message back to Terry Liversedge. Thereafter, heads close together over the marble table in our plush banquette corner, we talked in hoarse low voices, like conspirators.

'Have I missed anything?' I asked.

'Not yet, youth. Come on, Douglas, it's a fair question. How far have you got with Pauline? And slit my throat and hope to die, it won't go further than this bar.'

'It'd better not,' said Douglas. That sounded encouraging. He needed only a little egging on now.

'Speak now or forever hold your peace,' I said.

Douglas brushed flakes of potato crisp from his hairy upper lip, where he was covertly trying to grow a moustache although he had so far denied it. Cow-like, he slowly chomped the handful of crisps he had crammed into his mouth.

'How far, youth?' insisted Terry Liversedge. 'Give us a straightforward answer to a straightforward question.'

'All right, then, I will,' yielded Douglas at last. 'Let me put it this way, Terry. Further than I bet you've got with Esmé.'

'You can't know that, youth.'

'Yes I can.'

'You can't, you know.'

'I can, you know. How far have you got with Esme, then?'

'Further than you think.'

'That's not an answer. How far?'

'A lot farther than you have with Pauline. Anyway, I asked you first.'

Woodenly staring each other out like arm-wrestlers, Douglas and Terry Liversedge simultaneously lifted their glasses and drained them. Some arbitration was called for.

'We're getting nowhere,' I said soothingly. 'Let's take this step by step. You first, Douglas. All you've got to tell us is how far you've got. First base or second base? In other words above or below the waist?'

'This'd make a good wireless panel game to replace Twenty Questions!' giggled Douglas. The Irish whiskey was going to his head.

'Above or below the waist?'

'Both.'

'You're a liar,' said Terry Liversedge with heat.

'That proves one thing,' said Douglas. 'It proves that mon capitaine Terence Liversedge esquire hasn't got past first base with Esmé.'

'It doesn't prove anything of the sort, youth.'

I hadn't played poker since our College of Commerce days and not much then. But I felt like someone clutching a miserable pair of twos while the other players squared up as if holding royal flushes at worst. The difference was that I wouldn't be allowed to throw in my hand.

But it was not my turn yet. 'So what you're saying, Terry, is that you've been there below the waist with Esmé?'

'I didn't say that, Ray. I said *he* hadn't.'

'With Esmé? You're right,' cackled Douglas. He picked up his glass, realised it was empty, and crashed it back on the table. 'I wouldn't want to, either.'

'That'll do, Beckett. Watch it.'

I said pacifyingly, 'It's all right, Terry, I know his little game. He's just trying to wriggle out of telling us how far he's got with Pauline.'

'Au contraire, mon brave.'

'How far, then? Come on, Douglas, stop messing about. Both above and below the waist, that's what you said. Give us the gen.'

'Only if Terry gets another round in.'

'He'll get one in a minute. Give.'

Douglas gave. Getting to first base, he averred, had been a piece of cake. He had been on above-the-waist terms with Pauline Batty almost from the start, having been allowed on only their second date to fondle one breast briefly through her coat in the darkened telephone box at the corner of Iris Crescent. Thereafter he had progressed by easy stages to a point where slipping a hand inside Pauline's brassière for quite long periods had become so standard a feature of the evening as to be almost boring. On occasion, when wearing a garment with a difficult fastening, Pauline would even remove Douglas's stumbling, wart-encrusted fingers from her throat and, impatiently according to him, unfasten the troublesome hook and eye or button herself; he found this invigorating and would sometimes pretend to be having difficulty even when he wasn't. Given a dress or blouse that fastened to the waist, he had met little resistance in unbuttoning it all the way down, but Pauline would not yet allow him to slip her brassière straps off her shoulders so that her breasts could be seen as well as touched. This, however, was only self-consciousness on her part: she thought they were too small. Douglas was confident that had the weather not turned cold he would by now be feasting his eyes upon Pauline Batty's breasts any time he pleased. He was hoping either for an Indian summer or to discover some warm enclosed premises such as the cow-byre they had found on a small surviving dairy farm at the back of St Chad's church, ideal in every respect save that it was full of cows.

On the below-the-waist front, Douglas was more reticent. Progress, he said, was being made, but slowly.

'How slow is slow, youth?'

'Slow but sure, mon capitaine. I'll get to second base in the end.'

'Get there in the end, he says. I bet he's got as far as her knee.'

To stop Douglas coming back at him with, 'Which is further than you've got,' and starting the whole roundelay again, I interjected, 'At least he's come clean, Liversedge, which is more than you have.'

Too late I realised I was handing him his rejoinder on a plate. 'It's more than *you* have, Watmough, if it comes to that.'

Douglas came slyly to my rescue. 'What was Terry saying

about people wriggling out of giving us the griff?'

'I thought I'd already given you it, youth – I told you, I've got a naffing sight farther than you.'

'Below the waist, then?' I prompted.

'I didn't say below the waist. *He* hasn't got to second base, either. And isn't likely to.'

'Yet,' put in Douglas.

'Depends what you mean by yet, Douglas. How much do you want to bet I'll be there before you are?'

'Five bob.'

'You're on. That's a dollar you've lost.'

I thought of raising the delicate question of what was being defined, in below-the-waist terms, as getting there, but concluded on reflection that either Douglas or Terry Liversedge would know intuitively when the winning moment had arrived.

'Meanwhile,' I said, 'what about above the waist?'

'Above the waist, youth, I can do what I like with her.'

'Such as?' asked Douglas.

'Such as everything I was doing with Betty Parsons before I jacked her in.'

Perhaps he had forgotten admitting (although in the context of the time it had sounded like bragging) that his experience with Betty Parsons had been limited to touching one breast five times and both of them twice. It would not have been tactful to remind him.

'If you'd stuck with Betty Parsons, you'd have won that dollar before the bet was even made,' I said.

It was almost as undiplomatic an observation as the one I had just refrained from making. Terry Liversedge was at once plunged in alcoholic gloom.

'You don't have to tell me, kiddo, I know. Did I tell you I came across her a couple of Sundays ago, getting off a Textile District bus with that jammy devil Ralph Driver? She had straw on her back.' I had never seen Terry Liversedge look so woebegone.

'Fast worker,' I said enviously.

'Too true, youth.'

'Like Raymondo,' said Douglas mischievously.

Terry Liversedge's countenance lightened to express malevolent glee. 'Yes, he's been very quiet so far, hasn't he?

100

Sorry, Ray, you can't get out of it any longer. First base, second base, or jackpot?'

'First.'

'Hold it,' said Douglas, giving Terry Liversedge his empty glass. 'I thought a certain person was supposed to be getting them in.'

'Don't let him say anything till I get back, then,' said Terry Liversedge as he went across to the bar.

I asked Douglas, more as a conversation-maker than in anticipation of a proper reply, 'Have you really only got as far as her knee?'

'If you want daily bulletins, mon brave, you'll have to come in on the bet.'

'What – you'll make the same bet with me as you're making with Terry?'

'It's up to you, old bean, old boy. You know your prospects with Janet better than I do.'

I was pleased to be included, even as an afterthought. It had been rankling with me that both Douglas and Terry Liversedge seemed to be taking it as read that I was not in the running.

'Done,' I said. I would put half a crown away in my handkerchief drawer this week, and half a crown next week, then I wouldn't miss it so much when I had to pay out.

Terry Liversedge returned to the table, empty-handed. He did not sit down.

'The miserable sod won't serve us. He says we're making too much racket.'

Douglas and I looked towards the bar. The white-aproned dodo caught our eye and called across, 'You've had enough for one night, lads. Go watch the show – you've paid for it, you might as well see it.'

'Saved by the bell, eh, Raymondo?' murmured Douglas as we rose. 'Now we'll never know.'

'I bet he'd nothing to tell,' said Terry Liversedge.

I didn't rise to the bait, for we were passing through the thick velvet drapes into the circle. We stood at the back morosely watching a unicycle act but thinking thoughts that were far removed from the stage of the Palace of Varieties. In Terry Liversedge's case they probably centred on Betty Parsons with straw on her back. They certainly did in mine.

# 12

Above the neckline, rather than above the waist, would have been a more accurate way of describing the state of play with Janet Gill.

Janet's trouble was an irreverent disregard for convention. To restrain a wandering hand it was usual to seize it firmly and place it in some neutral, non-erogenous region, or in persistent cases to push it away altogether and sit bolt upright. That kind of rejection was straightforwardly met by recourse to the try-try-again policy of Bruce and the spider. It was more difficult to know how to counter Janet's idiosyncratic ploy of leaving the offending hand where it was – half inside her dress, as often as not, but no nearer journey's end than her collar-bone – while asking conversationally, 'Exploring?'

'Why – any objections?'

'Captain Cook was an explorer and look what happened to him.'

I hadn't done commercial geography for nothing – and now that I had got to know Janet, although not as intimately as I would have liked, I no longer feared my reply being sucked into a Sargasso Sea of dropped words and spoonerisms. 'He's supposed to have been eaten by cannibals – but not before anchoring on Point Venus.'

I thought that was rather neat but it cut no ice with Janet.

'Be that as it may, when I want my Point Venuses exploring, I'll let you know.'

Or she would say in a dreamy voice, so that it sounded like encouragement until the burden of what she was murmuring sank in, 'What's wrong – is your hand feeling cold?'

'Yes, since you ask. Would you like to warm it for me?'

'Seeing it's you, Ray, I'll knit you a pair of mittens for Christmas.'

Such dead-end exchanges left me in the awkward position of having to withdraw my straying hand voluntarily but without losing face. I usually got round it by lighting cigarettes, one for her and one for me. But it was on occasions

102

like these, I noticed, that cigarettes tended to stick to my lip.

I sometimes fretted in case any of this was getting back to Audrey Marsh. I knew the two of them had lunch regularly and Audrey would sometimes say, 'I hear you were doing your best to catch pneumonia up on Throstle Moor on Sunday,' or 'I'm surprised you can keep your eyes open, the time Janet says you kept her out till last night.' And she would smile her secret half-smile.

Was Janet giving her a running commentary on the non-progress of my left hand? (I had always engineered myself into a position where it would be the left hand that was brought into play, or not very much into play in Janet's case, ever since Douglas had advised that the fingertips of this hand were notoriously more sensitive, in right-handed persons, than those of the other which were invisibly calloused from daily use.) There was no reason to suppose she wasn't, since it was evident from the censored titbits she passed on to me that she was kept in close touch with all Audrey's doings with her fiancé Ronnie. Janet did not approve of him. He was, it seemed, of a vicious temperament, much given to issuing threats and making scenes. Once, suspecting that Audrey had been two-timing him with an old flame, he had burned her arm with a cigarette. It occurred to me that if Audrey couldn't resist two-timing despite the considerable risks, it might have paid to have been more persistent about asking her out. But Janet, probably interpreting my ruminative expression, hastened to give Audrey a glowing character-reference, saying that no matter how long it might be before his next leave, she always waited for him.

'Waits for him to do what?' I enquired acidly.

'I've no idea, I'm sure. But I don't suppose she looks forward to spending hour after hour in a freezing recreation ground.'

The recreation ground she referred to was the only secluded spot in the densely built-up area where Janet lived, a district of substantial terraces conveniently half-way between the town centre and the Crag Park trolley-bus terminus. For lack of a proper seat we had to make do with the seesaw – as comfortable, I reminded Janet, as any park bench, despite a tendency to edge us gradually to one end as it undulated slightly on the stout chains that moored it to a block of concrete. Admittedly, now that the November frosts were upon us, it could be cold sometimes when the rime began to permeate our clothing, but Janet was exaggerating when she called the recreation ground freezing. These were clear, crisp nights, seemingly forever moonlit, when even the fogs that rolled down from the moors were no more than a mist-smell and a nimbus of haze around the lamp-posts by the time they reached the footstep-echoing streets. The air was invigorating, like mountain air; I was always filled with exhilaration when I set off to meet Janet. If we were going to the recreation ground, as we did two or three times a week – 'going for a walk', we euphemistically called it – I always arranged to see her at seven outside a terrace-end sub-post-office. Waiting for her there I would check my watch against the electric clock in the window and work out that it would be four hours, call it three and three-quarters if we felt the need to warm ourselves up with a fish-and-chip supper, before we would have to leave the recreation ground. Four hours was two hundred and forty minutes. Anything was possible in two hundred and forty minutes. And as we huddled on the tethered seesaw with our breath curling like cigarette smoke, I would make out the hands of my watch and be relieved and delighted that only an hour had gone by and that there were still two hours to go before I began to be depressed at there being only one more hour left.

'Are you trying to pull that button off or just unfasten it?'

'Unfasten it, if it's all right by you.'

'Just so long as we know. You might do better if you blow on your hands first.'

Even though it was only the awkward top toggle-button of her thick winter coat, and she was wearing impenetrable layers of wool underneath, I would draw enormous encouragement from such words, sifting them for inference and savouring their potential. Three hours and twenty minutes left. An eternity of hope and endeavour.

'Do you know who you remind me of, Ray? Scott of the Antarctic.'

'Not Captain Cook this time?'

'No, Scott of the Antarctic. You never give up and you've got fingers like ice-cubes.'

Our other alfresco venue was Throstle Moor where, if it

104

were dry and fine enough on our weekend walks, Janet could be persuaded to lie down in the heather. She was not averse to having my arms around her, and it was while we were in this promising horizontal position one bright Sunday when the river far below us shone like metal and the curlews swirled overhead, that I thought I would short-circuit the delaying above-the-waist procedure and make a bold and direct attempt to win five shillings from Douglas. To no avail. 'Is that zip stiff, do you find, Ray?' – 'Not at all.' – 'Oh, good, you'll have no trouble zipping it up again, then.' But I wished when we got off the Textile District bus in Grippenshaw that Terry Liversedge would walk past and notice that Janet had straw on her back.

Twice a week we went to the pictures, sometimes in town but more often to Janet's local bughutch, the Renown, which despite being little more than a brick shed was much in demand because of its three back rows of double seats which were known as love-seats. To succeed in luring a date into a love-seat was supposedly tantamount to getting her into a four-poster, but I hadn't found it so. Janet was perfectly happy to share the red-plush intimacy of the back-row doubles but she always stated her terms while we were still in the queue: 'I don't mind sitting in the two-and-threes if you don't mind shelling out for them, but just because they put the lights out it doesn't mean you can start practising your Braille.'

I sometimes wondered if I did mind shelling out for the two-and-threes, let alone the more expensive seats at the Paramount and the Gaumont Coliseum. I had certainly seen very little return on my investment so far. I had been going out with Janet for a good three months now, quite long enough to fall into the category of 'going steady' and to be entitled to the privileges that customarily went with that role. But had Douglas and Terry Liversedge re-opened their interrogation, and had I been honest, I would have had to admit that the furthest I had got with Janet Gill so far was to insinuate three fingers under the lapel of her dress as far as the knuckles, and to be permitted to toy with the strap of her brassière. This, I calculated on a Moult & Sumpter billhead, adding up the cost of thirteen weeks' cinema outings, ices, fish suppers, cigarettes and bus fares, was for an outlay of around nine guineas, plus five shillings to Douglas when he inevitably won his bet.

Douglas himself, however, was far from sanguine when next we briefly compared notes. We had met in the doorway of the Sheepgate Lyons' one pelting, stony-broke Thursday evening for a complicated transaction whereby, in exchange for my shot-silk treasury-note-case that had once belonged to Douglas, plus two shillings, I took possession of Terry Liversedge's gunmetal cigarette-case that had likewise once belonged to Douglas; Terry Liversedge then gave Douglas the two shillings and nine Camels in payment for a packet of Chesterfield which Douglas had procured for him the previous week; and Douglas returned the two shillings to me in settlement of a debt.

'Now we're all straight again, I don't suppose there's any chance of borrowing it back, old bean, old boy, old man?'

'Sorry, Doug, I need every penny I've got - I'm taking Janet to the pix.'

'Can't you go in the one-and-nines?'

'What do you *think* we're going in on a Thursday night – the royal box? It's not even the one-and-nines. All I can stretch to is the stinking one-and-threes at the Renown, and that's only by walking home.'

'You're fizzing lucky to be going to the pictures at all, youth,' retorted Terry Liversedge. 'At least you'll keep dry – you won't be stuck under a frigging railway arch with the rain dripping off the end of your nose.'

Esmé Carpenter lived in an even more built-up part of Grippenshaw than Janet Gill. The Lane Ends viaduct was her and Terry Liversedge's winter quarters as the recreation ground was mine and Janet's. Douglas's and Pauline's was the lych-gate of St Chad's parish church where they had met. With its adequate cover, discreet location and wide stone-slab bench eminently suitable for lying down on, Terry Liversedge and I considered the lych-gate the best arrangement of the lot, but Douglas didn't seem to think so.

'The trouble is,' he complained, 'that it seems to be strategically placed so that whichever way the wind blows it always seems to be whistling round our ankles.'

'It would do, if you keep your feet on the floor, you dozey devil,' said Terry Liversedge.

'So would you, mon capitaine, if you had the perishing verger and the perishing vicar trotting backwards and

106

forwards at all hours. They don't mind couples snogging but they do draw the line at shafting. Besides, they know Pauline. So you see, we've got the two worst drawbacks it's possible to have – lack of warmth and lack of privacy. Did you know they're the biggest cause of non-consummation in marriage? It's a well-known medical fact.'

A dodo newspaper vendor with a sodden *Evening Argus* sack slung over his tarpaulin-bundle layer of coats and with droplets glistening on his nostril hairs, squelched between us and pushed open the aluminium barred doors of the Lyons' teashop. A smell of hot tea, chips, beans and boiling dishcloths steamed tantalisingly out to us. Terry Liversedge tipped water off the brim of his pork-pie hat. Douglas and I did not yet have hats. Small black rivulets, like mascara stains on the cheeks of a girl crying, trickled down Douglas's face from his damp, not-lately-washed hair.

We stared across Sheepgate at the rain bouncing off the fretted marquee of the Palace of Varieties, the trolley-bus queue huddling beneath it, and the shop-lights and the PK Chewing Gum neon sign reflecting shimmeringly on the gleaming bitumen. Terry Liversedge sneezed.

'We're all off our rockers,' said Douglas suddenly. 'Do you realise where we're making our big mistake? We're going out with dames who still live at home. That's no use to anyone, not in the middle of winter. We ought to get ourselves fixed up with three chicks who've got their own rooms.'

There was an extensive local mythology surrounding such creatures. The teacher-training college was supposed to house the overspill from its students' hostel in bed-sitters. Talent seen coming out of the stage doors of the Palace of Varieties and the Theatre Royal was said to live in theatrical digs, with the probable exception of some of the usherettes. Girl reporters on the *Argus*, said by Terry Liversedge to be earning eight pounds a week, young fashion buyers at Clough & Clough's, studious-looking chicks working in the Central Library and the Museum, were believed to have their own flats where they entertained suitors to candle-lit suppers with wine. We had never infiltrated these circles.

'Find them,' challenged Terry Liversedge.

'The other alternative,' mused Douglas, dabbing a balled-up handkerchief over his rain-spattered reading-glasses,

107

'would be for us to have a room where we could take them. How much do you suppose it would cost to rent a bed-sitter?'

'What – each?' asked Terry Liversedge incredulously.

'Between us. We could work a shift system.'

'It'd still take more than we earn between us – we're always skint as it is,' I pointed out. 'Besides, what landlady in her right mind's going to stand for three separate couples tramping up and down to the same fizzing room – not to mention never being there between eleven at night and six o'clock the next?'

'What's wrong with lunchtime?' said Douglas, defensively but unconvincingly. We could see he hadn't thought his idea through. 'Though I admit finance is a factor. Why don't we get engaged, all of us, then they'd have to let us do our courting in the front room?'

Terry Liversedge and I dismissed this latest proposal as frivolous, though coming from Douglas it was probably meant to be considered seriously.

'If it's a room we're after, youth,' Terry Liversedge said to me, 'I don't know why that tart of yours can't come up with one. There must be five hundred of them at the Metropole and they can't all be occupied. She must be able to get her mitts on a pass-key.'

I had already thought of that, frequently, though purely on my own behalf rather than Terry Liversedge's or Douglas's. But it would have to be approached delicately, gradually; there was no point in blundering into it. I had drawn up a timetable. The target date was the end of the month when it would be her seventeenth birthday. I would take her to the American Bar of the Hotel Metropole – a management that tolerated beautiful prostitutes could hardly be fussy about drinking under age, particularly where one of their own staff was concerned – and ply her with Sidecar cocktails. It would then be up to her to slip away to Reception, returning with some such enigmatic message as: 'Go up in the lift to the fifth floor and wait for me there.' She would have been primed in easy stages: I would have got to first base a month or so before her birthday and to second base about a fortnight before; by the third week of November the sentiment, 'Oh, if we only had somewhere to go to!' would have become a commonplace between us; and in the run-up to her birthday we should openly be discussing strategy.

I was badly behind schedule but still hoping to catch up.

'When Janet gets her mitts on a Metropole pass-key, Terry,' I said, 'you'll be the first to know. I don't think.'

On which flippant note, as we turned up our raincoat collars and hurried off in different directions, we relegated Douglas's talk of renting rooms to the realm of fancy. What even Douglas didn't realise on that rainy Thursday evening was that the seed he had planted in his own mind would burgeon into a scheme that, as the months passed, would obsessionally preoccupy us all – even to the exclusion, at times, of its own ultimate purpose.

As it happened, Janet Gill was obliged to celebrate her seventeenth birthday on a tethered seesaw in the corporation recreation ground rather than on a high chrome-legged stool in the American Bar of the Hotel Metropole, for the silver-plate bangle I had bought for her at Rabinowitcz's the Jeweller's had cost far more than I had budgeted for. But she was happy enough. 'It's lovely, Ray. You are good to me. But you shouldn't have spent all that money.' It was well-spent, though, for like all the other girls who met their dates at Rabinowitcz the Jeweller's Corner she was a keen student of the price-tickets in their brilliantly-lit barred windows, and would have seen her bangle expensively nestling there in that black-velvet grotto. She was beautiful when grateful.

It was the most serene of evenings, mild for the end of November and very still, so still that we could hear the rumble of shunting trains in the marshalling yards far across the town, beyond the viaduct where Terry Liversedge would be clasping Esmé Carpenter against a condensation-streaming wall. Good luck to him.

The moon was full and bright enough to throw shadows. With an arm around Janet, drawing her head to my shoulder, and toying with the bangle on her wrist to remind her I'd bought it for her, I murmured, 'Look, we make one big shadow.'

'Mm. Two hearts that beat as one.'

She seemed full of dreamy well-being. Encouraged, I thought I would egg her on to confess that this birthday with me in the recreation ground was the best one she'd ever spent.

With an induced note of self-pity in my voice I said, 'Not much of a birthday for you, sitting here, is it?'

Janet rose very nicely to the bait. 'There's nowhere else I'd rather be.'

'And nobody else you'd rather be with?'

'If there was, I'd be with them, wouldn't I? Silly.'

I brushed my lips against her forehead. 'Why do you like being with me, then?'

'Because I do.'

'Yes, but why?'

'I just do. If it comes to that, why do you like being with me?'

It was the cue I was waiting for. A cloud passed across the moon, bringing a welcome darkness. It was now virtually certain that I should reach first base with Janet Gill before her birthday was over. A little breathlessly I said, 'Oh, because I've never meant anyone like you.'

Happily she did not notice the nervous slip. 'Get away.'

'It's true. You have a very funny effect on my watch, do you know that, Janet?'

I paused, both to give her the chance to prompt me, which she at once did – 'Why do you say that?' – and to slow down my racing pulse. Pacing my words I went on, 'When I'm with you, an hour only seems like a minute. But when I'm not mint you, a minute only seems like an hour.'

She would have got the gist of it. I had used the line before, in a less garbled version, in one of my letters to Victoria Leadenbury in our first term at the College of Commerce. It had also gone down well with Doreen Theaker. But I meant it. I always had. And I was rewarded with a squeeze of the hand that was playing with her bangle.

'Thank you. That's one of the nicest things I've ever had said to me.'

'So now you've got to tell me why you like being with me.'

'Oh . . . I can't put it into words, Ray. Because you're you, I suppose.'

It was not as eloquent a reciprocal testimonial as I had got from Victoria Leadenbury, but I was well satisfied. She was still holding my hand. I manipulated my little finger into her palm and began ruminatively scratching it with my nail. This, according to Douglas, was a universally recognised signal

110

communicating intense sexual desire. The fact that she did not pull her hand away meant it was mutual.

Gently, after one last scratch that caused her to wince slightly, I withdrew my hand and brought it up to her chin, tilting back her head so that I could kiss her. Whatever her reservations hitherto about other forms of physical contact, Janet robustly enjoyed our necking sessions and was able to control her breathing so that we could keep them up for quite long periods. I let my hand brush from her chin to her throat but went on kissing her for a full minute before moving on again. Then I felt the ribbing of her corduroy collar and located the top button that secured it tightly at the neck. The coat was a new one, a birthday present from a family aborigine, and the briefest of scrutinies in the light of the sub-post-office window had left me still unfamiliar with its layout. I got the button undone with little difficulty, and no resistance, but the collar remained tightly fastened.

As I tried to decide between fumbling for what must have been a concealed press-stud arrangement or tugging the collar apart willy-nilly, Janet moved her hand up to mine, felt around it, and deftly unfastened her coat at the neck. It was the first time she had ever come to my aid in this way. Her lips still attached to mine, she traced her hand downwards along the now-released lapel, and I felt the coat loosen as she tugged open the second button. She brought her arm up around my neck and I slipped my hand, not to its accustomed station as far as the knuckle but as far as the wrist, in one clean movement, under the collar of her cardigan and blouse to her warm shoulder. I drew her even more tightly towards me, pressing my cheek against hers as we relinquished one another's numbed lips. I did not know whether the pounding I felt was my own heart or Janet's. Two hearts that beat as one, she'd said. Perhaps that was it.

The moon had come out from behind its screen of cloud again and I could see the whiteness of her shoulder where I had pushed back her blouse. Both it and the cardigan over it were V-necked so there would be no need of further fumbling with buttons. That hurdle circumvented, I went straight for the shoulder straps that had so far marked the limit of my explorations – this time, however, firmly striking out with my index finger and following them downwards with the

111

purposefulness of a traveller setting off along an unfamiliar but well-signposted country road.

I arrived at what felt from its soft scratchiness like lace, presumably the edging of a slip or petticoat. I allowed, and more significantly Janet allowed, two probing fingers to stray beneath it, expecting to reach, but not finding, the resistant perimeter of her Youngform brassière as strategically studied in the window of Clough & Clough's. Perhaps she was not wearing one, either because the slip or petticoat was an adequate winter substitute or – not so wildly improbable the way things were shaping up this evening – because she had left it off the better to accommodate this anticipated expedition. I pushed on, not too hurriedly, wishing to be sensitive and delicate, yet beginning to blunder a little as I realised I was losing my sense of direction. I felt a stitch or thread give as my knuckles pressed against the lace; then at last a fingertip brushed against a small, soft protuberance that seemed to be hardening to the touch.

The moonlight throwing shadows and picking up diamond-points of frost on the hard ground, the stillness, and the far-off sounds, all lent the night enchantment. Charitably, I hoped it was the same for Douglas over in St Chad's churchyard and for Terry Liversedge under the viaduct. Perhaps, even at this moment, they were getting there below the waist. I didn't mind. I had got there above the waist and that was all I cared about for one evening.

Janet, uttering for the first time since she had tried to tell me why she liked being with me, breathed into my ear, 'What do you find so fascinating about my mole, then?'

As if coming out from under an anaesthetic I was suddenly and simultaneously aware of the cold tautening my chest, the deadness in my feet, the cramp in the arm around her shoulder, and the lace edging of slip or petticoat grazing a small chilblain on one of my knuckles.

'Your what?'

Janet giggled, causing a ringing in my eardrum. '*Mole!* Under my armpit. Where you're just about to rip the top of my petticoat, if you're not careful when you pull your hand away. Why, what did you think it was?'

Please God, don't let this get back to Audrey Marsh.

# 13

Mimeographed invitations to the Youth Guild Christmas social were drawing-pinned to the bare trees along Crag Park Avenue. Douglas and I decided to go. Janet, after a succession of winter sniffles, had flu, and Pauline would be attending some seasonal function at St Chad's. To my surprise, considering how he had pooh-poohed the Youth Guild as a crèche for cradle-snatchers, Terry Liversedge said he would come too, declaring that if Esmé didn't like him going without her she could do the other thing.

'No point in dragging my own snogging-fodder along, youth – it'd be a case of taking coals to Newcastle. I want to see what crumpet's been accumulating during our absence.' And he made his salacious clicking noise.

It had been a long time. We felt like old boys revisiting the school for speech day. Our entrance was tentative: we stood just inside the scuffed swing doors of the corrugated iron porch, taking in a sea of mostly unknown faces as we fiddled with our Windsor knots, Terry Liversedge shrugging back the wide shoulders of his salmon-pink zoot jacket, Douglas zipping and unzipping his leatherette American bomber-pilot's jacket, I shivering slightly in my blue-and-white striped seersucker jacket. They had all come from the same source – the Lost Property Mart on the Aire Bridge, as had our amber cigarette-holders.

It was perhaps a mistake for us to light up simultaneously. As two council-school gargoyles carting out a crate of empty Tizer bottles barged past us through the swing doors, one of them all but knocking my Balkan Sobranie out of its holder, I heard an explosion of snorts and a guffawed jibe about the Three Stooges.

Looking around the swing-record-blaring hall with its roof girders draped with paper-chains, paper bells tied to the protective wire-mesh over imitation-snow-smeared windows still bearing the traces of last year's imitation snow, and trestle tables laden with school-bunfight food and clusters of beakers for soft drinks, I remembered Terry Liversedge's reservations about cradle-snatching. The doll-like chicks with bright red rosebud mouths rustling back and forth in their paper-stiff party clothes, all in twos, either heading for the Ladies' or aimlessly-purposefully crisscrossing the hall with no object but to get to the other side, looked as if they were awaiting the arrival of Uncle Jolly the entertainer. The dough-faced gargoyles in their first long trousers and chin-engulfing collars who clustered around the radiogram, making hissing timpani sounds and blowing imaginary trumpets in accompaniment to the Harry James and Gene Krupa records, could have been playing some obtuse school-playground game. The three or four midget couples trying to waltz to the Bugle Call Bop could have been waltzing with cane chairs; the tulle-encased chick blundering around the floor with the troglodyte youth leader looked like a little girl dancing with her father.

'I'm not too sure about this little scene, gentlemen,' drawled Douglas, peering through his thick reading-glasses. He drew on his amber cigarette-holder, unaware that his cigarette had fallen out of it.

'Neither am I,' I said. 'Come on, let's belt down into town and see what the action is at the Wine Lodge.'

'Just a tick,' said Terry Liversedge. When Terry Liversedge said 'Just a tick' in that furtive way, then screwed up his face as if repressing a cry of agony, it meant that talent was in the offing. In this case it was Betty Parsons. Carrying a big earthenware teapot she had come out of the little scullery behind the concert platform and was heading with her usual straight-backed briskness towards the chain of trestle tables where the food was laid out. Instead of wearing the standard starched party dress half-way to a full-blown crinoline, which would not only have been unsuitable for her height but would have crushed badly when pressed up against the nettle-infested back wall of the Crag Park Avenue Congregational Chapel, she had on a straight plain flannel skirt just wide enough to ride up around her hips, and a blue polo-neck jumper that would comfortably roll up to her armpits. She threw back a lock of long blonde hair and took command of the refreshments like a netball captain taking possession of the court.

'I see that twat Ralph Driver's not here,' noted Terry Liversedge. 'You two can do what you like – I'm staying.'

Without waiting for a reaction either way he darted off to the card-table directly around the corner from the porch entrance at which we stood, where Youth Guild members in relay were stationed to collect entrance money.

Moving a little further into the hall in the hope that Betty Parsons might spot me in my new seersucker jacket, I saw for the first time who was presently selling the tickets. It was Doreen Theaker, with the unnecessary assistance of Geoffrey Sissons. I had not set eyes on either of them for getting on for six months. Doreen, though it was improbable, seemed to have grown. Perhaps it was because her back-unzipping navy-blue wool dress was less Junior Miss-like than the things I had usually seen her in when she wasn't wearing school uniform; she looked more self-possessed, less vulnerable. I saw with a pang that she was laughing as she gave Terry Liversedge his ticket. It seemed to me altogether unreasonable that Doreen Theaker, since given the brush-off, should have anything to laugh about. Terry Liversedge said something to her and she responded by glancing in my direction then quickly away again, I thought with eyes downcast. She had stopped laughing. That was more like it.

Geoffrey Sissons too had changed. In his light blue gaberdenes and properly-fitting dark blue Technical College blazer which made me acutely aware that my seersucker sleeves were about an inch too long, he looked a much more imposing figure than the weedy youth who had hogged the ping-pong table in my Youth Guild days. His arm was around Doreen, his hand clutching not her waist as was customary but resting lightly on the small of her back at the furthermost point to which it was possible to unzip her dress. For someone who called himself a Young Communist he seemed remarkably possessive.

'We might as well stay for an hour, now we've come,' I said to Douglas.

'Why not, mon brave – after all, what's one-and-six? Easy come, easy go, that's my motto.' But despite the sarcasm, it was Douglas who was first across to the green baize table, thus giving me time to compose a suitable greeting to Doreen: 'Hello, strangely. Long time no seem.'

I needn't have bothered. Douglas, for the sake of impressing anyone who might be watching, took it into his head to produce his mock-crocodile wallet, formerly the property of Terry Liversedge, and extract from it a pound note. Unable to make change, Doreen was obliged to go and seek out the troglodyte youth leader, leaving me with no option but to hand my one and sixpence over to Geoffrey Sissons.

'Return of the three bad pennies, eh?' said Geoffrey Sissons, in what was not far off being a jibing voice. 'I'm afraid if you're looking for a pick-up you've come to the wrong shop.'

'You never know your luck,' I said sourly. I was surprised and pained that Doreen hadn't made Geoffrey Sissons go off and get the change for Douglas's pound note, thus giving herself the chance of a few moments of privacy with me.

Terry Liversedge, running his steel comb through his hair and keeping his eyes fixed steadily on Betty Parsons who, efficiently serving sausage rolls and lemonade to the first hungry wave of gargoyles, had either not seen him yet or was pretending not to, said, 'So that's two old flames under one roof. Pity Alma Tipper's not here, Duggerlugs. We could have had a reunion.'

Douglas said sententiously, 'Never try to relive the past, old bean, old boy. What's done is over.' There were probably further variations on this homily in the pipeline but he was interrupted by a gargoyle-child of about twelve, precociously powdered and lipsticked and clad in what looked like her nightdress.

' 'Lo, Douglas.'

Terry Liversedge, turning aside, dug me fiercely in the ribs and murmured into a cupped hand, 'I bet she's anybody's for a sherbert dab.'

Douglas, not surprisingly, seemed embarrassed. 'Oh, hello, Brenda.'

'Do you like my dress?'

'Very nice. Very nice indeed,' said Douglas with a kind of hearty sheepishness.

I took pity on him. 'Come on,' I said to Terry Liversedge who was making a big show of staring up at the rafters and whistling to himself. 'Let's have a cup of what passes for tea.'

'Not yet, youth, wait till all those bods have got served – I want to get Betty Parsons on her ownsome.'

So, pretending to watch the dancing but keeping our ears cocked in Douglas's direction, we stayed put. The piping voice continued: 'Shall I wear it on Sunday?'

Even without looking at him I could tell that Douglas was flushing deeply beneath his dark skin. He mumbled, hoping we wouldn't hear, 'I shouldn't, Brenda. It's not really suitable for daytime, is it?'

'It is if it's a special occasion.'

'I don't think so. I believe that young man wants the honour of this dance, Brenda!' Douglas spoke with desperate troglodyte-type chirpiness as a jug-eared gargoyle with plastered hair polished like a bootcap skulked into our line of vision.

'What – our Leonard? No, he's come to take me home, because our mam says I've got to be in by nine. Ta-ra, Douglas, see you on Sunday.'

'Good night, Brenda.'

As Douglas's elfin admirer was escorted off by her gnomic brother, and Douglas turned away with the understandable intention of losing himself among the throng at the refreshment tables, Terry Liversedge and I, with a practised pincer-movement, closed in on him.

'All right, Duggerlugs. What's it worth?'

It was unusual to see Douglas blustering. 'What? I'm not with you.'

'To keep our traps shut, youth.'

'About what? I don't know what you're going on about, old boy, old bean.'

'Look at him, Ray – the picture of innocence!' In a hideous high-pitched voice, clasping his hands under his chin like the heroine of a Victorian melodrama, Terry Liversedge trilled, ' "Shall I wear my lovely dress, Douglas?" '

'Keep your voice down, for Christ's sake!'

'Give us the griff, then,' I said.

'I've heard of catching them young, Douglas,' said Terry Liversedge. 'But you take the shortbread.'

'Don't talk so stupid.'

'Then what's all this "see you on Sunday" stuff?'

Douglas's swarthy face had gone almost black, like one who is choking. He was blushing again. 'If you must know,' he muttered, 'she was talking about the Sunday school treat.'

I looked at Terry Liversedge who shrugged expressively, copying a comic gesture of Red Skelton's which he much admired. 'I don't get it,' I said.

'There's nothing to get. It's the St Chad's Sunday school Christmas treat next week and I told Pauline I'd give her a hand.'

'What's the Sunday school treat got to do with Pauline?'

'Quite a lot, if it's any of your business.'

Terry Liversedge's flashes of intuition were as often as not wide of the mark. When he snapped his fingers triumphantly with a cry of, 'Got it! She's a fizzing Sunday school teacher!' I expected Douglas to come back with a snarled disclaimer.

Instead, trying to change his demeanour from hangdog to defiant, he said belligerently, 'What if she is?'

'Nothing at all, Douglas – you kept it very quiet, that's all. All credit to her. Anyway, *you* must be quids in, because from what I've heard, Sunday school teachers can be really hot stuff. In fact I think it was you who told us that.'

'It could have been. They *are* hot stuff.'

'But only from the waist up,' I couldn't resist saying, with a wink at Terry Liversedge. Then, more to stop Douglas retaliating than because I thought the question had any particular significance, 'So how did your little girl-friend know you'd be giving Pauline a hand on Sunday?'

'Because Douglas is a Sunday school teacher as well!' chortled Terry Liversedge. This time he wasn't even trying to be intuitive, only flippant. We were both unprepared for Douglas's reaction.

'So what?' he said with a fair attempt at coolness.

'He bloody *is*!' shouted Terry Liversedge, astounded. The frowning youth leader troglodyte, walking tightrope-fashion across the dance area bearing two brimming mugs and a plate piled high with fancy cakes, grimaced at Terry Liversedge to moderate his language and jerked his head to indicate the gyrating tots behind him, thereby creating a small tidal wave of tea which splashed at his feet.

We turned away and moved into a huddle by the ping-pong table which was stacked on its side against the end wall. One by one we produced our amber holders and lit cigarettes. Douglas, now we had got his confession out of him, seemed to be recovering his composure.

'I still can't get over it,' marvelled Terry Liversedge. 'Douglas Beckett a Sunday school teacher!'

'There does happen to be a reason,' said Douglas.

'What do you do, Douglas?' I asked, genuinely intrigued. 'Sit all these snotty-nosed kids in a circle and tell them a story?'

'It has been known,' he stonewalled.

'What – Bible stories?' pursued Terry Liversedge, still incredulous.

'As a general rule – yes.'

'What – Joseph and the coat of many colours and that?'

'That kind of thing.'

'Bloody hell fire,' said Terry Liversedge, awed.

'She really must be hot stuff,' I remarked, 'if she can talk you into doing that.'

'She didn't,' said Douglas, now with complete aplomb. He tapped his cigarette-holder with a grimy finger nail and was not even flustered when once again the cigarette fell out and rolled away under the stacked ping-pong table. 'I talked *her* into it. I did tell you, my friends,' he went on as we stared, our mouths dropping, 'there is a reason.'

Terry Liversedge narrowed his eyes. 'I'm beginning to see the light, you crafty devil, Beckett. Has this got anything to do with your idea of getting a room?'

'It could have,' said Douglas guardedly.

'So where does this Sunday school take place, then?'

'In the crypt.'

'Do you mean to stand there and tell us,' I said with tense incredulity, but keeping my voice down, 'that you've got yourself taken on as a Sunday school teacher, and you've made Pauline get herself taken on as a Sunday school teacher, just so that you can get her down in the church crypt and do her?'

'Something like that. As soon as the verger starts entrusting us with the key, that is.'

Terry Liversedge shook his head in wonder, admiration and disbelief. 'I don't know much about the Bible, Duggerlugs, but I do know that people have been turned into pillars of salt for less.'

Douglas, taking that as the compliment it was, smirked complacently as he bent to retrieve his cigarette.

There had been a brief respite between records. Now, as we drifted back towards the dance area, someone put on Glenn Miller playing 'In the Mood'.

'*In the mood, a-barby-darby, in the mood, a-booby-dooby,*' sang

Terry Liversedge, sachaying around to survey the talent. At once, he spotted Betty Parsons. So did I. Spellbound by Douglas's revelations he had temporarily forgotten about her. So had I. Then, across the hall, I saw Doreen Theaker. I had forgotten about her too. Betty Parsons, the rush for refreshments now temporarily assuaged, was standing alone at one of the trestle tables, rearranging cakes on a plate. Doreen Theaker was talking to a friend, there being no sign at present of Geoffrey Sissons. It was eminently the moment to accost either of them. It seemed monstrously unfair that I could not accost them both.

The dilemma was solved by Terry Liversedge. 'A-dooby-dooby-dooby-dooby-doo-bee-darboo. See you later.' And wriggling back his draped shoulders he half-walked, half-danced across to Betty Parsons.

'Do me a favour, Doug,' I said. 'Before you light that fag again, go and ask that dish standing with Doreen Theaker for a dance.'

'I'll clean your boots for fourpence,' said Douglas, but genially. Evidently he felt that on balance our interrogation had done his reputation more good than harm. I followed a step or two behind him, and as he took the floor with Doreen's friend I was on hand with my line almost pat: 'Hello, Doreen, could I have this chance?'

At least I had little trepidation about dancing with Doreen. She had once been my regular partner after all, though admittedly only at the Clock Saturday afternoon dancing class, beyond whose stilted one-two-three mechanics I had not progressed. Doreen, on the other hand, had come on a great deal. I wondered whether there were other directions in which she had come on. She was wearing a scent that was new to me, one that put me in mind of musk as conjured into my nostrils by Douglas's description. Her waist was pliant to my touch, indicative of a desire not to discourage Geoffrey Sissons's roving hands by the restriction of a roll-on girdle. Not that she had even worn one, but it was time she did.

'You dance very well these days,' I said.

'It must be the practice I'm getting – we go to the Clock every Saturday now.'

I had not imagined that she stayed in reading on Saturday nights, and I supposed she was better off in a warm public hall than in a draughty recreation ground, churchyard or viaduct, but I felt a dull pain in my chest. Steering Doreen in a gradual arc rather than committing myself to a spectacular corner turn I analysed the sentence. 'We', of course, was she and Geoffrey Sissons. It would be fruitless dwelling on the degree of intimacy implied. 'Now', however, could only have one meaning. It meant since I gave her the brush-off card. If I had not brushed her off, she would not now be going to the Clock every Saturday with Geoffrey Sissons.

Therefore he was only a substitute. Therefore –

Betty Parsons, standing chatting to Terry Liversedge, flashed me the warmest of smiles as we danced past her. I had only time to say, 'Hello, Petty,' but it seemed to me that she had understood my message, and that her eyes were following me, acknowledging its receipt. It was rather complicated. I was telling Betty Parsons that I would rather be dancing with her, but for the fact that I would rather be dancing with Doreen Theaker.

'Excuse me.' As we swayed past the door of the Gents', I felt a none-too-gentle tap on my shoulder. I tried to manipulate Doreen around, tripped, and stumbled against Geoffrey Sissons who was stamping out a cigarette end.

'This isn't an excuse-me dance, Sissons.'

'It is now, Watmough.'

'I thought you were supposed to be a Communist. Share and share alike.' But I was talking to myself. He held Doreen, I noticed as they swept away, more tightly than I had had the nerve to hold her, and she clung to him more closely than she had clung to me.

As I slouched off the floor Terry Liversedge and Betty Parsons were just beginning to dance. I stood near the door of the Gents' until they came round.

'Excuse me, Terry.'

'You'll be lucky, youth.'

# 14

We rounded off the evening with fish and chips. With no overcoats over our new jackets it was too cold to stand outside the Argosy Fish Saloon on The Parade, and so we hurried down to the Mermaid Supper Bar near the Gem, where you could perch at a narrow table. Douglas and I, that was – just as we were leaving the Youth Guild hut Terry Liversedge had said abruptly, 'I'll catch up with you,' and wheeled back inside, we supposed in the hope of walking Betty Parsons home. We got him a cod and threepennorth anyway – we could always find room for it ourselves if he didn't turn up – and squeezed ourselves along a bench jammed up against the tiled wall.

The Mermaid Supper Bar did not run to plates and it was good to feel the warmth of the parcels of fish and chips on chilblained hands. The night was one of the winter's coldest, with a sleet-flecked wind, and we were grateful for the bubbling heat of the frying range and the steam obscuring its tile-mosaic Neptune and attendant mermaids and the hanging blue and red placard for the George Formby double bill at the Gem.

'I give him three minutes,' I said to Douglas, still experiencing a tight chest pain from the chill that had cut through my seersucker. 'One minute to walk her across to Winifred Drive, if she lets him, one minute while they both freeze to death on the street corner, and one minute for him to belt down here.'

Sure enough, no sooner had we unwrapped our fish and chips and inhaled the savoury bouquet that the sprinkled salt and vinegar brought out as from a broken capsule, than I saw a salmon-pink sleeve rubbing the steamed-up window and Terry Liversedge's face, white with cold, peering in. The shop bell rang as he shoved open the door with a padded shoulder, both hands being drawn up into the sleeves of his zoot jacket. Squeezing alongside me on the narrow bench, he looked down ungratefully at the grease-exuding white paper parcel that awaited his arrival.

With heavy sarcasm he said, 'Oh, thank you. Thank you very much. That just goes to show how much faith my mates have in me. What made you so sure I was going to turn up? For all you knew I could have been getting in some crafty knee-trembling hours behind the Congregational Chapel.'

'If we hadn't got you any stinking fish and chips in, you'd have been saying, "Oo, pull the ladder up, Jack's in the lifeboat!" I retorted. 'Give us your tenpence and stop binding.'

It was in the best of humours, though, that Terry Liversedge paid up and commenced to drown his congealing supper in vinegar. 'These are frigging stone cold, youth,' he said, but without rancour.

'Complain to the management, not us, old fruit,' advised Douglas through a mouthful of chipped potato. 'We only beat you by about ten seconds.'

'Long enough, Duggerlugs.'

'Long enough for what?' I said. 'You haven't had time to get across Crag Park Avenue, let alone get across Betty Parsons.'

'Very witty, youth. Very droll. I know what I have had time for, though, and that's to ask her to start going out with me again. Guess what she said.'

'I'm sure it wasn't no, otherwise you wouldn't be telling us.'

'Too true. She's given that pratt Ralph Driver the brush-off. We're going to the Paramount on Boxing Day.'

'What about Esmé?'

'Esmé can go and stuff herself, Ray. I've had Esmé right up to here.'

Douglas was crammed up so close to me on the short bench that I didn't know whether he was kicking my ankle or just moving his foot. But I didn't pursue Esmé's destiny.

'They say it's a good picture – *Kiss Tomorrow Goodbye*. James Cagney,' went on Terry Liversedge, lowering his mouth to receive a steaming fragment of battered cod. 'Christ on crutches, this fish is hot!'

'It was cold a minute ago,' said Douglas laconically.

'Yes, well it's hot now. I don't suppose either of you wants to make up a foursome, by any chance?' The brazen casualness of the suggestion was calculated to lull us into thinking that it didn't matter to Terry Liversedge one way or the other. Again

I felt a tap on the ankle and this time I was left in no doubt that Douglas was kicking me.

'Sorry, mon capitaine, I've already made other arrangements,' said Douglas firmly. 'Besides, you don't want other bods playing gooseberry on your first date.'

'Ah, well, that's it, you see. For some unknown reason she wants it to be a foursome.' Terry Liversedge, sucking greasy fingers to hide his discomfiture, nudged my arm. 'Actually, youth, she said something about why didn't I invite you and Janet.'

I was going to enjoy this. 'She doesn't know Janet.'

'She knows you, though.'

That was hardly the case either. But it was flattering, if Betty Parsons had really said that, and her reasons for saying it would be the basis of some pleasant conjecture over Christmas. Meanwhile there was Terry Liversedge's blustering embarrassment to be relished.

'You don't half waffle, Liversedge. Why don't you just admit she's only agreed to go out with you on condition you make it a foursome?'

'I will admit it, youth. You know why, don't you? She can't trust herself to be alone with me.'

'Can't trust you to keep your mitts to yourself, more like.' I didn't believe either explanation, preferring to give more credibility to the possibility of her merely using Terry Liversedge to get better acquainted with me. We should have to see. 'All right, Terry, seeing it's you. We'll come to the Paramount with you if you pay for us in.'

'Get stuffed. Play your cards right and I might buy you an ice-cream.'

The shop bell was ringing intermittently as assorted fossils with blue-veined noses, streaming eyes and chattering false teeth, traipsed through the Mermaid Supper Bar, either guzzling their fish and chips at the other two tables or bearing steaming parcels home. It rang again now, as a female aborigine of vaguely familiar aspect, contracting her tweed-weighted shoulders in an elaborate stage shiver and making a pantomime face of protest against the cold, made her way to the counter in a facetious scutter.

She was familiar to Douglas, too. It was noticeable that he had brought up a blemished hand to shade his blemished face and that he was doing his best to withdraw his chin into his American bomber-pilot's jacket.

'Aye aye!' snickered Terry Liversedge. 'There's a piece of skirt come looking for you, Douglas. Did you stand her up tonight, then?'

'Quiet!' hissed Douglas.

Terry Liversedge, pleased that the limelight had shifted from his own confusion to Douglas's, refused to drop the joke. 'He goes from one extreme to the other, does our Douglas. First it's ten-year-olds he's after, then it's grand-mothers.'

Leaning against the counter as she waited for her order, the aborigine casually turned to look at the Gem Picture Palace placard. Both Terry Liversedge and I then recognised her from our one and only encounter, in St Chad's parish church. But of the three of us, Pauline's mother recognised only Douglas.

'Now then, Douglas – is it cold enough for you?'

With the beefy heartiness that we often adopted, chameleon-like, when addressing aborigines, Douglas responded, 'Now then, Mrs Batty – it's good weather for reindeer, isn't it?'

Two or three more such pleasantries were sufficient to cover her departure, much to Douglas's relief. As the door closed behind her Terry Liversedge uttered a triumphant squawk of laughter.

'Ha-har! It's just not your night, is it, Duggerlugs?'

All injured innocence, Douglas appealed to me. 'What's wrong with him? Can't I say good night to someone without his permission, now?'

'It's her saying good night to *you* that worries me, Beckett.' Terry Liversedge did have a point. Douglas was on a dangerous course. Exchanging smalltalk with a chick's mother was perilously on the way to being invited to Sunday tea, which in turn was only a few steps from the *Evening Argus* engagements column.

'What do you expect her to do – cut me dead?'

'Yes, I do, since you ask. How does she come to be so pally with you, that's what we want to know?'

'She isn't *all* that pally. It's just that she sees me in church every week.'

Terry Liversedge tutted and shook his head in a gesture of contempt. 'I might have fizzing known. Do you know what I'm beginning to think, Ray? It's all a lot of boloney about him trying to have it off with Pauline in the church crypt. He's got religion, that's about the size of it.'

The taunt wasn't supposed to be taken seriously, but Douglas, flushing again, evidently felt the need to justify himself. 'Very well, old bean, old boy. How much have you got says there isn't method in my madness?'

'Yes, we know, youth. That's what you said when we found out you were running a Sunday school on the quiet. What's the latest plan, then – getting Pauline's mother on her back in the vestry?'

'No, it's a plan that affects you two, actually.'

Terry Liversedge gave a sardonic sigh. 'Off we go.'

'Oh, don't you want to hear about it, Terence?' said Douglas with exaggerated blandness, picking scraps of batter from the grease-soaked wrappings of his supper. 'I thought you might have been curious, what with your being so interested in getting your oats.' Then, as if dismissing the subject entirely from his mind, 'I'm still hungry. Anyone fancy sharing another piece of cod?'

'Never mind pieces of cod,' I said, my interest aroused as Douglas had meant it to be. 'Shoot.'

'I bet he wants to get us into the choir so we can go on the church outing and have it off in a haystack,' scoffed Terry Liversedge.

'You may laugh and you may jeer, mon capitaine, but you are closer than you think.'

I tapped the tiled table imperatively. 'Get this, Beckett. We are not joining any fizzing church choir.'

'Forget the choir, mon brave. Concentrate on the Whitsun outing.'

'What Whitsun outing?'

'To the Festival of Britain.'

'What naffing Festival of Britain?' demanded Terry Liversedge, completely out of his depth.

'Come on, Terry,' I protested, 'even I know about that.' Although I never read the papers except for the weather forecast and the amusements guide, I was vaguely aware from newsreel shots of girders and puddles and workmen sloshing about in gumboots that the event was now very much in the offing. I had only the sketchiest idea what it was in aid of. Some political troglodytes were anxious to show that a new Britain was rising phoenix-like out of the ashes of war, if the hysterical commentator on British Movietone News had got it right. It was two hundred miles away in London so it didn't concern me. My only small interest in the Festival centred on our own town's sole contribution to it, the odd-looking building that was going up next to the Clock Ballroom behind the sign that said FESTIVAL OF BRITAIN 1951: SITE OF GRIPPEN-SHAW PAGEANT OF PROGRESS. An industrial exhibition, it was supposed to be. Where you had exhibitions, I had noted from the cage bird shows and other such events in the Corn Exchange, you had talent selling programmes.

'The whole beauty of it is this,' said Douglas. 'The last time they had a church outing to London they were there for five days. Apparently it takes some of them that long to recover from the journey.'

'We're not tagging along with a gang of old biddies, are we?' I objected, alarmed.

'What difference does it make? Once in London, we'll have nothing to do with them. We don't even have to go to the perishing Festival. Just think of it, my friends. The three of us in a hotel room apiece with three dames, and five days and nights of shafting to look forward to!'

We did think of it. Terry Liversedge at last broke our joint reverie.

'Yes. Good. Great. Fantastic. Only one thing, youth – why do we have to saddle ourselves with this Festival boloney at all? Why can't we just take our birds on holiday?'

'Oh, by all means, old bean, old boy,' said Douglas with airy sarcasm, running a greasy finger along his embryo moustache. 'And what would your folks say if you told them you were going to spend next Whitsun in Blackpool with a dame?'

'They wouldn't know. I'd say I was going with you.'

'All right, what would Esmé's folks say?'

'I don't go out with Esmé.'

'Betty Parsons, then.'

Terry Liversedge had the grace to grunt ruefully, conceding the point.

'Whereas, mon capitaine, if Betty announces to her folks that she'd like to go on an educational trip to the Festival of Britain at Whitsun, organised by St Chad's parish church no less, they'd probably pay for her ticket. It doesn't even matter if they come down to see her off. They'll just take one look at the vicar and all the rest of the travelling geriatric ward and think she must be in safe hands. You see, chaps, I've thought it all out.'

'I can see you have,' said Terry Liversedge with unstinting admiration. 'He's a clever devil on the quiet is our Douglas, isn't he, Ray?'

'What about the cost – have you thought that out?' I asked, putting my finger on a possible flaw.

'Ah. Now that's where you come in, Raymondo. I want you to find out.'

'Why – what's it got to do with me?'

'I thought if we hired one of Moult & Sumpter's coaches and we got them to arrange the hotel, they'd probably give you a favourable quotation.'

'Oh, I see. Yes, they probably – ' I was suddenly struck by the way he had phrased that request.'You say *you* thought, Douglas. Was this church outing your idea?'

'More or less.'

'So the whole point and purpose of driving all these toothless old sods all the way down the Great North Road and turning them loose on the Festival of Britain is so that we three can shag ourselves rotten in London?'

'More or less.'

'And you're the organiser, are you?'

'I will be, yes.'

'Will be, he says!' snorted Terry Liversedge with glee. 'I bet the poor buggers don't even know they're going yet.'

'Of course they fizzing don't!' I hooted, just as gleefully. I had just realised that myself. 'He's only just thought of it, while we've been sitting here eating fish and chips! Haven't you, Duggerlugs, you crafty swine?' It was quite plain: he'd dreamed up his scheme to stop Terry Liversedge riling him about Pauline's mother.

'I don't care when he thought of it, he's a frigging genius,' said Terry Liversedge. Then with unusual magnanimity he added, 'Did you say you wanted another cod, Douglas? Divvy up, Ray – we'll treat him between us.'

As I struggled to my feet, the better to dig coppers out of my pocket in the narrow space between bench and table, I said to Douglas, 'You'll look pretty silly if Pauline's mother decides to come on the trip.'

'She won't, mon brave. She gets car-sick. That's why we're not going by train.'

I put the pennies back in my pocket and tossed Terry Liversedge a sixpence. 'Get him some chips as well. He's earned them.'

# 15

'I didn't know you went to church,' said Audrey accusingly.

On the morning of Christmas Eve, Moult & Sumpter's was in comparatively festive mood. A limited amount of threadbare tinsel, dredged from a dusty cardboard box on top of the stationery cupboard, draped shelves and wall fittings, and we had garnished the pinned-up travel posters with clusters of imitation holly. Audrey had fetched in mince pies, bought from the petty cash, to supplement our coffee break. We would be finishing at lunchtime and the pterodactyls, in relaxed mood, were packed into the senior partner's cubicle where they were passing around the Wills' Whiffs and lacing their coffee with rum. Audrey half leant against, half perched upon, my desk, revealing an expanse of thirty-denier fully-fashioned almost up to the knee where her knife-pleated skirt had ridden up her crossed legs.

'I don't,' I hastened to say. 'It's for a friend.' We were talking about the quotation I had got for the Whitsun outing to the Festival of Britain. The pterodactyls, after humming and hawing, consulting their brochures and scribbling on bits of scrap paper, had come up with a figure of five and half guineas a head all in for five days, staying in the highly recommended Court Gardens Hotel quite near Marble Arch. Assuming I offered Janet Gill the inducement of going halves on her expenses, and allowing for incidentals such as snacks and contraceptives, I would have to put away around fifteen shillings a week between now and May. It was going to be worth it, though.

'But you'll be going on this trip yourself?' persisted Audrey.

'I might do,' I said evasively.

'Is Janet going?'

'I don't know, I haven't asked her yet.' It was none of Audrey's business.

'I'm not being nosey, Ray, it's just that if you do go, don't forget to get your twenty per cent staff discount. Because knowing this lot, they won't offer it if you don't ask for it.'

'Oh, thanks, Audrey, that should make a lot of difference.' I bit into a mince pie, clumsily scooping up the crust into a cupped hand as it disintegrated, and not heeding the powdered sugar that showered down my lapels. I had no need to make an impression on Audrey now. After some initial awkwardness on my part following her rebuff in the covered market, we had gradually developed an easy-going, bantering relationship. Our sporadic exchanges on non-office matters were based almost entirely on one another's supposed lack of sleep: Audrey had a running joke about transferring me from coffee to Horlicks in order to build up my stamina for my evenings with Janet; I had one about her mascara hiding rings under her eyes induced by weekends with Ronnie. It was wearing a little thin by now and it made a nice change to talk about something else.

'I wouldn't mind going to that Festival myself,' said Audrey. 'There's going to be coloured lights and open-air dancing and all sorts of things from what I've read.'

She certainly knew more about the Festival than I did. All I had was a vague picture of candy-striped pavilions filled with lathes. 'What's stopping you, then?'

'What – and play wallflower to you and Janet? I'm not that hard up, thank you very much, Raymond Watmough.'

'How do you know you'd have to? I might take you both on for all you know.' I ran the gallantry back through my mind to confirm that I'd said the words in the right order. I had, but they seemed too plodding for the lighthearted effect intended.

'It'd take a man, not his shirt,' scoffed Audrey with a momentary reversion to her natural mill-girl accent.

As she prised herself up from my desk and wandered across to her own, I felt obscurely that I had to retrieve some loss of face. I tried another oblique compliment: 'Anyway, I did ask you first, so you can't say I didn't.'

'What – to go down to London? Is that an invitation, you mad thing you?'

Surprising myself with my own boldness, and having no motive beyond adding a little spice to the moment to go with the unaccustomed treat of mince pies, I said, 'No, I meant to go out with me. Maybe you *would* be going down to London at Whitsun if you'd said yes.'

'Maybe I made a mistake then,' said Audrey, still jokingly.

Or, it was remotely possible, not jokingly.

'Maybe you did,' I said even more recklessly.

I brushed powdered sugar off my jacket. The pterodactyls were still lolling in the inner office, working up a blue fog of cigarillo smoke and now taking neat rum in their coffee cups. I was meeting Douglas in the Wine Lodge at lunchtime, to give him his quotation for the coach trip. I would have rum and blackcurrant and a packet of Whiffs.

Coquettishly, it sounded to me, Audrey said, 'Would you like this last mince pie?'

'No thanks, Audrey, I've had sufficient.'

'Come on, Ray, it's not Christmas every day – I'll share it with you.'

Crossing back to my desk, Audrey held the remaining mince pie at arm's length so as not to get crumbs on her clothes as she broke it in two. She muffed the operation and a dollop of mincemeat fell on to my inner thigh.

'Oh dear, I am sorry, Ray. I hope it doesn't stain.' She tore a piece off my blotter and handed it to me. 'Only I think you'd better wipe it off yourself under the circumstances rather than me. Otherwise certain persons might get the wrong idea.'

From the jerk of her head it was evident that the certain persons who might get the wrong idea were the pterodactyls, not me. Before dabbing the mincemeat off I had the wild notion of saying, 'They're not looking. Anywhere, you were the put who put it where.' It was perhaps as well that I abandoned the idea at once.

We had some discussion on the most efficacious way of removing stains, in the event of the damp spot on my gaberdine slacks leaving one. As I rubbed at it with my handkerchief Audrey said, 'Open wide!' and popped a segment of mince pie into my mouth. She sucked her fingers one by one, either in a child–like manner or a sensuous one, I could not make up my mind which. Though she had eaten her own piece of mince pie and we had both finished our coffee, she did not return to her own desk this time.

'You're not very observant, are you?' said Audrey as I rearranged my handkerchief in my top pocket.

'What's that?' I said indulgently. She had folded her arms and was leaning back against my desk drawers, looking down at me. We were in for a little game.

'Don't you notice anything?'

Yes. I noticed that the top two buttonholes of her yoked silk-crêpe blouse were misshapen where her fiancé had repeatedly but clumsily pulled open its pearl buttons. There was a mark on her neck which, unless he had taken a lighted cigarette to her again, was a lovebite. The zip of her skirt looked worn, as if from frequent use. She probably kept it oiled for him.

'You've done something with your hair.'

'I haven't done anything with my hair. I'll give you a clue. It's something I'm not wearing.'

Any underclothes?

'How would my know what you're not wearing?' I ventured falteringly. To my astonishment, Audrey gripped my shoulders and propelled herself forward from my desk so that her love-bitten or cigarette-burned neck was level with my face. 'Look.' For one excited and disturbing second I thought she had been at the pterodactyls' rum and was inviting me to peer down her blouse. I did in fact catch a disappointing glimpse of what looked to me like the top of a peach-coloured knitted vest before I realised what she was calling to my attention.

'That silver chain with your engagement ring on it.'

'Nobody can call you slow on the uptake, can they, Ray? Quite the Sexton Blake, aren't we?'

I was even slower on the uptake than Audrey knew. I had to squint at the third finger of her left hand before it dawned on me that she was not wearing her engagement ring at all.

'What's happened to it, then?'

'What usually happens when ladies break off their engagements. I've given it back to him. He's very fortunate I didn't throw it at him.'

With no apparent rancour or regret, Audrey gave me a brief summary of her broken romance. She said that without going into all the sordid details, he had nipped her arms just that once too often. Nipping her arms was seemingly what he did when holding her in a vice-like grip to grill her endlessly about her alleged two-timings – there were bruises she could show me, were she able to roll her sleeves up high enough. He had come home on Christmas leave and almost at once had begun to nip her arms and make his accusations, and she had had enough of it.

'Poor you,' was the only suitable comment that came to mind. I made it absently. I was thinking that anyone so tortured by suspicion, baseless or not, could only have reached such a demented state by having himself first savoured the pleasures that he feared others were now enjoying. I had to restrain myself from adding, 'Lucky him.'

'Poor me nothing,' said Audrey, quite vindictively. 'If he wants to be jealous, from now on he can have something to be jealous about.'

'That sounds as if you've got somebody else lined up already.' I was jealous myself, and I hadn't even touched her.

'Not yet. Let's just say I'm footloose and fancy-free. I've a good mind to go to the Christmas dance at the Mecca-Locarno tonight and get myself picked up.'

I would be free of Janet by six. I was meeting her only to give her her present – just a Picturegoer's Diary, following my extravagance on the silver-plated bangle – as I walked her down to the bus station. To my annoyance, she had refused to duck out of some fossilised home ritual involving exchanging presents under the Christmas tree, her excuse being that it was a family tradition and her aborigine parents would be hurt if she revealed a preference for spending Christmas Eve on the chained-down seesaw on the recreation ground.

I was on my own. Douglas, as he had shamefacedly had to admit, had committed himself to attending a midnight service at St Chad's with Pauline. Terry Liversedge would be at a loose end, but he would probably want to talk me into a Christmas Eve pub-crawl that would culminate with us throwing up into the privet. The prospect of a one-night stand, if that was what was on offer, with a piece of hot stuff capable of goading men into nipping her arms, was tempting.

But the nearest I could get to a decisive move was, 'You don't want to go on your own,' leaving her to respond to the hint or not, as she pleased.

'I couldn't even if I wanted to,' Audrey admitted ruefully. 'I don't know what it's like in your house at Christmas-time, but trying to get out of ours is like tunnelling out of Wakefield Gaol.'

It was as if the rum and blackcurrants I meant to drink with Douglas had gone to my head in advance. Unable to stop

134

myself, hearing my voice as if it were someone else's, I said, 'What wrong's with Boxing Day, then?'

'I thought you'd never ask,' said Audrey with alarming promptness. Too late, I realised I was catching her on the rebound.

Flushed with rum and clutching wet cigar-butts, the two pterodactyls who belonged at the big partner desk were about to return to it. In a moment they would be making guffawing innuendoes about what they would call the cosy tête-à-tête we had been having.

'That's if you haven't already got anything on on Boxing Day,' added Audrey coyly.

I had burned my boats. I riposted with stammering bravado, 'Nothing I can't get out of. The question that imperests me is whether *you'll* have anything on on, on Boxing May.'

'You'll have to wait and see, kid, won't you? Where do you want to meet?'

'Well, if you don't mind making up a foursome to see James Cagney in *Kiss Tomorrow Goodbye,* how about outside the Paramount?'

I was not being as rash as Terry Liversedge might have supposed, had he been privy to this slight change in his Boxing Day arrangements. Had I prudently decided to meet Audrey somewhere else, I knew I should have spent all Christmas vacillating and would have found myself on Boxing Day having to stand either her or Janet up, probably on the spin of a coin. Now, unless the two of them were to meet face to face outside the Paramount, I had to do something about Janet, although I had no idea what. A brush-off card was no longer appropriate, that I was sure of, but I didn't know what etiquette demanded in its place.

Some instinct told me not to ask Terry Liversedge, who unexpectedly turned up at the Wine Lodge with Douglas, they having stumbled across one another while admiring the same yellow waistcoat in the window of Horne Bros. It was hardly the place, anyway, for soliciting intimate advice. The Wine Lodge, a circular basement cavern almost the size of the Corn Exchange, had been built by some Victorian excavationist to dimensions that could comfortably entomb all the drinkers in Grippenshaw, and on this Christmas Eve lunchtime it looked as if most of them were fighting to be served. I had to bellow my news about Audrey against a marshalling-yard shunting of glasses and over an ocean-wave babble which itself was hard put to be heard above the robust wail of the carol-blaring Hammond organ between the ladies' snug and the pie counter.

Neither Terry Liversedge nor Douglas seemed surprised at my changing partners. I had the uneasy impression that they had already discussed my progress with Janet between themselves and reached the conclusion that I would get nowhere. Terry Liversedge's only concern was that I shouldn't let him down on his Boxing Day foursome with Betty Parsons; Douglas's, that I could still be counted on for his Festival of Britain church outing.

But when it was Terry Liversedge's turn to struggle towards the milling circular bar for three more rums, I jerked my head towards the Gents' as a signal for Douglas to thread his way after me across the packed cavern.

'I didn't like to ask Terry this,' I said as we stood side by side in the commodious slate stalls of a vast urinal, 'but how did he go about jacking it in with Esmé?'

'How do you know he did? How do you know she didn't jack him in?' said Douglas without expression.

My instinct had been right, then. 'Funny you should say that, Douglas. That's just the impression I got.'

'It's more than an impression, Raymondo. He got a Dear John letter.'

'What – and he showed it to you?' I asked unbelievingly. That would have been highly uncharacteristic.

'He didn't show it to me, no. I saw him reading it. I just happened to be going past Rabinowitcz the Jeweller's Corner, but on the other side of the road, just a couple of nights before that Youth Guild social. Who should be standing under the clock but Terry Liversedge and Esmé. She was diving into her handbag. I crossed over Albert Street and looked back, just in time to see her charging away up Sheepgate. And Terry was tearing open this letter and starting to read it. He doesn't know I know,' concluded Douglas, zipping up his flies. 'So don't tell him.'

'Poor Terry,' I said, meaning it. I had never had a Dear John letter myself but I could imagine what it would feel like to receive one. It would be doubly mortifying for Terry

Liversedge who could have had his pick, or pretty nearly his pick, of all the talent in Grippenshaw.

We crossed to the wash-basins and meticulously combed our hair in the curlicue-etched mirror.

'On the other hand,' I said, 'that's not much help to me. I was hoping for some tips on how to give Janet the brush-off.'

'Same method, old fruit. They send Dear John letters, we send Dear Jane ones. Or Dear Janet in your case.'

'What – and just hand it to her?' I asked dubiously.

'Good God, no! Post it.'

'Too late. No post till after Boxing Day.'

'Fret not. Leave it at the Metropole.'

'At the reception desk? They might take a dim view of being used as a private postbox for the junior staff.'

'Not at Christmas. They'll think it's a card.'

At Crag Park Secondary Modern, before we took our scholarships for the College of Commerce, the troglodyte whose form we were in had told Douglas that he had the kind of brain that would carry him to Leeds University if he worked hard. I had always endorsed that testimonial.

'So I send her a letter. What shall I put?'

'Oh, the usual things, Raymondo. Don't say you're not good enough for her, though, whatever you do, because she'll write straight back and say you are. Tell her you're both too young to be tied down.'

We pushed our way back through the crowded Wine Lodge to where Terry Liversedge was pinned against a gryphon-encrusted pillar, holding three glasses of rum aloft and looking impatient. We told him we had been going over the Moult & Sumpter quotation for the Festival of Britain outing.

Unlike me, both Douglas and Terry Liversedge had to go back to work after their lunch hour. I made the mistake of staying down in the Wine Lodge to finish the dregs of Douglas's rum and blackcurrant and to smoke another Wills' Whiff while I thought what to write to Janet. The din was stultifying. The body-warmth of the hordes of drinkers, all but climbing over one another like stag beetles as they struggled to and from the bar, was suffocating. The place was washed overall in a harsh yellow glow, with highlights in green, red and dancing orange from several dozen mechanical signs advertising beer and pies. The flashing images, combined with the trapped cigarette and panatella smoke, made my eyes burn. Feeling slightly sick, I headed for the nearest of the Wine Lodge's six exits.

I was still giddy as I turned into Sheepgate, pushing against the tide of homeward shoppers carrying turkeys in carrier bags, bunches of holly and giant teddy-bears. A little confused, I found myself in Woolworth's with no very clear idea of what I was doing there.

The letter to Janet, that was it. I had nothing to write it on. I shoved my way through to the stationery and greetings cards counter and was about to buy a wallet of Basildon Bond when I remembered Douglas saying something about a Christmas card. They had to think it was a Christmas card. That was it. I would write Janet's letter on a Christmas card.

With the last Christmas post gone the card counter was almost deserted and I was able to choose carefully, a good one costing sevenpence. Then I made my way through Woolworth's and cut down Exchange Row to the main post-office in Town Square. I was clearer-headed now. It was five unaccustomed cigars in successsion that had fuddled me, I decided, throwing the last one away half-finished.

I found a place at the long ledge under the windows where a few fossils were painstakingly writing telegrams or filling in forms, and spread out my card among the discarded bits of stamp-hinging. It was dusk already, and looking out across Town Square as I meditatively tapped my Biro against my teeth I could see the lighted-up Christmas trees on either side of the Hotel Metropole steps. I thought of Janet coming out of the hotel and down those steps, head bent, not seeing the Christmas trees, after she had read my letter. I would make it as kind a one as I could.

'. . . but have been thinking for quite a while now that . . . sure you must feel the same . . . unfair to take up so many of your evenings . . . must have other friends you would like to keep in touch with . . . young to be so involved . . . never forget you . . . really did mean it when I said . . . good while it lasted . . . time to call it a day . . .' No point in dragging Audrey Marsh into it. My letter had spilled over from the blank left-hand side of the card to the right-hand side with its printed greeting: 'Wishing you all that is bright and beautiful this joyful Christmastide.' I added ' – and always,' and signing the card, sealed it in its envelope and addressed it.

'Oh, excuse me,' I would say. 'Is it all bright if I just leave this card for Miss Janet Marsh, I mean mince Janet Gill?' I paused on the Metropole steps to rehearse the line once more, pretending to admire the Christmas trees, then pushed through the revolving doors with the easy familiarity of a guest.

My shoes sounded like clogs as I crossed the tiled floor of the reception area. The hotel seemed completely empty. There was no one to be seen in the palm-fringed lounge where I had sat with Douglas and Terry Liversedge, not even the old dodo with the frayed cuffs and the Benares-ware tray. The reception counter itself was unmanned, as were the porter's desk and the cashier's desk behind its golden grille.

There was an electric bell-push on the counter. I was unsure whether to press it or just leave my letter lying on the big blotter with its neatly arranged leather-bound register, twin pens, and twin glass inkwells. Then I saw the slight movement of a shadow in the arched doorway of some kind of office area beyond the reception counter, where strings of Christmas cards were hung along the wall. I touched the bell-push gingerly, and it resounded through the tiled hall like a fire alarm. The shadow stopped, then moved forward.

She wore the same blue glazed rayon dress as when we had first met, the one whose rounded neckline would just admit two fingers up to the knuckles.

'Oh, hello, early bird! I knew we couldn't be expecting a guest on Christmas Eve, otherwise they wouldn't have left me in charge. They're all up in the Airedale Suite, having a drink with the manager.'

My mouth felt very hot and dry, with a back-taste of rum, blackcurrant and cigar smoke. 'Didn't know you'd be here, I just came to leave you this,' I said, or some combination of those words.

To my further dismay, Janet registered comic concern as she took the envelope I was prodding at her. 'Oh dear. A Christmas card. Now that's one thing I *haven't* got you, Ray. I thought you might not want your mother and dad asking who Love Janet is when she's at home.'

One thing she hadn't got me meant there was one thing she had: a present. I hoped it wasn't an expensive one. I had torn the gift-wrapping off the Picturegoer's Diary I had bought for her and left it in my bottom desk drawer under the blotting-paper lining. I would probably give it to Audrey on New Year's Day. It was more her style than Janet's, anyway.

'You don't open to have to it now,' I jabbered, but too late. She had picked up a paper-knife from the pen-set on the blotter and was slitting open the envelope.

'It's a long time since I heard you talk Double Dutch. I bet you haven't had a drink with your pals this lunchtime, have you?' prattled Janet, drawing out the Christmas card. 'Oh, now this is nice, Ray. This is really nice. I love these old coaching scenes, they're traditional, aren't they?'

'I thought you'd like it,' I said vacuously, resisting the impulse to clear my throat with a high-pitched rasp.

It seemed an age before she opened the card, and even then she did not seem inclined to read it. Probably she meant to wait until I left and then enjoy it in privacy. It would be best for both of us, although getting away without re-committing myself to Boxing Day was going to be tricky.

'This looks a nice long message. Why have you brought it round now, though? Can't you make it at half-five?'

'Er – no, I'm afraid none.'

'You've got a frog in your throat. Don't smoke yourself to death over Christmas, will you? Which reminds me –'

She was going to give me a box of fifty or even a hundred cigarettes. Churchman No 1, probably, with a Dickensian wrapper to match my Christmas card. As Janet turned away to move into the back office I clutched her wrist across the blotter.

'I bet you think you'd read the card, Janny. Sorry. I think – you'd better – read – the card.'

At last she did. It took her such a long time that she probably read it more than once. Probably three times. A twisted little smile played on her lips, the same the-joke's-on-me smile as I had seen on Doreen Theaker's lips when finally she had understood the meaning of her brush-off card.

'Oh, I see. Well – what can I say? Merry Christmas, and thanks for telling me. At least you had the courage to come round with it personally.'

Ingratiatingly, with an unworthy desire to take any credit that was going, I said, 'I hope you don't mind it been in writing. It've come out Double Dutch other words.'

'I'm sure it would. Just a minute, Ray, I've still got something for you.'

Before I could stop her she darted into the back office area. I could have seized the moment to hurry away, but my shoes would have sounded on the tiled floor and I didn't want her calling me back across the echoing hall. I saw her shadow moving about: a shadow hand touched her shadow face. and in a moment, a little red-eyed, she reappeared. She handed me, not the chunky little parcel I had been expecting, but a creamy Hotel Metropole envelope with its crest embossed on the flap. It bulged a little. I felt the contours of the bulge and identified the silver-plated bangle I had given her for her birthday.

I couldn't give it to Audrey. She would probably recognise it.

'There's no need for this, Janet, I want you to keep it,' I shaped my lips to say. But I could only manage, 'Thank you.'

'Don't mention it.'

She was still holding her Christmas card, still open at my Dear Jane letter. Now she closed it and looked at the coaching scene again, as if still admiring it.

'It's a nice card, Ray, but I won't put it up with the others, if you don't mind.'

'No. Of course.' I understood perfectly.

# 16

In this country of ours we did not celebrate Christmas. On this one day we allowed ourselves to be taken prisoners of war, hostages to the promise of our resumed freedom. Sullenly we followed the customs of our captors, eating their aborigine food, talking their aborigine language, observing their aborigine ways, behaving like dwarf aborigines ourselves, but all the time thinking our own thoughts, and in those long, stuffy, tangerine-impregnated hours, pining for our own kind.

My thoughts were with Audrey Marsh, Betty Parsons, Doreen Theaker and Janet Gill. I missed them all, as keenly as any exile, but in their different ways. With Audrey, it was the pleasurable agony of anticipation; with Betty, the elusive, throat-tickling stimulus of unfocused possibilities; with Doreen, the sharp pang of jealousy; with Janet, the sweet pang of regret. I missed them all and wanted them all. I thought of them endlessly, exhaustingly, while outwardly I went through the aborigine motions of this aborigine day.

They too would be doing aborigine things. I thought of them in aborigine kitchens, playing at aborigines like little girls playing at houses, with an earnest enthusiasm that would fill me with excited melancholy if I could see it, because it would be an erotic facet of them that was tantalisingly out of reach. I thought of them wearing aprons that emphasised the swell of their bosoms and the roundness of their hips, tied at the back with bows that could be undone with one tug of the strings. So powerful was this multiple image that the smell of roasting turkey in my nostrils became an aphrodisiac. By the time my aborigine dinner was placed in front of me I was sated and could only peck at it for the sake of appearances.

The afternoon of Boxing Day saw us come blinking out into the cold sunlight again like survivors of an air-raid coming up out of the deep shelter. One by one, in a straggle that gradually became a stream, we returned to our country.

On The Parade, all aloof from the little gargoyles weaving

around them on new bicycles, waiting youths extracted new tortoiseshell combs from new stitched leather cases, complete with nail-files, and adjusted their partings; or they arranged the points of new Tootal handkerchieves in top pockets, consulted new Timex wristlet watches with expandable chromium straps, tucked new spun rayon ties into elasticated waists. Chicks carrying new zip shoulder-bags containing new compacts, new lipstick-holders, new manicure sets, and carrying under their arms gift boxes of Rowntree's Carefree Assortment against the rigours of the first house at the Gem or the Gainsborough, went to meet their dates. Crag Park Avenue was a boulevard as arm-in-arm twosomes reunited with other twosomes to become foursomes, when handing round cigarettes from boxes of fifty and lighting them with new Ronson lighters, they strolled off to swell the long queue for the skeleton-service trolley-bus into town. In every drive and close, front doors opened, gates banged on their springs, and the pavements, already a sounding-board for new skates and new scooters, reverberated now with the sound of new Cuban-heel suedette court shoes hurrying. Life stirred. It was as if it were spring already, in our country.

I was glad to find that Terry Liversedge had arrived at the trolley-bus terminus before me and was saving me a place almost at the head of the queue. While the chocolate-and-cream No 17 performed its complex turning operation on its umbilical scribble of wires, we appraised one another's sartorial arrangements.

Terry Liversedge had opted, rightly I thought for someone wishing to make the right impression on Betty Parsons, for a country look: green patch-pocket sports jacket, red-and-grey pullover with pegasus motif on either side of the V-neck, war-surplus army officer's shirt, open-necked, with his cravat; cavalry twill slacks and new ox-blood ghillie brogues; and a new brown corduroy Young Farmers' Club cap from Dunn's the hatters, its peak resting nicely on the bridge of his nose. For myself I had borrowed Douglas's American bomber-pilot's jacket, augmented by an oatmeal polo-neck sweater knitted by an aborigine, with a white silk evening scarf, found in a drawer, worn loosely over its shoulders; and my light blue gaberdines and crêpe soles. Audrey had only ever seen me in office clothes. I was quite pleased with the overall casual effect, though a little uneasy about the white silk scarf which she might think spivvish.

I was about to ask Terry Liversedge what he thought when he said, 'I'll tell you what, youth. I don't suppose you want to swop neckwear, do you?' So as the trolley-bus bounced and hummed down the Leeds Road to Grippenshaw, Terry Liversedge donned my silk evening scarf, tying it like a muffler and tucking it inside his officer's shirt, while I, with his help, arranged his cravat around my polo neck, zipped up my American bomber-pilot's jacket to hold the folds in position, and turned up the simulated fur collar. I was confident now.

The trolley-bus deposited us in the town centre and we walked, or rather strutted, down Sheepgate, part of a column of our own kind that divided and re-divided as different detachments headed for their different posts: the Gaumont Coliseum, the Paramount, the Rex, the Mecca-Locarno. We were like invaders as we marched past the locked arcades. This outpost of our country was, for a day, all ours. It was as if we had conquered it and its inhabitants fled. Except for us, and a Moult & Sumpter coachload of elderly fossils being decanted, late, for the early performance of *Mother Goose* at the Theatre Royal, the town centre was empty. On the outskirts, the aborigines snored through their wireless programmes. This was our day.

Long shuffling queues cordoned the Paramount, inching around its poster-encrusted side-street walls to converge on the corner entrance of Sheepgate where its canopy lights were watery in the dying winter sun.

Betty Parsons was there ahead of us, tossing back her blonde hair with each turn as she paced the foyer. She had untied the belt of her camelhair wrap-around coat, the better to enable Terry Liversedge to increase his total of having touched one breast five times and both of them twice to one of them six times or both of them three times. Her front-buttoning striped cotton dress made her look like a nurse. I was reminded of a discussion with Douglas about the sex-drive of nurses. It was reputedly so powerful that he had once given serious thought to getting himself run over in order to enjoy a spell in hospital.

'Hello, Terry, hello, Raymond. Did you have nice Christmases?'

Deadpan, Terry Liversedge, said, 'Why, how many Christmases have there been?'

'Raymond knows what I mean, don't you, Raymond?' She looked at me in the very direct way she had, smiling. At once my tongue felt the size of a fishcake.

'Yeth thank,' was all I could manage.

'I don't think I've met Janet, have I? What's she like?'

'She's wonderful,' I blurted, having no previous acquaintance with the words that fell out of my mouth.

'Except she isn't called Janet, she's called Audrey,' said Terry Liversedge in a meaningful tone that was directed at me. He was signalling the importance to him of not giving Betty the impression that I made a habit of casually switching dates. I supposed he thought a reputation for playing the field would rub off on him.

'What made me think her name was Janet?'

'I've no idea, my love. Audrey, I said.'

'She calls herself Janice for sure,' I said, contorting my mouth into a muscle-wrenching grimace to show Betty that it was a joke. She looked puzzled and I reviewed what I had just said. 'For short, I mean.'

'Still, it's nice to hear she's wonderful.'

'She isn't really,' I said.

Mercifully I was saved from further idiocies, or so I allowed myself briefly to imagine, by the arrival of Audrey herself. She had on a white raincoat, worn loose like Betty's camelhair and with, I was entitled to hope, the same object. Her pale green cotton frock was unbuttonable to the waist. That, reasonably enough, would be as far as she was prepared to go on a first encounter, for fear of getting herself talked about.

'Ah. Now then. Audrey, this is Betty and this is Janet. Betty, this is Audrey and this is Raymond.'

'Has he been at the Christmas sherry?' cracked Audrey, in rather too much of a mill girl's accent for my liking. It contrasted unfavourably with Betty's almost southern, rather bossy yet warm-sounding voice. A question such as, 'Why have you taken your hand away?' would sound far more sensuous in Betty's voice than in Audrey's. I also thought that Audrey was rather too much at ease with people she had just met – another mill girl tendency. Like Terry Liversedge, I was anxious that Betty shouldn't judge me by association.

We joined the shorter of the two queues, the one for the two-and-nines or three-and-sixes – back stalls or balcony. The queue was slow-moving and it would be a matter of taking what seats would be available when we reached the pay-box. I was in two minds which I would prefer. The steeply-raked balcony, being more public, allowed little scope for intimacy beyond hand-holding or an arm around the shoulders at best. Sinking into the darkened back stalls, and particularly the back row of the back stalls, was by comparison like nestling into a red plush burrow. But when I drew Audrey Marsh's head down on my chest, with a view to seeing if I could get further towards first base with her than I had got with Janet Gill, I wasn't sure that I wanted Betty Parsons observing our progress from an adjoining seat; or, even worse, not observing it, in that she could well be engrossed in her own progress with Terry Liversedge.

'Will you two think it rude if I whisper something to him?' piped up Audrey as we edged slowly forward. I was only relieved she hadn't used the mill-dialect 'summat'. It was remarkable how outside office hours Audrey's secretarial college veneer dropped away. She was beginning to sound like one of the brassy chicks encountered at the Clock Ballroom.

'Aye aye!' sang Terry Liversedge with unwarranted suggestiveness. He too could be quite coarse when he wanted to be. I wished I could be granted one more switch of partners. He would get Audrey Marsh and I would get Betty Parsons. She was my type.

'Don't mind us,' smiled Betty, and to afford us more privacy, took Terry Liversedge's elbow and propelled him ahead of us in the queue, so that we were now two separate couples instead of the foursome she had been the one to insist on.

Audrey, clutching the sleeve of my borrowed bomber-pilot's jacket, brought her mouth close to my ear in a waft of presentation-box eau-de-cologne. 'What did you say to Janet?'

The dispensation to whisper did not, I felt, apply to me. I replied with a non-commital, 'Nothing much.'

In a stage-whisper that sounded to me as loud as the dodo voice shouting, 'Have your correct change ready please!' at the head of the queue, Audrey elaborated, 'She rang me up on Christmas Eve. She was quite upset. You didn't tell me you were going to stop going out with her.'

146

'You didn't ask.' Even though Betty Parsons, ostentatiously studying a glue-streaked portrait of James Cagney in prison clothes, was making a point of trying not to listen, I thought my next words had better be restricted to Audrey's scent-splashed ear only. A hand over my mouth, I breathed, 'I'm like you. I don't go in for two-timing.'

This time making no effort whatever not to be overheard, Audrey said carelessly, 'I didn't even know we were one-timing, kid.' Then louder, to Terry Liversedge and Betty Parsons: 'It's all right, I was just asking him why he's come out dressed like a dog's dinner.' And she laughed gratingly.

If we finished up in the balcony, and I could maneouvre it so that I sat with Betty Parsons on my left and Audrey Marsh on my right, I would not even hold hands with her. I would smoke with my right hand and let my left hand hang loosely so that if Betty Parsons cared to brush against it with any part of her anatomy, she would be free to do so.

But by the time the Paramount foyer came in sight there was no longer any possibility of the four of us sitting together. The cinema was full, and only as couples who had dawdled on from the first performance came blinking out into the daylight did the uniformed dodo controlling the queue permit a replacement couple to move forward to the pay-box, a frogged sleeve keeping the rest at bay.

Terry Liversedge and Betty, still ahead of us, got balcony seats. Audrey and I found ourselves in the back row of the stalls.

'I'm glad we don't have to sit with them,' she said as we crossed the foyer's wide expanse of springy carpet. 'I always feel like something out of a zoo when I'm in a foursome.'

'Maybe they're just as glad they don't have to sit with us,' I said distantly.

'Maybe they are. She's a bit on the la-di-da side is Betty, isn't she? Is she always like that or was she putting it on for my benefit?'

At least Audrey's easy familiarity had worked the trick of unknotting my tongue. I said, cuttingly, 'How do you want her to sound – as if she were selling fruit and veg at the back of the market?'

Audrey laughed carelessly, mistaking rudeness for repartee. Irked at her refusal to take offence, I barged through the curtained swing doors into the auditorium, leaving her to follow. It was going to be a wasted evening. I couldn't help wondering what Audrey herself thought she was getting out of it. Why, if to quote her own words she 'didn't even know we were one-timing', had she bothered to make a date with someone who, again in her own words, she regarded as looking 'like a dog's dinner'? As an alternative to spending Boxing Night painting her toenails, I had to suppose.

But as the red plush swallowed us up and Audrey shrugged out of the sleeves of her raincoat to release a nosegay of eau-de-cologne, talcum powder and bath crystals, it crossed my mind that she had a more interesting motive than the one she had put forward for being glad that we did not have to sit with Betty Parsons and Terry Liversedge.

It would be standoffish, churlish even, not to seize whatever opportunity Audrey might contemplate putting on offer. Moreover, we were sitting at the very end of the row where the usherette's torch swept over us as she went back and forth along the aisle – she would think it very odd if she were to see us sitting bolt upright. She might even feel entitled to direct us to other seats, relinquishing our privileged back-row position to those who had need of it.

I would wait until the main feature began and the lights had stopped fading up and down, then I would ease my arm around Audrey's shoulders and see how we got on from there. Meanwhile, as a James A. Fitzpatrick Traveltalk droned towards its guitar-twanging climax, I sought her hand. She let me take it without demur. Clutching it firmly, I positioned our forearms along the prickly arm-rest between us. It would have been a tactical error to let our clasped hands fall either into her lap or mine at so early a stage.

The travelogue gave way to the British Movietone News, and the newsreel to next week's trailer. The lights came up for the last time. I gave Audrey's hand a final squeeze and relinquished it to light a cigarette. The squeeze had been reciprocated; progress was being made. Audrey, who didn't smoke for all that she had the husky voice of someone on forty a day, delved into her bag. I did hope she wasn't proposing to start sucking boiled sweets, for according to my timetable I would be kissing her quite shortly. Instead, she took out a demure little folded handkerchief with her initial embroidered upon it in blue silk, and dabbed her palm with it.

'You haven't half got sweaty hands, haven't you?' observed Audrey.

Expelling smoke in a long, whistling sigh, I said nothing. The Paramount's proscenium curtains shimmered from green to pink to blue to orange and back to pink, the Wurlitzer organ ascended moaning from its pit, and spotlights picked out the ice-cream girls taking up their stations in the aisles. I was not going to ask her if she would like one. It would be throwing good money after bad.

'You're never ogling that ice-cream tray, are you, Ray?'

'No,' I said curtly.

'You're the same as me. By the time Christmas is over I've had enough sweet stuff to last me a lifetime.' Audrey yawned, making only the most perfunctory gesture of masking her mouth. 'The only thing I've gone short of is sleep. Once all my aunties and uncles get their feet under the table there's no getting rid of them.'

Audrey babbled on. I fell to wondering how Janet was spending her Boxing Night. Listening to the Light Programme probably – she liked the comedy shows. I could have had her sitting next to me instead of Audrey. At least I would have been repulsed with style. I lit a fresh cigarette from my glowing stub.

'I think I've seen this,' Audrey said as the big picture began.

'You can't have done. It's just been released.'

'Escaped, more like. You didn't tell me it was a prison picture. I hate prison pictures.'

'Sssh!'

I ground out my cigarette in the ashtray on the second-row seat-back. My knuckles contacted serge where the youth in front already had his arm around his date. I toyed with the thought of putting an arm around Audrey, just for the sake of passing the time. She wouldn't object, would expect it even; but then she would come out with one of her common remarks to arrest further developments as effectively as Janet murmuring, 'Dr. Livingstone, I presume.'

I decided to chain-smoke instead. But as I rustled open my packet of twenty again I felt Audrey's hand touch mine. 'I've seen mill-chimneys smoke less than you, lad!' She lifted my hand and adeptly draped it across her shoulders.

It was probably only to stop me blowing smoke in her eyes but there was no point in letting the advantage go to waste. I drew her towards me, meeting such lack of resistance that it was probable she was already heading in that direction voluntarily.

Now, as her cheek made contact with Douglas's American bomber-pilot's jacket, she gave a little shudder. 'Ooh! Cold leather!' As silently as I could I unzipped it and tugged it apart so that she was nestling partly against my oatmeal polo-neck sweater and partly against Terry Liversedge's cravat. 'Mm. Better.'

My original schedule had to be hastily revised. What should have been the kissing stage had already been passed – strictly speaking, she should not have reached the position she was in without first being softened up by a fairly long necking session. I would have to take care not to be too precipitous. On the other hand there seemed little to be gained from back-tracking; I therefore rejected, even as I formulated it, a scheme whereby I would gently but firmly push at her chin until I had got her mouth at the angle required for the omission to be rectified. I contented myself, and I hoped Audrey too, by pecking abstractedly at her hair. She responded by pressing herself closer to me, bending her head slightly so that I could kiss her neck too, and bringing her arm forward to grasp my elbow. By now she was lying against the left side of my chest and would be able to feel my heart thumping like a drum. She could be in no possible doubt what I was up to.

Egged on, I fancied, by gentle pressure on my elbow, I raised my free hand and stroked her hair. Unlike Janet Gill's and Doreen Theaker's hair it was rather greasy and not very pleasant to the touch. As soon as I felt able to I let my fingers stray to her shoulder, kneading it rhythmically as I had always done with Janet's shoulder preparatory to slipping them under her neckline as far as the knuckles. Aware that my palm and finger-joints had begun to sweat profusely, I wiped them surreptitiously on her sleeve under cover of massaging her upper arm. Then, gliding from the back of her ear down the side of her neck and under her chin, I slipped three middle fingers under her dress as far as the knuckles and beyond, and reached first base with such ease that for a few seconds I could not properly comprehend that I was there.

150

It was not a mole. I was there. To double-check I encompassed her entire breast with my hand. The way she was lying across me made the manoeuvre easy: a simple slipping-down of a shiny-feeling strap over her shoulder and the breast was resting in my palm, like a fruit being weighed or judged for ripeness. I wished now that Terry Liversedge and Betty Parsons were sitting next to us, though with Betty on the far side out of sight. He would chance to glance through the darkness in my direction and would be left in no doubt that on my first date with Audrey Marsh and within the space of less than an hour, I had already got there above the waist.

I stroked and squeezed the breast with what I hoped was appropriate tenderness, seeking a response though unclear what kind of response to expect. Somewhat at a loss, I decided to try the other one. Now that I was on course to match Terry Liversedge's tally I should have a good head start with a count of touching both breasts once. I slid my hand down from her unencumbered right breast towards her left one which, in consequence of her sprawling across my chest, was pressed hard against the arm-rest between us. I waited expectantly, the nerves of my hand ticking over like a car at traffic lights, confident that she would raise herself slightly to allow me free access. She didn't move, and I suddenly realised from the little snort that she gave that Audrey was fast asleep.

Feeling like a necrophiliac I withdrew my hand and fumbled for the packet of cigarettes in my lap, knocking them on the floor as I fished one out. I managed to unzip a pocket and get my petrol lighter out, but it needed a new flint and I could not light it with one hand. The arm around Audrey, I knew from experience with Janet who was also given to falling asleep in cinemas, would soon be numb with cramp.

# 17

One Saturday morning early in the New Year, Douglas, Terry Liversedge and I took the trolley-bus down to the Aire Bridge to buy a rolled umbrella each at the Lost Property Mart. It was a fine crisp day and after we had chosen them we took a stroll through the town centre to look at clothes in the arcade shops.

A change had come over Terry Liversedge. It was noticeable when we stopped at the Snuff Shop in Town Arcade. Although its bow windows were so lit as to act as perfect mirrors from a particular angle, Terry Liversedge glanced at his reflection only perfunctorily before adjusting his grip on his new umbrella and moving on. He showed no interest in the little tins of snuff on display, nor in the fanned-out arrangement of florid snuff handkerchieves. It had been the same in the Lost Property Mart when he had bought almost the first umbrella to hand. He was listless and moody.

'How are you getting on with Betty?' I asked casually as Douglas and I caught up with him.

'All right, youth,' answered Terry Liversedge shortly.

The ferrules of our umbrellas tapped the arcade's fleur-de-lis mosaic in unison as we marched in step towards Exchange Row. 'Only all right?' ventured Douglas.

'Better than all right, Duggerlugs. In fact I'll be wanting that five bob off you very shortly, so you can divvy up now if you like.'

'What's the score now?' I asked. It was a full three weeks since Terry Liversedge had resumed his relationship with Betty Parsons, and it was to be expected that we could look for an improvement on his tally of one breast five times, both breasts twice. Date for date and breast for breast, he would certainly have surpassed my own miserable record with Audrey Marsh.

'I've stopped counting, youth. I got straight back to first base that night we all went to the Paramount, and it's only a question of time now before I get there below the waist. The only reason she's holding out is that she doesn't want to seem too eager.'

I repressed a stab of jealousy. I was going to have to resign myself to the fact that Betty Parsons was spoken for. 'So why are you looking so brassed-off, then?' I asked.

'I don't know what you're talking about.'

We crossed Exchange Row. It was not until our umbrellas had tapped to a halt outside Jerome Bros' menswear shop in Exchange Arcade, where foulard silk pyjamas and matching dressing-gowns were on offer in the winter sale, that Terry Liversedge spoke again.

He did not respond when I suggested, 'We could do with one of those outfits each on that Festival trip.' Nor when Douglas, in a faraway voice, said, 'Dressing-gowns yes, pyjamas no.'

We stared in the window, savouring the potentiality of silk dressing-gowns minus pyjamas. Then abruptly, as if this exchange had not taken place, or as if he had not heard it, Terry Liversedge said, 'I'll tell you what bothers me, if you really want to know. If she's so easy with me, how do I know she isn't just as easy with other bods?'

The idea did not disturb me as much as it seemed to disturb Terry Liversedge, but it was depressing all the same. 'Such as who?'

'Such as that lamebrain she was going out with – Ralph Driver. She had quite a crush on him while it lasted, you know. You can't tell me she didn't let him get to first base, so how do I know he didn't get to second base?'

I left the answer to Douglas. Logic and hypothesis were his domain. 'You can't know she let him get to first base if she hasn't admitted it, Terence,' he said in reasoning, soothing tones. 'And as for getting to second base, she's known you longer and she hasn't even let you get there yet.'

'No, but she's going to,' said Terry Liversedge gloomily, unconsoled.

'Audrey had a bloke just like you, and she ditched him,' I warned him, quite sharply. I didn't know whether Terry Liversedge went in for nipping Betty Parsons' arms when questioning her about past encounters, but I would not have put it past him.

'That's one thing she won't do, youth. She'd have to find

somebody else first.'

'That's not impossible.'

'It is, you know. For one thing, she never goes anywhere without me, and for another, I've stopped her wearing lipstick.'

Douglas and I, leaning on our umbrellas and staring intently at the display of nightware in Jerome Bros' window, caught one another's eye in the reflective glass.

'Oh, yes? What's the idea of that, old bean, old boy?'

'To stop her giving the come-on to other blokes.'

Douglas nodded slowly and judiciously, as one who has been made privy to a great pearl of wisdom.

'As a matter of interest, Terence, when you were going out with Esmé Carpenter, did you stop her wearing lipstick?'

'As a matter of interest, Douglas, I did. It's the only way, with a certain type of dame. Why?'

'I just wondered.' Like me, Douglas had probably noticed with what quick and furtive strides Terry Liversedge had a few moments ago slipped past the sheet-music shop in Town Arcade where Esmé, lipsticked, rouged and powdered, could be seen polishing the grand piano.

We moved on again.

Terry Liversedge, as always when justly or unjustly, explicitly or implicitly, he sensed he was under attack, tried to turn the tables on me. His opening shot as we passed under the Exchange Arcade's bronze Gog and Magog striking clock into Museum Street, was, 'What's the griff on Audrey, then? She looks like hot stuff to me, youth.'

'She is,' I said smugly. 'Didn't I tell you, I was there above the waist within an hour of first going out with her?' I knew I had, but I thought it would bear repetition.

'We know, Watmough, you've told us six times. At that rate of progress you should have hit the jackpot by now. You haven't though, have you? You haven't even got to second base.'

No, I hadn't. I had not even, though there was no point in admitting it to Terry Liversedge, got to first base in Audrey's waking hours, either. I had not cared to try.

I was in what seemed to me a highly ambivalent situation with Audrey Marsh. Seeing her home that night after our first, narcotic date, I had asked her, 'So what gives with this stuff about us not even one-timing?'

'Well we're not, Ray, are we? We don't go out with each other.'

'But we *are* out with each other.'

She nudged me significantly. 'Tell you later.' She meant she didn't want the taxi driver to overhear our business. There had been such a throng heading for the bus station when we came out of the Paramount that I had splashed out on a Silver Line radio cab which chanced to be depositing a party of fossils at the Mechanics Institute. Douglas would have approved of my not wanting to waste valuable snogging time in a mile-long trolley-bus queue. Nor did I propose to have much of it wasted on the semantic question of whether we were going out with one another or not.

The corner of Cemetery Road and Glasshouse Street, she had instructed the peak-capped dodo. It was an area of working-class terraces which I knew only from Cemetery Road being on the route out to the estate of bungalows where Victoria Leadenbury used to live. (Although I had never walked Victoria Leadenbury home during our first-term courtship at Grippenshaw College of Commerce, I had found out her address and gone and stood opposite her bungalow for an hour or so whenever I had the time available.) I rapidly constituted a sketch map in my mind's eye. There was the cemetery itself, if Audrey knew of any way through the high railings. There was a Victorian-vintage board-school, with the possibility of an alley behind its high playground wall. There were some allotments: she might even conceivably have access to a cosy shed built of old doors and tarpaulin. Provided she could stay awake, the night was not yet a write-off.

'This next corner, please.' Audrey was leaning forward over the dodo driver's seat to direct him. But then, as if jolted by sudden braking, she threw herself back in her seat. 'On second thoughts, could you drive on a bit?' she called in some agitation.

Cowering in the back of the taxi, Audrey pressed her face against my chest as she had done in the Paramount, while we sped past a terrace-end wall with the words 'Bile Beans' painted in huge flaking letters. Out of the back window I studied the big thick-set airman standing in a pool of lamplight, boots gleaming. It was possible that his burliness

155

could have been exaggerated by the thickness of his blue greatcoat.

'Do I take it that's Ronnie?'

'It's not King Kong, is it?'

We turned a bend in the road. Audrey instructed the dodo driver to pull up outside a corner pub. The allotments, I fancied, were just past the dye-works opposite.

But Audrey, instead of getting out, turned to me as if to receive the chastest of good-night kisses. 'Listen, I know that Ronnie. He'll stand there and stand there till two in the morning if he has to – just for the satisfaction of catching me out with another chap. You'd better go. My auntie works in the pub – I'll walk back with her.'

It had cost three-and-nine to get Audrey home by taxi and I had not planned on spending another three-and-nine getting myself home, especially if I had to return so to speak empty-handed. But I had not planned on a confrontation with her ex-fiancé, either.

'When shall I see you again, then?'

'At work, I suppose.'

Our dodo, probably thinking himself the soul of tact, had slippped into the pub's off-licence to buy cigarettes. I could see him holding the door ajar and keeping an eye on us while he waited to be served, in case we ran off without paying. 'Look, Ray,' said Audrey. 'I've enjoyed tonight, I really have. If it hadn't been for you I'd have sat at home twiddling my thumbs. But if I see you again I don't want you to run away with the idea that I'm going out with you.'

'I may be dense,' I said, feeling it, 'but I can't see what the difference is.'

'You've got to remember I've just broken off my engagement, Ray. If I went out with you seriously, it'd just be on the rebound from that big lunk. You wouldn't want that, would you?'

'Oh, I don't know,' I said magnanimously.

'I should never have led you on in the first place. I was feeling browned-off, I suppose. You'd be far better off with Janet, you know.'

'That's for me to judge. What are you doing tomorrow night?'

And so, on the understanding that we were going together

156

but not going out together, I had continued to see Audrey on about three evenings a week. They were expensive evenings, for implicit in not going out with one another was the condition that we had to go somewhere specific – it would not do, for example, to suggest a walk in the hope of finishing up in a tarred shed on the allotments. So far we had been to the pictures six times and to the Clock Ballroom four, including the Gala New Year's Eve Dance at seven and sixpence a ticket. Apart from conquering my fear of dancing I had nothing to show for the considerable outlay involved, which incidentally was seriously constricting the funds I was trying to put by for the Festival of Britain trip.

Going with someone but not going out with them seemed to confer no rights or privileges, and so while in the back rows of the Paramount and the Gaumont Coliseum she would slip my arm around her shoulder with the familiar ease of someone throwing on an old cardigan, I had made no further effort to return to first base with Audrey. I did permit myself to hope that when she thought a suitable period had elapsed, or when she could resist the urge no longer, whichever was the sooner, she would take the initiative herself. Meanwhile, the only progress I could claim was the odd fairly prolonged kiss under the Bile Beans sign at the end of her street, and that only after Ronnie had safely returned to camp after his Christmas leave.

Answering Terry Liversedge's taunting as we entered Museum Arcade I said, 'I'll tell you what, bighead. I've already got five bob with Douglas that I get to second base before he does –'

'So have I, youth. But you lose, because you were betting on Janet Gill.'

'If it comes to that, you were betting on Esmé Carpenter. But as a matter of fact, no names were specified. So I'll have the same bet with you.'

'On Audrey Marsh?'

'On anybody,' I said prudently, but trying to sound as if I were saying it wildly.

'You're on, kiddo. When I have a dance with Audrey at the Clock tonight, I'll tell her you've got a dollar riding on her.'

'You do that. Why, are you and Betty going?'

'Too true.'

I was now less inclined to begrudge the six shillings it would cost for an evening at the Clock. I had yet to dance with Betty, though since the Gala New Year's Eve Dance she and Terry Liversedge, too, were becoming ballroom regulars. I now thought I had the proficiency to approach her. It would be interesting to judge, by reconnoitring her waist as I had done with Doreen Theaker at the Youth Guild Christmas social, whether she was wearing a roll-on or similar device to inhibit Terry Liversedge from winning his bets. Not that it was an infallible rule of thumb. At the New Year's Eve Dance I had convinced myself that Audrey Marsh was wearing nothing whatever under her shot-silk dress, but the conjecture had led nowhere.

'Why don't you and Pauline come, and make it a sixsome?' I said to Douglas. I had never danced with Pauline either. In fact, apart from an occasional glimpse of her walking arm-in-arm with Douglas down Crag Park Avenue or standing hand-in-hand with him in the Gainsborough cinema queue, we saw nothing of Pauline at all. From those glimpses, though, of her pale face and generous red lips framed by her black hair which she wore longer now, and the neat removable suit of some pale shade which was her customary outfit, she seemed even more attractive than when we'd first seen her at St Chad's church. Perhaps it was her elusiveness. It was a pity we never met: she was my type.

'Sorry, old fruit, we've got other fish to fry.' Or perhaps it was Douglas's evasiveness that made Pauline so intriguing. We never knew for sure what the two of them were up to.

By now we had walked up Museum Arcade and come out under its whirring clockwork carillon, which played a fragment of 'Sweet Lass of Richmond Hill' on the hour and had always seemed to be doing so in the days when we had clattered up the arcade on the way to the College of Commerce from the No 19A Circular stop at Rabinowitcz the Jeweller's Corner, or a fraction more punctually had cruised past on the platform of the No 17 that would deposit us near the College gates.

Crossing Cloth Hall Lane now to the request stop almost opposite, we could look towards Infirmary Hill and see those very gates, locked for the weekend, and behind them the College of Commerce itself, its tall windows already looking smaller than we remembered them and its blackened façade

158

less like the workhouse or prison with which we had habitually made comparison.

I conjured up the chalkdust smell and the lavender smell of Victoria Leadenbury's pale mauve scalloped notepaper with matching envelopes, and the nail-varnish smell of the Gestetner stencil correction fluid in the typing-room which I had knocked over with my elbow in the excitement of hearing, from an intermediary who was sucking wine gums, that she would go out with me. I could smell the wine gums too. 'I see Dotheboys Hall still stands,' I said in an offhand voice.

'Do-the-girls Hall, that's where we should have gone,' quipped Terry Liversedge. He seemed a little more cheerful now.

Standing at the request stop, leaning back on his umbrella as it if were a shooting-stick and raising his thick reading-glasses to his forehead in order to see beyond his nose, Douglas was staring with solemn intensity up the hill as if the College of Commerce were some famous edifice he'd never seen before.

'Just think,' said Douglas softly, almost reverently, without shifting his gaze. 'Six months ago we were sitting at our little school desks with our little satchels hanging on our little chairbacks, scribbling in our little exercise books and putting our little pens away when the bell rang. And less than four months from now we'll be shacked up in the Court Gardens Hotel near Marble Arch, poking ourselves cross-eyed.'

'Roll on Whitsun,' said Terry Liversedge, with more loyalty than enthusiasm, I thought. Douglas's glasses flashed as he shot him a suspicious glance.

'I take it you've asked Betty? She definitely leaves school at Easter, does she?'

'Yes.'

'Yes she does, or yes you've asked her?'

'Keep your shirt on, Duggerlugs. Both.'

'And —?'

'She's thinking about it,' said Terry Liversedge evasively.

Far from satisfied, Douglas turned almost accusingly to me. 'What about you and Audrey?'

'Oh, she's all for it,' I said, telling the truth to some extent. After all, she had been quite envious when she had heard me outlining the plan, or what she and the pterodactyls thought

159

was the plan, down at Moult & Sumpter's. 'The only problem is whether, working in the same office, we can both get time off together.' That was not the only problem, it was one problem. The other was whether Audrey would come to London. I would ask her tonight. If she assented, even on the basis that it would not constitute a going-out-with-one-another contract, I was prepared to take pot luck with her in London. If not, I should have to find another partner. There was plenty of time.

'Look,' said Douglas with some heat. 'I hope you're not going to let me make all these elaborate arrangements and then drop me in it. I'm putting a lot of work into this, you know, Ray. And that goes for you too, Terry. I've already got fifteen old-age pensioners signed up, which means I'm committed to going down to the St Chad's Silver Threads Circle every Monday night to round up their five bobs. Pauline's mother takes care of collecting for the Mothers' Union, thank Christ, but I've still got nearly two dozen seats to get rid of if we're going to get this off the ground, which means I've still got to suck up to the choir and the Churchmen's Guild and whoever else might fall for it. So don't let me down, will you?'

Both Terry Liversedge and I were impressed, touched and awed by Douglas's dedication.

'You worry too much, youth,' said Terry Liversedge.

'We'll be there,' I pledged. 'We might not know who with just at the present moment, Douglas, but we'll be there all right.'

'Thank you, my friends. That's all I wanted to know.'

A chocolate-and-cream No 17 was approaching the request stop. Three furled umbrellas were raised in unison, like swords at a wedding.

# 18

I met Audrey as she stepped off the trolley-bus with a chiffon headscarf protecting her perm, an inch of dance frock showing below her raincoat, and the heels of a pair of silver sandals jutting from her bucket-bag, and conducted her across the acre of once-derelict ground where a Meccano-grid of rusted girders had gone up behind the sign that said FESTIVAL OF BRITAIN 1951: SITE OF GRIPPENSHAW PAGEANT OF PROGRESS.

I could just as well have met her inside the Clock Ballroom and saved myself three shillings, but that would probably not have been good manners even though I was only going with her and not going out with her. Audrey certainly wouldn't have stood for it. 'I don't believe in going Dutch,' she had informed me one evening apropros of nothing very much, as if making a general ethical statement. 'If a chap can't pay for a girl he shouldn't take her out.' Or not take her out, I thought, but said nothing.

A familiar sensation of shallow exultation laced with melancholy came over me as we neared the Clock Ballroom's aircraft hangar frontage with its fluorescent hour and minute hands set in the flickering neon 'O' of CLOCK, and the big-band thump we could hear all the way from the trolley-bus terminus defined itself into an over-saxophoned arrangement of 'Souvenirs', a mournful standard that had served me well. Beginning with Victoria Leadenbury, 'Souvenirs' had been 'our tune' with a succession of girl-friends including Doreen Theaker and Janet Gill. By humming it at what I judged to be appropriate moments, I hoped that it would eventually, perhaps subliminally, become 'our tune' with Audrey Marsh.

While Audrey changed out of her bootees behind the red quilted door of the Ladies' Powder Room, I stood on the metalled fringe of the undulating maple-sprung dance floor, scanning each cluster of gilt cane chairs and little round coffee-tables for Terry Liversedge and Betty Parsons. Presently, the spotlight bouncing off the revolving ball of mirrors on to bobbing, brilliantined heads, picked out my candy-striped seersucker jacket, and Terry Liversedge, who was wearing it on this occasion, came foxtrotting by with Betty held far too close in his arms for my liking. She was wearing something white, but how it fastened I could not make out in the flickering light, and she had done something with her hair, I didn't know what. Terry Liversedge caught my wave and gesticulated towards four empty chairs near the buffet counter, which he had reserved by tilting them forward over the coffee table where Betty had left her handbag.

Audrey, as she stepped off the conveyor-belt line of chicks streaming in and out of the Powder Room, proved to be wearing the same shot-silk frock, back press-stud fastening with nothing whatever underneath it, that she had worn at the New Year's Eve Dance. It no longer excited me to see her in it although I expected my pulse would in due course quicken for a moment or so, between us taking the floor and her passing her usual remark about it being like dancing with a gorilla.

I reached for her hand to lead her through the horde of gum-chewing, shoulder-twitching bystanders to our table, but instead she put her arms up around the neck of Terry Liversedge's salmon-pink zoot jacket, which I was afraid did not fit me as well as it fitted him, and launched me with a few deft steps on to the dance floor.

Audrey was drenched in the upstairs smell of all the things she put in her bath and sprayed on her hair and rolled under her arms, and was almost certainly naked beneath her dress. 'Keep your hands still,' she protested, as trying to verify this I located a disappointing ridge of elastic. 'You're like a flipping octopus.'

'Just exploring,' I said.

'Yes, well don't.' As repartee it was not much but it did prove, to my relief, that she hadn't been exchanging notes with Janet. Perhaps, though apparently they'd gone through secretarial college together, she was not on such close terms with Janet as I'd thought. Now that I knew Audrey better, though not well enough, it had come to puzzle me how she and Janet were friends. Janet, for instance, did not chew gum: Audrey did. It occurred to me, watching her jaws move in the slow-quick-quick-slow tempo of the foxtrot we were dancing, that if she'd been a couple of years older she would have been a GI bride living in a shack in Kentucky.

We performed, moderately successfully, the outside swivel that Audrey had taught me, repeated it, then settled down into a routine sway along the soccer-pitch-length floor. I tried to increase speed to catch up with Betty Parsons and Terry Liversedge who were just executing a natural turn by the bandstand, but Audrey kept me back.

'I didn't tell you,' she said as she always did when she had something to tell me, 'Ronnie's home on leave again.'

'It's only five minutes since he went back,' I said grumpily.

'He must be on a forty-eight. My auntie saw him in Cemetery Road.'

'What do you want me to do about it – come out in spots?'

'I don't want you to do anything, Ray, but you'd better not see me home tonight. You know what he's like.'

I had embarked on an attempt to emulate Terry Liversedge's natural turn. I misjudged it and was obliged to perform an awkward shuffling adjustment of my feet to get back on course. The manoeuvre left me nettled.

'No, I don't know what he's like Audrey. Am I supposed to go in fear and trembling every time the bloke you were once engaged to comes home on leave?'

'I just don't want you to get tangled up with him, that's all.'

'How do you know he'd be all that eager to get tangled up with me?' I blustered. 'He might wish he'd stayed in camp before I've done with him.'

'Don't talk so daft.'

I was content to leave it at that. Not seeing Audrey home would save me enough to buy a couple of Kunzle cakes at the buffet counter.

But I could not resist one final little grumble as the dance came to an end and the band in their powder-blue jackets sorted sheet-music behind their plywood stands. 'He must think a lot about you, to be carrying a torch for so long.'

'He must do, mustn't he?' said Audrey, chewing nonchalantly. One of us, and I thought it was Audrey, had begun to smell faintly of sweat. Her facepowder was too thick, and too orange-looking. Her secret half-smile suddenly looked like a lopsided leer. And all at once, as I followed her across the floor to the table where Terry Liversedge and Betty Parsons were already sitting, and I noticed for the first time the spread of her hips where she refused to wear a girdle, I realised why Janet was her best friend. It was what Douglas called the Duck-walk syndrome: the presentable one paired off with the plain one. I had decided my own destiny, turning my back on the Leeds branch of the Bank of England and settling for a tinpot little travel agency, on the strength of a glimpse on a Corn Exchange balcony of one of a Duck-walk pair who turned out, on closer examination, to be the plain one of the two – and moreover I had turned away from the presentable one to get her. Douglas wouldn't have complained at the compromising of his entire future career in exchange for being saddled with the plain one – he would have preferred it that way. But I wasn't saddled with her. I wasn't even going out with her.

I did not, for once, instantly register how Betty Parsons was dressed. A remarkable change had come over her face. It was devoid even of the little make-up she usually wore. It looked scrubbed, like a child's. Her loose blonde hair had been tugged back into the severest of buns. She looked like a young prison wardress in mufti.

Against this, I now saw that the mufti was a plain white dress which buttoned all the way down the front, thus completely negating the offputting effect hoped for by Terry Liversedge. Such erotic garments were often to be seen on the Junior Miss dummies in Clough & Clough's windows, but it was rarely that they were encountered in real life. It was Douglas's contention that any chick wearing a dress that buttoned all the way down the front was so blatantly advertising her desires that she might just as well carry it folded over her arm.

'I like your hair, Betty,' said Audrey unconvincingly. I could already hear her saying to me, as we or they took the floor again, 'Well I had to say *something*, Ray, and I couldn't say she looked like death warmed up, could I?' (I could also, as Betty gave her a wan smile, hear her saying, 'Whose idea was it to sit with that stuck-up cat anyway?')

'Keep telling her that, Audrey!' exclaimed Terry Liversedge, rubbing his hands with unnatural heartiness. 'Don't *you* like it, Ray?'

'Every nice,' I blurred, offering Betty one of my grimace-smiles.

We made some smalltalk, or rather Audrey did, then Terry

164

Liversedge again brought his hands together, this time with a resounding smack and a cry of, 'Well come on, Audrey, are you and me getting up or not?' A chameleon uncouthness seemed to come over Terry Liversedge when he spoke to Audrey. She really was his type. It was a pity he hadn't taken the short cut through the Corn Exchange that morning instead of me.

Audrey, coquettishly responding to Terry Liversedge as if he had come up in a Hussar's uniform and clicked his heels, allowed herself to be led off; but not before Terry Liversedge had said to Betty with his accustomed grace, 'You can dance with Ray if you like.'

I rose, hoping that she would follow suit and I would not have to put the invitation on a verbal footing.

'You don't have to,' Betty Parsons smiled.

'I'd have to.'

We had waltzed halfway around the floor before it filtered back to me that I hadn't said, 'I'd love to' as I'd set off to do. I decided to let it go. To forestall further journeys into the conversational unknown I held her as close as seemed permissible and half-hummed, half-sung where I knew the words, 'The Tennessee Waltz'.

Betty was slightly taller than me and her grip was firm. Her long legs carried her effortlessly before me with such confident, wide-sweeping steps that although I was technically leading, she seemed to be making the running. My moist palm pressing her midriff encountered what felt like elasticated armour beneath the white dress that buttoned all the way down. My reactions were mixed. This solid, unyielding proof that she did not after all keep herself in permanent, ecstatic readiness for a below-the-waist exploration was dispiriting; yet the fact that she could not have rebuffed Terry Liversedge's advances more had she been wearing a chastity belt was vastly encouraging.

'You dance quite well,' said Betty.

I hummed on.

'All you need is a better sense of rhythm. I'll lend you some of my Victor Sylvester records if you like, then you can practise with a chair like we used to at dancing class.'

'Is that what you still do?'

'Sometimes. Don't tell Terry, though – he'd be jealous.'

165

'Of a *chair*?'

Betty didn't laugh. 'I meant of me lending you my records. But since you mention it, he *is* quite capable of being jealous of a chair.'

'Funny bloke.'

'Still, so long as he doesn't mind my dancing with you . . .'

I was still trying to evaluate how well I came out of this double-edged compliment when the waltz came to an end. Concurrently, I was already elatedly cobbling together the scenario for an elaborately clandestine rendezvous with Betty on the excuse of borrowing her records. I felt a flush of guilt as I saw Terry Liversedge standing by our table, jangling his change and looking impatient.

Audrey was not with him. She would be on one of her frequent trips to the Powder Room. Although Audrey was one of those who liked to go to the Ladies' in twos like animals going into the ark, she would not have felt at ease making the expedition with Betty.

'Don't sit down, youth, you can help me get the coffees in.'

'Bit early, isn't it?'

'There'll be a queue a mile long if we wait for the band-break. Come on – get fell in.'

I saw that behind Betty's back Terry Liversedge was making a pantomime of head-jerks and gesticulations. I took the hint and followed him.

Taking my elbow and hustling me towards the long buffet counter with the same conspiratorial urgency as when we were schoolboys and he was concealing a bottle of milk snatched from a doorstep under his blazer, Terry Liversedge uttered what sounded like, 'Quick, youth, I've got her diary!'

'You've done what?'

What I thought he had mumbled was what he had mumbled. 'Quiet, she'll hear us! Her diary! I snitched it out of her handbag while you were dancing with her.'

'What in God's name for? And how could you have done, when you were dancing with Audrey?'

'Ah, but I wasn't, you see, because she let this big twerp cut in.'

'What big twerp?'

'Never mind that now – is Betty looking?' For her benefit, Terry Liversedge was pretending to study a display of Kunzle

166

cakes and slices of gâteaux, even going to the extent of moving slowly along the counter and pointing at them to suggest that we were discussing our selection.

With some of his furtiveness rubbing off on me I revolved slowly on my heel as if admiring the Clock Ballroom's decor.

'No, but she's looking in her handbag.'

I felt the chunkiness of the fat little pocket diary as he thrust it into my hand. 'Put it away, quick, Ray! I'll pick it up later.'

'Before you get me mixed up in this, would you mind telling me exactly what you're playing at?' I protested. Nevertheless I slid the diary into my side pocket, or rather Terry Liversedge's side pocket since it was his jacket I was wearing.

'I want to see what she's written about Ralph Driver.'

'Your fizzing mind's going, Liversedge – do you know that? You're the one she's been going out with since Boxing Day – why should she write anything about Ralph Driver in a new 1951 diary?'

'Because if she's still carrying a torch for him, there'll be some mention of him, won't there? Such as his phone number at the Library. Whereas if she's got over him, there won't be. It's no use looking at me like that, Ray – I've got to find out and that's all there is to it.'

I was shaking my head in uncomprehending pity. 'You're cracking up, Terry. You really are. You're going doolally.'

We bought four Pyrex cups of coffee and four Kunzle cakes, distributed on two trays to justify Terry Liversedge's insistence that he needed my help in getting them. I was acutely conscious of Betty's diary in my pocket and could not be altogether sure that its contours pressing against the thin salmon-pink cloth would not be as revealing to her as any X-ray.

'That's the big twerp I was telling you about,' said Terry Liversedge as we reached our table. The next dance had not yet started and the floor was empty except for a couple diagonally crossing it from the vicinity of the entrance lobby, hand in hand, her engagement ring flashing where it caught the light from the revolving ball of mirrors. They had evidently got pass-outs and had stepped outside for a moment. Audrey's companion looked just as burly in his dark utility suit as in his RAF greatcoat.

'There you are, Ray – this is Ronnie. Ronnie, this is Ray. Is there somewhere where we can have a quick word with you, Ray?' Audrey didn't bother introducing Betty Parsons or Terry Liversedge.

'Sure.' Looking, I was afraid, like a schoolboy who has been called up to the headmaster's dais for scufflling during assembly, I led the way back to the vicinity of the buffet counter, where a queue was beginning to form. I reasoned that the more public our confrontation, the less likely was there to be a scene.

Ronnie, however, seemed just as nervous as I was. His coal-heaver's hand pulled at the white starched collar that he had evidently outgrown. I noticed that he too wore a ring, of dull white metal that would double as a serviceable knuckle-duster.

'It comes to this, Ray,' he said familiarly, as if we had often played ping-pong together at the Youth Guild. 'I think Audrey's got something to say to you.'

Audrey, rather flustered, obeyed her cue. 'I'm sorry to say I'm starting going out with Ronnie again. Well not sorry, glad really, but you know what I mean.'

'Oh, I see,' was the only observation I felt it safe to make.

'She's giving me one more chance,' said Ronnie.

'Good for you,' I said, and feeling that it was required of me, extended my hand, shooting back a good two inches of Terry Liversedge's salmon-pink cuff.

Ronnie gripped my hand as if for a bout of all-in wrestling. 'No hard feelings?'

'None at all, youth.' The Terry Liversedge mode of address seemed toughly appropriate.

'Just one more thing, Ray. Is it all right if I see Audrey home?' asked Ronnie formally, as if I were her father.

'Be my guest, youth.'

'Sorry, Ray,' said Audrey with a rueful wag of her perm to suggest sympathy. 'You must have known it was Ronnie, all along. That was why I'd never go out with you.'

That, I probably judged correctly, was for Ronnie's consumption. I wondered how long it would be before he was pinning her against a wall, nipping her arms, and asking her how far she had gone with me. I did hope I didn't feature in the Picturegoer's Diary I had given her.

'Easy come, easy go, eh?' I said relieved to find my heavy humour going down well with Ronnie, who grinned oafishly. 'Ah, well, there's always Janet.'

'I'm afraid you've missed the bus there, Ray,' said Audrey with a touch of malice. 'She's going out with Ronnie's best pal now, isn't she, Ronnie? That's how he knew we'd be here tonight.'

I gave an expansive, arm-loping shrug to show that I could take such blows philosophically. 'Well, see you around,' I said lamely.

'Take care, Ray.'

'See you, Ray.'

Hand in hand again, they turned away to join the queue at the buffet counter. Terry Liversedge and Betty Parsons, I found as I swaggered back to our table as if nothing untoward had happened, had had their coffee and were dancing. Betty had put saucers over the other two cups of coffee to keep them warm. There were two cellophane-wrapped Kunzle cakes left on the plate. I pocketed them and walked purposefully around the perimeter of the dance floor, ostensibly heading for the Gents' but keeping up my brisk pace until I was outside, clutching an unneeded pass-out.

There was enough light in the trolley-bus shelter to read Betty Parsons' diary – a blue-bound Letts Schoolgirl's Diary as it proved to be. I had long stopped thinking of her as a schoolgirl and the reminder induced an obscure heart-lurch of poignancy.

Nibbling the chocolate off a Kunzle cake, I fingered through its pages. There were very few entries. Schoolgirl though Betty may still have been, she had only one more term to go and she had passed the stage of filling her diary with a cramped record of her daily doings. ('Went to pix. K. Douglas in *Young Man With Horn*. V. good.' Doreen Theaker had shown me her diary voluntarily, at my insistence. It was not very interesting.)

There were dentist's appointments, exam dates, reminders of various aborigine birthdays, the usual cryptic circles to record her monthly periods, and one exuberant, *Girls' Own*-type note for March 21, the Wednesday before Easter: 'Leave school. Hip hip hooray!' I leafed on to May 11, the day for setting off on the Festival of Britain outing. It was blank.

169

Either Terry Liversedge had never asked her or she had turned him down.

There were a few pages for addresses and telephone numbers at the back of the diary. These too were not very interesting. Ralph Driver's name was not there, as feared by Terry Liversedge, but then neither was Terry Liversedge's. The names were mainly those of school friends: Jennifer, Jacqueline, Margaret, Madge, Olive, Sue. They were listed in the indexed pages only by their Christian names.

Cramming the half-eaten Kunzle cake into my mouth, and wiping a smear of chocolate on my sock where it wouldn't show, I turned to the last pages. Wendy. Winifred, Raymond Watmough. And, in her neat round hand, there was my address: 21 Edith Close, followed by my home telephone number which she had troubled to copy out of the directory, and the number of Moult & Sumpter's which she had also bothered to look up.

Later that evening I put Betty Parsons' diary away in the little locked valuables drawer of my dressing-table where I kept my private things: Janet Gill's silver-plated bangle, one or two surviving letters from Victoria Leadenbury, Terry Liversedge's obscene shorthand epistle to Miss Cohen. When I met him on The Parade on the following morning, Sunday, to lend him his cravat back, I said I was sorry and he was going to kill me for this, but I had lost the diary.

'Skip it, youth. I've jacked her in.'

# 19

Having told Terry Liversedge I'd lost Betty Parsons' diary, I told Betty Parsons I'd found it.

It was, I thought, a masterstroke, cutting out as it did the necessity for waylaying her with a formal, burbling request for a date, which I should have had to repeat three times before she knew what I was driving at. All I had to do was loaf around The Parade for most of the rest of Sunday until she finally emerged from Winifred Avenue with a gargoyle dog on a lead, fall into step with her, return the diary with a yarn about having found it on the waste ground by the Clock Ballroom, and remind her that she had promised to borrow some Victor Sylvester records. We could take the whole thing from there.

'Lend, not borrow,' Betty smiled.

'That's what I mend.'

'You're the only person I know who speaks in misprints.' She had a quick tongue, like Janet. I trusted she wasn't proposing to put it to the same inhibiting use when we sat in the back row of the Gainsborough.

Walking her up to the top of Crag Park Avenue and back, I expanded on the story I had told her about her diary, incorporating into it an explanation for my abrupt departure from the Clock Ballroom the previous evening. I had, I said, felt giddy from too much smoking and had gone out for a breath of fresh air, forgetting however to obtain a pass-out.

'Too many cigarettes are bad for you,' said Betty in her bossy, prefectorial way. 'How many do you smoke a day?'

'Forty.'

'That's enough to make anyone giddy.' She was quite plainly making a note to herself to nag me into cutting down when she knew me better. I would let her get me down to the fifteen a day I really smoked. We would both enjoy that.

I was quite proud to be seen out with Betty Parsons. She had abandoned her prison-wardress look of the night before. Her blonde hair once more waved like corn and she had resumed her accustomed touch of make-up, with just enough lipstick to be removed by one long kiss. Not expecting to see me, she had not bothered much about her clothes, however. She was wearing her unprepossessing school mac against the threat of January rain, her long stride as the dog tugged her along the avenue revealing a comfortable-looking tweedy skirt. It would be interesting to see what she would regard as suitable attire for handing over her Victor Sylvester collection, which without need of any further prompting from me she arranged to do outside the Royal Coronation branch library the next evening.

It was a choice of venue that suited me. It was a long time since I had stood on the brick steps of the library, inhaling the distilled night smells of frost, creosote and promise. It was also pleasant to reflect that beyond the glass-bricked entrance lobby through which the library's diffused lights glowed cheerfully, Ralph Driver was assiduously stamping the returned books of the High School chicks who scampered the gauntlet of dawdling youths in the shadows. One or other was bound to tell him that Betty Parsons was meeting her new steady not ten yards away.

A further and unexpected pleasure was the discovery of Geoffrey Sissons, a bundle of thick political-looking tomes under his arm, among the hair-primping loiterers on the library steps. With any luck my date would arrive before his, leaving him to impart to Doreen Theaker the same news as one of the High School chicks would be imparting to Ralph Driver. This would impel her to spend some portion of the evening brooding on where I had taken Betty Parsons on this dark night and what we were doing, and whether if she had shown more willingness to do those same things she could still be meeting me herself instead of having to make do with Geoffrey Sissons.

In a moment I saw why he was sheepishly averting his face in the pretence of fingering a spot. The duffel-coated, bespectacled chick who loped on flat heels up the steps to meet him was certainly not Doreen Theaker: she looked more like one of the Monkey-walk also-rans who at one time would have been automatically assigned to Douglas. I knew that Geoffrey Sissons was still going out with Doreen, for I had seen them at the Clock Ballroom on Saturday, so it could only be that he was two-timing her, either because he was making no progress with her or because had had made such good progress that he had now got the taste for it. His new companion was likewise toting a consignment of heavy books. Douglas always said that the more intelligent a chick, the higher was her sex drive and the more imaginative she was in satisfying it. It was possible, I conceded as she and Geoffrey Sissons entered the library, that she was completely naked under her duffel-coat. But if that was the case, why were they wasting time exchanging library books? It was difficult to know what to think.

Betty Parsons, to my disappointment, was still wearing her old school mac, with her school uniform under it. But at once I was able to appreciate her difficulty: the process of changing, involving as it did taking all her clothes off then going slowly through her wardrobe to select her most alluring underwear and then the dress that was most provocative and unbuttoned the easiest, yet did not look cheap and common, would have left her with very little time to do her homework before coming out.

'I can't stay out long, I'm afraid, I've still got an essay to write.' I was only slightly dismayed. The clear implication was that if she hadn't had an essay to write, she would have arrived with the full intention of staying out until midnight.

'I'll walk you back along Crag Park Avenue,' I said, and was delighted to hear Betty counter-propose, 'I'm not in all *that* much of a hurry. Why don't we walk along Parkview Gardens and up Elm Tree Drive?' That was the long way. If I could persuade Betty to scale her long-legged stride down to mine I could spin it out to twenty minutes, as against five the direct route.

We set off at an amble, Betty hugging her slim stack of Victor Sylvester records in their tattered brown-paper sleeves. I was glad she had not handed them over at once: it was a tiny acknowledgement that lending them to me was only a pretext for seeing me. Against that, until she did hand them over I wouldn't be able to get off my chest the little speech I had polished, suggesting another meeting to return them, and I didn't want it lying there much longer, curdling.

'Thanks for the records, Betty. Shall I take them off your hands?'

'So long as you don't drop them. Don't worry about

173

returning them – there's no hurry.'

'Ah, but the sooner I give them back, the sooner I'll be label to give them back.'

'That sounds like another misprint.'

'I should have sped the schooner I give them back, the sooner I'll be able to see you again.'

'Oh, so that's what you meant,' said Betty gravely. There was a delicious little pause before she went on to say in surprisingly matter-of-fact tones, 'You don't really need an excuse for seeing me again, do you, Raymond?'

It would go into the archives. It beat anything said by Pauline Batty to Douglas at the bottom of Iris Crescent or by Janet Gill to me upon introducing herself in the Hotel Metropole. Betty Parsons had spoken my name, making Raymond in full sound ten times more intimate than anyone had ever managed to make the familiar Ray sound, and she had said that I didn't need an excuse for seeing her again. It was as if she had come right out and moaned, 'You don't really need an excuse for touching one of my breasts five times and both of them twice, oh my darling, and that will only be the beginning.'

'Not if you say so, Breasty.'

'What are you doing on Friday, then?'

'Friday? By Friday, my dear Betty, I shall have expired from impatience at not having seen you on Tuesday, Wednesday and Thursday.' I would have to remember that, perhaps putting it in a love-letter.

'Nothing,' I said. I was just about capable of adding, 'Why don't we see that picture at the Gainsborough?' but I wanted her to say it.

'We could go to the pix if you like.'

'Fine.' Now I was going to make her say, 'Which one, the Gem or the Gainsborough?' and following that, 'What time?'

'Does Terry know?' asked Betty after I had got these concessions out of her. I was tempted to parry with, 'Does Terry know what?', thus forcing her to make a formal admission that we were going out with one another. But I had probably gone far enough on those lines for one night. Besides, I found the prospect of murmuring, 'I'll tell him tomorrow' an appealing one. The words would be spiced with intrigue and velvety with the promise of romance.

174

'Not that it makes any difference now,' said Betty, when I had murmured them and they had sounded to my ear no more romantic than an undertaking to have a tooth filled. 'Has he told you I've stopped seeing him?'

'He mentioned it, yes.' And barely that: he had not expanded on that curt 'I've jacked her in'. I added, curious, 'He didn't say why, though.'

'Oh, it was just getting silly. I didn't mind not wearing lipstick and changing my hairstyle to please him, but when he told me on Saturday he wanted me to start wearing glasses, I thought it was time to put my foot down.'

I felt the small, hurtful pain in my chest. Terry Liversedge must have had something of a hold over her if she had really adopted that prison-wardress appearance to please him, and not merely because she had been worn down by threats or nagging. I didn't understand about the glasses, though. 'Why – was he worried about your eyesight?'

'No, he was worried about boys looking at me. He wanted me to wear National Health specs with plain lenses so they wouldn't fall prey to my fatal charms.'

Though she spoke ironically, it was evident that Betty Parsons had a cool awareness of her own attractions. Again I felt a prod of jealousy.

'In one way I don't blame him,' I said, the gallantry sounding ponderous, though lucid.

'Even that wasn't the last straw. You know I leave school at Easter? He wanted me to promise I wouldn't take a job where I'd be working with men.'

So did I, if it came to that, and I would probably make my views known at the appropriate time. Trying to make her wear spectacles, though, was absurd. It was an open incitement to any Tom, Dick or Harry to slip them gently off and ask if she knew how beautiful she was without her glasses. Nor – though I was tempted not only to stop her using lipstick but to make her have all her hair cut off just to see if she would do more to please me than she had done to please Terry Liversedge – did I think it wise to have her going around looking as she had done at the Clock dance on Saturday. Chicks who didn't wear make-up had a powerful attraction to some types. Douglas said it was because not wearing make-up was suggestive of going to bed.

'I'm afraid Terry's going round the twist,' I said. We had already reached the end of Winifred Drive where Betty lived, to my chagrin in about twelve minutes rather than the anticipated twenty, thanks to her long legs which I was surprised Terry Liversedge hadn't made her encase in slacks.

'I'm afraid he is. When you asked if he was jealous of my dancing with a chair, you thought you were joking, didn't you?'

'Oh, I don't know,' I said, making a wild lunge at a compliment, and missing: 'I think it depends on the chair.'

'I've no idea what that means but I'm sure it was something nice,' said Betty with smiling graveness. Her hair shone gold under the street corner lamplight. 'Did Terry put you up to taking my diary, by the way?'

Her own directness of manner inhibited bluff. Besides, I thought something approximating the truth could do me no harm. I told her roughly how I had really come by her diary.

'I thought it was something like that. I have to go in now, but can I ask you something? You didn't ask me out just because you found your name in it, did you? That's assuming you did read it, as I certainly would have done?'

'Yes, I did, and no I didn't,' I said accurately, though unclearly. But she seemed to know what I meant: 'Why *did* you ask me out, then?'

So as to be able to do the things detailed in Terry Liversedge's shorthand missive to Miss Cohen, which incidentally I had better return to him before we set off for a dirty Whitsun in the Court Gardens Hotel and the coach crashes into a lorry and we're all killed and my aborigine mother gets someone who understands shorthand to translate what she thinks are her only son's last words. Placing my tongue inside your mouth, I would slip your silken robe off your white shoulders, at the same time urgently –

'Because I've always wanted to go out with you,' I said, again truthfully.

'I'm glad.'

'My turn to ask you something. What *is* my name doing in your diary?'

'Perhaps I'm starting a list of boys who fish for compliments,' said Betty impishly. 'Now I really must go.'

'Till Friday, then.' An impulse told me to kiss her on the

cheek. I did so, lightly, standing on tiptoe to do so. I had never kissed a girl on the cheek before, only on the mouth or neck, and it was probable that she had never been kissed there before, either. I hoped that the electric charge that went through me was a two-way one. I was fairly sure, anyway, that when Betty Parsons broke into a long-legged run as she receded along Winifred Drive, it was out of elation and not because she was late.

I did not fulfil my promise to tell Terry Liversedge about us. As Betty had said, it made no difference now, and I saw little point in seeking him out just for the sake of stammering an awkward confession. I had the impression, anyway, shared by Douglas, that after being given the brush-off by Betty, or 'jacking her in' as he preferred us to believe, he wanted to keep out of our way for a while. It was not for over a fortnight that all three of us met again, early one evening in the Wine Lodge. By that time, and helped by a fortifying pint of draught Guinness, it was relatively easy to drop Betty casually into the conversation as if our going out together was common knowledge.

Terry Liversedge didn't seem to mind. The bank had transferred him to a new department recently, thus opening up, he claimed, a whole new seam of talent. There was one in particular, identified only as 'this red-headed bint' of whom he entertained high hopes. As for Betty, it was obvious that his only concern was with what she might have told me about him. 'Is she still carrying a torch for her old flame, youth?' he asked with bantering anxiety. I assured him that she never mentioned him. (Nor had she, after that first evening.) Terry Liversedge became cocky in his relief. 'That proves it, youth. She can't even bear to mention my name. She's pining for me.' He then hastily changed the subject back to the fresh talent at the Pennines Linen Bank.

Though relieved at the way Terry Liversedge was taking it, I was to some degree disappointed that he hadn't asked if I had yet got to first base with Betty Parsons. The truth was that I had, with surprising ease, and on only our second proper date. Kissing her lightly on the cheek that night at the corner of Winifred Drive had somehow broken the ice in a way that sweatingly waiting for the right moment to kiss her full square on the mouth could never have done. In the back row of the

Gainsborough, slipping an arm around her had been effected with none of the usual jerky awkwardness. After that, when her head was on my shoulder and I had kissed her clean hair once or twice, she had raised her lips to mine so naturally that in closing in on them I had avoided completely the usual first-attempt glancing slobber at chin or nose. I had to keep my eyes open to remind myself that it was Betty Parsons and not Audrey Marsh or Janet Gill or Doreen Theaker I was kissing. It was all going so smoothly and swimmingly that I refrained from trying for first base there and then only because I wanted to save something to look forward to on our next date.

We had now been out four times and I had touched one breast three times and both of them once, if I was allowed to include touching both of them once in either category. Whether or not, I would soon be passing Terry Liversedge's original score with Betty Parsons and should be well on the way to winning those five-shilling bets.

The Wine Lodge meeting had been convened by Douglas to discuss the business of the Festival of Britain expedition. There were only three months to Whitsun now and he was anxious to get our participation on a sound footing. Every seat, he reported, had now been taken. He had been collecting the required deposits from the St Chad's parish church's Silver Threads Circle and other fossilised groups in weekly dribs and drabs, and he wanted me to pay them in to Moult & Sumpter's and clinch the deal. 'So if either of you has cold feet, now's the time to say so. Otherwise, my friends, you can poppy up your thirty-bob deposits.'

I took out the shot-silk treasury-note-case that had once been Douglas's, now back in my possession after being owned for a time by Terry Liversedge, and extracted the three ten-shilling notes I had painstakingly managed to save. If I did not eat lunch again between now and Whitsun I could just about manage the balance, plus essential expenses.

'That'll do to be going on with, Raymondo, but don't forget you're down as a couple. You'll be taking Betty Parsons now, I suppose?'

'I hope so. I haven't asked her yet.' I glanced surreptitiously at Terry Liversedge but his lean jaw remained impassive.

'What about you, mon capitaine?'

'I'll pay you next week without fail, Douglas,' said Terry

Liversedge, not entirely convincingly.

'Who are you taking – have you decided yet?'

'I'm giving it deep thought, youth. Probably this red-headed bint at work.'

Douglas had brought along his College of Commerce satchel, its strap cut away and an old suitcase handle stapled to its flap so that it could pass as a businessman's briefcase. I wished now that my own satchel hadn't gone to the jumble sale. He drew from it several cyclostyled quarto sheets which he fanned out on the beer-sticky table. They were home-made handbills for the Festival outing. *'NB,'* I read, *'Ladies are advised to take flat shoes for touring the exhibition, also a shawl for open-air evening concerts on the river.'* It was fortunate that the trip was already booked up, for Douglas's prose, surprisingly for one who had a way with words, made it sound like a very tame affair.

'Exactement, mon brave! Without actually saying so in so many words, this guff subtly suggests we're going to have culture rammed down our throats morning, noon and night, with no time for what you might describe as other activities.'

Terry Liversedge looked doubtfully at the sheaf of handbills which Douglas now thrust at him. 'What do you want us to do with them, youth? Hand them out in the bus queue, or what?'

'Just leave them lying about on the doormat as if they've been shoved through the letter box, and get your dames to do the same,' advised Douglas. 'It's what is known as the softening-up process.'

'You think of everything,' I said admiringly.

'Very necessary, Raymondo, as the aforementioned dames may find when they break the news to their everloving parents that they're going down to London with a trio of sex maniacs. In fact,' said Douglas, with a studied airiness which immediately aroused my worst suspicions, 'I've already had some trouble in that direction with Pauline's dragon of a mother.'

'What did she say?'

'Oh, the kind of tripe you'd expect. Darling daughter never been away from home on her own et cetera et cetera. Fret not,' cooed Douglas, shiftily soothing. 'We worked out a compromise.'

'What fizzing compromise?' Terry Liversedge was now as

179

alarmed as I was.

'One that should benefit us financially, as a matter of fact, old bean, old boy. That's if Ray can persuade Moult & Sumpter's to give the six of us a special rate if we don't stay at the Court Gardens Hotel.'

'But we *are* staying at the Court Gardens Hotel,' I pointed out. 'That's the whole frigging purpose of the whole frigging enterprise.'

'Ah, well that's it, you see, Raymondo. Pauline's mother unfortunately has the idea that all London hotels are more or less on a level with Port Said knocking-shops. So the upshot is she'll only let Pauline off the apron-strings on condition that we stay with her Auntie May in Hounslow.'

Terry Liversedge and I exchanged the Laurel and Hardy long-suffering sigh we had perfected for moments such as these, of which there had been several since we'd known Douglas.

'We've been had,' said Terry Liversedge.

'Not so fast, Terry,' I said, still ready to give Douglas the benefit of the now considerable doubt. 'By "us", Douglas, you mean all of us?'

'Natch. It's a big house.'

'So we'll still have a room each?'

'Ah, well it's not quite as big as that. The three of us will share one room and the three dames will share another.'

'We *have* been had,' I said.

'Don't be like that, Raymondo. Think of it this way – the three of us, with the three dames of our choice, all under the same roof in what apparently is a very big house.'

'But not all that big,' I said drily.

'Big enough for our purposes. She's got to go out sometime, hasn't she – shopping et cetera? And there's no one else in the house except her old mother, who's eighty-odd and bedridden, so she'll be no trouble –'

'Have you got the key to that church crypt yet, Douglas?' asked Terry Liversedge abruptly, coming out of a morose silence.

'What's that got to do with it?'

'Because if you have, just get a duplicate made for me and you can keep the naffing Festival of Britain. It's going to be a waste of money, youth.'

'You're not being constructive, mon capitaine. Look – supposing the worst comes to the worst, which it won't, and there's no actual opportunity to get your actual oats in the actual house, which there will be –'

With the air of a conjuror producing the flags of all nations out of a hat, Douglas drew out of his makeshift briefcase a folded map. The Wine Lodge was doing little business so early in the evening and we had a booth to ourselves. He spread the map out on the table in front of us, using our Guinness glasses to hold down the corners.

'Now, my friends. This is the official Ordnance Survey map of Richmond Park, which as you may or may not know is but a short bus-ride from Hounslow. According to Pauline's mother who's been there, it's exactly like being in the middle of the country.' A wart-festooned forefinger circled a section of the map. 'All these are woods and conifer plantations. You can spend all day flat on your back in this part without seeing a living soul.'

'Oh, yes? Did Pauline's mother tell you that?'

'You may laugh and you may jeer, mon brave, but I am probably pointing at the very spot where twelve weeks from now you'll be lying with your trousers round your ankles.'

'Yes – with a gnat biting his arse,' scoffed Terry Liversedge.

'All right, Terence, it may not have the comfort of a sprung mattress in a two-star hotel,' conceded Douglas, folding up his map. 'But what you've both got to keep in mind is that with all the slight drawbacks of this revised arrangement, you will still be spending five solid days, on the trot, with the dame of your choice, two hundred miles from home. If you know of a more golden opportunity for getting your leg across, I wish you'd tell me about it.'

Douglas had a point there, as, in the end, he usually did. Mollified, I collected our glasses and went over to the bar for refills. But Terry Liversedge remained doubtful. As I returned, Douglas was still working on him:

'. . . greatest advantage is that the dames, in complete honesty, can say not only that it's a church outing to a cultural festival with a gang of old fogeys, but that they'll be sharing a room with two other God-fearing bints in a respectable suburban house, with Pauline's Auntie May and Pauline's Auntie May's old lady as chaperones. Address, phone number and references supplied if needed. What more could a cautious mum and dad ask for?'

Terry Liversedge capitulated, raising his glass in a grudging toast. 'You know, Duggerlugs, you're wasting your time at that building society you crack on your work for. You ought to be flogging patent medicines at the back of Grippenshaw Market.'

Douglas, through the moustache of Guinness froth that clung to the one he was trying to grow, beamed his gratification at the tribute.

# 20

Fired anew by Douglas's single-minded enthusiasm, I put the Festival of Britain idea to Betty Parsons that same night.

Betty had met me off the trolley-bus, our plan being to have high tea at the Mermaid Supper Bar and then go for a walk on the municipal golf course, which, according to intelligence received by Terry Liversedge, had lately become accessible in the night hours via a gate with a broken lock. But a sudden cloudburst first stranded us under the canopy of the Gem Picture Palace and ultimately, as it developed into a steady, remorseless downpour, drove us into the little fleapot cinema.

The British Movietone News, as nearly always these days, gave the latest report on how the Festival of Britain was taking shape. I had a watery sensation in my stomach as the shots of a science-fiction-looking structure called the Dome of Discovery and a cigar-shaped affair known as the Skylon brought home to me how near it all was now. During the ice-cream interval I gave Betty one of Douglas's handbills to read while I fetched two tubs. As I'd guessed, she had learned nothing of the expedition from Terry Liversedge. But I didn't even need to ask if she would like to go.

'If this is an invitation, Raymond, I'd love to say yes, but I have an awful feeling that's not the answer I'll get from the committee.' That was what she called her aborigine parents.

'Why not?'

'Well, it's not that they don't trust me, but after all I shall be only just turned seventeen. They'd take a dim view of their baby daughter swanning off to London on her own.'

'But you wouldn't be on your own.'

'That's what they'd be afraid of.'

I told her about the house in Hounslow and Pauline Batty's Auntie May, adding that it would be practically like staying in a youth hostel.

'In that case,' said Betty without further hesitation, 'I should think they might be persuaded. I shall tell them it's my last girlish fling before I settle down to earning a living.' She folded the handbill carefully away in her bag. 'I'd love to go, Raymond, I really would.'

'Mark you,' I said, encouraged into daring, 'I don't expose Auntie May will be keeping her beamy eye on us from morning till nine.'

'I should hope not,' said Betty demurely.

The supporting programme began – a 'This Is Britain' miscellany that neither we nor anyone else in the sparse audience had any interest in watching. The rain beat down on the Gem's tin roof. I slipped my arm around Betty and, unbidden, she pressed her hair, clean and damp, against my cheek. I liften her chin and kissed her.

'You've been drinking,' murmured Betty, not disapprovingly.

'Only Guinness.'

Having skipped lunch that day for reasons of economy, I had embarked upon my Wine Lodge session with Douglas and Terry Liversedge on an empty stomach. Betty and I had not made it to the Mermaid Supper Bar where the three pints swilling about inside me would have been mopped up wholesomely by cod, chips, and bread and butter. The tub of ice-cream I had just finished was all I had eaten since a skimpy breakfast. And – as I wished Betty would hurry up and express warm concern about before I really did feel ill – I was smoking too much. It was the wooziness thereby induced that emboldened me, after another fervent kiss, to relocate the arm that was around Betty Parsons' shoulder to the area of her waist, thereupon rotating my outspread hand until it spanned her hip. Receiving no rebuff from Betty personally, I was altogether sure of receiving one from the elasticated fortifications protecting her. Nevertheless I applied gentle pressure, expecting the same resistance I had met when dancing with her at the Clock Ballroom. There was none.

There could only be one logical yet incredible explanation, more intoxicating even than three pints on an empty stomach. Having girdled herself against the unwelcome attentions of Terry Liversedge, she had now liberated her body to await the welcome attentions of Raymond Watmough.

Made reckless by drink, desire and self-confidence, I kneaded the softness of her hip where my hand rested. 'You

184

don't wear armour-plating,' I murmured, under cover of the subdued babble of muttering, shuffling and match-scraping that always accompanied the 'This Is Britain' documentary.

'I hope I don't need to.'

'You did that night at the Clock.'

'You mean I happened to be wearing a dress with an elasticated bodice,' whispered Betty. The clinical accuracy of the reply was not as dispiriting as it might have been. Though she had put paid to my heated fancies, there was something intimate about a murmured discussion about elasticated bodices in a darkened cinema. It was with a distinct thrill that I heard her continue, quite brazenly, 'Anyway, why are you so interested in my foundation garments, or lack of them?'

'Never mime,' was all I dared commit myself to saying.

The 'This is Britain' miscellany, after short items on silver-beating and training in the use of artificial limbs, had now got its teeth into the subject of biscuit manufacture. It had reached the point where the biscuits had come out of the ovens and were being funnelled down the assembly line to be packed in tins. The tins would have to be sealed, then fork-lifted into a van, and the van would have to be seen driving up the A.1 and delivering them to a shop, and then we would have to see an aristocratic-looking fossil buying them and serving them for tea before the short bored itself to a stop. That should give me a good four or five minutes before the lights came up for the last time. Just enough for an exploratory foray, to be followed by the main expedition during the big picture.

Now that it had come to it, I had very little idea how to set about reaching second base in the present circumstances. Given the semi-vertical position we found ourselves in – as distinct from the horizontal position we would have proceeded from had we made it to a sand bunker on the municipal golf course – I had always assumed that below the waist would be reached from the waist itself, with a hand sidling under a loosened waistband down a satin curve of stomach. But Betty was wearing her school gymslip, with no visible access between neckline and hem. The packed biscuit tins were tumbling off the assembly line before I had totally discarded the insane notion of thrusting down the front of her gymslip as far as my armpit. As the fork-lift truck ploughed towards a cliff of rich tea assortment, I saw that I had but one course available – what I had hitherto thought of as the Throstle Moor, sewage farm or, more recently, sand bunker approach.

Keeping one eye on the 'This Is Britain' footage, I kissed Betty perfunctorily. After a token brushing of my disengaged hand against her breast – a gesture I obscurely sensed to be following established protocol whereby a courtesy visit had to be paid to first base before second base was embarked upon – I lowered it rapidly to her lap, burrowing under her folded raincoat until I found her knee.

I satisfied myself that it was in fact a kneecap I was holding, and not for example her handbag, part of the furnishings or any other below-the-waist equivalent of Janet Gill's mole. This exploration was permitted. But as I was about to consolidate my position by extending a roving thumb towards her other knee, she seized my wrist so firmly that my hand hung limp as she brought it up to the seat-rest between us. Yet at the same time she turned her face towards me and whispered, '*Not here.*'

'Not here' could only mean 'Somewhere else'. It was as if she had given me an engraved, gilt-edged invitation to avail myself of second base rights, with only the date and the place left blank.

The rain beat down on the old tin roof of the ramshackle Gem Picture Palace, drowning even the comic backfiring of the biscuit van proceeding over the horizon as the 'This Is Britain' short reached another of its many false endings.

'I wish it wasn't raining,' I murmured.

She whispered something, so low that I couldn't make out what at first. Then, in retrospect, I heard, '*It won't rain for ever.*' They were the most seductive five words that had ever come my way, including anything that Terry Liversedge had written in shorthand.

But it did rain for ever, or seemed to be doing. It rained all the weekend, so that Saturday evening had to be spent at the Clock Ballroom with my arm clasping what I now under-stood to be an elasticated bodice, and Sunday evening at the Gainsborough where my above-the-waist figures, if I could count the two performances we sat through as separate occasions, rose to match Terry Liversedge's, while my below-the-waist count remained at zero. The rain varied in

186

strength between drizzle and downpour, but never completely stopped except, perversely, when we were not together.

Four times a week Betty allowed herself, or was allowed, to go out with me. Each Monday, Thursday, Friday and Saturday evening I scanned the next day's weather forecast on the back page of the *Argus*, allowing its lies to seduce my despair into hope. Each Tuesday, Friday, Saturday and Sunday I threw back my bedroom curtain and looked out, with frustration, exasperation and resignation melting into a dull rage, at the water seething along the gutters of Edith Close. Sometimes the rain was teeming down, sometimes only pitter-pattering, sometimes it played a trick: the puddle that had formed in an area of pavement subsidence out in the street would be as calm and still and glistening with sunshine as the Crag Park boating-lake on an August bank holiday. Then, even as I watched semi-mesmerised, dressing by the window for fear of the mirage dissolving, there would be a small plopping splash in the puddle as if someone had dropped a tiny stone into it; then a scattered sequence of splashes as if it were a bucket-spray of gravel that was being dropped now; then the splashes grew faster, their little waves dancing upwards, until the puddle began to resemble, in miniature, a storm at sea.

Behind the streaked sign announcing FESTIVAL OF BRITAIN 1951: SITE OF GRIPPENSHAW PAGEANT OF PROGRESS, a pagoda of rain-buckled plywood and plastic panels had begun to swaddle the rusty girders which rose like a derrick out of a lake of mud. On the newsreels, every shot of the Festival of Britain sites on the South Bank and in Battersea Park, wherever that was, featured squelching gumboots. With each Festival item, its soundtrack accompaniment of 'Holiday For Strings' half-drowned by the hammering of rain on the Gem's tin roof, Betty Parsons and I would squeeze hands along the neutral zone of the dividing seat-rest.

She sustained me with a series of obliquely provocative, even teasing, observations. 'Perhaps I was wrong – perhaps it *can* rain for ever,' she sighed jokingly one evening. That meant she had a clear memory of what she had said in the Gem the night I had had the three pints of Guinness, total recall of the circumstances in which she had said it, and an awareness of the

187

implication contained in her repetition of it. On another occasion she complained, 'Even when it does stop, it'll be ages before the ground dries out.' By ground she meant grass: she was saying it would be a long time before we could lie down on it, even with the protection of two raincoats. 'Do you think somebody up there doesn't like us, Raymond?' Did I think there was a conspiracy of fate preventing me getting to second base? 'I hope it's not like this in London.' That meant she was looking forward to spending a good part of our visit in the conifer plantations of Richmond Park, which I had explained was like open country and very convenient from Hounslow.

I was now very pleased by the Hounslow turn of events. Douglas's insight into aborigine thought-processes had proved unwaveringly perceptive – Betty's 'committee' had been so impressed by his handbill and the careful arrangements made to place the younger Festival excursionists under the wing of Pauline Batty's Auntie May, that they had told her she would be foolish not to seize such an opportunity of broadening her mind. Moult & Sumpter's, after some initial grumbling, had agreed to charge the Hounslow contingent only their basic coach fares, less, in my case, staff discount, which meant I could eat lunch again. The outlook was sunny. Only the weather forecast remained bleak.

As the rain continued, inducing a state of restlessness of probably the same order as that experienced by planters during the long monsoon, I was constantly invigorated by the thought of Betty Parsons thinking of me. On the nights we were not together I would visualise her sitting at a polished dining-table with a satchel-load of school books spread out before her, sucking a pen as she wrestled with a French grammar but quite unable to stop her mind wandering off to what we would be doing when the rain stopped, and perhaps committing certain words and phrases to French as Terry Liversedge had committed them to shorthand.

Curiously, this was only a nocturnal image. By day, mooning at my office desk and indulgently suffering Audrey's waggish speculation on the cause of it (our former bantering neutrality having been happily, and less awkwardly than I had feared, restored), I could not imagine Betty Parsons at her school desk. She did not exist for me until her long-legged, straight-backed, hair-tossing walk carried her through the

High School gates and into my country.

At last there came a Saturday when I bought the Buff Sports Final of the *Evening Argus* and turned to the weather forecast in the shelter of the Chocolate Cabin doorway. Looking over my shoulder, Betty read it out, '"Sunny intervals at first, becoming cloudy with a little rain in places." Do you think we dare risk an afternoon walk?'

# 21

That March Sunday dawned like an August one. The sun was watery but brilliant. By eleven in the morning the puddle out in Edith Close had a two-inch cracked-mud tidemark where the water had begun to evaporate. By noon, except for the puddle and the depressed corners of uneven paving stones, the street was dry. By one, when I went out to the back lawn to test the weather on the pretext of feeding birds, the grass was still spongily damp but no longer glistening with dewdrops of accumulated rain. By two-thirty, when I left the house, the wooden garden-bench was bone dry. By three, as I paced the brick steps of the Royal Coronation branch library, with my mac folded over the arm of Terry Liversedge's salmon-pink zoot jacket, an armada of grey cloud had begun to cruise across the sky from somewhere behind the Pennines. I felt a stray fleck of moisture on my face as Betty, hurrying as she always did when coming to meet me, as if she wanted to demonstrate that it was an occasion she'd been looking forward to, strode along the green rubber-tiled promenade.

The skirts of her buttoned-up and belted school raincoat parting slightly as she skipped up the library steps towards me showed that she was wearing the white dress I had once seen on her at the Clock Ballroom. My delight was not total. Buttoning as it did all the way down, it indicated a willingness amounting to eagerness on Betty's part to facilitate the process of getting to second base. But, only hazily familiar with the interior geography of dresses, I had no idea how I was going to get on with its forbidding elasticated bodice, a probable formidable hazard that, she surely must have known, could have been specifically designed to repel potential below-the-waist boarders. A further discouraging sign was that the clouds were now directly overhead.

'Well, it did say cloudy, and it did say a *little* rain,' said Betty cheerfully. 'So if the weather forecast goes on keeping its word, we might be in for another of those sunny intervals it promised.'

'Otherwise I suppose there's always the park shelters,' I said with no great enthusiasm. The park shelters, one by the playground, one by the old fossils' bowling-green, and one by the municipal rose garden, were as often as not infested with pram-rocking aborigines or penknife-wielding council school gargoyles. The substitute hope that I had allowed to foster as the sky darkened, of finding a tree with foliage enough to keep the rain off and spending the afternoon pressed against it with one arm around her elasticated waist, foundered as I glanced down at her shoes. Betty, with surprising stupidity, had elected to wear white suedette basket-weave sandals, thoroughly unsuitable for trekking through the wet grass of the bluebell woods. But the error was mitigated by her absence of stockings. The potential, in more clement conditions, of Betty Parsons' long, bare limbs under her crisp white frock was almost too painful to contemplate: I all but shook my fist in fury at the lowering sky as we moved off towards Crag Park Avenue.

By the time the park came in sight, what had started as a tentative smattering of rain had resolved itself into a fine thin drizzle, a prolonged and premature April shower not wet enough to drench but wet enough to re-saturate the grass and to varnish the park benches with a thin layer of moistness as if they had been wiped over with a damp cloth. Rain droplets shone in Betty's hair like Christmas glitter-dust. As we reached the park gates the Petrocelli's ice-cream dodo, draped in oilskins like a lifeboatman, was pushing away his cart. I thought of the hot day last summer after Terry Liversedge had given Betty Parsons her brush-off card and we had seen her walking hand-in-hand into the park with Ralph Driver, licking the ice-cream cone he had bought her, and I thought of her strawberry-flavoured tongue flicking into Ralph Driver's mouth before they sank down in the soft, and at that time dry, grass of the bluebell woods.

'What do you reckon?' I said dully, as we hovered indecisively at the park gates.

'Oh, it's only rain,' said Betty.

I didn't want her to think I could be put off by the weather. Twelve-foot snowdrifts would not have kept me out of the park. My only purpose in hesitating was to decide which of the three park shelters we should head for. With any luck the

191

pram-rockers and penknife-wielders would have been rained off by now and we should have to watch out only for the prowling peaked-cap dodo who was the park ranger. We would be operating in first-base conditions rather than second-base ones, but it would be better than nothing.

But Betty resisted my gently tugging hand. 'Just a second, Raymond, I'm thinking.' After a momentary hesitation she continued briskly, as if she had been debating with herself and reached a decision, 'Let's go this way. After all, what's a little pneumonia between friends?' And now it was my own hand that was tugged, and we were walking along Parkside through the drizzle, following the line of the park's low stone wall topped by green spiked railings where it swept round in a long, gradual arc to meet the golf course.

'I don't mind getting wet if you don't, Betty,' I said, sounding and feeling valiant as she slipped her arm through mine, 'but you do know there's no shelter on the golf course, if it starts coming down like the clappers as it has been doing?'

'Ah, but we're not going to the golf course,' said Betty teasingly.

'Where are we going, then?'

'Wait and see.'

'Give me a clue.'

My hands, as we hurried along arm-in-arm, were plunged into the pockets of my mac. Betty's hand, clutching my inner arm, travelled down my sleeve until it seized my wrist, then nestled into my pocket where her fingers intertwined with mine. It was a voluptuous, getting on for lustful gesture, complementing the playful suggestiveness in her voice as she said bewilderingly, '*I thought I'd show you how the committee used to take me to Scarborough.*'

I had not the slightest notion what she was talking about, except that her aborigine parents came into it somewhere. A confused and alarming suspicion that I was being hustled off to have tea in an uncut-moquette-stuffed lounge was allayed at once by the seductive pressure of her hand. But she would say no more, except, 'You'll see when we get there.'

We skirted the mesh fence of the golf course, finally turning down a paved walk that separated it from the long glasshouses and outbuildings of a nursery garden. We reached the side gate with its broken lock where Terry Liversedge had promised

192

access could be gained to the golf course by night. But we were not going on the golf course. We strode on, purposefully like hikers, past a splintered noticeboard announcing in half-flaked-off letters, 'Private Property – Keep Out'. It had looked imposing enough to be taken seriously the last time I had ventured this far, but now it lay unregarded in the ditch.

The paved walk had already reduced itself to a single line of paving-stones laid out like duckboards on a camp-site along a ribbon of churned-up clay, deeply troughed with water-filled tyre-tracks. Now the paving gave way to cinders. On one side, where the nursery garden petered out into a no-man's-land of compost heaps and fenced-in dumps of sacks of fertiliser, we were now passing a wire-fenced scrapyard. On the other, the blackberry-bush thicket marking the golf course boundary was strewn with the scrapyard's overspill of oil drums and festering mattresses.

The drizzle had all but stopped at last. Betty's clay-splashed suedette sandals and my nigger-brown twill Dunlop bunjees crunched over the cinders. It was the only sound, except for a blackbird far off across the golf course. Neither of us spoke. Betty's long strides always gave the impression that she was hurrying, and that impression, and the silence, and the expectation, created a tension that almost crackled between us as we walked along to wherever we were going. As Betty half-stumbled on the bumpy cinder path, I drew her warm hand out of my mac pocket and slipped my arm around her waist. Her foot twisted slightly and she lurched towards me, and my arm slipped as of its own accord to her hip. I pressed my hand against it as we walked and was surprised not to meet the armoured resistance I had expected. Even through her raincoat the contours of her hip felt soft and supple.

'Hello!' I said, venturing speech. If I sounded breathless she would think it was from the exertion of walking. 'What happened to the elasticated what-d'you-call-it?'

'I thought you didn't approve of it, so I cut it out.'

'Very thoughtful of you.'

'Besides which, it was beginning to shrink and pucker up the material of the dress.'

She had felt obliged to add that out of modesty, to make it sound as if she had ripped the elasticated bodice out of her button-all-the-way-down dress in something less than a frenzy of desire to be arrived at second base with. But she could not seriously think I was taken in. For when her slipping on the cinders had precipitated my hand across her hip, it had pressed her other hip close to mine, and far from showing any signs of pulling away from me she was still actively pressing against me as we moved along. I returned the pressure. Her stride being so much longer than mine meant I had to develop a kind of loping gait to keep up with her along the cinder path, but I was determined to remain in bodily contact, hip to hip.

As we crunched on in this manner, like contestants in a three-legged race, Betty dropped another of her inscrutable and tantalising remarks. 'Mark you, I've no evidence that it's still here.'

'What?'

'We'll see. If not, there are plenty of others.'

A moment later the cinders had petered out altogether, and we were picking our way across a flattened farm gate into what had once been a field, then had seemingly started a new career as an ash-tip and was now a dump for old cars, vans and lorries. Stripped of their wheels and headlamps they were strewn about the site haphazardly where they had sputtered to their final stop, some of them tilted at crazy angles where they had fetched up against piles of clinker. Car seats and springs were strewn about where children had played. A trampled Durex packet showed that other games were played here. My heart lurched at the sight of it, but I was glad that Betty either hadn't noticed it or didn't know what it was.

'This is where our little Morris came to die,' said Betty softly, her hand seeking mine. 'The committee used to take me to Scarborough in her every year, when I was little. Then one day Daddy drove her down here and she didn't come back. Poor Bruno. That's what we used to call her.'

'Sounds like a dog,' I said fatuously.

'No. Pipe tobacco. It was what Daddy used to smoke, and the car reeked of it. I wonder if it still does.'

We were carefully not looking at one another. 'Only one way to find out,' I said.

I tried to gauge whether it was with a practised tread that she guided me across the wasteland of crunching cinders and scraps of upholstery flock that were lying about like sodden tumbleweed. She was certainly unerring in heading for the black Morris Eight that was lurched up against a bank of ash and cinders, its running boards rotted, its tyres gone, its windshield shattered and the driver's door hanging on one hinge like a stamp in an album.

We clambered into the back seat, finding it intact though slashed with criss-cross knife-strokes. The leather was still slithery and the tilt of the abandoned car brought Betty sliding towards me as she climbed in through the buckled offside door. I put my arm around her.

'That's a good start,' I said with the heavy-handed lightness of a failed soufflé, hoping to sound like a man of the world.

'Mm. Comfy. And I can still smell Bruno. Can you?'

In dreamy tones, Betty began to talk about the runs to the dales and such places she had been taken on in the old Morris Eight when younger. But her mind, I hoped and believed, was not on motoring matters, for as she spoke she was slowly unbuttoning her raincoat. I had already unbuttoned mine and when she had completed the operation I drew her to me, pulling her shoulders so that her arm came up around my neck and her forearm was resting on my pumping chest. Then I brought her reminiscences to an end by kissing her.

Very soon the score, for Terry Liversedge's information, was one breast touched either eleven or twelve times, I could no longer remember which, and both breasts touched five times. This stage had been reached effortlessly without any unbuttoning of buttons or disengaging of shoulder-straps, and we both knew it was merely a preliminary. I had already mapped out my plan of campaign for reaching second base. Instead of fudging around at knee or waist level I proposed boldly to unbutton her dress all the way down, and then take whatever follow-up action was suggested by her response and the number and variety of garments thus revealed.

Sucking saliva into my mouth I counted silently to five, then said, 'When you unbutton this dress, do you unbutton it up from the tomp, or fom the bomtom?'

'Oh dear, what a lot of misprints!' said Betty with mocking gravity. She was stroking the shaking hand that was trying to toy with her top button. 'I think you'd better take a deep breath and start again.'

'I'll take it snowly. When. You unbutton. This dress. Do you unbutton it. From the top. Or from the bontom?'

'Oh, I see.' It was a far-off seductive murmur in my ear. 'Sometimes one, sometimes the other. But I suppose if one hand started at the top and the other at the bottom, they'd meet in the middle, wouldn't they?'

Croaking that I supposed they would, or something approximating to that, I steadied my hand beneath hers and pincered forefinger and thumb over her top button. She gripped them together tightly, detaining my purchase on the button.

'Raymond. You're not going to ask me to go all the way, are you?'

Not yet. Not until the Festival of Britain. Say the second or third day.

'I wouldn't do that, Betty.'

'There's something else.' My heart felt weighty at the expectation of her being about to tell me that whatever we were going to do short of going all the way, it would not be her first time. 'I don't want you to think this is a regular haunt of mine.'

'I don't.'

'For instance, that I ever brought Terry Liversedge here.'

'I know you didn't.' She had taken him, or he had taken her, to the various park shelters, to the alley of high weeds behind the Crag Park Avenue Congregational Chapel, to the lych-gate of St Chad's parish church by prior arrangement with Douglas, and to Throstle Moor in our long-ago existence of last summer. But he knew nothing about the car dump. It was already a source of smug glee with me.

'Or Ralph Driver?' I couldn't resist asking, in a thick, resigned voice. I was relieved to hear a small inward chuckle reverberate against my chest.

'Ralph Driver just happened to be the first person who came along after Terry Liversedge.'

'So he caught you on the rebound?' I asked jealously, wishing I had been the one to catch her on the rebound instead of wasting my time chasing after Audrey Marsh and Janet Gill.

'Not even that. Hurt pride, I suppose. It was such a slap in the face when Terry gave me that brush-off card, I wanted to show him that I didn't care.'

'Why did you start going out with him again, then?'

'I thought I was still fond of him.'

'But you weren't?'

'Well,' Betty hedged, to my annoyance. 'Certainly not enough to bring him down here.'

'Or anyone else?'

Betty looked up into my face, her blue-grey eyes steady, but with a hint of amusement in them. 'Listen, silly billy. The last time I was anywhere near here was when I came blackberrying with the Girl Guides. And another thing. If we sit here just talking for the rest of the day, I shan't have any reason for wanting to come here again. Now shall I?'

I closed my lips on hers. The hand that was gripping my hand at her throat fell away, giving me permission to commence unbuttoning her dress from the top. Making slits of my eyes I saw, over my elbow, that her hand rested for a moment on her flank and then groped towards the hem of her dress to begin unbuttoning it from the bottom. Then there was a slithering crunch of cinders, and she pulled away.

'Someone coming.'

'Damn and blast.'

I craned my head round, following Betty's gaze which was, I was glad to note, an exasperated one. A gargoyle dog on a rope lead, followed by an ancient fossil in a long, oil-impregnated raincoat also tied with rope, and a shapeless flat cap pulled halfway over his hair-sprouting ears, came into view around an overturned lorry. The fossil carried a length of broom-handle with which he prodded a pile of clinker as the dog tugged him along.

'Ratting,' said Betty, with impatient resignation. 'That's a Norwich terrier. They won't be long, touch wood.'

'Do you know something, Betty?' I said, hugging her arm. 'You say really marvellous things sometimes.'

'That's news to me, though I'm very pleased to hear it. Like what, for instance?'

' "They won't be long, touch wood." '

'What's so marvellous about that?'

'It's difficult to explain. You say ordinary things, but they have extraordinary meanings.' I was glad I had been able to get through so many syllables without mishap. Having jumped those half a dozen fences, I could jump any, at least for the moment. 'For instance, "they won't be long" and "touch wood" seem to suggest that you're hoping against hope they'll

197

go, so that we can start again where we left off.'

'That's what I *am* hoping. It's not extraordinary.'

When I got home I was going to take down the kittens-in-a-basket calendar with the date of the Festival of Britain outing circled in Biro, and I was going to work out the exact number of days before we would be setting off, adding a further day to arrive at the moment when Betty and I would lie down beneath the conifers of Richmond Park, then I would multiply the days by twenty-four, the hours by sixty, and the minutes again by sixty.

'I love you, Betty,' I was on the verge of saying, but she suddenly made a performance of straightening up as best she could on the sloping back seat and brushing back her hair as the fossil and his gargoyle dog pottered towards us, then veered off with a stare and a growl to begin poking about in the heap of ash and cinders on which the Morris Eight was foundered. It seemed a good moment to have a cigarette, which I badly needed by now.

'Would your car object to tobacco smoke that wasn't Bruno?'

'I should think she'd quite like it.'

'Can I tempt you to one for a change?' Betty never having shown any real inclination to stop me smoking, it had become an ambition of mine to get her to take it up. She was so much the type who didn't smoke that it would be a small ego-victory for me. It was, I fully recognised, my own variation on Terry Liversedge stopping her using lipstick.

'No thanks, but let me light it for you.'

She relieved me of the petrol lighter I had started fiddling with, then felt for my cigarettes in the inside pocket of Terry Liversedge's salmon-pink zoot jacket. Her fingers closed not on my gunmetal cigarette-case but on a plain cream-laid envelope, sealed, unaddressed and bearing the trademark of Moult & Sumpter, and bulging, it must have seemed to her intriguingly, with its undivulged contents.

'Hello! What's this – a love letter?'

It was the sheaf of obscene shorthand notes I had been looking after for Terry Liversedge. I was meeting him on The Parade before supper to return his jacket and recover my own, for he was off to a jazz evening at the Pack Horse Tavern off Sheepgate and thought the zoot cut and shrieking salmon-pink more hep than my subdued candy-striped seersucker. I would, I had decided, leave the notes in the inside pocket so that his taking receipt of them would become a *fait accompli*. It was all very well his wanting me to go on looking after them for fear that his shorthand-reading aborigines at home would read them, but I had now become seized by the notion that in the event of my ending up dead or in hospital, my own aborigines would have them translated.

Betty was balancing the quite weighty packet in her hand.

'It *is* a sort of love letter, since you ask,' I said.

'So I've caught you out, have I, Raymond Watmough?'

She was teasing but curious. 'What makes you say that?' I found it necessary to say.

'Well, the envelope's blank. How am I to know who it's meant for?'

'Why don't you open it and see?'

It was very fortunate, I reflected as she slit open the envelope, that shorthand was not on the curriculum of Grippenshaw Girls' High School. I would tell her that they were some private thoughts I had scribbled down after one of the endless rainy evenings when we had longed to be in some such private place as the one we found ourselves in now, or in which we were about to find ourselves when the old fossil and his gargoyle dog had pleased to move on. Perhaps, in view of everything she had said about top and bottom buttons and the presence of fossil and dog not lasting long touch wood, and so forth, I could give her an extemporarily edited version of the letter's actual contents. I looked down at the folded notebook pages as she smoothed them out and brushed off her lap the curling paper shreds from the top spiralled edges. '*Thrusting into your yielding loins while you moan with ecstasy, I would then* –' Perhaps not.

Wondering how, then, to explain the copious notes, and hovering between an arch and leering refusal to read out what I seemed to have drifted into claiming I'd written, and offhand denial that they were anything very interesting after all – some notes for a Moult & Sumpter travel brochure, perhaps, the office equivalent of homework: and I was sorry to have led her to expect a love letter but I would write her one tonight, in longhand – I did not realise until she had turned over two pages that she was actually reading Terry Liversedge's

Pitman.

'This is filthy,' said Betty with a chill in her voice I had never heard before. Perhaps latecomers to assembly at Grippenshaw Girls' High School had.

'But you don't know what it says!'

'It's more than filthy, it's downright disgusting.'

She turned over another page, and I glimpsed the elaborate outline for *soixante-neuf*. 'I did a crash course in Pitman at night school last winter, if you want to know, to qualify for a job at the Prudential.'

'You never told me you were going to work at the Pru!' I said in an injured voice. I could perhaps deflect her anger with a sulking accusation that she kept things from me, though perhaps this was not the moment to protest that she would be thrown into the lustful company of men.

But Betty was not to be headed off.

'I don't want to read any more. Did you really write this to me, Raymond? I shall hate you if you did.'

'Of course I didn't,' I mumbled. 'I have more respent for you Nan gnat.'

'Who did write it, then, and what is it doing in your possession?' She sounded like the head prefect she was, questioning a first-form shrimp after confiscating her bubble-gum.

I had nothing to lose by coming clean. With a sigh of exasperation: 'Terry Liversedge wrote it, if you must know.'

'You don't surprise me, it's just about his mark. Why should he give it to you?'

'To look after. He was going to give it to someone, the shorthand teacher at Commerce when we were leaving, but he didn't have the nerve. Look, Betty, you're making heavy weather of this – it's only a joke, you know.'

She riffled through the shorthand manuscript as if prefectorially examining the school imposition that, now I remembered, it should have been had Terry Liversedge not taken it into his head to act the fool that day at the end of term. I caught the word *pulsating*. And then Betty took an unexpected, wholly intuitive leap into my mind.

'You two talk about me, don't you?'

'No we don't.'

'Yes you do, you compare notes.'

'We *don't*, Betty. Be told.'

'You mean he gives you this sort of filth – "I would like to do this, that and the other" – but you never talk about what you really do do?'

There was a rising indignation in her voice that disturbed, even frightened me. She had got herself so wound up that she was all uncaring of the old fossil who was still prodding into the cinders, well within hearing distance.

'Calm down, Betty. We never talk about you.'

'Then how do you come to know I never brought Terry Liversedge down here?'

'I didn't know. You told me.'

'I said I never brought Terry Liversedge here and you said "I know". How could you know if he hadn't given you a running commentary on the places I *have* been to with him?'

My tongue was swelling again. I would have to keep my sentences concise. 'I didn't mean I *mew*, Benny. I meant I mew you *wouldn't* have.'

'*How* do you know? I'll tell you how you know, Raymond. Because he would have told you if I had.'

'No he wouldn't.'

'I don't believe you. What does Terry Liversedge say he's done with me?'

'Nothing.'

'Did he tell you I was easy?'

'Of course not.'

'Why of course? I am with you – why shouldn't I be with him?'

Remembering how the same question, though in respect of himself and Ralph Driver, had exercised Terry Liversedge, I paused for one fatal moment before replying.

'Because I know you weren't.'

'Yes, I *know* you know. Because he told you just how far I'd allowed him to get with me, didn't he?'

'All right, then, he told me!'

It was easy to see why they'd made her head prefect. She wouldn't need proof of who had skipped netball practice – she would just question the form one by one and goad them all into a full confession.

She was buttoning up her raincoat now in fast, angry jerks. 'And I suppose you give *him* progress reports now, do you,

201

telling him how far you've got? You know, Raymond, somebody warned me about Terry Liversedge boasting about his conquests, but I never dreamed you'd do it too.' She pulled her belt tight in a vicious, garrotting gesture. 'Now I wouldn't be surprised to hear you have a half-crown bet on who's got the furthest with Betty Parsons!'

The old fossil poking about in the cinder pile with the gargoyle dog at his heels was quite clearly listening to every word. For a reason unknown to me I wanted, as a wave of irritation swept over me, to impress on him that I was more than a match for Betty Parsons' withering scorn.

I said, regretting it even as the words came out of my mouth, 'Five bob, actually.'

Betty dropped, not threw, the shorthand notes into my lap – lightly, as if releasing feathers. She gave me the rueful smile that, on various faces and in various circumstances, I had come to recognise. But then the smile grew sweetly venomous as she said, 'Close the door when you leave, won't you? We don't want Bruno getting rusty – I might need her again.'

And she was gone, her long bare legs striding off across the cinders.

I lit the cigarette I had meant to light when all this had started. It began to pitter-patter with rain again, and the old fossil and his gargoyle dog scurried off like the rats they were seeking.

I sat in the back of an abandoned Morris Eight that a chick I had once known had fancifully said smelled of Bruno Flake, and which smelled now of Player's Airman. Aimlessly, I whistled a few bars of 'Souvenirs', even though it had never been 'our tune' with Betty. We had never needed one. '. . . There's nothing left for me . . .' I stopped whistling, realising that I had nothing to whistle about. I had been brushed off.

# 22

The days and hours and minutes to the Festival of Britain outing, which I had been on the verge of counting up in eager expectation, I now counted up in panic. Subject to a re-check with the kittens-in-a-basket calendar, I had less than eight weeks left – fifty-four days, to be precise – before I would have to be lying with a chick, any chick, in a conifer plantation in Richmond Park as described by Douglas from information supplied by Pauline's mother.

'Why don't you advertise?' suggested Douglas.

'Be serious.'

'I am serious.'

He probably was, too. It was only a few hours after Betty had walked out on me, and we were on The Parade where I was exchanging jackets with Terry Liversedge. Douglas – on his way to take Pauline to church in order, so he said, to oil the wheels by keeping in with her aborigine mother, the troglodyte vicar and the dodo verger – had joined us, wishing to borrow my seersucker jacket now that Terry Liversedge had finished with it, in return for the renewed loan of his leatherette American bomber-pilot's jacket which had become a particular favourite of mine.

The rain had stopped again but a stiff breeze had got up. It sucked up water from the puddles and blew film-thin, shimmering ripples across the empty Parade, which in the ghost-light of the fluorescent tubes in the windows of Moffat's Radio & Electrical, looked as forlorn as a seaside promenade out of season. Compounding the forlornness was the indigenous melancholy of Sunday evening, with the bleak sound of wireless sets behind the bay windows accentuating the ticking stillness; and adding to the melancholy was the private sadness that had weighed down on me ever since I had watched Betty walking away from me out of the car dump that was to have been our secret place.

Shivering, we stood in shirt sleeves outside the Chocolate Cabin, discarded macs tossed over the battery of *Yorkshire Post* and *Argus* placards, while I handed Terry Liversedge back his salmon-pink zoot jacket, he handed me my candy-striped seersucker jacket, I handed the seersucker jacket to Douglas, and he handed me his American bomber-pilot's jacket.

As we completed the transaction Douglas said, 'You still haven't told me why Betty Parsons has dropped out. If she's having trouble with her folks, I can get Pauline's mother to have a word with them and persuade them it's on the level.'

'Duggerlugs, it'd make no difference if you got Pope Pius the Twelfth to have a word with them – he's jacked her in,' reported Terry Liversedge with satisfaction. I had been in the course of telling him this as Douglas came out. It seemed to cheer him up. 'So what happened, youth? Did you find she was padlocked from the waist down?'

'Something like that,' I muttered, shamefaced.

'I could have warned you about that, Ray. I think she's frigid on the quiet, don't you?'

I gave him the minimal response of a noncommittal shrug. Then, to give Terry Liversedge something else to talk about, I said, trying to sound curt rather than ingratiating, 'While we're on the subject of you-know-what, you'll find that shorthand diatribe of yours in your inside pocket. I reckon I've looked after it long enough.'

'Looked after it till you know it off by heart, you mean. Thanks anyway, youth – I've been wanting to get my dawks on this again. Did I tell you I saw Rebecca Redlips a couple of days ago? She's moved to that secretarial college on Cloth Hall Lane.'

'How do you know?' I asked, not caring but glad to keep the conversation away from the subject of Betty.

'Because, old bean, old boy, he drools outside the main door every lunchtime, watching the little college chicks going in and out in their little gymslips,' drawled Douglas, admiring the fit of my seersucker jacket in the Post Office window.

The jibe seemed to hit home. At any rate, Terry Liversedge found it more politic to ignore it than to challenge it. 'The point is, youth, now I know where she is I can deliver her love letter. Touch wood, she could finish up at the Festival of Britain with us – legs wide open round the back of Battersea Fun Fair, eh?'

'You're not still going on about that, are you, Liversedge?'

Perhaps it was the way he had been talking about Betty, or perhaps the way Betty had talked about him, or perhaps that it was too cold to be standing out on the windswept Parade listening to schoolboy smut, but I was finding it increasingly easy to be irritated by Terry Liversedge.

'Seriously, Terry, I'd still like to know who you *are* taking,' nagged Douglas.

'Don't worry about me, youth – it's Watmough you should be worrying about,' said Terry Liversedge defensively. 'Ask him who *he's* taking.'

'I'm working on it,' I said.

As usual, when under embarrassing scrutiny, he had tried to switch the limelight on to me. But without knowing it Terry Liversedge was to solve my problem.

After we had parted company with Douglas I walked a little way with him, I towards Edith Close, he towards the terminus where he was catching the trolley-bus to his jazz concert.

'You don't really think I hang about outside that secretarial college?' pleaded Terry Liversedge, with a wheedling snigger.

I was not going to help him. 'I've no idea, Terry – it's all the same to me whether you do or not.'

'I'm not that hard up, kiddo. I'll tell you who I have seen lurking about there, though – Geoffrey Sissons. He meets a bird there.'

'With glasses? Wears a duffel-coat?'

'That's her – looks like something the cat's dragged in. I thought he was still going out with Doreen Theaker, though?'

'He is. He's two-timing her.'

'What is known as dipping his wick at both ends of the candle,' said Terry Liversedge with his accustomed crudeness. We had reached the corner of Edith Close. 'You're not going home, are you, Ray? Why don't you come and take in the Grippenshaw Magnolia Band at the Pack Horse – there's a lot of talent goes in there, you might get yourself fixed up.'

'I could be fixed up already,' I said.

I was ninety per cent certain that Geoffrey Sissons and Doreen Theaker would have gone to the Gainsborough. It was too wet and windy for sitting out on the porched bench outside the Cragside Crematorium where I happened to know they passed some of their evenings, and the pictures was their only real alternative. They would not have gone to the Gem, for the Gem was showing *Battleground* with Van Johnson, and Geoffrey Sissons, as well as being a Young Communist, was a pacifist and a conscientious objector who keenly looked forward to going to prison for refusing to do his National Service. That left the Gainsborough. *The Happiest Days Of Your Life* with Margaret Rutherford and Alastair Sim. They would be playing 'God Save The King' at around ten.

I went in and had my supper, dozed through the Grand Hotel Orchestra on the Light Programme, then came out again. First I went back to The Parade and tried the cigarette machine outside the Chocolate Cabin. As usual, it was empty. It was going to be a long wait and I wished now I had bought a fresh packet while there were shops still open. I had six cigarettes left. I would smoke one on the walk up to the Gainsborough, half of one at nine o'clock, the other half at half-past nine, another whole one when I saw them coming out and followed them, and one more while waiting for them to say good-night. That would leave two – one for me and one for Geoffrey Sissons.

I positioned myself on the Clock Ballroom side of the road from the Gainsborough, with my back to the fence of wooden hoardings surrounding the structure that was being completed behind the FESTIVAL OF BRITAIN 1951: SITE OF GRIPPENSHAW PAGEANT OF PROGRESS sign. From here I could look out across the wet tarmac and see both the front entrance and the side doors. The programme was continuous and I had no proof that Geoffrey Sissons and Doreen had gone in at the very start of the last performance, so if they had already seen part of the big film they might emerge any time between now and the end. The thin, mean drizzle was starting up again and I had left my mac at home, but I could not risk shifting from my vantage point in case they came out. I turned up the simulated fur collar of Douglas's American bomber-pilot's jacket, and waited. In twenty minutes I should be able to have half a cigarette.

Behind me the patchwork edifice of plywood and plastic panels that was to house the Pageant of Progress had begun to look something like a building. It had a roof on now, a huge drape of what looked like parachute silk stretched over a skeleton gable of girders, the idea being to create a marquee effect. By the time we set off for the Festival of Britain proper in London, the Pageant of Progress Pavilion's undercoat stripes of pink and white would be properly painted, the hoardings would have come down, and where I was standing now there would be chicks in red, white and blue uniforms selling tickets, souvenirs and programmes, and making dates with the youths who would add this to their list of Duck-walk and Monkey-walk meeting-places while ever the pageant lasted. A specimen uniform, draped on a Clough & Clough's dummy, was on display in the window of the temporary Pageant office in a vacant shop in Albert Street: white scarf-blouse with two buttons that would unfasten it to the waist after the scarf had been untied: blue linen suit with a close-fitting skirt featuring an unusual front panel unbuttoning from midriff to thigh; and red stockings, the first ever seen in Grippenshaw. We didn't know what adventures we might be in for this summer.

And all across Britain, according to a special Pathe Pictorial on the topic I had seen recently, other pavilions and marquees and temporary halls were going up, or existing ones were being made ready, and maypoles were being erected, for the subsidiary pageants, exhibitions, displays, fêtes and galas that would be the regional contribution to the Festival. And all across Britain, youths flocking to these events, that were said to distil the spirit of a new chapter in our island story, would be wondering what the School of Music chicks singing madrigals had on under their long dirndl skirts, what the School of Drama chicks representing Britannia and Boadicea had on under their flowing cheesecloth robes, and whether the chicks selling programmes wore red, white and blue suspenders under their red, white and blue uniforms.

Then there was the Festival of Britain itself, the main and central function: over and over again the breathless newsreel troglodytes had gabbled its statistics until it was possible to know them by heart. Six million pounds. Four million man-hours. A million bricks. Six thousand six hundred tons of cement. Four thousand tons of steel. Four hundred of aluminium. Fifteen thousand exhibits. Two thousand two hundred and eighty-five employees. One hundred and fifty thousand planted flowers. And all so that Douglas Beckett, Terry Liversedge and Raymond Watmough could lose their virginity in the conifer plantations of Richmond Park.

The extinguished two-inch stub of a Player's Airman in my mouth, I looked at my watch to see if it was time to relight it. Still only ten-past nine: either time was dragging or it had stopped. Lighting up, I stepped out from the shelter of the placard fence into the drizzle to see if I could make out the clock-hands set in the O of the Clock Ballroom neon sign, unilluminated when there was no dance on. Even as I peered through the wet murk, I heard the crash of the push-bars on the Gainsborough's side doors, and the faint strains of the National Anthem. It was nearly ten. I hurried across the road to the glistening tarmac forecourt of the Gainsborough, which abruptly ceased to glisten as its neon sign and floodlighting were snapped off. In the dark, lighting the fresh cigarette I was now entitled to from the long stub I had just belatedly got through in half a dozen long, grateful drags, I monitored the crowd trickling and then pouring out of the cinema. I judged that from whatever exit they left, Geoffrey Sissons and Doreen would cross the tarmac at just about this point if they were heading straight for Pearl Grove and not for the crematorium. In the rain, which had now taken such a hold that the leatherette of Douglas's bomber-pilot's jacket had begun to gleam like sealskin, it was inconceivable that Geoffrey Sissons wouldn't be taking her straight home. Besides, she had school tomorrow and wouldn't be allowed to stay out too late.

Just as the stream had subsided back to a trickle, and I had begun to wonder whether Geoffrey Sissons had overcome his pacifist scruples and taken her to the Gem, I saw them emerging from the furthermost set of side doors, clear evidence that they must have been sitting in the back rows. Doreen was buttoning up her raincoat, having previously buttoned up whatever was beneath it; Geoffrey Sissons was buckling the belt of his. Falling back among a straggle of fossils crossing the tarmac from the front entrance, I followed them.

The telephone box on the corner of Pearl Grove and Crag Park Avenue, discreetly set back in the high privet hedge of the end house, was lacking a light, like the one on the corner of Iris Crescent and Station Approach where Pauline Batty had advised Douglas that having kissed her at one end of the

Crescent did not disqualify him from kissing her at the other. It had certainly not been unlit in the days when I had been accustomed to saying good-night to Doreen on this selfsame spot. I suspected Geoffrey Sissons of removing the bulb.

I had still not wound up my watch and so didn't know how long they had been in the phone box, but it seemed a good half hour. I couldn't see what they were up to, for I dared not go near enough to be seen. I loitered around the corner of Crag Park Avenue from which I could see the top of the phone box across the privet. I should just be able to make out its door creaking open when at last Doreen was able to tear herself away from Geoffrey Sissons' octopus embrace. My last cigarette, apart from the two I was saving, was long finished. The drizzling rain trickled down my face and I could shake water off Douglas's bomber-pilot's jacket like a spaniel coming out of the boating-lake. Tomorrow, my squelching twill Dunlop bunjees would have a white tidemark where the rain had soaked in.

At last the squeak of the phone box door alerted me. There was another long pause while Doreen and Geoffrey Sissons accomplished their final interminable goodbye, then at last I heard their cries of 'Good-night' and the sound of her heels clacking at a run along Pearl Grove. In a moment Geoffrey Sissons, complacently running a comb through damp ruffled hair, turned the corner into Crag Park Avenue, heading away from me towards Parkview Gardens where he lived.

Walking briskly, hands plunged into my pockets as if hurrying home through the rain, I caught up with him.

'Good weather for ducks, eh, youth? How's it going?' I had decided on the Terry Liversedge mode of address and general swaggering manner of speech. It would efficiently mask any nervousness that might come over me, as well as showing Geoffrey Sissons that he was dealing with someone out of his class. I was, after all, his senior: he had not even left technical college yet.

'Can't grumble,' he said tersely. He made no pretence of being pleased to see me, not that I blamed him for that. There was little love lost between us. Whenever I saw him I wondered what favours Doreen Theaker had granted him that she hadn't granted me, and I had no doubt that he wondered the same.

'Wasn't that Doreen Theaker I just saw scooting down Pearl Grove?' I went on chattily.

'Who do you think it was – Minnie Mouse?'

'No, I thought it was Doreen, youth,' I said, enjoying the line I had decided to pursue. 'But I couldn't be sure because she wasn't wearing specs.'

'She doesn't wear specs.'

'Doesn't she? I could have sworn she'd started wearing them. Because don't you remember I once saw you meeting her outside the library, with a big pile of books under your arm? And she was wearing specs, I'm sure of it. And a duffel-coat.'

We had got to the corner of Parkview Gardens, where Geoffrey Sissons stopped and faced me in the drizzle.

'All right, Watmough. What do you want?'

'I don't want anything, youth. I'm just walking home, the same as you.'

'You don't live in this direction.'

'So I'm going the long way round – there's no law against it.' I had taken out my gunmetal cigarette-case. I pressed it open revealing my last two remaining Player's Airman under its yellow band of elastic. 'Have a fag.'

'I don't smoke.'

The possibility had not occurred to me. All youths smoked. It would be pleasant to have an unexpected cigarette in reserve but it did weaken my negotiating position.

'Pity about that, youth. I was going to ask you if you could use this ciggy case. Holds twenty. Feel it – real gunmetal. And this little shiny square is where you can get your initials engraved.'

It was fortunate that neither Douglas, Terry Liversedge nor I had ever had funds available for such a luxury during its various ownerships.

'It's not much good to me if I don't smoke, is it?'

'You could swop it for something.'

'Why should I buy something I don't want to swop for something I do want?'

The cigarette I was trying to light had stuck to my upper lip. As I pulled it away, I thought I might as well turn my wincing grimace into something approximating Humphrey Bogart's twisted smile.

210

'You wouldn't be buying it, kiddo. You'd be getting it given.'

Geoffrey Sissons' face twitched into the sardonic sneer I had seen on it at Youth Guild debates when he was launching upon one of his attacks on capitalist mill-owners.

'I know what your game is, Watmough. They don't call *me* Douglas Beckett, you know.' I looked suitably innocent. 'You think I don't know about you giving him an electric razor to take a certain bird off his hands, don't you?'

'Did she tell you about that, then?' I was quite gratified. It was always pleasant to hear that chicks had been talking about one.

'Yes, she did, and she's never forgotten it – the same as she's never forgotten you giving her that brush-off card. So your chances of getting back with Doreen Theaker are zero. Nix.'

I didn't take the same pessimistic view, if what he said was true and these things still rankled. A more positive interpretation was that Doreen was carrying a torch for me.

'That's for me to find out, youth. I'll tell you what I'll do – I'll chuck in my petrol lighter.'

'How many more times – I don't smoke!'

'Well start smoking!' I snapped in a gush of exasperation as a cold rivulet trickled under my collar and down my spine. It was all right for Geoffrey Sissons: his raincoat was buttoned to the throat. Then, in more conciliatory, even pleading tones: 'Look, Geoff – *you* know you're two-timing Doreen and I know you are. You don't want to go out with both of them.'

'That's for me to decide.'

I blew out smoke, trying for the Bogart effect again. 'Not necessarily. It might be for Doreen to decide.'

'Meaning you'd tell her.'

'Somebody might.'

'If somebody does, Watmough, you'll know about it.'

Geoffrey Sissons visibly pouted out his concave chest. I realised that it was only by this considerable effort that he had managed to look bigger than I remembered him when I had met him with Doreen at the Youth Guild Christmas social. But his clenched fists were still puny.

'I thought you were supposed to be a conchie, youth.'

'Yes, I am, and in case you'd forgotten I'm also a member of the Young Communists' League. So if you do go telling tales out of school, all you'll be letting Doreen Theaker know is that I sometimes have to meet the YCL treasurer on YCL business.'

'Don't give me that, Sissons!' But even to me it had the makings of a convincing explanation. In something of a panic I extended my wrist. 'All right, so you don't smoke, so you don't need a ciggy-case. This is a stainless steel waterproof Timex, fifteen jewels, luminous, chrome expanding strap, new last Christmas. It's yours.'

Geoffrey Sissons took one covetous, then scornful, glance at my watch.

'Ten-past nine? It's conked out, man!'

'I forgot to wind it up, that's all. Look, Geoff, I'm not even asking you to stop going out with her. Just give me the chance to ask her to go out with me, and let her make her own mind up. She can go out with both of us if that's what she wants. And if that's not communism, I don't know what is.'

He was wavering. He took hold of my extended wrist and turned it over to examine the clasp of the expanding metal strap.

'You'll have to offer me something more than a watch that goes on teacakes.'

I had won. 'I've got nothing else.'

'That jacket you're wearing. Is it real leather?'

'It's real leatherette, youth. Not only that, it's a genuine Yankee bomber-pilot's jacket. Flying jacket,' I amended, remembering Geoffrey Sissons' pacifist leanings.

'Give me that and the watch and she's all yours.'

'You're on.'

I had only a moment of misgiving. It wasn't what I was going to say to the aborigines to explain how I came to be arriving home in my shirtsleeves in the driving rain that concerned me, it was how I was going to break it to Douglas. As well as being my favourite jacket, it was his too. I supposed I would have to let him keep my seersucker, now.

# 23

'You've changed.'

'So have you.'

It didn't matter who said which to whom. We had both changed. She was more mature. I, more desperate.

My state of mind had not been helped by the lapse of over a month before I was able to make contact with Doreen Theaker, leaving a bare three weeks in hand before she and I, or I and somebody, were supposed to be rolling down the Great North Road in a streamlined Moult & Sumpter coach.

In the first place, the disastrous Sunday that had begun in the car dump with Betty and culminated in my running home through the rain minus Douglas's jacket, had left me with a heavy cold which had developed into flu. It was after Easter when I was at last allowed to get up, after a prolonged and inexplicable fever which the baffled troglodyte doctor could not account for. Evidently I could not have been crying out 'Festival of Britain!' in my sweat-drenched sleep.

It transpired that Doreen, like Betty Parsons a school-leaver that term, had gone with her aborigine parents for a holiday in Morecambe before starting work. Moult & Sumpter ran weekend excursions to Morecambe and I thought seriously about cadging a lift on one of the firm's coaches, if necessary travelling as luggage. I could haunt the sands until I found her alone, then pour out the confession that when languishing close to death with a temperature of a hundred and four I had come to realise that I could not live without her.

By the time Doreen returned I had almost persuaded myself that this was, indeed, the case. Thinking about her, I remembered with extraordinary vividness how she looked, talked and smelled, how we had huddled all day by the electricity sub-station on the edge of Throstle Moor, hoping for the rain to stop, and how she had asked me, upon receipt of her brush-off card, if it was something she hadn't done and whether it would have made a difference had it not rained that day.

I had learned from Geoffrey Sissons, in exchange for a small contribution towards the repair of my watch which it seemed had been overwound, that she had taken a job in the cashier's department at Clough & Clough's. I wasted several more precious days trying to get in touch with her there.

Waiting for her outside the store at six o'clock, I discovered after two days, was hopeless. Clough & Clough's had a good dozen exits, public and private, and the staff came swarming out of them all. It was like keeping watch on a beehive. After another fruitless evening spent hanging around Pearl Grove, it then occurred to me that she must go to work on the No 17 trolley-bus, which stopped directly outside Clough & Clough's. One more day slipped by after I had stood forlornly at the trolley-bus terminus until the hands in the O of the Clock Ballroom neon sign reached nine, subsequently arriving for work half an hour late. Then, on the Friday morning, having realised in a flash of inspiration that although Clough & Clough's did not open its multitudinous doors until nine, the staff would be required to get there earlier, I reached the trolley-bus terminus at eight and was rewarded by the sight of her hurrying for the twenty-past No 17.

She carried the light raincoat that four weeks hence would be spread out on the grass in a Richmond Park conifer plantation, and wore a Clough & Clough Junior Miss tailored grey flannel suit, close-fitting but with side pleats to allow easy access of a hand upon her knee. Her stockings, I saw as I followed her up the stairs to the top deck, were fully-fashioned, straight seams tapering down to the first proper high heels I had ever seen her in. She had grown up considerably even since I had danced with her at the Youth Guild Christmas social. She smelled of the same scent she had worn then, the one that put me in mind of musk. She was my type.

It was a twenty-minute journey at most to Clough & Clough's and I was obliged to use up a good five of them in smalltalk, asking about her holiday and how she was enjoying work and so on. The time was not wasted, though, for it gave me the chance to put myself at ease with Doreen and get my breath back to normal. It would be an advantage, when I got round to asking her for a date, for her to be able to understand what I was saying.

Having prepared the way by insisting on paying her fare, I said nonchalantly, as the trolley-bus hissed down the Leeds Road past the stone terraces near the recreation ground where I used to sit on the tethered seesaw with Janet Gill: 'Well, now you're a working girl, Janeen, we must have lunch sometime.'

It was a novel and, I thought, an audacious approach, showing that I had become possessed of a certain urbane flair since the old days. No one ever took chicks to lunch. It was a cardinal rule laid down by Douglas and I had never questioned it. Yet why not? The impossibility of making a pass either during lunch or in the crowded town centre after it – that was the reason for the embargo – was all the evidence that could possibly be needed of being interested in the chick's mind as well as her body, of wishing to pander to the desire that all chicks seemed to have of being liked for themselves. Besides, time was short, and I would be able to broach the Festival of Britain question more easily over lunch than during an evening at the Gainsborough, the only other option available. I wondered if I dared take her to the Kismet Café, provided we steered well clear of Madge's tables.

'We have a very nice canteen, actually,' said Doreen, to my intense irritation.

'But you don't *have* to eat there, do you?' I asked plaintively, repressing an impulse to snap back that she was missing the whole fizzing point.

'We don't have to, no, but it's so cheap. It seems silly to go out to a café when they give you a proper hot lunch for sevenpence.'

'Oh, well, it was just a thought.'

I blamed Douglas. Chicks were so conditioned to not being invited to lunch that they were incapable of recognising a sophisticated gesture when they saw one.

The terraces were giving way to warehouses and mills. The whiff of blood from the corporation abattoir, as alarming to my nostrils as to the pigs that were slaughtered there, told me that we were getting dangerously near the town centre.

I tried a different tack altogether. 'That's a nice costume you're wearing, Doreen. Did you get it at Clough & Clough's?'

'I'd be silly not to, wouldn't I?'

'Why, do they give you a discount?'

'Yes – a third off.'

'*Infirmary next stop!*' the ticket-punching dodo sang from his platform. I had to work fast.

'I don't suppose you'd like to get me one of those American zip-up sports shirts they've got in the Cross Street windows, would you?'

Doreen gave an eye-rolling sigh of comic impatience that was not very encouraging, given that we were only two stops from Clough & Clough's by now. 'You men! The minute you hear I'm entitled to a staff discount, it's can you get me this, can you get me that! It seems to be all you ever think about – clothes! You're all the same!'

All, I speculated, would include Geoffrey Sissons, but who else?

Putting the question aside as an irrelevance, I started to hatch out a gallantry on the lines of, on the first rough draft, 'At least it makes a change from what girls usually tell us is usually all it's ever we think about.' I abandoned the effort on a dodo cry of '*Corn Exchange.*'

'Your stop, isn't it?' said Doreen. I was flattered that she remembered where I worked.

'It's all right, I'm early – I can walk back through the arcades. So what do you usually say when all these people ask you to get them things?'

'I say, "What's in it for me?" ' Although this was only a joke, she was not the Doreen I had once known. The hardness in her voice was a flippant hardness, but it was there all the same.

Taking my bantering tone from her, I said, 'I'll tell you that when you deliver the goods.'

'*Cross Street next stop.*'

As Doreen shuffled her raincoat over her arm and hoisted up the strap of her shoulder-bag, I gabbled, 'Any colour, preferably green, neck size fourteen. I'll pay you when I see you – six o'clock outside the library tomorrow night.'

'I haven't said I'll get it yet.'

'No, but you will though, won't you?'

'*Cross Street. Clough & Clough's.*'

'You forget some of us have to work on Saturday afternoons. I'll meet you at half-seven.'

Although I was there an hour early I was curiously

unexpectant, and had been ever since, in a surprisingly short time, the initial elation of making a date with Doreen Theaker had worn off. The scents of promise that always accumulated around the library's green rubberised boulevards were muted. I lit a cigarette and inhaled the smoke, but it lacked the sharp taste that went with first dates on spring Saturday evenings. I had known more excitement waiting to barter socks and ties with Douglas and Terry Liversedge.

To pass the time, I meandered around the outside of the library building, following the Monkey-walk past the French-windowed reading-room where young High School chicks could be seen pretending to read *Britannia and Eve* and *Vanity Fair* at the yellow polished tables, while the blazered youths whose prey they were let them stew while pretending to read *Punch* and *Blackwood's*, just as Doreen Theaker and I and scores and hundreds had done over the years, although in our case I had let her stew for so long that the bell had rung for closing-time, and it had subsequently cost me a second-hand electric razor to make her acquaintance. Tonight, though, not even the Monkey-walk raised my spirits. The sight of Ralph Driver stamping library books certainly didn't. I had heard that Betty Parsons was going out with him again.

When I came around the corner, back to the brick steps of the library, Doreen was waiting for me, in the same tailored suit she had worn the day before. She was certainly not putting herself out to impress or stimulate me with her wardrobe, although I supposed the suit would be a kind of office uniform and she would not have had time to change. I saw that she had got the sports shirt, which she was hugging, in its green Clough & Clough's paper bag, to her chest. And it was then that the Saturday evening scents came into full bloom as I remembered Betty Parsons standing on just the same spot, holding her Victor Sylvester records in their paper sleeves in just the same way, and saying that although she could not stay out she was not in so much of a hurry as all that.

'It's all right, I know I'm early,' was the bald way Doreen chose to greet me, as if we had been going out four or five times a week for the last year. 'Only our clock's fast at home and I haven't a watch.'

I didn't expect shyness, since we knew one another of old, but I did feel entitled to a certain demureness.

217

'Neither have I,' I said distantly.

She thrust the package into my hands. 'I hope it's all right – I can change it if it isn't.' It was a good thing, I reflected, studying the receipt, that she didn't know the full extent to which our resuming relationship had depended on various items of clothing passing from hand to hand.

I drew a ten-shilling note out of my shot-silk treasury-note-case and took a perfunctory look at the shirt. Preferably green, I had said, and she had got blue. Still, she had turned up.

'Thanks a lot. Right – where shall we go?'

Doreen, burrowing the ten-shilling note into her purse so that her gaze was averted, now provided a little of the demureness element that had earlier been missing.

'Am I supposed to be going out with you again, then?'

'That's the general idea.'

'Just so long as we know.'

'Always assuming,' I said lightly, 'that Geoffrey Sissons has no say in the matter.' He had assured me that he had kept his side of the bargain, using the method of getting a third party to tell Doreen that he was two-timing her and then allowing her to walk out on him, but there was no harm in cross-checking.

'I haven't been out with Geoffrey Sissons for ages.'

It was not quite the confirmation I was looking for, but aside from the nagging possibility that I had parted with my Timex watch and Douglas's bomber-pilot's jacket unnecessarily, I was not really interested in further details.

'Shall we go across to the Gainsborough, then? We should just about catch the big picture.'

'If we can get in.'

It seemed a listless, lackadaisical way of taking up again where we had so painfully left off in Crag Park all those months ago. I couldn't make Doreen out. Although, after fate had thrown us together again insofar as she knew anything about it, we had both directly acknowledged that we were going out together again and the way was now formally open for sorties of first an above-the-waist and then a below-the-waist nature, it was as if she were engaged in nothing more stimulating than signing up for one more season at the tennis club. Douglas contended that chicks who were outwardly cool and detached often had hidden and fiery depths, but I was not sure that this held good in the case of chicks who appeared to have acquired their coolness and detachment on a shopping spree along with their first grown-up hair-do and proper high heels.

As we walked across to the Gainsborough I said, 'By the way, I don't want to rush you into anything, Doreen, but as you've only just joined Clough & Clough's, do you think they'd let you take off the Friday and Saturday before Whitsun, and the Tuesday after it?'

'Well, I do know I'm entitled to a week's holiday in my first year, and they don't seem to mind staff taking split weeks. Why, where are you taking me?' This was the comic hardness again, as if Doreen Theaker from Pearl Grove were trying to sound like Audrey Marsh from Cemetery Road.

'What would you say to the Festival of Britain?' I asked with impressive casualness.

'In London? Oh, yes, I can see my mum and dad agreeing to that – I don't think. It took me all my time to persuade them to let me go to the school camp at Grange-over-Sands last August.'

'If they'll let you go to a school camp they can't object to a church outing with a pack of old women. And me, of course, but you don't need to mention that. You'll be staying with two other girls at Douglas Beckett's girl-friend's auntie's in Hounslow, so you can't come to any harm.'

'Not much point in going, then.' That was another almost millgirlish crack that Doreen wouldn't have made a year ago.

'You know what I mean.'

'I'll certainly try, Ray. They can only say no.' And again she sounded no more thrilled than if I had invited her to a Whit Sunday swim at Cragside Lido.

'If they do say no, let me know as soon as you possibly can because I've got to make the arrangements.' Fortunately, Doreen missed the ambiguity of this request.

We got into the Gainsborough during the trailer and were settled in the last two remaining seats at the end of an aisle as the lights went up. For the first time that evening I felt an upsurge of excitement as, drawing my sports shirt out of its bag to have a proper look at it, I was distracted by the sight of Doreen's crossed legs where the side pleat of her tailored skirt had fallen away to expose the tempting sheen of a nylon-sheathed knee. I ran my eye appreciatively from knee to ankle and back again. In a dark age of ballerina-length dresses, such a feast was a rarity.

'Is something wrong?' asked Doreen.

'I was admiring you legs, to sell you the truth,' I said recklessly, and indistinctly.

'Oh, I thought for a minute I had a ladder,' said Doreen, as if admiration of her legs was a matter of everyday comment, and casually she flapped the pleat back across her knee as the lights went down.

I had thought, as we took our seats, that in the subdued atmosphere in which our reunion was being conducted, putting an arm around Doreen would be a mere gesture, an expected courtesy, and there would be no point in making any advances of a first-base nature. But my arousal at the sight of her knee had been only partly dowsed by her matter-of-fact response. Before the credit titles of a film which appeared to be called *Something Boulevard* with Gloria Swanson were off the screen, I had got my arm around her shoulder, then around her waist, had manipulated her head towards my chest with only the merest of tugs, and was nipping out my cigarette preparatory to putting my free hand on her neck. If she was going to object, it was at this stage that she would be doing it, since a hand on the neck could not be construed as going in any direction except that of first base. But she did not object. Nor, however, did she fondle the hand for a moment as Betty Parsons would have done, as if to wish it bon voyage.

Doreen Theaker's tailored suit was also tailor-made for above-the-waist activity, and the deep V-necked blouse beneath her jacket offered no obstacle. Within moments her right breast was cupped in my hand.

I had a sensation, as I listlessly squeezed and caressed it, with none of the shivering, arm-clutching response I had been accustomed to from Betty Parsons, not only of anti-climax but of déjà vu. Then, as I ran an abstracted finger back and forth over a pulpy-feeling area that was presumably her nipple, I remembered. Audrey Marsh, on Boxing Night in the back row of the Paramount, when she had proved to be asleep.

Doreen's rigidly permed hair against my upper chest and neck was pressing my head back in such a way that it was impossible to peer round at her face to confirm that her eyes were open. Nor did I like to ask. There was only one way to

220

test her consciousness and that was to see what happened if I tried to upgrade my score, on a Terry Liversedge reading, from one breast once to both breasts once. I slid my hand down over the cleft of her bosom until it met the resistance of the arm-rest against which she was lying. At this point Doreen shifted slightly so that my journey could continue unimpeded.

'Thank you,' I whispered oafishly.

After repeating the squeezing, caressing and stroking exercises with the same lack of drive and purpose, and receiving the same lack of acknowledgment, I began to realise despondently that I could become extremely bored with Doreen Theaker's breasts before what threatened to be a very long film was over.

Contemplating alternative diversions, and rejecting a second-base attempt as being out of the question in our exposed situation at the end of the aisle, I brought to mind another similarity with the Audrey Marsh evening. I had not yet kissed her. But where failure to kiss Audrey Marsh had excusably arisen out of too-precipitous manoevring, this was nothing more nor less than forgetfulness.

I was quite shocked at myself. Getting to first base without going through the preliminaries seemed a discourtesy, a neglect of the social obligations. I was uncomfortably reminded of the joke which had gone round the Youth Guild and the College of Commerce in many variations, defining a gentleman as one who took his hat off while on the job. But when I tried to extract my hand from Doreen's blouse with the object of tilting back her head to repair the omission, I realised that it was firmly pinned against the arm-rest where she had resumed her position after allowing me access to her left breast.

'Are you all right?' I murmured.

'Yes, thank you.'

'I'm not. I've got pins and needles.'

Without complaint or comment she sat up and shrugged away the arm that was around her, not with any sense of repulsion or of having taken offence at my lack of grace, but rather as if we were having a break for refreshments, which in effect we were. Non-too-surreptitiously shaking the life back into my tingling hand I smoked a cigarette while Doreen ate a bar of Motoring Chocolate I had bought for her in the kiosk.

Then I put my arm around her again and, after a suitable interval, kissed her. I hoped it was because her tongue was coated with chocolate that she was holding back, but I was afraid such wasn't the case. I could not say she was not returning my kiss, only that she was not returning it with interest. To enliven the proceedings I slipped a hand inside her blouse again. As, once again, I closed on the grapefruit-like dead weight of Doreen's right breast, I was seized by a kind of desperate inertia. Opening one eye and squinting to focus on the square green glass clock over the emergency exit to one side of the screen, I saw that *Something Boulevard* still had over an hour to run.

On the whole I was glad, when I had walked Doreen back to Pearl Grove in arm-in-arm silence, that she did not invite me into the darkened telephone box. She probably considered that I had had my ration for the evening. All the same, I did feel the need for some further communication between us before I left her. I had a sense of unease that I could not define. The impropriety of not having kissed her before getting to first base came into it somewhere, I knew that. I hoped she could help.

I said, after a desultory exchange of views on Gloria Swanson had petered out like a sputtering match, 'Doreen. I sincerely hope you haven't got the impression I've become a fast worker since last time we were out together.'

'Become one? I thought you always were one.' It was the Audrey Marsh-type wisecrack again. Tinged with bitterness, it sounded.

'I mean I didn't set out with the intention of making a play at you tonight. It just happened that way.'

'I've no complaints if you haven't.'

She was so unlike the Doreen I'd known, so unlike anyone I'd known, so disinterested, or affecting to sound disinterested, that I was baffled. On the defensive, I nearly said, 'You don't think I'm cheap, do you?' but recalled just in time that that was the kind of thing she ought to be saying, if anyone should. I said instead, fiddling with the sports shirt she had got me in its crumpled bag, 'It was only because I'd been missing you, Doreen. I mean that I worked so fast.'

'That's all right. Still, you won't have to miss me any longer now, will you?'

It could have sounded as Betty Parsons would have said it. Instead it sounded flat and resigned – almost, I would have imagined, like one of the beautiful prostitutes in the lounge of the Hotel Metropole saying the lines expected of her.

Perhaps Geoffrey Sissons, preaching and no doubt practising free love along with his pacifism and Communism, was to blame for this.

'Doreen, all I'm trying to say in a roundabout way is that I don't want you to do anything you don't want to do.'

'Tell me that when you're walking away,' said Doreen with what seemed to me a sadness that ought to have been outside her range.

'I'm not walking away.'

'You did before. So did Geoffrey Sissons, in case it's not all over Crag Park.'

Twenty-five years on, visiting Grippenshaw and returning to old haunts, I saw Doreen coming out of the windowless blue-brick supermarket that now sprawls over where the Pageant of Progress Pavilion and the old Clock Ballroom used to be. She had been plumply shopping for her grown-up family. She didn't recognise me and we didn't speak. She looked bovinely contented: the rounded, comfortable well-being of one who never asked for much but to whom nothing very unpleasant ever happened in consequence. But her smart if matronly grey flannel coat reminded me of the tailored grey suit she had worn this night when we stood, not touching, outside the darkened telephone box when we should have been inside it, kissing. And watching her then I could smell her musk scent and the evening privet, its sweetness brought out by little buds of rain. But here and now I could not smell it at all, and in the distorting light of the street lamp her tailored suit had changed colour, so that it looked like a school uniform. She looked young, waif-like and vulnerable.

Unexpectedly she threw, or rather placed, her arms around my shoulders, clasping her hands behind my neck.

'There's no need to look so solemn about it, Ray, you know. If I can make *you* happy, it makes *me* happy.'

'Does it?'

'Of course it does.'

I kissed her then, as I was expected to. This time she tried her best to put warmth into it, but succeeded only in a bruising pressure of mouth against mouth. I thought, relevantly, of Betty Parsons' darting tongue.

'Shall we go out tomorrow, Doreen?'

'Why not? Afternoon or evening?'

'I thought afternoon. We could get a bus up to Throstle Moor if it's fine.'

Arms still around my neck, Doreen Theaker attempted arch knowingness: 'Oh, yes. We have some unfinished business, don't we?'

Early the next Thursday evening, when I met Douglas and Terry Liversedge for half an hour in the matter of our Festival of Britain outing, my voice was far less shaky with triumph than anticipated when I announced, 'Oh, by the way, sorry to spring this on you the day before payday, chaps, but you both owe me five bob.'

# 24

This was in the Lyons' teashop fronting Sheepgate, which we had taken up as a low-budget rendezvous since Terry Liversedge's discovery that by nipping in through the side entrance in Pack Horse Passage you could avoid having to buy anything. The cafeteria was L-shaped, so that if you chose a cup-littered table out of sight of the troglodyte manageress at her chromium battery of urns and hot-plates, you could sit there until closing-time if you wished, like the near-down-and-out fossils and dodo newsvendors who sat muttering to themselves and stacking up piles of pennies.

The meeting had been called by Douglas, who seemed to need constant reassurance of our serious intent regarding the Festival of Britain outing. Terry Liversedge had yet to pay his contribution, although he seemed to have pretty well decided that his choice of companion would be the chick identified only as 'that red-headed bint at work'. He had never told us her name and I for one had entertained doubts as to her existence, but Douglas had seen the pair of them going into the Pack Horse one evening. He reported that the red-headed bint was a lot older than Terry Liversedge, about twenty in fact, and that she was rouged to the eyebrows, wore net stockings and looked like a whore. But at least there was evidence that he was going steady again. I was relieved, for Terry Liversedge's sake, that he had not lost his touch.

As far as I was concerned, Douglas had no cause for complaint. I had already got a firm commitment from Doreen Theaker, whose task in winning parental approval had been made considerably easier by her aborigine mother having read a glowing preview of the outing in the parish magazine. That would flatter Douglas: he had written the paragraph himself.

I had also done all that was required of me at Moult & Sumpter's. I had procured for Douglas an itinerary, an invoice ('In Account With St Chad's Church Festival of Britain Cttee') for the balance of the fossils' dues, and a batch of enticing Festival brochures to distribute among any last-minute fainthearts among his flock. All was running smoothly. There were fifteen days to go.

'So if you give the five bob you owe me to Douglas, Terry,' I continued in the gratifyingly stunned silence that went some way towards kindling the smug glow that had so far been lacking, 'and you, Douglas, add it to the five bob you owe me yourself, that's ten bob you can knock off what I've got to pay you for Doreen's ticket. And you can take the rest out of what you owe me for that camera.'

The elaborate personal transactions by which I was now having to float my Festival expenses, the weeks having somehow slipped by without my adding appreciably to my savings, embraced a Coronet Rapide folding camera in canvas case, as new, from the same source as the second-hand Remington razor for which Douglas had once traded Doreen Theaker. He had conceived an equally consuming passion for the camera and had offered me two pounds for it.

'Yes,' said Douglas weightily. Elbows resting on the Formica table, he gazed abstractedly at the congealed plates of the table's previous occupants. His mental calculations, unusually for him, seemed to be giving him trouble.

Meanwhile, Terry Liversedge's eyes bulged in a prolonged, histrionic stare that was meant to convey the extremes of incredulity at my news of having got to second base with Doreen Theaker.

'Yes,' said Douglas again. 'There's just one snag, old bean, old boy, old fruit. Well, two snags really. You see, if you really want to insist on honouring that bet, I don't owe *you* five bob – you owe *me* five bob. Added to which, I'm afraid I have to give you back word on the camera, for the very simple reason that as things turn out I can't afford it.'

The technicalities of who had got to second base first could wait. What most concerned me was the two pounds I had been banking upon raising on my camera. My budget depended on it.

'But you reckoned you were going to make a profit on it, taking souvenir snaps of the coach trip.'

'So I should have done, Raymondo – if I were going on the coach trip.'

My gaping expression must have looked as asinine to Douglas as Terry Liversedge's unbroken disbelieving stare looked to me.

'What – you mean it's off?'

'Au contraire, mon brave. Fret not. Everything proceeds as normal. Pauline phoned up her Auntie May in Hounslow last night, and she's very kindly confirmed that as she can't get to the wedding because of the old lady being bedridden, you two and Doreen and Terry's red-headed bint are still welcome to stay with her if you don't mind paying a pound each for your board and –'

'*What stinking wedding?*' The question, angrily bemused, came from Terry Liversedge. I was so stunned I hadn't grasped that a wedding had been mentioned.

Douglas, as always when he had had to wriggle his way out of a tight corner, while perhaps leaving others in it, was looking apologetically, perspiringly, relieved. It was, I judged, with authentic rather than affected offhandedness that he said:

'Mine, actually, mon capitaine.'

'Bollocks, youth! You – getting married? You never bloody are!'

'I bloody am, you know.'

Finding voice of a sort, I squeaked in stupefaction: 'To Pauline?'

'Natch. On Whit Monday as ever was – which unfortunately clashes with the Festival jaunt. The difficulty is that for what are delicately known as obvious reasons, ahem ahem' – here Douglas gave vent to a chortling cough – 'we want to get married as soon as poss, and that's the first available date after the banns have been read. The first reading's this Sunday, by the way – I don't suppose you'd like to come, Raymondo?'

'No thanks,' I said, dazed.

'Well I'll be knackered!' said Terry Liversedge. We exchanged a version of our Laurel and Hardy look, expressing pitying incredulity.

'Oh, well if that's your only comment . . .' said Douglas, pretending to look injured. Terry Liversedge, genuinely, looked blank.

'I think we're supposed to congratulate him, Terry,' I said. 'Many congrats, Douglas.'

'Oh, I see. Many congrats, Duggerlugs.'

'That's better. Sorry you'll miss the beanfeast, mes amis,

but at least it'll save you falling out over who's to be best man. Never mind – I'll think of you both shafting yourself rotten in Richmond Park.'

Terry Liversedge and I again exchanged looks, semaphoring that we were on delicate ground here. The occasion demanded a reciprocation of Douglas's good wishes, but instinctive etiquette told us that in his new circumstances it would be inappropriate to echo their robustness.

'We'll be thinking of you too,' I said, with the kind of wooden courtesy normally reserved for aborigines. 'Are you going on honeymoon?'

'No spondulicks, Raymondo. Besides which we've got to save up towards getting a flat of our own. We don't want to live with Pauline's mother all our lives – for one thing, the bedroom walls are very thin, so my future bride assures me.'

Douglas's swarthy countenance, beetle brows, and the thick reading glasses he now wore all the time had always made him look far older than his years. Now, however, as he tossed off the words 'so my future bride assures me' with self-conscious glibness, he seemed absurdly, preposterously young, like a grave-faced child absorbed in a game of soldiers when he thinks no one is looking. Even his moustache, which had now grown to tolerable proportions, suddenly looked glued on.

Or so it seemed to me. The phrase exercising Terry Liversedge, on the other hand, was 'thin bedroom walls'. He seized on it as licence to raise, in a suitably roundabout way, the point of information that had been exercising us both after the initial shock of Douglas's announcement.

'You kept fizzing quiet about all this, didn't you, youth?'

'Well, it was all a bit sudden, you know, mon capitaine.'

'*You* know what I'm talking about. So you've got the key to the crypt, then?'

'Oh, I see. Yes, it has come into my possession.' Douglas, perhaps forgetting that the debris of plates and cups and saucers in front of us was not our own, abstractedly chiselled a cold bean off a crust of toast with his thumb nail and popped it into his mouth like a cocktail snack.

Terry Liversedge fell reluctantly silent, but I knew the questions that were swirling about in his mind. They were the same as were swirling about in mine. Two years ago we had

228

acquired, from a dustbin outside the rubber goods shop in Aire Bridge Passage, an imperfect copy of a little book called *The Red Light* whose contents we had devoured and learned by rote before dropping it into the river. Although we had mastered the mysteries of foreplay, contraception, climax, anxiety, premature ejaculation, frigidity, hymens, vulvas, Vaseline and blood, it was all theory. Douglas was now in a position to confirm or correct everything we knew from the standpoint of practical experience. But already there was an inhibiting gulf between us.

'How long have you had it?' I asked with something like timidity.

'The crypt key? Oh, quite a while, actually.'

'You never mentioned it.'

'Didn't I? Oh, I do apologise, old bean, old boy.' Douglas was unusually withering in his sarcasm. 'Very remiss of me, I'm sure – I should have sent you a postcard.'

'We did have a bet.'

'Which as I've pointed out, mon brave, you've lost.'

'Yes – he's stolen your thunder there, youth!' brayed Terry Liversedge. 'Poor Ray! He gets to second base with Doreen Theaker, or so he cracks on, and nobody wants to hear about it!'

As to that, I was very relieved that they didn't. 'I still think you could have told us,' I said to Douglas, diffidently persistent. 'You wouldn't have had to go into all the sordid details.'

'They're not sordid,' said Douglas lightly, gnawing with thick-lipped delicacy at a piece of bacon rind he had prised off a congealed plate. 'Also, I don't think Pauline would have liked it.'

From Terry Liversedge's astonished expression I was sure he was about to explode, 'What the naffing hell has it got to do with her?' Douglas was evidently of the same impression, for throwing down his piece of bacon rind he turned on Terry Liversedge with a kind of embarrassed ferociousness. 'Look, Liversedge! And you too, Watmough, while we're about it. I'm very sorry if it offends you in any way, but I do happen to be in fizzing love with the girl. All right? And if you don't like it you can stick it!'

Scowling, Douglas turned his close attention back to the

229

litter of discarded plates. Probably more to avoid our eyes after this outburst than because even he had any real appetite for it, he dunked a crust of toast in a smear of petrified egg-yolk and proceeded to nibble it with epicurean concentration.

He need not have put himself to the ordeal, for we were avoiding Douglas's gaze, as well as one another's, as much as he was avoiding ours. Love was a taboo subject in our country. It was as an open discussion of cancer would have been among the aborigines, troglodytes and dodoes. Some of us had had a glancing acquaintanceship with love – I thought I probably had, with Betty Parsons – and some of us had properly loved or still did love, deeply love as distinct from have a crush on, go a bundle on, carry a torch for, think a lot about or even be very fond of, but it was a painful and private thing, not to be admitted or talked about.

After a suitable pause to neutralise the effect of Douglas's uncalled-for confession, Terry Liversedge said, 'Even so, youth. Married at seventeen, what? I mean to say!'

'What's wrong with being married at seventeen?'

'Well . . .' said Terry Liversedge lamely. 'I mean to say, think what you'll be missing.'

'But I shan't be missing it, mon capitaine, I'll be getting it,' Douglas pointed out with malicious logic. 'As I told the old man when he was binding on about how I'd made my bed and would have to lie on it – that's precisely what I intend to do.'

'You never said that, Douglas!'

'I bet he did, youth!'

'In any case,' said Douglas, with a greasy-lipped smirk, either of recollection of the riposte to his aborigine father or of pleasure at our admiration for his audacity, 'it might as well be now as later. We intended to get married anyway as soon as I'd done my National Service. As it turns out, I'll come back to civvy street an old married man, and if I go back to the Grippenshaw Permanent they'll have no option but to grant me a staff mortgage. Which means we'll be setting up house while you lot are still scratching about in furnished rooms.'

'He's got it all worked out, hasn't he, Terry?'

'He always has, youth.'

'I think,' said Douglas, his spectacles flashing like headlights from Terry Liversedge to me in pleased acknowledgment, 'that's what persuaded Pauline's mother to give her permission.'

Douglas never failed to astonish me. It had not occurred to me, even after he had gone on about loving Pauline and how they had meant to get married in due course anyway, that the wedding hadn't been forced upon them by the aborigines.

Nor to Terry Liversedge. 'So it's not what you might call a shotgun wedding, Douglas?'

'Good gracious, no, old bean, old boy,' said Douglas, a touch patronisingly. 'As I said, the old man insisted on my doing the honourable thing et cetera et cetera, but Pauline's mother wouldn't hear of it at first. She was all for having the baby adopted and me never darkening her doorstep again. Still, we talked her round in the end. She's quite looking forward to being a grandmother now.'

'I bet she flaming is,' said Terry Liversedge, pushing back his chair. 'If you'd told her you were having Siamese twins, the pair of you, she'd be knitting four-legged fizzing romper-suits by now. I'll tell you what, youth – although I suppose I shouldn't call you youth now you're nearly a daddy: this calls for a celebration. Skint or not, I'm going to treat us all to a coffee – so you can stop chewing that bacon-rind and move to a clean table.'

Sally Beckett, born December 1951, is a beautiful young woman now, a publicist for a television company, living in London. I have lunch with her occasionally in the role of a useful old friend of her father's who can get her cheap air tickets and last-minute villa holidays. She looks very much like Pauline, with the same jet-black hair, yearning look and full lips. She grew up in Grippenshaw, at various addresses all in the Crag Park area, and went to the Girls' High School, although by then it was called something else. She knew, because I asked her, the Royal Coronation branch library, the Gainsborough before it became a furniture warehouse, The Parade where her aborigine grandfather kept the Chocolate Cabin, St Chad's church where her mother and father met and the lych-gate where they had told her they had done their courting, and Crag Park itself. She told me about Sunday afternoon walks around the boating lake, the boys walking clockwise, the girls anti-clockwise. The Duck-walk, it was called, she said.

'Can you remember what it smelled like?' I asked.

'That's easy. Rhododendrons and cut grass. Even in winter.'

'What about the Monkey-walk? How did that smell?'

'No, I don't remember the Monkey-walk. I remember the library reading-room, though, where we used to go to get picked up. That smelled of lavender polish.'

'Does it all seem like another country now, Sally?'

'Oh, it *was* another country. My dear man, it was another world.'

While Terry Liversedge fetched the coffees, Douglas and I moved as bidden to a clean table, bumping past other tables where the demented-looking fossils nursed their cold cups of tea, spoke to thin air, and fiddled with their carrier bags of rubbish. As we sat down I thought Douglas was grinning and was about to warn him against laughing at the fossils, some of whom could turn ugly when mocked. Then I realised that it was not really a grin at all, more of a diffused radiance really. His swarthy face was alight with what I could only suppose was happiness.

'So instead of you owing me five bob,' I said awkwardly, for want of anything else to say, 'I owe you five bob.'

'You'll need that for tube fares, Raymondo,' said Douglas, tugging an oblong, concertinaed document from his pocket and pushing it across the newly-swabbed Formica table. 'This belongs to my future mother-in-law, by the way, so let me have it back in due course, won't you?'

It was an Ordnance Survey map of Richmond Park, showing its various gates, woods, walks and conifer plantations in the scale of ten inches to one mile.

# 25

It was when the three of us met on the Aire Bridge on the sunny, May-warming Saturday morning before the Festival of Britain outing that, as soon as I saw him, I knew for sure that Terry Liversedge was dropping out.

We had all been on our various errands about the town – Terry Liversedge to get his hair cut at Maison Charles of Leeds in Market Street; Douglas, who seemed to be supervising the wedding arrangements on Pauline's mother's behalf, to check details of the reception with Betty's Café; I to feed furtive half-crowns into the contraceptive machine outside the rubber goods shop. The plan now was to pay a visit to Rabinowitcz the Jeweller's Aire Bridge branch next door to the Lost Property Mart, with the object of pawning most of our belongings.

Terry Liversedge had learned the pledging procedure from someone he knew – it was, he assured us, almost as easy as depositing a suitcase at the Central Station luggage office. And we desperately needed the money: Terry Liversedge and I to finance the expedition to London, Douglas because he was going to have a use for every penny he could raise.

Much of my life was in the stout Grippenshaw Co-op carrier bag I lugged down to the Aire Bridge. Besides the Coronet Rapide folding camera I had failed to sell to Douglas, and the gunmetal cigarette-case and lighter which Geoffrey Sissons had refused to accept in exchange for Doreen Theaker, I had fished out my chrome tie-clip with chain, my stainless steel armbands, my Rhodium-plated Biro, the Waterman pen and propelling pencil in presentation case I had got for my fifteenth birthday, the set of ivory-backed hairbrushes an aborigine aunt had sent me for my sixteenth, my amber cigarette-holder, some of my shoes, a glass paperweight, and a few nondescript trinkets including the silver-plated bangle I had once given to Janet Gill. My rolled umbrella I carried. Now, leaning against the iron parapet of the Aire Bridge with the carrier bag between my feet, I emptied the shot-silk treasury-note-case that had belonged to all three of us in turn, buckled it open and blew out the fluff, and added that to the stockpile. I would have nothing left except my clothes and one or two little things that were broken or valueless. I didn't care. I would start all over again from scratch, beginning perhaps with a souvenir wallet from the Festival of Britain.

Douglas arrived carrying not one but two carrier bags, with his own rolled umbrella crooked over one arm and six feet or so of flex trailing behind him from the portable electric fire he was humping under the other. In one bag was stuffed a jumble-sale dinner-jacket which, together with his crippling patent leather shoes which were in the other, had been intended as the nucleus of a dress suit. All his other things, his pens, his watch, a pair of field-glasses, his school prizes, his tie-pins and cufflinks, everything except the medallion key-ring Pauline had given him for Christmas – on which to hang the crypt key, it was to be supposed – made up the rest of his burden.

Terry Liversedge came empty-handed, and that was how we knew.

Wreathed in a nimbus of violet pomade and bay rum, out-stenching even the tannery and dyeworks effluent that sludged along the river, Terry Liversedge approached stiff-leggedly with his hands held high like a captured German in a war picture, crying, 'Kamerad! Kamerad!' That meant he had let us down and was going to try to bluff his way through what for anyone else would have been a shamefaced confession.

'All right, Liversedge, let's hear the worst,' I said with a resigned sigh.

'You're going to kill me for this, youth.'

'I'm sure we are.'

'He's going to tell us he can't go,' said Douglas.

Terry Liversedge nodded, setting his lean jaw in a grotesque, clown-like affectation of glumness. As a rare damson-liveried tram rocked over the bridge, groaning and whining and clanging its bell mournfully like the ghost-train it nearly was, he nervously licked his lips in rehearsal of what he had to tell us.

'Well, chaps. In short, the balloon's gone up,' said Terry Liversedge when we could hear ourselves speak.

234

He waited for us to prompt him with, 'What naffing balloon?' or, 'Go on – we'll buy it.' Neither of us did.

'You know that shorthand letter I wrote to Rebecca Redlips. I told you I sent it to her, didn't I?'

'No. You didn't.'

'Anyway, I did. I didn't know what else to do with it after you gave it back to me, youth, so I blame you in part. I couldn't leave it at home, I couldn't leave it in my desk at work where nearly everybody reads Pitman, so I thought I'd post it. Just for a laugh.'

'Do you remember what we did with that *Red Light* book we once had?' enquired Douglas coldly.

'I'm not with you, Douglas.'

'We chucked it in the river, where we're standing now,' I reminded him, equally coldly.

'It would have been a waste of a good letter, youth. It took me ages to write. And how was I to know she'd trace it back to me?'

'I thought that was the general idea,' I said.

'It was and it wasn't, Ray. I thought she might suspect without really knowing for sure. Then when I happened to accidentally on purpose bump into her as she was coming out of the secretarial college, I'd know it'd be in the back of her mind, and that all the time we were chatting she'd be thinking about me doing her. *Coarr!*' Terry Liversedge made a lewd gesture with his fist, causing passing fossils to frown their disapproval.

'You know what, Liversedge?' said Douglas. 'You ought to be locked up.'

'I nearly was, don't you worry!'

'So what *did* happen?' I asked, too curious now to be able to resist prompting him.

'She said,' - and here he attempted a grotesque falsetto parody of Miss Cohen - ' "Yes, I was ninety per cent certain you were the culprit, Liversedge, from the way your D-strokes slope backwards like Bs. Now I find you here I'm a hundred per cent certain." '

'And –?'

'I said, "If you mean D for 'do', Miss, you're *supposed* to slope backwards." '

'No you didn't.'

'Do you want to bet?'

'Get to the point,' said Douglas.

'That's what I'm doing, kiddo. So she rings up the old man and says if I ever pester her again, she'll call the police. Talk about blue murder. He went doolally! He did – he was frothing at the mouth.'

'It must run in the family,' said Douglas unkindly. 'So the upshot is he won't let you go to London?'

'He won't let me go anywhere. He even cracks on I've got to stay in every night for a month, like a fizzing schoolboy.'

'Serve you right – you behave like one,' I said.

'It's what I'm going to tell that red-headed bint at work that's worrying me,' said Terry Liversedge bluffly, choosing to ignore this little sideswipe.

'Oh, really?' said Douglas, at his loftiest. 'I thought you might have been worrying about telling us.'

'Which I was – I've had a sleepless night, youth, I can tell you. Still, I've told you both now, haven't I? Sorry and all that, fellows. And there's one way of looking at it, Douglas – you won't go short of a best man now.'

If this typical piece of Terry Liversedge cheek was supposed to make us shake our heads in rueful wonder at his incorrigible ways, it failed. We continued to regard him stonily.

'Well say something, if it's only goodbye!'

'Goodbye,' I said pointedly.

'Aw, come on, Ray, don't be like that. Why do you need my company, anyway – do you want me to hold your coat while you're doing Doreen Theaker?'

An absurd image of him actually doing so, like a second at a duel, thawed me a little. I thought of the three packets of gossamer in my inside pocket that were not really bulging my jacket but only felt as if they were. Terry Liversedge was right, I wouldn't need him.

'All right, you daft bugger – but if you want Moult & Sumpter to give you a refund you can go and ask them yourself, because I'm not doing it.'

'And I'll tell you something else he can do, Raymondo.' Though refusing to speak to Terry Liversedge directly, Douglas was extending a grudging olive branch. 'Seeing it was his brilliant idea to pawn all our stuff, he can be the one to go in and do the dirty work.'

This was quite a little brainwave of Douglas's, for while waiting for Terry Liversedge we had confessed our mutual diffidence about negotiating with the pawnbroker.

'All right, seeing it's you two, but don't blame me if I only get ten bob for the lot.' To our relief, and probably to his own at being able to perform this small act of contrition, Terry Liversedge encumbered himself with our carrier bags, umbrellas, and Douglas's electric fire, and skulked off along the dank Aire Bridge Passage, where two doors below the rubber goods shop a discreetly-painted arrow pointed to Rabinowitcz the Jeweller's pledge office.

'Do you believe him?' asked Douglas as we heard the tinkle of a Dickensian-sounding shop bell.

'What – about him sending Rebecca Redlips that letter? He's mad enough to.'

'I meant about her complaining to his dad so that he very conveniently can't make the Festival trip. If you ask me, he couldn't get anyone to go with him.'

'You said it, Douglas, I didn't.' I felt more charitable towards Terry Liversedge, even sorry for him. 'You know, the funny thing is, we can both remember when he could get practically any dame he wanted.'

'That was back in our College of Commerce days, mon brave. The trouble is, he behaves as if he's still there.' With these sage words Douglas dismissed the subject of Terry Liversedge and turned his attention to me. 'Well, there's only you now, Raymondo, old bean, old boy. I hope you're not going to let me down, or this whole cunning wheeze will have counted for nothing.'

Forbearing to remind Douglas who had dropped out first, I merely said, 'I'm counting the hours.'

Pushing up his glasses in order to be able to see further than the end of the bridge, Douglas squinted one eye along the tramlines to the brewery clock far down Airegate.

His lips moved. 'One hundred and thirty-nine hours, twenty-six minutes,' he announced after a moment.

'Thank you, Professor Einstein.' Actually, it was a hundred and seventy-three hours, twenty-six minutes. Douglas's calculations took him to seven on Friday morning when the coach would be pulling away from St Chad's; mine, to five the following afternoon when, if on schedule and weather

237

permitting, Doreen Theaker and I should be making the preparatory moves towards going all the way.

I had fixed on five pm as giving us a reasonable time for sightseeing. Doreen had expressed an interest in seeing the Tower of London, Big Ben, Trafalgar Square, the Zoo, Piccadilly Circus, Madame Tussaud's and Speakers' Corner. With the aid of the Ward Lock *Guide to London* in the reference room of the Royal Coronation branch library, I had worked out that we could cover all these attractions, have late lunch or early tea at the Strand Corner House, and be on the District Railway or water-bus for Richmond by four. The previous afternoon and evening would have been occupied in settling in at Hounslow and seeing as much as we needed of the Festival of Britain, culminating in some heavy petting in one of the darker corners of the Battersea Park Pleasure Gardens. The following day, Whit Sunday, we would take a picnic and spend the whole day in Richmond Park. On Whit Monday, Douglas's wedding day, we would rush round Windsor Castle in the morning, have a quick bite somewhere, and get to Richmond Park by about noon. On Tuesday, sated, we should return home.

I had not put this itinerary to Doreen in detail but I was left in no doubt as to her approval in principle. On the previous Sunday, the one following the second-base breakthrough on Throstle Moor, I had taken her on the dark blue Textile District bus to the field of long grass near the corporation sewage farm which I had once long ago earmarked for Audrey Marsh. I knew, by the way she sank back with her arms behind her head, her blouse open almost to the waist where I had unbuttoned it and her twill skirt riding up to her stockingless knees, that she would have gone all the way there and then. But the Festival of Britain had been the goal now for so long that I was incapable of readjusting my sights to this nearer opportunity. Richmond Park was now journey's end, its conifer plantations Mecca. I recalled that among my confused feelings when given the news about Douglas and Pauline had been a small sense of betrayal at Douglas having, so to speak, jumped the gun. He should have waited, as I was prepared to wait, whether Doreen was prepared to go through with it here and now or not. She would thank me for it in due course. Like a bride who has saved herself for the marriage

238

bed, she would be glad she had saved herself for the Festival of Britain.

Meanwhile, she didn't really seem to mind one way or the other. On evenings when inclement weather or other circumstances had prevented me from re-reaching the evermore familiar territory of second base, she displayed no outward signs of frustration. On other evenings, when the Throstle Moor exercise was repeated with such variations as I could remember from the chapter on foreplay in *The Red Light*, she betrayed no inner sense of intense pleasure. I had to admit to myself that my own responses followed the same pretty-well neutral line. The might-have-been with Betty Parsons in an abandoned Morris Eight called Bruno was forever a more exciting prospect than the here-and-now in the bluebell woods with Doreen Theaker. But I rejected as perverse the temptation to take her down to the old car dump beyond the golf course, and concentrated on thinking about the conifer plantations of Richmond, now so vivid in my mind that I could smell the pine needles. It would all be different there, after the first or second time.

'Are you bored with me?' Doreen had asked in the long grass near the sewage farm, after I had done everything I could think of short of the one thing that had to be kept.

'How could I be?' seemed a weak and unconvincing reply, especially since I had been on the verge of sleep, with a cold hand lying lifelessly between her cold thighs. I searched for an appropriate compliment to keep her happy, and remembered one that was usually well received. Even Audrey Marsh had thought it quite neat. I had never tried it on Betty Parsons.

'You have a very funny effect on my watch, do you know that, Doreen?'

'How do you mean?'

'When I'm with you, an hour only seems like a minute. But when I'm not with you, a minute seems like an hour.'

It was the first time, I realised with dull self-congratulation, that I could remember having got through this pretty little speech word-perfect, except with Victoria Leadenbury to whom I had put the point in writing.

'But you don't have a watch,' Doreen pointed out.

'No. I meant if I did have a wash.'

'You used to have one. What happened to it?'

'Lost it.'

Doreen gave me one of the little pecking kisses that were as near as she ever got to using her own initiative.

'I know you had a watch, because you once said that to me before, ages and ages ago. Do you remember?'

'Did I?'

'At least I think you did. I couldn't really understand what you were saying, and I didn't know you well enough to ask.'

'You known be benter now,' I said. Anxious to get off the subject, I clawed indiscriminately at her thighs. A circling rook cawed sardonically.

Still waiting for Terry Liversedge, I said to Douglas as we gazed idly in the barred windows of Rabinowitcz the Jeweller's at the cheaper range of jewellery they stocked in their Aire Bridge branch: 'You see that woman's cocktail watch with the green cord strap, fifty-four and a tanner? If Terry Liversedge gets more than eight quid for me, I'm going to buy it for Doreen.'

Douglas, pricing wedding rings, said absently: 'What? Why?'

'She's got to have *some* reward for losing her virginity,' I said, and having said it, felt so shoddy that I added at once, as a triumphant Terry Liversedge swaggered out of Aire Bridge Passage brandishing three white five-pound notes and some ten-shilling and pound notes, 'Joke over. No, it's to make sure we don't get locked in Richmond Park after closing-time.'

'I heard that, you mucky devil!' crowed Terry Liversedge, and I still felt shoddy. I would have liked to have said, emulating Douglas, 'Look, I do happen to be in fizzing love with the girl!' but it so happened that I didn't.

240

In the dawning light I made out the silver-gilt hands of the cocktail watch's tiny oblong face with difficulty. Coming up to half-past, if it was still keeping proper time. Thirty-six and a half hours to go. To Richmond Park, that was: the coach would be leaving two and a half hours from now.

The aborigines' alarm clock which I had borrowed and set for half-past four clanged tinnily on the sounding-board of my chest of drawers across the bedroom. I prised myself off the bed and turned it off, then switched on the overhead light and looked in the tallboy mirror.

The yellow tie, which had seemed to go very well with Terry Liversedge's re-requisitioned salmon-pink zoot jacket when dressing an hour or so earlier, seemed less of a striking choice now that the hard electric light was compromised by half-daylight. I unclasped the aborigines' fibre suitcase, took out the clip-on black bow tie that Douglas, disposing of the last remnants of the evening-dress wardrobe he had been building up, had sold me for threepence, and exchanged it for the yellow one. The rest of the ensemble – the blue Clough & Clough's sports shirt that Doreen had got for me, the navy barathea slacks, the brown grain leather sandals over yellow socks – was just about right.

I recombed my hair, felt my chin for five am shadow after last night's shave, and opened the window to let out the cigarette smoke. I had had seven since waking just after three and was feeling queasy. I tiptoed downstairs and had finished a breakfast of cornflakes and milk before the aborigines stirred and forced me to eat another one of eggs, bacon, toast and coffee. I silently vomited in the bathroom, cleaned my teeth with my finger since my toothbrush was packed, placed an Amplex tablet on my tongue, suffered a catalogue of strictures, warnings and advice from the aborigines, and was striding out along Edith Close with my mac over my shoulder and my suitcase swinging as Big Ben chimed six-thirty on some early riser's wireless.

Despite having checked and re-checked my itinerary, I was anxious in case for some unfathomable reason the coach might have already left, but not so anxious that I could not appreciate the smell of privet, as sweet at this hour of the morning as it ever was at this hour in the evening, in blackbird-chirruping Crag Park Avenue.

The pang that I felt when I strode past Winifred Drive where Betty Parsons lived diminished then vanished as I passed Pearl Grove where Doreen Theaker lived. I could just see the side of her house from the corner of the Avenue. A wisp of steam filtered out of the ventilator brick by the bathroom window. If she was still having a bath I hoped she knew what time it was. Thoughts of Doreen in her bath, and the soapy water lapping areas now familiar to me, overcame an incipient neurosis on that score, and sustained me to the end of Station Approach where, by previous arrangement with myself, I lit the last of my cigarettes, bought a new twenty-packet of Three Castles at the station kiosk, then took a deep breath and humped my suitcase over the level crossing into Church Street.

The Moult & Sumpter coach was reassuringly parked outside St Chad's, its cream bodywork and flashy green streamlining contrasting sinfully with the black stump tower behind it. A dozen or so of the fossils who were to be my travelling companions were doddering about on the pavement in their thick pastel coats and raspberry-whirl hats, or in the case of the smattering of male fossils among them, black funeral suits just out of mothballs and new cloth caps. Roughly the same number of younger fossils, in all essential respects their replicas, had assembled to see them off. As I crossed Church Street towards the coach I saw that it was already more than half full, with antimacassared, uncut-moquette row upon row of glinting spectacles and white false teeth catching the morning sun.

I walked round the back of the coach to the other side, where enough strap-tied cardboard suitcases and war-surplus canvas grips to service a world cruise lined the pavement awaiting loading, while the white-coated dodo who was the Moult & Sumpter driver sweated an actual tin cabin trunk into the luggage hold.

The fossils wobbling on to the coach on their bad feet,

242

clutching the chrome handrails as if climbing out of a saline bath, were being marked off on a clipboard by the troglodyte vicar's wife, who was deputising for Douglas as outing marshal. Douglas himself had been very positive that he would not be coming down to see us off and run the gauntlet of cackling fossils wishing to proffer their nudging, watery-winking congratulations on his impending wedding. I was therefore very surprised to see him, sheepishly thwacking a rolled-up magazine against his hip as he suffered their jocular good wishes and cry upon chuckled cry of, 'Don't do owt I wouldn't do, lad – that'll give him plenty of leeway!' as they were helped aboard.

There was no sign of Doreen yet. I dumped my suitcase with the others then stood round the back of the coach, on the offside, where I would be able to see her coming along Church Street. If she turned out to be accompanied by either or both of her aborigine parents, it was arranged that I should slip on to the coach, sit next to an apple-cheeked fossil and look as much like her grandson as possible until they had waved Doreen off.

The sweating Moult & Sumpter dodo, whom I knew slightly from my visits to the booking-office down at the coach station, pushed back his peaked cap between bouts of loading. 'Bit out of your line, young Raymond, this lot, isn't it?'

'Don't worry, Len,' I said with the bluffness expected of me. 'Once in London you won't see me for dust.'

'Aye aye! Like that, is it!' he said knowingly, to my considerable pleasure.

I saw that Douglas, still fiddling with his rolled-up magazine, had detached himself from the cloying attentions of the fossils and was hovering near at hand.

'There you are, mon brave. Could I have a quick word?'

Taking my elbow he led me a yard or two away from the coach. By his ingratiating grin I could see at once that something had gone wrong.

'Fret not . . . '

'Oh, by the left, Beckett! What's up now?'

'Nothing to worry about, Raymondo – one slight change in the arrangements. It's just that Pauline's Auntie May has decided to come up for the wedding after all. She's had to put the old lady in hospital.'

'I don't care if she's had to put her in the naffing dustbin. Does that mean this isn't worth the fizzing paper it's written on?'

I brandished the envelope containing a note of introduction from Pauline's mother to Pauline's Auntie May, on which Douglas had jotted the address in Hounslow and the instructions for getting there by tube train from Lancaster Gate where the fossils would be disembarking for the Court Garden Hotel.

'Well, not unless you're going to break in through the kitchen window, old fruit.'

'What are we going to do, then?'

Douglas's voice was low and soothing, in not absolute contrast to mine which was low and horrified.

'I've told you, old bean, old boy, fret not!'

'Never mind fret fizzing not! And don't tell me we can stay at the Court Gardens Hotel with this lot because they've told Moult & Sumpter they're turning bookings away. And even if we could find a hotel that wasn't full, what are we going to use for dough?'

Douglas, on the verge of saying 'Fret not' again, caught my eye and changed his mind. He unrolled the magazine he had been playing around with, revealing it to be a dog-eared but recent copy of *John Bull*. A gay picture of the Festival of Britain by night, with the Skylon reflecting in the Thames and the Dome of Discovery glowing like a landed flying saucer among the teeming promenades and terraces, decorated the cover. I was unimpressed.

'What's this in aid of?'

'Just cast your eye over this, mon brave.' Douglas's wart-barnacled fingers leafed through the periodical until he located an article in the middle. Folding back the page he handed it to me. I read the headline, 'AT THE SIGN OF THE DEEP SHELTER'.

'What's this to me?'

'All will become clear if you'll only read it.'

I skimmed the first few paragraphs. Clapham South Deep Shelter . . . unique hotel . . . deep sleep indeed . . . 120 feet below ground level . . . built during war at cost of £3,000,000 and now planned as future part of the underground . . . at present run by London County Council as hostel . . .

fifty thousand Festival visitors expected . . .

'Douglas,' I said, starting with sardonic calm but unable to prevent my voice rising shrilly. 'Are you suggesting that because you've made a complete cock-up of this whole trip from start to finish, I should ask Doreen Theaker to kip down in an air-raid shelter?'

'Why not?'

I tried to think of a reason. The bunk beds would be segregated, but then so would Pauline's Auntie May's house be segregated. And Clapham sounded more Londonish than Hounslow. And we wouldn't have to bother what time we got in at night.

'It'll be full.'

'Never in this world, Raymondo.' He prodded a paragraph I hadn't reached yet. 'Eight thousand beds, see?'

'What's Doreen's mother going to say?'

'Doreen's mother won't know.'

'What if she rings up Pauline's Auntie May?'

'Pauline's Auntie May won't be there, will she? If Doreen's worried about that she can ring home from a call-box and say the phone's out of order. It just goes on ringing even after she's answered it, she could say . . .'

As Douglas developed further ingenious skeins to this web of deceit, I scanned the article for further objections. I found one.

'Just a minute. It costs five bob a night.'

'Very reasonable.'

'But Pauline's Auntie May was only going to charge us a quid apiece for the five days, full board.'

'Ah, but she's a relative,' said Douglas with sweet reasonableness.

Through gritted teeth I said: 'I'm going to get you for this, Beckett.' Nevertheless, I folded the magazine up and stuffed it in the pocket of Terry Liversedge's zoot jacket. Churlishly mollified, I asked: 'Is Clapham anywhere near Richmond Park, do you happen to know?'

'Better than that, Raymondo. It's near Clapham Common, which apparently is not only just as big and just as secluded as Richmond Park, but doesn't have railings round it.'

To congratulate Douglas, I decided on the verge of doing so, would be overdoing it. But it couldn't be denied that the

Hobson's choice I was having to settle for was a probable improvement on the original plan, or at least on the original revised one.

Not too grudgingly I said, 'Well, so long as Doreen doesn't mind . . . Which reminds me, it's about time she was here, isn't it?'

'You've got stacks of time yet,' said Douglas, peering along Church Street through his thick lenses. 'In fact, isn't this her coming now?'

'Not unless she's gained half a stone, you blind bat.'

Yet there was something familiar about the chick who was approaching the coach. And she was carrying a suitcase.

Allowing Douglas to be shanghaied by the white-smocked Moult & Sumpter dodo into helping him hoist aboard the last galley-load of baggage, I studied her as she came nearer. I definitely knew her from somewhere.

'Hello, Raymond.'

'Oh. Hello.'

'I knew you wouldn't remember me.' She was going pink.

'Yes I do.'

'Vicky,' she said. There was a label tied to the handle of the suitcase she was wriggling in front of her with both hands, and I took in the name on it at a glance.

*Oh, my darling sweetheart, what can I say except that I love you with every atom of my heart. When I am not with you every minute seems like an hour, yet when we are together every hour is but a minute. Oh, my precious . . .*

'If it isn't Victoria Leadenbury!' I knew she lived somewhere in the neighbourhood these days, but I had not set eyes on her since leaving the College of Commerce.

'Only Doreen can't come,' she said, and placed her suitcase at my feet, like a cat putting a dead mouse on a doorstep.

I thought, 'Oh, Christ!' but said, trying to keep the shrillness out of my voice, 'Oh dear.'

She was breathing heavily, either from the exertion of having carried her quite largish suitcase, or from nervousness.

'Yes, she stripped over the corn of her dressing-down last nine and strained her nankle.'

She tripped over the cord of her dressing-gown, like Victoria Leadenbury tripping over her words, and strained or sprained, it didn't matter which, her ankle. Victoria's lisp had always given her a tendency to garble her speech. It seemed worse now.

She took a deep breath. 'She was going *up*stairs, strainly enough, not drown. It just grows to show, doesn't it?'

'I didn't know you knew Doreen,' I said with wooden pointlessness.

'Fullyny enough I didn't until, oh, two or three weeks since ago, even though we work in the same deparntment.'

'In Clough & Clough's?'

'Yes, but with Doreen being a relatively nude arrival I didn't take much notice of her.' Having succeeded in making a more or less fair copy of that sentence encouraged her to simmer down a little. I knew the feeling. 'Then I heard her making a phone call to Moult & Sumpter and asking for Mr Raymond Watmough.' The pinkness that had left her face came flooding back momentarily as she spoke my name.

'That would be me,' I said with flirting jocularity. Victoria was still plumpish but not unreasonably so. There was a waistline there now. And the tweed coat she wore was a very thick one. She would be even slimmer, or less plump, underneath. She wore a perky red beret. You didn't often see chicks wearing hats these days.

'Yes, I thought it might be,' smiled Victoria, responding to my jokiness. Nice smile, too. And she had shed her squint, more or less, with her specs. 'So then I main myself known, and we started having our coffin breaks together.'

'She didn't mention it.'

Victoria, fluttering what I now saw were quite reasonably long eyelashes, looked as if she were riffling through a mental repertoire of coy remarks. But she settled for, 'Anyway, she sent me.'

I thought I understood at once, but at once thought I couldn't possibly have understood.

'Flattered, I'm sure, but I don't get it.'

'She didn't want to let you down.'

'So she rang you up?'

I had the whole picture in my mind, then, stage by stage like the Horlicks strip that was probably on the back pages of the *John Bull* magazine in my pocket. She wouldn't ring me at home because she never had and would know that the sound of a chick's voice on the eve of the Festival expedition would arouse the aborigines' basest suspicions. She would wait for the right guarded moment then hobble into the hall and ring Victoria Leadenbury, in whispers. And Victoria, conspiratorially whispering back, would have said, 'Yes, all right.'

It was very nice and appealing of Doreen not to want to let me down. And, I well appreciated, typical. She was always anxious to please. I didn't know what footing it was supposed to leave us on – whether, for instance, Victoria was merely on loan or whether this was supposed to be a permanent transaction. We would sort all that out when we came back.

'That's rhyme. And she send there was mince strip to the Fencimence – '

Flushing and wriggling, Victoria broke off in a little sneeze of giggles.

'Do what I do, Vicky,' I said with great kindliness. 'Breathe in through your mouth. Breathe out. Then take it very slowly.'

Gratefully she followed the recommended exercises.

'She said. There was this trip. To the Festival of Britain . . . '

'. . . And how would you like to go on it, and you said yes. What did your folks say?'

'Oh, they were all for it – said it would be a great experience for me and they'd ring up Clough & Clough's today and say I was poorly. That was once they knew it was a church trip, and that we'd be straying with Pauline Batty's auntie.'

I would mention the Clapham deep shelter when we got to the other side of Doncaster.

'You know Pauline Batty too, then?'

'No, but my mother knows her mother.'

'We'd better get on the coach,' I said. I swung Victoria's case into the luggage compartment where the Moult & Sumpter dodo was slamming down the hatches.

I had been noticing, out of the corner of my eye, the quizzical looks that Douglas had been giving us. Now, as we approached the front of the coach where he was standing with the troglodyte vicar's wife and the guard of honour of younger fossils, he raised a bushy eyebrow for an explanation. I gave him our tell-you-later signal, and he shrugged in comic mystification.

'And you must be R. Watmough and D. Theaker, is it?' said

the troglodyte, making ticks.

'That's right.'

I hustled Victoria Leadenbury on to the coach, gave Douglas a wave and a casual 'So long' as I boarded myself, then remembered that he would be a married man the next time I saw him. I turned back down the metalled step and gestured him closer to murmur in his ear.

'Good luck with the wedding, mate, and if you see Victoria Leadenbury's mother chucking confetti after you've tied the knot, for Christ's sake keep her away from Pauline's Auntie May.'

I followed Victoria down the coach through a double cordon of spectacles and teeth. There were senile murmurings of 'Here come the lovebirds!' and the like which I ignored, though Victoria's shoulders heaved in silent giggles. The back offside seat had been left for us.

'Just like the pictures,' I said, settling in. We would begin to hold hands south of Wakefield. Sooner or later she would begin to nod off and I would put my arm around her and draw her head to my shoulder, if it was not already there. 'Why don't you take your coat off and make yourself comfortable?'

She was wearing a blue lift-up jumper and lighter blue lift-up skirt. The soft plumpness of her hips and stomach showed that she was not much over-encumbered underneath.

'Do you have the time, Vicky?' I asked.

Her watch looked quite a good one. I fingered the cheap cocktail watch in my pocket. It would come in useful one of these days, I supposed, like Janet Gill's silver-plated bangle.

'Coming up to seven,' said Victoria. 'We should be off in a minim.'

Twelve hours, say, before we were lying under a bush on Clapham Common.

'Isn't it exciting, Ray?'

'Isn't it just?'

With much waving and cheerioing from the old fossils within and the younger fossils without, and with a wart-studded thumbs-up from Douglas into which it was possible to read volumes of innuendo, we pulled away along Church Street and humped over the level-crossing into Station Approach. Then, ponderously trundling round into Crag Park Avenue, we were on our way.

The handkerchief-waving fossils had wound down several windows and through them, as we gathered speed, we sucked in the expected scent of the Crag Park Avenue privet, then of the creosoted chestnut pailings and the May blossom, with the exhaust fumes of the coach adding to the swelling symphony of smells.

Then the hint of musk scent as we passed Doreen Theaker Grove, the smell of clean hair as we passed Betty Parsons Drive, the tang of salt and vinegar and batter from the Argosy Fish Bar, and the cigarette smoke from The Parade curling in with my own cigarette smoke. Turning around the grass roundabout with its own cut-grass smell, we gathered in the brick and green rubber and roses and lavender polish smell of the Royal Coronation branch library, then chocolate-cream and orange peel from the Gainsborough, and French chalk and sweat from the Clock Ballroom. Now we were passing the spanking pink and white pavilion of the Grippenshaw Pageant of Progress where Terry Liversedge had reported much promising talent was to be seen: the smell of new paint added, and belonged, to the pot pourri.

All the scents were still with us as we speeded along the Leeds Road, past Janet Gill Terrace with its frost-smell from the recreation ground, and on towards the stale-beer-smelling town. Soon we would turn off for the ring road that would take us along Audrey Marsh Road with those upstairs smells of talc and bath salts and roll-on deodorant, and towards the Doncaster by-pass that would lead us into the A1, the Great North Road. We were far from home now yet all the home scents kept wafting in as we bowled along like a rolling pommander.

'Can you smell anything, Vicky?'

'Pooh, yes! The slaughterhouse!'

But it wasn't that, it was creosote, privet, frost in May and all the rest of it. That portable scent of promise was coming with us, all the way down the Great North Road.